VULGAR GENRES

VULGAR GENRES

*Gay Pornographic Writing and
Contemporary Fiction*

Steven Ruszczycky

THE UNIVERSITY OF CHICAGO PRESS

CHICAGO AND LONDON

The University of Chicago Press, Chicago 60637
The University of Chicago Press, Ltd., London
© 2021 by The University of Chicago
Published 2021
Printed in the United States of America

30 29 28 27 26 25 24 23 22 21   1 2 3 4 5

ISBN-13: 978-0-226-78861-6 (cloth)
ISBN-13: 978-0-226-78875-3 (paper)
ISBN-13: 978-0-226-78889-0 (e-book)
DOI: https://doi.org/10.7208/chicago
/9780226788890.001.0001

Library of Congress Cataloging-in-Publication Data

Names: Ruszczycky, Steven, 1981– author.
Title: Vulgar genres : gay pornographic writing and
contemporary fiction / Steven Ruszczycky.
Other titles: Gay pornographic writing and contemporary
fiction
Description: Chicago ; London : The University of Chicago
Press, 2021. | Includes bibliographical references and index.
Identifiers: LCCN 2021016875 | ISBN 9780226788616 (cloth) |
ISBN 9780226788753 (paperback) | ISBN 9780226788890
(ebook)
Subjects: LCSH: American literature—20th century—History
and criticism. | American literature—21st century—History
and criticism. | Gay pornography—United States—History—
20th century. | Gay pornography—United States—History—
21st century. | Homosexuality in literature. | Pornography in
literature.
Classification: LCC PS228.G38 R87 2021 | DDC
810.9/3538086642—dc23
LC record available at https://lccn.loc.gov/2021016875

♾ This paper meets the requirements of ANSI/NISO
Z39.48-1992 (Permanence of Paper).

Contents

Figures

Introduction

In the United States in the mid-1960s, a case came before the Supreme Court, one intended to settle the question of obscenity addressed by the famous Roth decision of 1957. The nine quarrelsome old men now came to the conclusion that obscenity required a work to be utterly without any redeeming social value.

Whammo! There was a thoughtful pause whilst the country digested that—and came to the conclusion that of course there was a revelatory and redeeming social value to even the lousiest suckee-fuckee books. The gates were opened. The flood began. Suddenly all the old four-letter words (and some new ones) appeared in print, almost overnight. Publishers no longer had to write prefatory notes condemning what they were printing; they could merely suggest the social significance of erotica, and lo! all was satisfied. The court's decision had more holes in it than a colander, and publishing houses sprang up like mushrooms after rain.[1]

In the passage above, pornographer, tattoo artist, and erstwhile literature professor Samuel Steward reflects on a moment whose import for our understanding of gay literary fiction, pornography, and print culture has been largely underappreciated. Steward has in mind the rapid attenuation of US obscenity law at midcentury, when the state's waning interest in censoring sexually explicit media led to a remarkable change in the kinds of texts available to a general readership. Of course, his account of that transformation is less than precise: the explosion in pornographic writing in the US was the consequence of not one but a string of interrelated Supreme Court decisions delivered between 1957 and 1966, which were themselves the product of numerous courtroom battles stretching back well into the early twentieth century. While Steward fudges the historical details, his account of what those changes meant for publishers, writers, and readers is accurate. The court's protracted development of a new framework for assessing obscenity not only enabled the rapid proliferation of markets for pornography, which included both homegrown varieties and imports from around the world, but also allowed publishers, and Grove Press in particular, to popularize the texts of the modernist avant-garde, many of which had been banned in the US for pushing the boundaries of sexual propriety in the name of art.[2] In response to the freedoms afforded to publishers and writers by this new legal context, the First Amendment lawyer Charles Rembar triumphantly declared this moment "the end of obscenity" and predicted that the censorship of sexually explicit writing might soon be a thing of the past.[3]

Given the significance that such legal changes had for writers, it's tempting to follow Rembar in construing the end of obscenity more or less in terms of a progress narrative. However, over the past twenty years, a number of scholars, including Florence Dore, Loren Glass, Elizabeth Ladenson, Allison Pease, and Rachel Potter, have highlighted the extent to in which the interrelated notions of obscenity, pornography, and censorship in fact, not only drove the formation of an elite literary modernism, but also had a key role in its wider dissemination. According to Pease, the aesthetic theory of the eighteenth and nineteenth centuries relied on pornography to clarify the specific, and specifically aesthetic, value of literary writing.[4] Where the latter engaged the reader in the disinterested contemplation of beauty, the former turned one's attention toward the self-interested pleasures of the flesh. Beyond being a mere description of particular textual properties, the distinction between literature and pornography also served the ideological ends of class differentiation. While perceived as the means by which one expressed one's elite standing, the ability to produce and recognize texts with distinctly literary value was also understood to be available only to the population of White male property holders largely responsible for articulating such theories of value. In contrast, pornography increasingly described an aesthetically inferior form of writing associated with the popular entertainments of the working classes.[5] Thus, pornography was recognizable, not only in terms of its crudeness, but also in terms of the relations of power that subordinated it to literature as the thinking man's art.

By the early twentieth century, writers sought to push both aesthetic and social boundaries through the deliberate incorporation of explicit sex into their work.[6] The goal was not to arouse the reader but to bring the aesthetic to bear on the subject's sexualized interiority: unlike the pornographer who wallowed in filth, literary genius sublimated sex into art. Such literary innovation set the scene for the US obscenity trials of the early twentieth century, which in turn drove the growth of an internationalized professional culture of writers, publishers, and First Amendment lawyers seeking to combat not only censorship but also the unauthorized sale of pirated editions.[7] By the mid-twentieth century, writers, critics, and academics had successfully popularized the values of social realism, according to which literature should represent life in all its sordid detail, and of literary modernism, which championed "art for art's sake," such that they could serve as persuasive arguments for the defense of controversial texts in the nation's courtrooms.[8] By 1966, the growing acceptance of literature's capacity to represent human sexuality would lead Steven Marcus to argue that arousal was itself an acceptable response to literature. Moreover, once liberal democratic societies finally came to terms with that fact, then pornography itself would cease to exist: "Pornography is, after all, nothing more than a representation of the fantasies of infantile sexual life," Marcus observed in the conclusion to his study of Victorian pornography. "Every man who grows up must pass through a phase of his existence, and I can see no reason for supposing that our society, in the history of its own life, should not have to pass through such a phase as well."[9]

Of course, Marcus's prediction did not come true, and scholars have explained why by offering detailed accounts of the history of that moment. However, we know far less about what happened after, when "pornography" was no longer simply the slur of "aesthetic immaturity" that forewarned an obscenity charge but increasingly referred to a genre of representation and a semi-legitimate niche market for specific populations of readers. In continuing to neglect these materials, scholars risk tracking too closely with the law, losing interest in pornographic writing when, as Pease declares, "specific and overt references to sex acts and sexualized bodies [are] so much a part of literature, including works of high-cultural aesthetic status, that today they hardly seem worth notice."[10] For Steward, the end of obscenity was not so much an ending but a beginning, something worth noticing, especially for the many gay men who were becoming increasingly conscious of themselves as members of a distinct minority by reading the books that writers like Steward were beginning to publish. His account of that change is also suggestive: the mycological metaphor he employs prevents him from falling easily into the kind of straightforward narrative of de-repression favored by writers such as Rembar and Marcus. Instead of unrestricted speech, there is a sense of something changed by the wash of four-letter words and the clusters of smut peddlers that sprouted up across the nation's publishing landscape. Within the new cultural ecology that Steward imagines, the meaning and import of all those four-letter words is far from clear.

This book offers a preliminary foray into the subject of gay pornographic writing after obscenity through an examination of its relation to gay literary fiction. The principal argument is this: the attenuation of federal obscenity law established the conditions for gay pornographic writing and gay literary fiction to emerge in relation to one another; thus, any attempt to understand contemporary gay literary production must do so through an understanding of its fundamental connection to the genre of gay pornographic writing. Contemporary literary studies tend to ignore this relation, thereby preserving an erroneous assumption that gay pornographic writing was an immature form of culture whose popularity inhibited the commercial and critical success of gay literary fiction. While it's unlikely that anyone would make that argument in precisely those terms today, its implicit force is still palpable, especially in studies of gay print culture that construe pornographic writing published after 1970 as little more than a private, masturbatory pleasure. Even the field of porn studies, which has done more than any other field to describe pornography's social and political significance, has by and large neglected to account for pornographic writing published in the contemporary period. Owing to the ways in which that field took shape within film and media studies departments during the 1980s, contemporary pornography has become more or less synonymous with the pornographic image, while pornographic writing becomes a quaint relic from the pre-Stonewall era.

This book builds its argument through close readings of work by a number of writers, including William Carney, Dennis Cooper, Samuel Delany, John Rechy, and Matthew Stadler. While some actively distanced their work from porn, others embraced the genre through the deliberate incorporation of its formal and thematic conventions within their novels. Many of them also directly benefited from the reception contexts and markets for their writing that gay porn helped to carve out, especially during the late 1960s and early 1970s when writers were forced to contend with the heteronormativity of a literary public sphere that construed the value of their work in normalizing terms. However, regardless of their respective attitudes, these writers share in common an understanding of the ways that gay pornographic writing was hardly a private pleasure, but instead provided the material basis for pornographic counterpublics: modes of print-mediated stranger sociability that played a central role in the self-understanding and practices for a wide range of readers. This book provides the first full-length account of these various pornographic counterpublics in arguing that pornographic writing's sociocultural significance derived from its subordinated status: its vulgarity, commercialism, pragmatic associations, and indifference to politics nonetheless enabled readers to imagine forms of gay subjectivity and sociability that were often unrecognizable elsewhere. It's no secret that many gay men are avid consumers and producers of porn. In its turn to the contemporary history of gay pornographic writing, this book seeks to find out why.

VULGAR GENRES

In order to conceptualize the relationship between literary and pornographic fiction, this book uses the term "vulgar genres," where "vulgar" connotes not only the potential offensiveness of pornographic representation but also the colloquialisms, argot, and clichés that characterize nonexpert discourses about sexuality. Consider, for example, the scene from Steward's *San Francisco Hustler* (1970), in which readers received an impromptu lesson from regular protagonist Phil Andros on the pleasures and practicality of "le petit souper," or the act of ingesting semen out of someone's rectum.[11] The term's vulgarity derives from at least two different sources. The first pertains to the use of a language with significant culinary cachet to describe a practice some readers will likely find unappetizing. The second derives from the scene's erotic pedagogy, which subtly evokes porn's own historical associations with the rise of public education and print literacy during the nineteenth century.[12] In the fall of 1953, Steward had contracted hepatitis after spending a sex-filled summer in San Francisco. According to Steward's biographer, Justin Spring, Steward fondly remembered his time in the city, yet his infection with hepatitis was an unpleasant souvenir that he believed he had acquired while orally stimulating another man's anus. As a result, Steward resolved to "never [rim] anyone" ever again.[13] However, as Phil explains to the men who have just ejaculated in his own ass, the risk of contracting hepatitis from oral-anal contact did not necessarily rule oral-anal eroticism out of the question. As a demonstration, Phil then flips his legs back over his own head and allows the other men's semen to dribble into his own mouth.

By the time Steward published his novel, such brazen representations of gay sexuality had begun to proliferate as a partial consequence of the rapid attenuation of federal obscenity law. As the historian John D'Emilio succinctly puts it: "In pornography, literature, and the mass media, portrayals of gay life multiplied."[14] In turn, those materials played a significant role in shaping the formation of contemporary gay identities and communities. "These books," according to the cultural historian Michael Bronski, "were the maps and the signposts, the etiquette manuals and the foreign-phrase books, for gay men entering the half-hidden world of homosexuality."[15] Of course, censorship did not come to an end at this point, and over the next thirty years, entities from the local police to postal inspectors to US senators seeking to safeguard the nation's moral fabric would target the gay and lesbian press as well as the venues that distributed their materials, from bookstores to bathhouses. Yet those acts of censorship often themselves initiated tense legal trials and facilitated the formation of oppositional social identities, as sexual and gender dissidents understood the efforts of the police and other regulatory entities as attacks on their hard-won sexual and expressive freedoms. The right to pornographic representation was something that needed to be defended.

At the same time, gay pornographic writing itself posed a problem for many writers seeking to write openly about gay sexuality in literary fiction. The attenuation of US obscenity law had also entailed a weakening of the association between the legal concept of obscenity, understood as a threat to social norms so harmful that it required the state's intervention, and pornography, which operated for much of the late nineteenth and early twentieth century as a term for controversial texts thought to be both aesthetically inferior to literature and potentially obscene. More or less freed from its juridical meanings, pornography could function as a genre and a marketing category that, according to some critics, posed an obstacle to greater critical and commercial recognition of gay literary fiction. As Roger Austen argued in his landmark study *Playing the Game: The Homosexual Novel in America* (1977): "Gay men now buy novels more for titillation than for story line and, like their straight counterparts, are willing and even eager to subsidize fiction that descends to the eternally common denominator of sex. As a result, the more serious and literate gay writer has found himself the victim of a paradox: with the wide-open acceptance of frankly homosexual fiction, the future of his sort of novel is threatened by its lurid competition."[16] Gay readers can stimulate their minds or their bodies, but they cannot do both: when it comes to one-handed reading, the other hand better be taking notes.

Setting Austen's distaste for porn aside, he was nonetheless correct that much of pornographic writing produced over the late twentieth century evinced a single-minded focus on sex, a fact that pornographers themselves lamented. In the August 19, 1970, issue of the *Advocate*, the writer Larry Townsend reported on a panel of pornographers featuring Richard Amory, Dirk Vanden, and Steward who together described the limitations they faced in their efforts to write books with "frankly homosexual themes." "Most of us have been forced into the 'adult' or 'porno' market," Townsend observed: "None of us are overly pleased with this, as it restricts our range of expression. As Dirk Vanden noted, we are limited to an exposition of 50,000 to 65,000 words—too short for proper development of characters and plot, especially when it is necessary to devote approximately 20 per cent of our text to 'hots' (sex)." "The net result," Townsend concluded, "is a series of stories with less literary merit then we want to see within the covers that bear our names."[17] Writing approximately ten years later, Steward observed how little things seemed to have changed: "Contemporary publishers of pornography demand from 50 per cent to 75 per cent actual page count of sex scenes in a 35,000-word novel. As in Denmark, the quality of American erotic writing diminished within a few years after the ban against pornography/erotica was lifted. And we may also look forward, if the trend toward these miserable productions continues, to the near-complete extinction of the genre."[18] The striking implication in Steward's remark is that things had been better for gay writers in the moment prior to the end of obscenity.

As a consequence of both porn's crudeness and its associations with crass commercialism, many writers sought to distance themselves from porn by referencing a specific range of other genres. For example, John Rechy's *The Sexual Outlaw: A Documentary* (1977) declared its genre in its subtitle, even as the novel's account of gay sex was so explicit that some bookstores refused to stock it.[19] Similarly, Boyd McDonald's underground zine *Straight to Hell* proclaimed to publish only reader-submitted true accounts of sex between men, which it described as a documentary project via an array of semi-ironized subtitles, including *Archives of the American Academy of Sexual Evidence* and *Sex Research (Men)*. In the introduction to the fourth edition of the popular anthology *Flesh and the Word* (1997), Mike Lowenthal bemoaned the fact that "the vast majority of published pornography is—like any other kind of genre writing—formulaic, stale, cancerous with clichés."[20] In order to distinguish *Flesh and the Word* from the "preponderance of bad erotic writing" flooding the market, Lowenthal redescribed it as a collection of "gay erotic confessionals" containing only "first-person, nonfiction sexual memoirs."[21] "Stripped of their fictional defenses and their pornographic smoke-and-mirrors," Lowenthal explained to his readers, "the contributors to this volume bare themselves at their most vulnerable." Yet despite the fact that each narrative was grounded in the life of its writer, "absolute veracity is not the point. As Toni Morrison has pointed out, there is a crucial difference between 'fact' and 'truth.' The memoirs you will read in this collection are undeniably 'true.'"[22] In what is likely Toni Morrison's only appearance within an anthology of gay "sexual memoirs," Lowenthal works to distance the writing collected in his book from smut: if the latter gets one off, then *Flesh and the Word* will reveal a truth about the world and its relation to the lives of its writers.

At the same time, not everyone was so critical of porn or its relation to literary production. When, in 1983, the former Grove Press editor Donald Allen solicited a number of writers, including Samuel Delany, Patrick Califia, Samuel Steward, and Michael Rumaker, for their thoughts on the powers of erotic representation, he received a wide range of responses.[23] Michael Rumaker answered affirmatively: "[eros] wants to be free to have a good time; it opens the floodgates of playful disobedience and reminds us to treat one another with trust and respect."[24] Steward proffered a similar argument by describing the modern human condition as a "spherical ball, an uncomfortable mesh of steel bonds" that only erotic writing could break: "It frees the spirit, dissolves the bondage. For erotica allows him to escape—through the imagination and the communication between it and the immediate response, simple and direct, much more effective and exact than through music."[25] Meanwhile, Califia and Delany offered more ambivalent takes. The "radical potential" of erotica, argued Califia, depended on the media: the "patina of high art" that clung to painting and sculpture dulled their transgressive force. Film and photography were more likely than other forms to incite calls for censorship, and thus were more immediately powerful. As for writing, the need for literacy rendered it less efficacious than visual media, yet nonetheless it had an edge in its unique ability to capture "the feeling aroused by or the meaning of particular forbidden acts."[26] Finally, Delany's five-page letter, by far the longest of the replies, explained that erotic texts, whatever shape or form they took, could neither "suppress or liberate. They stabilize and destabilize. That is all."[27]

Far from being a settled matter with the end of obscenity, pornographic writing lay at the center of debates and discussions that spanned the final decades of the twentieth century, and which were preoccupied with its relations to literature, power, and gay sexuality. However, we know far less about those debates or their significance for gay cultural production more generally than we do about the wealth of gay print culture during the mid-twentieth century. During the 1970s, a first wave of openly gay critics had characterized pulp novels and physique magazines as shame-ridden consumer culture that quickly diminished into irrelevance following the explosion of sexually explicit films of the post-Stonewall era. Beginning in the late 1990s, scholars such as David Bergman, Michael Bronski, Christopher Nealon, and Susan Stryker sought to counter the elitism of such critiques by not only identifying midcentury pulp writers' literary influences but also revealing the ways that pulp novels and physique magazines often affirmed queer desires while eluding detection by censors.[28] Subsequent work by David K. Johnson, Martin Meeker, and Whitney Strub has elaborated on those insights while highlighting significant connections between pulp publishers and the period's homophile organizations, whose leadership frequently envied the successes of their entrepreneurial colleagues.[29] Moreover, the courtroom victories of gay publishers over obscenity charges helped to install the legal framework necessary for the relatively untroubled proliferation of sexually explicit media in subsequent decades. The writers and activists of the post-Stonewall era, Johnson argued, owed much to the sex-driven consumer culture that came before them.

Reevaluations of gay print culture have greatly deepened our understanding of pulp's role in shaping the sexual politics and culture of that period, yet they have far less frequently carried those insights forward into the final decades of the twentieth century.[30] As an unintended consequence, scholars otherwise attentive to the complex relation between gay literary and popular writing are at risk of uncritically preserving problematic narratives of literary and cultural history, such that pornographic writing becomes an embarrassing relic of the past unable to compete, either politically or commercially, with film and video. For example, in their introduction to the edited collection *1960s Gay Pulp Fiction: The Misplaced Heritage*, Drewey Wayne Gunn and Jamie Harker declare that "the majority of the hundreds and hundreds of books churned out in the 1970s served as little more than masturbatory aids, their quality degenerating further in the 1980s when publishers tried to compete with videotapes as erotic stimuli."[31] On the one hand, Gunn and Harker are correct that the profitability of sexually explicit photographic media did encourage publishers to demand more explicit sex scenes from writers, as Townsend and other writers would complain, and readers certainly employed these materials in acts of masturbation. However, to conceptualize them as mere "masturbatory aids" and "erotic stimuli" drains them of their status as culture. In the search for a misplaced heritage, the true site of literary value, gay pornographic writing becomes little else than a "degenerate" anachronism, seemingly despite its mushrooming across the cultural landscape.

In contrast, this book seeks to restore gay pornographic writing's status as culture by redescribing it as a genre, whose marginality derives, not only from its repertoire of vulgar and potentially offensive conventions, but also from the subordinated social worlds those conventions mediate. In doing so, this book draws inspiration from a number of scholars, including Mary Poovey and Ross Chambers, who have approached the question of genre in sociohistorical terms. According to Poovey, genre refers to an

> ensemble of formal features that are ranked hierarchically within the genre in order to perform a social function; these features are also interrelated with the features of other forms of writing produced at the same time. One advantage of this understanding of genre is that it enables us to view each text both as a member of a larger set (its genre) and in relation to other texts produced at the same time that belong to other genres. Another advantage is that it enables us to see that genres change: as the social function of a par-

ticular genre changes, the hierarchy of its features and its relation to other genres change too.[32]

In *Genres of the Credit Economy: Mediating Value in Eighteenth- and Nineteenth-Century Britain* (2008), Poovey proffered this notion of genre to explain how eighteenth- and nineteenth-century genres of writing mediating reader's understandings of value, including not only aesthetic value but also value as defined in terms of the emerging credit economy. Admittedly, her study is about as far from the subject of this book as one might get, yet her account of genre nonetheless remains a useful means to describe gay pornographic writing because it emphasizes thinking about genres in terms of both their features and their uses.

Understood in those terms, it becomes easier to recognize not only the conventions of gay pornographic writing, but also how those conventions were linked to particular, historically conditioned uses. As I explore in chapter 3, "Samuel Delany, Scott O'Hara, and the Counterpublic of Sleaze-hounds: On the Risks of Public Sex in AIDS-Era Pornography," the out-break of the HIV/AIDS epidemic intensified gay pornography's pedagogical function, evident in Steward's account of *le petite souper*, as activists sought to promote erotic practices among gay men that might prevent the transmission of HIV. As a consequence, the status accorded to condom use as the preferred safer-sex technique led to a general mandate from publishers that writers include conspicuous acts of condom use in their writing. If writers failed to do so, they put the publication of their writing at risk. At the same time, the rearrangement of gay pornographic writing's formal features during the epidemic also reveals something of the ways that genre mediated readers' understandings of value, as a failure to adhere to those new conventions could also induce confusion among readers. Running over five-hundred pages in length, containing few instances of penetrative anal sex, and expressing remarkable ambivalence toward condom use, Samuel Delany's *The Mad Man* (1994) explicitly identified itself as "pornotopic fantasy," yet some prominent gay critics had a hard time recognizing it as such and instead sought to redeem it as a life-affirming work of gay literary realism.[33] Delany continued to challenge such readings and, in doing so, proffered a different understanding of not only what pornography was but also what it did and could do for readers during the epidemic, particularly those men for whom infection with HIV in the era prior to effective treatment paradoxically comprised a source of empowerment.

Delany's minor dustup with his critics over *The Mad Man* highlights the relationship between genres and their social function, as well as how each may change in relation to the other. However, Poovey's formulation of genre doesn't quite explain the visceral response that readers had to Delany's novel or the various ways that writers and readers often understood the transgressive force of their work. As I consider in chapter 4, "Boy Problems: Boyd McDonald's *Straight to Hell*, Matthew Stadler's *Allan Stein*, and the Becoming Historical of Intergenerational Intimacy," Boyd McDonald's underground zine frequently published narratives featuring sex between adults and adolescent boys and did so at a moment in which the category of child pornography was itself taking shape in US jurisprudence. Just as the law increasingly understood the presence of children in suspect images as evidence of a criminal pathology, McDonald construed his zine in documentary terms, asserting that *Straight to Hell* featured not escapist fantasies but "true tales" reported by the many men whose alleged contributions comprised the bulk of the zine's content. The presence of male youth lent *Straight to Hell* a sense of indexicality, itself complicated by the use of other conventions common to gay pornographic writing (if it wasn't porn, then it sure read like it). In subsequent decades, Matthew Stadler would put pressure on such documentary fantasies as they permeated the cultural touchstones of the North American Man/Boy Love Association and its fascination with the impossible genre of boy porn: the depiction of boys in porn depended on their exclusion from the means to create pornography by and for themselves. However, at the same time that McDonald sought to put boys in porn, the law was working to take them out in ways that have rendered McDonald's zine a source of continued unease for contemporary readers.

In *Untimely Interventions: AIDS Writing, Testimonial, and the Rhetoric of Haunting* (2004), Ross Chambers provides a helpful means to understand the visceral force associated with such instances of gay pornographic writing when he conceptualizes genres in terms of their normative qualities. Genre, Chambers explains, consists of a "conventional habitus entailing understandings and agreements that don't need to be specifically negotiated concerning the 'kinds' of social interaction that are possible under the aegis of that culture. Interactions that are nongeneric in a given culture are those that are culturally 'out of bounds,' although they may be generic—that is, they may be regarded as appropriate—in another culture, including one quite proximate to the culture in question."[34] For that reason, a text that works against the norms of its genre qualifies as "*edgy*' writing. Edgy in that it is liminal, writing 'from' the periphery but 'in' language and genres that are simultaneously recognizable and familiar, but 'turned' and strange. Edgy because it is anxious writing from the perspective of its subjects, and because it induces anxious responses in its audience."[35] Chambers has in mind the disturbing qualities of writing that seeks to attest to an event whose atrocity defies resources available to a culture in order to make sense of that trauma, but his account of "edgy writing" might just as readily explain the generic normativity shaping the production and reception of gay pornographic writing. When critics encountered Delany's pornographic novel, they responded by resolving its anxiogenic depictions of risky promiscuity within the genre of literary realism. When McDonald integrated adolescent boys into scenes of gay sex, he sought to marshal the transgressive force of a feature rapidly becoming nongeneric for the purposes of sociopolitical documentary. Like testimonial, gay pornographic writing becomes a genre seemingly defined by its paradoxical willingness to engage in deliberate misuse.

GAY PORNOGRAPHY'S RISKY FANTASIES

It perhaps goes without saying that McDonald's zine raises a number of thorny ethical and political questions. While I will attend to some of those questions, I am more interested in clarifying what writers like McDonald were after in composing pornography that was often not only vulgar and offensive, but also erotically exciting. To do so, this book draws on the conceptual resources of porn studies, which has done more than any other field to broadened our understandings of porn's historical, social, and political significance beyond the terms specified within the feminist sex wars. During the late 1970s and early 1980s, the proliferation of sexually explicit media over the previous decade had provoked responses from a number of feminist critics, most notably Andrea Dworkin, Robin Morgan, and Catherine MacKinnon, who conceptualized pornography as a form of patriarchal violence that individually and systematically disadvantaged women and thus demanded legal redress. In response, libertarian and sex-radical feminists highlighted porn's political and economic significance for women while challenging the paternal role that their opponents assigned to the state. By the mid-1980s these debates seemingly had calcified into a set of antiporn and anticensorship positions, which energized a younger generation of feminist critics working primarily within academic departments of film and media studies to seek out alternative approaches to theorizing porn.[36] In doing so, they crucially reframed pornography as neither a harm nor an uncomplicated form of sexual expression, but as a form of culture whose meanings and uses were far from self-explanatory. The point was not to excuse pornography of its political or ethical implications. Rather, those implications could only become clear through a closer analysis of pornographic representations themselves.

One of the important conceptual moves that some feminist porn critics made was to redescribe pornographic representations in terms of the psychoanalytic concept of fantasy. This concept held particular appeal because it challenged the ways that antiporn critics routinely understood porn spectatorship in terms of the viewer's simplistic desire to emulate the acts depicted on screen. As Laura Kipnis explained: "[fantasies] *don't in any literal way represent desires*: they're the setting for desires. What looks straightforward, like, say, a victim fantasy or a rape fantasy, isn't."[37] Drawing explicitly on the work of French psychoanalysts Jean Laplanche and Bertrand Pontalis, Elizabeth Cowie similarly argued that pornographic fantasy was "characterized not by the achievement of wished-for objects but by the arranging of, a setting out of, the desire for certain objects. It is a veritable a *mise en scène* of desire, a staging of a scene."[38] While not necessarily straightforward depictions of wish fulfillment, fantasies also were not merely escapist pleasures. Instead, as Kipnis argues: "Pornography, then, is profoundly and paradoxically social, but even more than that, it's acutely historical. It's an archive of data about both our history as a culture and our own individual histories—our formation as selves. Pornography's favorite terrain is the tender spots where the individual psyche collides with the historical process of molding social subjects."[39] Understood in terms of fantasy, pornography ceased to be either the authentic expression of a violent desire or a degenerate form of culture. Instead, its vulgar representations engaged the subject's mental life in complex ways, even as it induced seemingly simplistic acts of self-pleasure.

The concept of fantasy, as well as psychoanalytic theory more generally, has also been of use to scholars of gay pornography, such that gay porn studies comprises one of the largest and most active subfields within porn studies itself. Over the past twenty-five years, scholars have highlighted porn's significance for gay subcultures, particularly those for which sexual risk plays a key role in the production of subjectivity and intimacy between men. Following the publication of Tim Dean's *Unlimited Intimacy: Reflections on the Subculture of Barebacking* (2009), scholars have been particularly interested in elaborating pornography's role in the development of organized erotic practices conducted with either an indifference to HIV transmission or a desire to have the virus inside one's body.[40] In doing so, they have effectively countered interpretations of such subcultural practices in terms of the failures of safe-sex education, internalized homophobia, or moral weakness, and instead have offered complex readings of the ethics of risk imagined through bareback pornography.[41] As Dean's account of bareback porn itself demonstrates, the bareback porn of the late 1990s and early 2000s envisioned the act of viral transmission as the basis for homosocial modes of intimacy in which the bodies of women are not necessarily at stake. While the traffic in women has more or less provided the dominant logic structuring forms of male same-sex kinship in the West since antiquity, barebackers joined together in a form of biosociality, according to which the fantasized exchange of a virus links participants together in kinship networks that extend both horizontally in space and vertically across generations.[42] Understood as a form of culture, porn's unseemly fantasies mediated men's understanding of risk in often surprising ways, including the production of benign and even salutary forms of same-sex intimacy.

At the same time, and regardless of whether or not scholars make use of an explicitly psychoanalytic vocabulary, both the field of porn studies and the subfield of gay porn studies suffer from a remarkable bias toward photographic media, such that gay porn has become synonymous with pornographic photography, film, and video.[43] There are of course a number of notable exceptions to that trend, including important work by Lucas Hilderbrand, Earl Jackson Jr., and Darieck Scott, yet the field's narrow focus has led scholars to underappreciate the function of gay pornographic writing in the contemporary period.[44] Moreover, owing to bareback porn's highly controversial, and occasionally sensational, status, it has crowded out considerations of the other ways in which gay porn has mediated men's relation to sexual risk. This variety becomes clearer when one shifts one's attention to the preceding decades, prior to barebacking's emergence as a subculture, and also toward the wealth of other pornographic texts that comprise this book's archive.

I have already alluded to some of those kinds of risk in my brief discussions of Delany's *The Mad Man* and McDonald's zine. However, I explore this problem most fully in chapter 2, "Police Cruisers: John Rechy and Samuel Steward Take on the Hot Cop," which considers how two writers positioned very differently in the field of gay cultural production each addressed the vexed problem of gay men's erotic fascination with cops. Among all the pornographers I discuss in this book, Steward's name likely will be most familiar to readers, as Spring's biography of Steward renewed popular and scholarly interest in his work, yet efforts to recover Steward's life and writing have often framed his novels and short fiction as the happy, sex-positive answer to Rechy's dark and brooding *City of Night*. In doing so, critics have overlooked the frequency with which Steward's regular protagonist remains enamored with the macho "straight" cop, whose dangerousness comprises a significant source of his appeal. Steward was not alone in his cop lust, and both he and Rechy reflected on its bizarre prevalence among gay men who frequently suffered at the hands of cops seeking to entrap, blackmail, or otherwise brutalize gay men by participating in their cruising practices. Both arrived at a similar conclusion: cops provided a form to imagine same-sex intimacy mediated through a kind of hierarchy that made certain kinds of pleasure possible. While they differed on its implications, both conceptualized a practice of gay promiscuity as a means of resistance, doing so in ways that were deeply shaped by the respective genres in which they worked. Rechy's promiscuous, documentary outlaw was the political counterpart to Steward's ethically promiscuous, pornographic hustler.

Writing from socially and politically marginalized positions, porn's defenders often sought to specify its political value in terms of its ability to violate the norms of sexual propriety that structured national culture more generally. By asserting alternative modes of collectivity that differed from either the family, the police force, or the corporation, gay pornography offered an escape from the stifling conditions in which readers otherwise found themselves. However, the transgressive meanings associated with male homosexuality in US Cold War culture were not always or unambiguously aligned with revolution. As Michael Davidson has shown, homoeroticism had an important role to play in "the creation of new artistic modalities and social positions" via the formation of male homosocial communities, such as the Black Mountain school and Jack Spicer's San Francisco scene, yet those communities also trafficked in their own forms of exclusion, including attacks on women poets and brash denunciations of "effeminate" gay writers, including Paul Goodman and Frank O'Hara.[45] In fact, the Cold War culture those poets rejected was itself fascinated by outlaw masculinities, including depictions of dangerous male homosexuals who were able to "blend in" among other, "normal" men. The dangerous homosexual was a staple of pulp novels and popular reportage, but it was also useful for publishers such as Grove Press who were eager to capitalize on the nascent energies of the counterculture. As Glass has shown, Grove deliberately promoted the work of "vulgar modernists," writers who brought avant-garde techniques to bear on representations of transgressive male sexuality.[46] In doing so, the press introduced US readers to not only Henry Miller and D. H. Lawrence, but also Jean Genet, William Burroughs, and John Rechy, whose depictions of criminal homosexuality held significant appeal for White male audiences otherwise chaffing against the suburban normalcy of middle-class American life.[47]

Both pornography and representations of male homosexuality could be very good for business, a fact that both pulp and literary publishers understood quite well. Nonetheless, publishers exploited US readers' interest in sexual nonconformity by leveraging a pervasive heteronormativity against the Supreme Court's new obscenity test, according to which such texts acquire redeeming social value in terms of their value for normal readers. As Glass notes, "Grove marketed [Rechy] in the 1960s as a chronicler of the homosexual world" yet Rechy "struggled against this pigeonholing."[48] "Mr. Rechy can hardly be called a novelist," argued Peter Buitenhuis of the *New York Times*, but, as he went on to claim, *City of Night* had an "unmistakable ring of candor and truth. [. . .] Perhaps, then, the book should be regarded more as sociology than as a novel."[49] Far less generous readers denounced the novel in similar terms. In "Fruit Salad," Alfred Chester's notoriously nasty review for the *New York Review of Books*, Chester dismissed *City of Night* for its failure to "bring anything new to literature, homosexual, socio- logical or American."[50] Himself gay, Chester added insult to injury by going on to call both Rechy's outlaw masculinity and his very existence into ques- tion: "This is the worst confection yet devised by the masterminds behind the Grove *epater-la-post-office* Machine. So fabricated is it that, despite the adorable photograph on the rear of the dust jacket, I can hardly believe there is a real John Rechy—and if there is, he would probably be the first to agree that there isn't—for *City of Night* reads like the unTrue Confessions of a Male Whore."[51] In sum, Rechy was less beefcake than cream puff.

Despite those troubles, Rechy's debut novel was commercially success- ful, and he has since become an important name within the canons of multi- ethnic and gay US literatures. However, not all writers enjoyed the same success. When G. P. Putnam's Sons framed the value of William Carney's *The Real Thing* (1968) in similarly quasi-sociological terms, critics resound- ingly rejected the novel's account of a clandestine homosexual underworld dedicated to high-risk BDSM precisely for the ludicrousness of the world it ostensibly purported to describe. The novel did receive a warmer reception among gay leather and BDSM practitioners, yet Carney remained unsatis- fied insofar as they appreciated the novel not for its aesthetic value, but for what it might contribute to their erotic practices. On the one hand, read- ers' tendency to value literature in terms of its social practicality reflected a broader a shift in reading practices taking place during the early years of the Cold War. As Merve Emre has shown, a variety of civic and economic institutions eager to promote international relations during that period did so by pressuring readers to become competent cross-cultural communica- tors. Instead of learning to recognize the value of literature in terms of its formal complexity, readers learned to read fiction and nonfiction writing alike in ways that emphasized "the cultivation of publicly oriented schemes of action, a weakened commitment to fictionality, a newfound attentiveness to the political temporalities of texts, and the juggling of distinct documen- tary genres."[52] On the other hand, even as Carney's fans were becoming the kinds of adept "paraliterary" readers that Emre describes, their enthusiastic uptake of *The Real Thing* served a very different kind of project, articulated in and through a very different range of genres that included not only literary fiction, but also tracts on animal husbandry, histories of flagellation, and a growing body of gay pornographic writing.

Chapter 1, "William Carney and the Leathermen: Revaluing BDSM in the Pornographic Counterpublics of the 1970s," uses the publication history of Carney's novel to consider how gay pornographic writing provided a queer cultural register in which to revalue gay masculinity, often doing so against a literary public sphere that linked homosexuality to not only effeminacy and pathology, but also fantasy, dishonesty, and unreality.[53] As Martin Levine has shown, the urban gay subculture of the macho clone frequently posited the rhetoric of realness in opposition to the association of homosexuality with failed masculinity: "[Clones] were real men—and in their presentational styles they set about demonstrating their newfound and hard-fought conformity to traditional norms of masculinity."[54] While clones tended to "disfavor 'heavy S&M,'" the rhetoric of realness nevertheless frequently described those practices, as the title of Carney's novel makes clear. In ways that scholars of gay leather and kink have underappreciated, realness also provided a language to imagine gay subjectivity and practices in terms of the risks inherent in print mediation, including the risk that one's arranged date may not be as experienced or as butch as he claimed to be in his letter or classified ad. Readers construed such dissimulation as undesirably effeminizing, and so a general hostility to effeminacy was present throughout the genre. However, and at the same time, writers also utilized the conventions of pornography in other ways, suggesting a profound political ambivalence that cuts through much gay pornographic writing. In addition to being members of a "noble" leather fraternity, participants also often imagined themselves in far stranger terms, as slaves, dismembered bodies, and throbbing objects that spoke to intimacies not necessarily reducible to femme-phobia.

FROM IMAGINED COMMUNITIES TO PORNOGRAPHIC COUNTERPUBLICS

The pornographic writing associated with the gay BDSM and leather subcultures of the 1970s and 1980s was not new, and in many ways its project of trans-valuing gay masculinity was itself an extension and transformation of the gay consumer culture that had emerged and expanded in the US during the preceding decades. In fact, as early as 1951, gay entrepreneurs such as Bob Mizer began building extensive networks of print-mediated gay sociability by publishing physique magazines, subscription book services, travel guides, and consumer catalogs targeted at gay readers and readily available on local newsstands or via mail order. The growth of editorial pages and pen-pal clubs further encouraged forms of exchange not only between physique photographers and their readers, but also among consumers, who occasionally gathered at small conferences dedicated to the appreciation of the male physique. As David K. Johnson writes in the conclusion to his detailed study of midcentury gay consumer culture: "Through these magazines, they learned there were other men out there collecting the same images, wearing the same clothes, reading the same books, decorating their apartments with similar statues. They enjoyed being part of an 'imagined community,' one that had noble roots in an ancient Greek and Roman culture, as these magazines informed them. Perhaps most important, they understood themselves as part of a minority group under attack by forces that consider their desires pathological and illegal. Through these periodicals, a community of men who enjoyed viewing other men's bodies literally became visible."[55]

In many ways, this book picks up where Johnson's study concludes. At the same time, I utilize a different conceptual vocabulary in order to understand how gay pornographic writing continued and revised the project of community formation that Johnson ascribes to midcentury gay print culture. In thinking in terms of the "imagined community," Johnson draws on Benedict Anderson's highly influential *Imagined Communities: Reflections on the Origins and Spread of Nationalism* (1983), in which Anderson coined the term in order to describe how "[the] development of print-as-commodity" during the eighteenth and nineteenth centuries indirectly cultivated a sense of national belonging among populations of readers that were otherwise demographically disparate and geographically dispersed.[56] However, as Michael Warner pointed out, Anderson's account of that process, while highly generative, was also fairly loose, leaving its claims "relatively undeveloped and [the term "imagined community"] undefined."[57] Consequently, scholars of gay print culture who have adopted it have retained its insensitivity to the dynamism that characterizes the social and subjective processes at stake in readers' specific interactions with print and writing, including the ways in which the boundaries and qualities of an imagined community are often unstable and open to constant renegotiation.[58] In contrast, this book prefers the term "counterpublics," which better accounts for how a genre's relation to other genres deployed across a range of print and written media could feed the production of not only identities, but also modes of intimacy often at odds with those very identities.

The concept of the counterpublic itself initially emerged within feminist critiques of Jürgen Habermas's *The Structural Transformation of the Public Sphere* (1962), which described the emergence of the modern public sphere toward the end of the eighteenth century as Western democratic states gradually displaced absolutist forms of rule. If the public sphere had previously referred to the court in which the monarchy presented itself to the aristocracy, then with the rise of print literacy, the public sphere morphed into a space of discursive exchange among citizens who kept the state in check through a practice of disinterested rational-critical debate. The rise of the public sphere was only one feature of the structural transformation Habermas described, as it was divided off from not only the private sphere of the market, which provided the proper domain of self-interest, but also the intimate sphere of the home, in which matters of gender, sexuality, and kinship provided the universal ground of the abstract citizen's humanity. While Habermas initially envisioned that structural transformation as a political ideal, whose full democratic potential had rapidly faded with the rise of consumer-oriented mass cultures, critics subsequently took him to task for ignoring how the demand to bracket one's particularities in fact reinscribed the White male property holder as the unmarked, universal subject of political life.[59] The bourgeois public sphere, in other words, was far from being the site of disinterested public debate that Habermas and others understood it to be.

In addition to exposing the false universalization at the core of the public sphere, critics also focused their attention on exploring how marginalized subjects have devised oppositional networks of discursive exchange, often doing so by way of the mass consumer cultures frequently associated with the decline of the public sphere's full democratic potential. Subsequent work by queer theorists, including Lauren Berlant, Eric O. Clarke, and Warner, further specified the heteronormativity shaping social theory's formulations of the public sphere, arguing that despite the ideological containment of sex within the intimate sphere of the home and family, sexuality was itself mediated through various publics and institutions, including those that promoted forms of US national culture that seemed to have very little to do with sex at all.[60] In the context of those interventions, Warner elaborated on the concept of the counterpublic itself, emphasizing that counterpublics are not only oppositional in the sense that they may consist of statements that challenge the dominant public. Counterpublics are also "counter" because they operate according to pragmatics, "speech genres, idioms, stylistic markers, address, temporality, mise-en-scène, citational field, interlocutory protocols, lexicon and so on," regularly disqualified as improper, offensive, or simply meaningless according to the system of intelligibility that defines the dominant public.[61] In other words, and in contrast to the idealization of disinterested rational-critical debate, counterpublics employ modes of "intimate association, vocabularies of affect, styles of embodiment, erotic practices, and relations of care and pedagogy" to aggregate otherwise unaffili-

FIGURE 0.1. Cover for *Malebox News* 1, no. 2 (1979).

ated subjects in meaningful ways.[62] From that perspective, it becomes easier to recognize how a genre may obtain a social function precisely because it is useful as a "masturbatory aid."

Consider, for example, *Malebox News*, which launched in 1979 and billed itself as "America's most widely circulated direct 'non-coded' personal ad newspaper for gay and bi-sexual men everywhere" (figure 0.1). The phrase "non-coded" indicated that readers perusing the classified ads would not

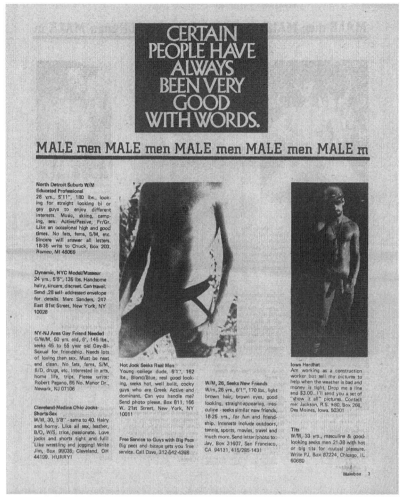

FIGURE O.2. Classified section from *Malebox News* 1, no. 2 (1979): 3.

need to decipher short alphanumeric codes such as "M4M" but instead would find short, sometimes sexually explicit descriptions of what other lonely hearts were looking for. Beyond its promise of erotic contact, the publication also drew in readers for other reasons, including its advertisements for "models" and "masseurs," bar reviews, porn performer interviews, reader-submitted photos, nude artwork, and short pornographic fiction. *Malebox News* thus not only addressed its audience as mere readers, but also imagined them as crucial to its function. As editor Beau Lewis declared at the start of each issue: "Certain people have always been very good with words" (figure O.2). That claim seems to mark out the boundaries of an imagined community, yet it does so by tying membership not to an identity per se, but to a practice — a skilled way "with words." The editor does not specify what that means, exactly, but the statement's context assigns value to writing that has less to do with traditional markers, such as clarity or formal complexity, than with a capacity to incite one's desire. While *Malebox News* pitches itself as being for "gay and bi-sexual men," the coy ambiguity of the phrase "certain people" renders the boundaries of that imagined community far fuzzier than it may initially seem.

The quality of indefinite address that characterizes a counterpublic also highlights one additional feature that will be important for this study: counterpublics are defined by risk. As modes of mediated stranger sociability conducted according to specific temporal rhythms, counterpublics invite transformation by virtue of addressing themselves to strangers. Warner theorized that transformative potential in political terms: unlike the dominant public, which misrecognizes "the indefinite scope of [its] expansive address as universality or normalcy," counterpublics "are spaces of circulation in which it is hoped that the poesis of scene making will be transformative, not replicative, merely."[63] In ways that I will explore, the worlds that readers and writers projected through gay pornographic writing were often very strange indeed. However, I avoid construing gay pornographic writing's vulgar conventions as examples of transgressive sexual politics, whose apparent violation of social and political norms marks the beginning of a queerer world for all: there is no shortage of examples of writers and readers who acted in ways that reflected an investment in oppressive regimes. In many ways, social transgression was itself a key convention of the genre. However, while I recognize that gay pornographic writing was shaped in and through the same ideologies that structure US culture more generally, including the interlinked ideologies of neoliberalism, patriarchy, White supremacy, and settler colonialism, I refrain from reducing the genre's vulgar fantasies in terms of internalized homophobia, political quietism, or false consciousness, as they often gave expression to desires that were difficult to express in any other terms and whose ethical and political implications were often unclear.[64] If gay pornographic writing is vulgar, then it is so because it maintains an intimacy with the limits of sense that seems to adhere within eroticism itself.

This book begins thinking about those limits with its initial foray into the counterpublics of gay BDSM and leather pornography that comprise the subject of chapter 1. Chapters 2, 3, and 4 proceed more or less chronologically, examining different ways in which writers have engaged across the literary-pornographic divide, which lead up to the book's conclusion, "Going Online: Dennis Cooper and the Piglets," which sketches out the literary and erotic implications of pornographic writing's ongoing transition from print to digital publication. The internet itself has shaped gay subjectivities in ways that we are still coming to understand, yet one of the most notable consequences has been the emergence of what João Florêncio terms pig masculinity, which rejects the standards of youth, health, and fitness promoted in mainstream urban gay cultures in favor of risk, sexual fluidity, and corporeal porousness.[65] In my final chapter, I consider how Dennis Cooper's *The Sluts* (2004), which details the erotic exchange conducted over a website dedicated to reviewing young gay escorts, presages the emergence of pig masculinities over the next decade, thereby bringing them into genealogical alignment with those explored in the previous chapters. Critics tend to read the novel's digitally mediated collectivity as queerly transgressive, yet they overlook the ways in which its online community depends on the exclusive inclusion of the adolescent boy, who is a persistent object of fascination for the website's users yet who remains both prohibited from and disdainfully uninterested in participating within its online discourse. While historically porn has been constructed as a form of representation for "adults only," Cooper's novel hints at the ways in which pornography also may provide the primary terms and narratives that have shaped our understandings of growth and development for much of the twentieth century.

To elaborate those meanings, the final two chapters of this book bring its history of gay pornographic writing and literary fiction into preliminary conversation with another genre central to modern notions of selfhood: the bildungsroman. While not a focus of this book, my readings of Stadler's *Allan Stein*, McDonald's *Straight to Hell*, and Cooper's *The Sluts* consider the role that pornography itself has played in narratives of gay self-formation, particularly those that have posed challenges to the idealized form of linear development with accounts of frozen adolescence and sideways growth explored by scholars such as Jed Esty and Kathryn Bond Stockton. As the rapid proliferation of digitally mediated pornography continues to outpace the strictures that adults have devised to limit youth's access to it, pornography may continue to serve as an important source of inspiration in stories of queer self-development. Remaining attentive to the ways that gay pornographic writing has fulfilled a similar role in the past will help scholars better understand such engagements, particularly as the internet has triggered yet another series of moral panics regarding what will happen should minors be exposed to porn too soon. In ways that are highly racialized and gendered, the public imagines such harms in a variety of ways, from the traditional stranger danger to the insidious pathology of porn addiction. My conclusion advocates neither for nor against allowing minors' access to porn. The question is largely moot, and it also distracts us from asking more meaningful questions about pornography's relation to twentieth-century narratives of subject formation and the notions of youth, adolescence, and adulthood that have been so important for them. As one crucial site in which men have imagined what it means to become gay, pornographic writing may also clue us into the ways that current and future generations of writers may answer that question in wholly new and unexpected ways.

CHAPTER 1

William Carney and
the Leathermen

Revaluing BDSM in the Pornographic Counterpublics of the 1970s

This chapter explores how gay pornographic writing comprised counter-publics through a focused analysis of the print culture associated with the gay BDSM and leather subcultures of the 1970s and early 1980s. I begin here for three reasons. First, the amount of pornographic writing produced after the US Supreme Court decriminalized sexually explicit writing is vast, and so some focus is necessary, yet the writers associated with gay BDSM, leather, and other kink-centered subcultures also produced an extraordinary amount of discourse about their fantasies and erotic practices. In addition to the numerous pornographic novels featuring scenes of gay BDSM, that discourse also consisted of conduct manuals, newspapers, and lifestyle magazines, which featured a variety of genres including advice columns, editorials, feature stories, reviews of literature and film, public correspondence, classified ads, short fiction, and serialized novels. Second, the print culture associated with gay BDSM and leather was highly self-reflexive: far from being a mode of solipsistic enjoyment, writers and readers maintained a keen awareness of how print forms fostered imaginary relations between themselves and readers, even if one's interest in BDSM never went any further than an interest in its pornographic representation. Third, in keeping with that self-reflexivity, writers and readers also understood how their fantasies and erotic practices left them doubly stigmatized: they not only faced persecution from police agencies and popular media outlets, which viewed gay BDSM as a source of rhetorically powerful and politically useful sensationalism, but also risked rejection by other gender and sexual minorities who understood kink itself as an inherently oppressive or pathological practice.[1]

Taken together, print mediation, self-reflexivity, and an understanding of one's marginalization are features of the pornographic counterpublics examined throughout this book, yet their interrelation is particularly salient within those of gay leather and BDSM pornography. Counterpublics, as Michael Warner has argued, are forms of culturally and politically subordinated stranger sociability whose "protocols of discourse and debate remain open to affective and expressive dimensions of language."[2] In contrast to public sphere ideology that sets the bracketing of particularities and the use of deliberative reason as conditions for determining the validity and intelligibility of one's discourse, counterpublics treat poetic language, gestures, embodiments, and affects, among many other things, as capable of not only having meaning but also aggregating social life in meaningful ways. Like other counterpublics, the counterpublics of leather and BDSM pornography violated the normative demand to bracket one's particularities, yet they do so via fantasies and practices that are themselves a frequent source of controversy. While the exact terminology can and has varied over the past century, terms such as S&M or BDSM designate a range of roles and practices that employ power differentials in the service of pleasure, often to the point of troubling conventionally liberal notions of consent or erotic mutuality. For example, the letters in the abbreviation BDSM can refer to any one or more of the following: bondage, boy, daddy, discipline, domination, submission, slave, sadist, master, and masochist. An interest in "discipline and submission," which emphasize power, does not necessarily entail a corresponding interest in "sadism and masochism," which emphasize the giving and experiencing of pain. Moreover, the fact that a single letter might refer to two seemingly mutually exclusive roles hints at the erotic mobility such practices can entail. A man who begins a scene as slave might end up as the master by its end.

One of the primary ways that men have signaled their interest in BDSM practices to other men is through the semiotic codes of leather styles. However, while leather and BDSM are closely related, they are not synonymous. BDSM practices predate the twentieth century, yet they acquired their association with leather when the latter emerged in gay male subcultures in the US during the mid-1940s. Following the end of World War II, many gay men who had served in the armed forces found themselves at a loss for the kinds of male homosocial intimacy that had been a regular feature of their lives within a gender-segregated military.[3] In the working-class bars where soldiers and sailors on leave had once mingled with the city's sexual demimonde, leather styles broadcasted one's interest in men whose masculinity had been shaped by similar working-class or wartime experiences. Leather's association with BDSM developed out of that context. Part of BDSM's appeal for leather men pertained to its intensification of, not only the order and discipline that characterized military life, but also the intimacy and vulnerability experienced during affectively intense combat situations. BDSM also provided an outlet for both the specialized technical knowledge gained while working with complex heavy machinery and the pride that came with it: it wasn't enough to hold a whip; one also needed to know how to use it. Finally, the matters of technical knowledge and a desire for affectively intense homosocial intimacy were interrelated: BDSM entailed another man skillfully bringing one to one's physical, mental, and erotic limits without inflicting permanent damage. Sometimes treated as an erotic sport, BDSM for some men more closely approximated a spiritual or aesthetic practice.

While visions of gay leather found their way into the queer avant-garde creations of filmmakers like Kenneth Anger, the growth of markets for pornographic writing during the 1970s would help drive the popularization of leather styles during that decade and beyond. Social scientists such as Gayle Rubin and Peter Hennen have performed invaluable work in tracing out the intertwined histories of gay leather and BDSM practices, yet the importance of gay pornographic writing, and print culture in general, for the development of contemporary gay leather subjectivity and BDSM practices has been underappreciated by scholars of the subculture. In fact, porn appealed to readers because it provided a language for them to manage the "historically sedimented connection between same-sex desire and effeminacy" that Hennen has termed the "effeminacy effect."[4] As a consequence, the close association between BDSM and leather styles would weaken not only as leather styles themselves proliferated, but also as many men found themselves attracted to leather's "dark world of masculinity," but with little corresponding interest in BDSM practices.[5] At the same time that leather was giving many middle-class gay men a chance to be "real men," its pornography also cultivated a way of relating to others that took far stranger forms, providing another perspective on the vexed relation between male homosocial desire and aesthetic innovation that Michael Davidson associates with the masculinist poetic communities of the Cold War.[6] While often resembling forms of violence or gross dehumanization that contrasted starkly with norms of safety, consent, and erotic mutuality, porn provided a language for modes of sociality that resembled kinds of objectification, degradation, and dehumanization and whose logic was best expressed in a phrase that appeared in an advertisement for an anthology of pornographic letters: "I am not just a human being, I am a piece of meat."[7]

In addition to showing how gay pornographic writing mediated forms of gay subjectivity and intimacy during the 1970s, this chapter concludes by exploring its budding relation to gay literary fiction through a study of

William Carney's debut novel *The Real Thing*. Published in 1968 by G. P. Putnam's Sons, Carney's compact novel told a story of intrigue and revenge set within a clandestine gay leather and BDSM subculture. While Carney understood his novel as a complex modernist work, Putnam framed it for readers as a mix of fiction, sociology, and psychological case study that promised a slumming tour through one of the nation's most perverse and thus most fascinating sexual underworlds. Unfortunately, critics failed to take the novel seriously, and it likely would have fallen into obscurity if not for the enthusiastic reception it received within the burgeoning pornographic counterpublics. As one pornographer put it, *The Real Thing* was "a landmark book for the leather set."[8] However, more than simply providing a register in which to revalue a novel that had struggled against the heteronormativity of the public sphere, gay pornographic writing also drew inspiration from Carney's depictions of a "dark world of masculinity," and the novel inspired at least one writer to adopt the plot for his own pornographic novel. As the history of Carney's novel shows, gay pornographic writing was, in a sense, marginal, yet as such it provided an alternative means to value representations of gay BDSM that fed the production of markets for gay literary fiction and laid the groundwork for its legitimization, such that new editions of Carney's novel could reappear as a "gay classic" marketed to gay readers by the end of the twentieth century.

HANDBOOKS, CLASSIFIED ADS, AND A MAGAZINE FOR THE MACHO MALE

Neither Carney's novel nor the wealth of gay pornographic writing it inspired were the first instances in which gay leather itself went public. By the early 1960s, mainstream publications had introduced their audiences to the leatherman through reportage ostensibly meant to educate readers on the general danger that male homosexuality posed to the moral fabric of the nation while titillating them with firsthand accounts of its underworlds. Perhaps the most infamous example appeared in the form of a pair of feature stories for the June 26, 1964, issue of *Life* magazine under the headline "Homosexuality in America": "A secret world grows bolder. Society is forced to look at it—and try to understand it."[9] As Lee Edelman has argued, the feature exploited the anxiety generated by "the cultural invisibility enjoyed by homosexuals" by taking readers on a slumming tour through gay subcultural spaces,[10] yet it opened with a photo taken inside San Francisco's Tool Box, glossed as one of many "S&M bars ('S' for sadism and 'M' for masochism)," thereby identifying the leatherman as the exposé's central emblem of maladjustment.[11] Playing on the theme of indiscernible danger, the photo depicted a group of young men dressed in jeans, white T-shirts, and leather jackets milling about the bar's darkened interior, thereby infusing an image of rebellious White male youth with a sense of perversity. With their faces shrouded by cigarette smoke and shadows, the men exude a conspiratorial feel, yet the journalist Paul Welch tempered any anxiety the photo might generate by noting the "obsessiveness" of the men's efforts to "appear manly," reassuring readers that despite such posturing homosexuals were doomed to a "furtive, hazardous, and lonely" existence.[12] When the leatherman stepped onto the national stage, he did so unintentionally, as an example of social menace at once terribly thrilling and utterly impotent.

At the same time that mainstream publications were enlightening readers about the varieties of sexual perversion infiltrating polite society, many gay men were taking advantage of the changing legal and social context in order to produce a range of publications by and about themselves, often with mixed results. As David K. Johnson has shown, the 1950s and 1960s witnessed the efflorescence of a gay consumer culture premised on readers' enjoyment of the male physique. Originating out of the health and fitness publications that had been a staple of the male bodybuilding cultures of the 1930s and 1940s, physique magazines appealed to readers with an interest in the male form. Widely available on newsstands and through subscription mail order, physique magazines sometimes utilized bodybuilding culture as a cover for readers with decidedly more erotic interests, yet the magazines themselves were not always so shy about their endorsement and promotion of male homoeroticism. "Far from being in the closet," Johnson explains, "gay men's place in bodybuilding culture was part of public discourse—the subject of frequent editorials, pop culture depictions, and discussions in both mainstream and gay circles."[13] Moreover, physique entrepreneurs were also interested in facilitating connections and exchanges among readers, which readers heartily welcomed. According to Johnson: "Physique customers responded to and encouraged these efforts as they came to understand themselves as part of a community of 'physique enthusiasts' enjoying and being excited by the same images, and being marginalized for that desire—even if it went unnamed."[14]

The physique magazines, and gay print culture more generally, provided more than just an opportunity to connect with other men over the enjoyment of the male form. They also provided a shared set of images and language through which to imagine a kind of transhistorical sexual and gender identity. With titles such as *Grecian Guild Pictorial*, the physique magazines cultivated a sense of imagined community by constructing a collective history for readers rooted in notions of Greek homoeroticism, which it merged surprisingly with contemporary notions of Christian fellowship that val-

ued exercise, clean living, and spiritual discipline.[15] The manly comrad-
ery among physique aficionados provided an alternative means for many
middle-class gay men to imagine a mode of homosexuality distinct from,
not only the pathologized version circulating in popular discourse, but also
the effeminacy embodied by the pansies and fairies of the working-class bar
scene.[16] "While those communities centered around bars and other sites of
urban leisure," observes Johnson, "the more masculine-identified gay men
of the post-war period found community through a network of gyms, physique magazines, homophile organizations, and other nonbar settings."[17]
At the same time, physique publishers such as Bob Mizer often employed
young working-class men as models but presented them to readers in terms
of a middle-class wholesomeness.[18] Such effacements of the models' class
position both consolidated the physique magazines' imagined community
of masculine-identified gay men and mitigated the stigma of working-class
queerness. In doing so, publishers also protected themselves from the threat
of censorship that such vulgar association might engender. By the late 1960s,
physique publishers had scored a number of courtroom victories, including
those associated with *MANual Enterprises v. Day* (1962) and *U.S. v. Spinar
and Germain* (1967), thereby clearing the way for the generally untroubled
proliferation of print cultures devoted to the sexually explicit elaboration of
gay masculinity in subsequent decades.

The classically inflected fantasies of the physique magazines, as well as
the various problems that characterized their production, served as a precursor to many of the gay publications of the 1970s and beyond, including those associated with the leather subcultures. John Embry's *Drummer*,
which announced itself as "America's mag for the macho male" is perhaps
the best-known example. The magazine began its run following Embry's
work during the early 1970s with the Homophile Effort for Legal Protection
(HELP), an organization founded in 1968 to provide legal services to gay
men arrested in Los Angeles.[19] After briefly helming editorial duties for the
HELP Newsletter, which Embry had renamed *HELP Drummer*, Embry left
that project to found *Drummer* in 1975. According to Jack Fritscher, who
served as editor in chief of *Drummer* between 1977 and 1979, Embry largely
abandoned any pretense to serious political discussion and reframed the
magazine as a lifestyle publication dedicated to the elaboration of "homo-
masculinity." The magazine's title announced that project in two ways: it
was at once a nod to Clark Polak's Philadelphia-based physique magazine
Drum and to the famous passage from the conclusion of Thoreau's *Walden*:
"If a man does not keep pace with his companions, perhaps it is because he
hears a different drummer," which editors regularly quoted in the magazine's masthead.[20] In doing so, *Drummer* sought to counter the pathologiza-

tion of male homosexuality while retaining its sense of antisocial danger. In the wake of *Drummer* and other instance of leather print culture, men such as Fritscher could look back on *Life* magazine's "Homosexuality in America" and find a radically different meaning: "Long before the gay press was 'legal,' *Life* had discovered the Art and Lifestyle boom that something butch this way comes demanding civil rights. What a shock to American culture: Sissies weren't the only fags."[21]

In thinking about the shift from physique to leather magazines, Johnson notes that publications such as *Drummer* often "featured frequent nostalgic odes to physique artists and photographers," thereby maintaining a connection to the print culture that came before.[22] However, the focus on images distracts from how those images existed within a body of print-mediated discourse that proved instrumental not only for mediating forms of post-Stonewall gay masculinity but also for producing the kind of transvaluation evident in Fritscher's rereading of "Homosexuality in America." Put differently, the imagined community mediated through physique magazines was itself a product of a counterpublic composed of not only its photographs and illustration but also the message services, book clubs, catalogs, and other forms that Johnson's study amply documents. A similar diversity of genres and media also characterized the counterpublics of leather print media. For example, *Drummer* often featured photospreads, but it also printed short fiction and serialized novels, comics, news reports, photo essays, reviews of various kinds, classified ads, and letters to the editor, which often complained about the kinds of bodies that the magazine regularly featured. Like physique culture, *Drummer* skewed White, and readers occasionally wrote in asking for more diverse representation. However, in keeping with the homogenizing trends at work in the physique magazines, *Drummer*'s readers at times also demanded the opposite. For example, in October of 1976, *Drummer* ran a cover story on the Cycle Sluts, a drag troupe of bearded men who complemented sequins, boots, and big hair with BDSM accoutrement.[23] The cover of that issue depicted a close-up shot of the Cycle Sluts' members, yet, as Fritscher reports, "this was *Drummer* magazine's most unpopular cover ever. Leather animus against gender-fucking anima began in the next issue and simmered for years."[24]

In addition to facilitating debates that policed the content and contours of homomasculine identity, *Drummer* also provided a venue for readers to argue over the meanings of particular fantasies and erotic practices. For example, in his review of Richard Plante's historical study *The Pink Triangle: The Nazi War against Homosexuals* for *Drummer* magazine, the pornographer T. R. Witomski used his conclusion to take aim at the use of fascist iconography in BDSM, arguing that "[gays] who embrace the Nazi mystique vilify themselves; accepting the straight world's condemnation of homosexuals"; while those fantasies were the consequence of gay men's existence within a homophobic culture, Witomski argued, gay men's use of them reflected a dangerous complacency: "Nazi-loving gays are walking into the ovens of a new Auschwitz."[25] In subsequent issues a number of readers responded. Patrick Califia pointed to Witomski's authorship of stories about Roman gladiators, crucifixion, and erotic torture to question whether or not he was making a special case of the Nazis: "Does he really want to be a galley slave (or a Roman centurion)?"[26] Califia then concluded by arguing for greater conceptual clarity in political analyses of porn and the erotic practices they inspired. Similarly, Eric Rofes observed that there was a "tremendous difference between our sexual fantasies and our politics"; moreover, fantasizing about oppression was one manner in which sexual minorities survived it: "I know leading gay activists who spend their days fighting anti-gay bigotry and spend their nights turning on to a fist pounding their stomachs as a 'fag-basher' calls them 'queer' and 'cunt' and 'sissy.'"[27] The magazine's publisher also weighed in, declaring that what one did or consumed didn't matter as long as it was done so in an appropriate fashion: "if two people participate in such a fantasy scene safely and by mutual consent, that is their own erotic trip and none of my or anyone else's business."[28]

The heat of the debate over Nazi-themed fantasies derived from a general sense that there was some kind of connection between such fantasies and one's historical experience, even if that connection was far from clear. In other words, fantasies were not simply private pleasures, but an aspect of erotic life that mediated one's relationship both to oneself and to others. While some participants in the leather counterpublics were most concerned with the political and ethical implications of men's fantasies, others were far more interested in exploring their value for the cultivation of particular erotic practices. For example, Larry Townsend's *The Leatherman's Handbook* (1972) explained a variety of BDSM practices and leather styles to readers while following each section with a short pornographic narrative, allegedly culled from either Townsend's own experience or that of a friend, meant to serve as an illustrative example. As the pornographer and leatherman John Preston put it: "*The Handbook* not only delivered information on what to wear, where to go, how to act, it was still spiced with stories that created a narrative which a man could use to understand and envision his fantasies. (Or, if he wanted to, he could simply enjoy the erotic story telling and leave it at that. He did not need to physically enter the realm if he didn't want to.)"[29] A self-styled leather and BDSM guru, Townsend was also a prolific writer of gay pornographic fiction and a frequent contributor to *Drummer*, helming an advice column titled "The Leather Notebook" that ran in the magazine from 1979 to 1992. However, he is perhaps best known for his handbook, which was and remains a popular text: It was reprinted three times between 1974 and 1993. In 2000, it was reissued as a silver jubilee edition. In 1983, Townsend published *The Leatherman's Handbook II*, which updated much of the material while also addressing the implications of HIV for kink, suggesting the ongoing significance that such publications had in mediating subcultural norms and practices.

"LIKE SOME WILD MOVIE, OR THE PICTURES THEY SELL IN ADULT BOOKSTORES"

Examples like *The Leatherman's Handbook* or *Drummer* magazine highlight the role that print culture played in the formation of gay masculine identities and the mediation of subcultural erotic practices. A closer look at some of its pornography reveals how that process occurred in and through the properties of print publics as it's through the conventions of pornography that the qualities of print publicity, such as an openness to strangers, come to adhere within various forms of leather sex. For example, Townsend's 1970 *Leather Ad: M* adopted the conceit of the classified ad and message service as a means for structuring its episodic narrative. The novel also served as a guide about the risks and rewards of arranging BDSM encounters not at the bar but through the mail. Its plot follows the handsome young Johnny as he arranges a series of sexual encounters with other men in order to explore his budding interest in masochism and submission. In one scene, Johnny arranges to meet Rick through the mail service, but he is dismayed to find that, in contrast to the handsome stud that Rick described himself as being, he is instead overweight, much older than he claimed, and "though he wore boots, he was also somewhat nelly."[30] The scene is significant because it locates the risk of arranging anonymous BDSM encounters not in the physical danger that a stranger might pose, but in the possibility that one's potential sexual partner has used the limitations of the genre to deceive. Significantly, the scene also polices the boundaries of gay masculinity by construing Rick's deception as effeminizing: while Rick may entice his tricks with his sexy writing style, it masks a style of comportment at odds with Johnny's vision of a real man. Real men, in a sense, were men of their word.

The problem of misrepresentation occurs frequently throughout *Leather Ad: M* and, to a lesser extent, in the novel's 1972 sequel *Leather Ad: S*, but the scene with Rick is the only one in which sex does not follow. More often than not, the novels underscore the value of sex with strangers, despite the risks and despite not necessarily getting what one originally had in mind. Other scenes address issues that might occur within cruising venues. For example, after spending some time at a local bar, Johnny picks up a dominant young hitchhiker whose rough sex verges on abuse. "That I live to tell about it was sheer luck and certainly not the reward for any responsible judgment," Johnny states of the encounter, but the absence of lasting repercussions suggests that while the sex was not something to repeat, it was also not regrettable (40). A similar scene occurs in a later chapter, after Johnny and his lover Bobby (the dominant/sadist protagonist of the sequel) attend a hippie house party that quickly turns into a drug-fueled BDSM orgy. The chapter ends with the following "solemn oath": "Our single experiment with drugs would be our last. For us, at least, pot and leather would never combine again" (157). However, it is difficult to say that these scenes function as cautionary examples of what the reader should avoid. The qualification "for us, at least" limits the scope of the couple's oath, leaving intact the suggestion that some forms of erotic risk-taking are valuable in and of themselves.

These examples highlight a number of different risks that might attend men's participation in a public practice of leather sex. Those risks include the possibility that one's partner might misrepresent himself, that one might not enjoy the experience as much as one thought one might, and that one's partner might not demonstrate the practical skills or attentiveness necessary to perform BDSM practices without damaging one's trick. In addition to those, some notable examples of leather pornography approached another kind of risk, which had less to do with one's partner than the particular risks that one posed to oneself during the encounter. In *Leather Ad: M*, the most significant—if also most extreme—example of an erotic encounter ostensibly gone wrong occurs when Johnny and Bobby arrange a threesome with a sadist named Tim, hosted in a modified warehouse loft in the city's industrial district. Tim begins the evening's scene by serving his guests cocktails and showing them his slideshow of homemade pornography: photos he has taken with previous guests. However, the seemingly generous host has spiked Johnny and Bobby's drinks, and when the two regain consciousness they find themselves restrained in preparation for a series of erotic torments. It is the only scene in which Johnny and Bobby endure practices such as suspension (being hung by the limbs), piercing, and branding committed explicitly against their will. To that extent, it serves much like earlier scenes that highlight everything that could possibly go wrong with public leather sex: don't meet men in their own homes, don't accept drinks you didn't make yourself, and only arrange encounters with people you know and trust.

Despite those warnings, the scene takes a more complex stance toward the encounter, doing so by way of an extended reflection on pornography's capacity to recast actions that seem unappealing, terrifying, or violent in erotic and potentially salutary terms. The scene hints at its own pornographic transvaluation in a number of ways, including the pornographic slide show with which Tim seduces his soon-to-be captives, yet the most obvious comes in Johnny's repeated comparisons of the scene itself to pornography. As he puts it, the ordeal is, "Christ, like some wild movie, or the pictures they sell in adult bookstores . . . but real; it's real! My cock's getting hard . . . if he sees it . . . Jesus!" (165). On the one hand, the comparison acknowledges how Tim's actions lack the effort necessary to inflict real damage on Johnny and Bobby, even as they nonetheless solicit a variety of protestations. For example, while Tim states that he has fastened "piano wire" around the base of Johnny's cock and balls, Johnny quickly realizes that it is not the razor-sharp material his captor claims it to be. Similarly, Tim also employs a noticeable degree of restraint in his use of the whip: "I knew that he wasn't hitting me nearly as hard as he might. That weapon would easily have taken off a layer of skin had it been laid on with any degree of force. This realization, plus the entire atmosphere, sustained my level of excitement. My cock, despite my conscious wish to the contrary, continued to remain hard and pointed" (166). To inflict irreparable damage on Johnny and Bobby would violate the scene's logic, transforming it from pornography into something more akin to a horror film.

Recast as pornography, volitional acts such as Tim's actions acquire new meaning, yet so too do the involuntary movements of the body. Hence, Johnny's enduring concern for both the presence and visibility of his erection, which under Tim's ministrations "continued to swell, obstinately refusing to heed the commands of my brain. *Quit it! Soft! SOFT!* Still, it continued to rise" (165). On the one hand, the visibility of Johnny's erection reflects the masculine version of what Linda Williams has described as a pornographic will to knowledge regarding feminine pleasure. "Hard core," Williams writes, "desires assurance that it is witnessing not the voluntary performance of feminine pleasure, but its involuntary confession."[31] While hardcore pornography must engage a number of formal strategies in order to render visible the elusive truth of feminine pleasure, masculine pleasure has the ready signifiers of erection and, most spectacularly, ejaculation. Yet in *Leather Ad: M*, the visibility of Johnny's involuntary pleasure does not serve as an indicator of truth, but as a kind of instantaneous feedback mechanism that guides Tim's actions. For that reason, whenever Johnny's or Bobby's erections begin to deflate, such as when Johnny realizes the piano wire is not as sharp as Tim claims it to be, Tim will switch tactics. To that extent, Tim is less the sadist or sexologist than a participant within a pornographic structure, where intentions matter far less than the value, or sexiness, assigned to one's actions. The erection as a barometer of arousal displaces ejaculation as the signifier for masculine pleasure, as the goal is to take Johnny and Bobby to the maximal limits of their pleasure and keep them there for as long as possible.

The final but perhaps most significant reflexive comment the narrative makes about pornographic mediation comes at the conclusion of the Tim chapter. Tim's torments exhaust Bobby and Johnny to the point where they can continue no further. Their captor sedates them once more, and the two men awaken the next morning in the car they left parked outside Tim's now-darkened and seemingly abandoned warehouse loft. They are largely unsure of what to make of their experience until a few days later, when they receive a package from Tim containing "a full dozen eight-by-tens of our experience" (173). Johnny responds enthusiastically: "The pictures were sexy! There was no disputing that, and the photo technique, using the available light so we were never aware that they were being taken, made them all the more exciting" (174). In fact, Tim's photos are so good that Bobby and Johnny find themselves aroused and, accordingly, retire to their bedroom. The images help the couple to reconceptualize their experience with Tim: "the memory of our night with Tim, terrifying as it was when it happened, gradually assumed a different proportion for both of us. [. . .] As with all things, the passage of time increased the pleasure recall and blunted the painful aspects until they were nearly forgotten" (174). Johnny's comment regarding the "different proportion" the events obtain in light of the photographs hints at the importance of pornographic aesthetic for producing that transvaluation. Pornography helps Johnny and Bobby to rethink and revalue their experience without ever completely losing sight of its more troubling dimensions. They are "nearly," not entirely, forgotten.

The fact that Johnny and Bobby remain unsettled regarding the meaning of both the photographs and their experience with Tim prevents its easy recuperation as consensual kink. Instead, it highlights the ways in which such experiences might be both desirable for their intensity but also undesirable for the disturbing effects they produce. To that extent, Johnny and Bobby's experience resembles what the sociologist Staci Newmahr, in her ethnography of a pansexual S&M community, calls intimate edgework. According to Newmahr, "[intimate edgework] exists on and *for* the edges of what people should and should not feel in given situations. This is distinct from the emotional culture of edgework [among] rescue workers. This emotional edgework is not about the emotions that come with edgework or their management [i.e., the rush of being a race car driver or the soldier's thrill of mastering his fears during combat], but about the risk in emotional experiences. Emotional edgework explores the line between emotional chaos and emotional order, between emotional form and emotional formlessness, between the self and the obliteration of the self."[32] Another term for emotional edgework might be what Leo Bersani described as pleasure's capacity to momentarily shatter the ego. For Bersani, self-shattering harbors an ethical potential alternative to sexuality's ego-inflating pleasures and the normative masculinity that traditionally incorporates practices of erotic dominance and self-assertion. Subsequent theorists have figured shattering in terms of orgasm, either to develop it into a traumatic encounter with jouissance or to critique it as an overvaluation of sex's potential for radical change. However, Newmahr's intimate edgework helps to redescribe shattering not as a spectacular instant but as a durational practice, which provides an emotionally intense "rest" from one's masculinized ego but which cannot be easily assimilated into the ego. Thus, Johnny and Bobby are never quite sure what to make of their experience with Tim, despite the fact that both find the photos "sexy."

To be sure, Townsend's novel holds its print-mediated debasement of masculine gay identity in tension with the consolidation that identity. Throughout *Leather Ad: M*, Townsend holds up normative values of sexual autonomy and self-respect as important for gay men, and the novel ends with a sunny endorsement of these values when Johnny delivers an impassioned declaration of his newfound and well-cherished identities: "I'm an M, bottom man, masochist. And I've found [in Bobby] my boss, my master, my lover . . . and I'm happy!" (201). I don't want to be (too) cynical about the novel's conclusion or the representations of subcultural identities it provides. Narratives such as *Leather Ad: M* likely supported important survival strategies for many men even as the novel's conventional, marriage-plot-like conclusion treats episodes such as the Tim scene as if they were an afterthought, equivalent to a collection of pornographic photos or novels that one can easily stash in a bedside table when one no longer has a need for them. For example, a significant conflict in *Leather Ad: S* involves Bobby's concern that his love for leather will ruin his ability to enjoy and perform more conventionally intimate practices. Yet the novel concludes with Bobby staring tenderly at Johnny beside him, realizing that "I like leather-sex, like being S . . . even M, sometimes. But with this guy I love, it doesn't make any difference. It doesn't matter. When sex and love are one, it simply doesn't matter" (192). The conclusion provides a powerful contrast against the dual stigmatization of kink and homosexuality, even as it leaves the more troubling encounters in Johnny and Bobby's lives and gay masculine identities unexamined.

Not all leather pornography concluded with such sunny endings, and one of the more popular stories from the period provides a far better example of the ways in which pornographers leveraged BDSM against a gay macho identity. Perhaps the best known is Aaron Travis's short story "Blue Light," which more clearly captures the intense pleasures of leather sex by way of conventions more proper to the fantasy genre. "Blue Light" first appeared in the July 1980 issue of *Malebox*, but it was reprinted in various gay life-style magazines after its initial publication and is frequently anthologized in contemporary collections of gay pornographic fiction.[33] The story follows a self-styled gay macho sadist named Bill who has rented a room in a large Houston house occupied by a butch lesbian couple and a mysterious hunk named Michael, who resides on the house's top floor. After spying a half-naked Michael at work in the garden, Bill gets the idea to seduce and dominate him sexually, yet things don't go as planned. As it turns out, Michael is a mystical rent boy who uses his powers to give his clients "special" experiences. In the midst of their sexual contest, Michael places a spell on Bill that magically separates his head and cock from his body, and renders the now-smooth patch of skin between his legs into a site of penetration. While Bill still perceives every smack and caress delivered to his various parts, they refuse to obey his increasingly panicked thoughts. Michael warns Bill that if he orgasms before the spell is removed, then Bill will live out the rest of his days as a castrated sex toy, his permanently erect cock kept in a velvet bag stashed in Michael's dresser alongside the severed erections of his other sexual conquests. The story's conflict thus derives from the fact that Bill is unmanned, literally and figuratively, but finds the experience so seductively pleasurable.

"Blue Light" exhibits a reflexive orientation similar to the Tim episode, yet while the latter mediates Johnny's experience through Tim's photographs, the former employs the conceit of the magic spell. In doing so, it literalizes Bill's self-observation but also underscores that act as an estranging experience when Michael instructs Bill that he'll find his shattering easier to handle if he imagines that his body is another man. As Bill does so, the various parts acquire a life of their own:

> It was crazy; something was wrong in my head that I could look at my body and feel such cool detachment. At the time, I didn't realize that. I was where Michael had put me, in some strange psychic zone.
>
> That body turned me on. The hairlessness showed off my muscles, as Michael had said it would. Everything looked larger, fuller. Especially my pecs, big mounds of sleek muscle. The nipples, normally buried in swirls of hair, stood out from the flesh taut, looking exquisitely sensitive, begging to be touched. My cock and balls, hairless and chained, looked larger than life, but not commanding; exposed and vulnerable. *Do it*, I begged silently. *I want to see it crawl. I want it.*[34] (42–43)

In this passage, Bill undergoes an experience of self-shattering similar to that of Johnny's, such that his encounter with Michael's magic causes him not only to break into literal pieces but also experience a durational period of psychic fragmentation and disorganization. As a consequence, it becomes difficult to locate Bill as a speaking subject at any point in the narrative, as his account consists of disorienting shifts in perspective and verb tense as well as pronoun use that slides between the demonstrative, possessive, and third person. Moreover, the passage's turn toward present-tense italics further suggests that Bill is experiencing something of the fantasy scene's disturbing effects in the present time of his narration. It's as if telling a story about disturbing sex can be just as disorienting as the sex itself.

Bill's pornographic fantasy demonstrates the disruptive effects that desire has on his pretense to gay masculinity, which he sought to reaffirm through his sexual conquest of Michael. Luckily, things turn out well for Bill in the end; he manages to keep it together just long enough that Michael reassembles him into a whole body, but Bill does not suddenly see himself as in possession of a newer, more progressive sexuality that reconciles his investments in conventional masculinity with the pleasures of emasculation. Rather, Bill's intense and unexpected enjoyment of the scene leaves him shaken. The story's conclusion highlights this point through the contrast it establishes between Bill and Carl, the previous tenant of the room in the house where Bill now lives. After recovering from his bout with Michael, Bill secretly watches as Carl makes a late-night visit to Michael, pleading for sex. Eventually, Michael complies, retrieving Carl's severed erection from his dresser drawer, where he keeps it reverently "wrapped in blue silk." The sight is too much for Bill. He moves out of the house that night but confesses an "urge to see Michael again—a glimpse of his broad shoulders, from a safe distance, would do" (56). The point being, of course, that no amount of distance would ever be safe for Bill if he wanted to maintain his masculine sense of self. There is no possibility of reconciling his macho identity with his desires, yet that impossibility itself serves as an intense source of pleasure, repeatable in a somewhat safer form via its narration to others.

Both of the scenes that I have discussed so far depict intimate edgework as a strangely social experience. While sometimes viewed as solipsistic, self-shattering in those scenes encompasses an encounter with what stubbornly resists going public. Each scene imagines such an encounter by positing that "something else" seems both present yet occluded to the action taking place. On the one hand, literal others such as Tim, Bobby, and Michael are present to the action. On the other hand, both scenes register a more enigmatic presence in the experience of self-fragmentation, according to which each character seems doubled—or tripled—by both Johnny's unruly erection and Bill's spectacular dismemberment. Each character beholds something that makes itself perceptible within the stylized movements of their own bodies, even as that enigmatic presence remains hidden from view. At the same time, each narrative contains an additional layer of publicness insofar as each character's seemingly solitary experience seems open to the view of others. This is less conspicuous in "Blue Light," but I have in mind Bill's past-tense narration, the trophies that Michael displays to his visitors, and the moment in which Bill spies on Carl's return. The sense that one's experience is not necessarily one's own is more explicit in *Leather Ad: M*, which reproduces Johnny's torments as a pornographic text: Johnny's experience is not only like some "wild movie"; it *is* a set of wild photographs that arrive in the mail and, one might also assume, have worked their way into the slide show that Tim regularly exhibits to his victims. Put differently, leather pornographers imagined modes of counterpublic sex for which one's own objectification constituted a condition of participation.

In order to clarify that point, I'd like to briefly examine its succinct expression in one last example: an advertisement for Boyd McDonald's *Meat*, an anthology of erotic letters collected from his liberationist magazine *Straight to Hell: The Manhattan Review of Unnatural Acts. Straight to Hell*, which first appeared in 1973, disdained fiction and rejected sexual identity categories as a basis for representation. Instead, it consisted entirely of readers' reports of true-life sexual encounters that were occasionally reprinted on the pages of more overtly BDSM-themed publications such as *Drummer*. The quote in question appears next to a male figure with an appended speech bubble: "I am not just a human being, I am a piece of meat" (figure 1.1). The ad poses a series of correspondences that descend the slight S-curve of the model's body, beginning with his head and speech bubble, extending through his hands and the text box he holds, and finishing with the bulge in his underwear and the text that floats freely next to it. A different sense of "meat" dominates at each level: meat signifies the man's enthusiastic self-debasement, his inclusion within the anthology, and his cock. The man is objectified as meat. The ad ties this objectification to his status as an object available for public circulation: just as his finger points at the text box, his shadow's phallic-shaped finger points at the mail-order form. However, the result is not a subtraction of humanity from one's person but the addition of something else expressed in the statement's implicit syntax: not just human, but also meat. The advertisement, like both *Leather Ad: M* and "Blue Light," thus proposes a form of public objectification, in which one's exposure before a public becomes at once a means of degradation and exaltation.

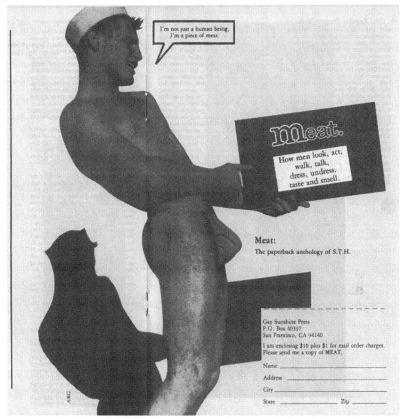

FIGURE 1.1. Advertisement for *Meat: How Men Look, Act, Walk, Talk, Dress, Undress, Taste, & Smell: True Homosexual Experiences* (San Francisco: Gay Sunshine Press, 1981). From *Straight to Hell* 1, no. 48 (1980): n.p. Reproduced with the permission of Billy Miller. Photograph: Leather Archives and Museum, Chicago.

RECOMMENDED READING: *THE REAL THING*

The modes of erotic practice imagined in and through the pornography of the leather counterpublics were not exactly new, and in many they had literary forebearers in the kinds of transgressive, self-annihilating masculine sexualities depicted within the novels of the many writers popularized by Grove Press during the 1950s and 1960s. As both Loren Glass and Jordan Carroll have argued, Grove Press marketed "vulgar modernists" such as Henry Miller, Jean Genet, John Rechy, Hubert Selby, and William Burroughs by hitching their novels to the period's growing countercultural energies, yet those books most often appealed to a male readership safely if also listlessly ensconced within the professional security of a manage-rial career and the quiet monotony of the suburbs.[35] Far from being politi-cally transformative, the transgressive erotics of Grove's vulgar modernism did little to challenge the status quo, even as Grove itself had dramatically expanded the range of writers available to a general reading public. Yet that isn't the whole story, and the counterpublics of leather pornography drew inspiration from a far wider body of nonfiction and fiction than only Grove's catalog. In fact, a frequent source of inspiration was William Carney's *The Real Thing* (1968), which explicitly tied the intimate edgework of BDSM to one's objectification before a shadowy public of leathermen. However, Car-ney's novel would not enjoy the same kinds of success, whether commercial or critical, that Grove's vulgar modernists enjoyed. Nonetheless, the novel did not fall into complete obscurity, and its persistence owed much to the leather publications that paved the way for its revival as a gay cult classic in the 1990s.

In this final section, I explore that history in order to consider how por-nographic counterpublics were an important yet overlooked component in the formation of gay literary fiction during the late twentieth century. Yet I begin here with a brief biography of Carney for readers who may be unfa-miliar with him. Like many of the men who participated in the gay leather scene of the 1950s and 1960s, William Carney had been a military man. Born in Alabama in 1922, Carney served as a gunner in the US Air Force during the Second World War. Afterward, he obtained a bachelor's degree from the Missouri School of Journalism and then spent some time in New York where he pursued additional studies and worked as a translator and edito-rial assistant for a scientific journal. He divided the remainder of his adult life between Paris and California's Bay Area, where he obtained a master's degree in French literature from the University of California, Berkeley, and then worked as instructor for the university's extension. Carney was also a prolific writer, having produced in his lifetime manuscripts for several novels and a biography of the French playwright Pierre Beaumarchais, yet he published very little of that work. By the end of his life, he had managed to see only three of his novels into print: *The Real Thing* (1968), *A Year in a Closet* (1972), and *The Rose Exterminator* (1983), each of which comprised a chapter within what Carney had envisioned as a massive literary saga whose narrative spanned the entire twentieth century.

Carney's fiction blended his intellectual, literary, and erotic interests. Most noticeably, the title of *The Real Thing* is a direct reference to Henry James's novella of the same name, yet where the latter offered a meditation on the aesthetic by way of an artist's musings about his models, Carney's novel did so through its account of a clandestine leather subculture. *The*

Real Thing is a slim epistolary novel made up of a series of letters sent from an estranged uncle to his nephew intended to introduce the young man into the ways and means of the real thing: a form of intense BDSM believed to cultivate the self through the rigorous testing of the limits of one's mind and body, such that recreational sex gives way to highly aestheticized rituals of pleasure and pain. In each chapter, the uncle unveils new aspects of the real thing, or "the Way," while providing feedback on his nephew's actions, which he observes anonymously and at a distance, from the darkened corners of bars, clubs, and parties where the adherents of the Way practice their erotic art. As the protégé grows in skill and experience, the pedagogical plot gives way to one about family revenge: the uncle's former student in the Way was the brother of his current protégé. The former student died under mysterious circumstances, and the new protégé and his mother, the uncle's sister, believe that the uncle is responsible for his death. The nephew's efforts to ingratiate himself to his teacher amount to an attempt to maneuver him into a vulnerable position wherein he and his mother can enact their own murderous retribution.

The novel's pedagogical plot creates an explicit contrast between the family and the real thing, two modes of cultural transmission that the uncle considers to be mutually exclusive. When the nephew-cum-student expresses concern about having his uncle initiate him into the world of gay BDSM, the uncle responds by dissolving their familial bond: "Your newfound interest and my abiding one will form a common ground placing us beyond such considerations. I feel actually that I have no family, and that is exactly as I and they wish it to be."[36] This change is further emphasized in the anonymity that surrounds its characters. While names are important for families, being the primary means by which they designate a sense of shared identity, names are far less significant in the uncle's world; they are never revealed, and individuals are only ever referred to in the uncle's letters with an initial, such as "J." or "H." In fact, one's name matters far less than one's actions, which other members subject to stringent evaluation. The uncle provides a description of that process in response to his nephew's mistaken belief that his recent failure to seduce a more experienced man will go unnoticed:

> You are and will be from now on the property, and in a manner of speaking the common property, of this clan of which you have made yourself a part. Knowledge of your private actions, your manner of approaching arrangements, your successes and failures, are of interest for reasons far beyond any slight considerations of petty gossip, slander, or violated privacy. And, privacy? Here there is no privacy, not even when you are, as you were (or

were you? do you really *know* whether or not someone might have been observing?), alone with a partner. A crowd of ghostly witnesses will always be at hand, for your own mind will summon up surrogates, as it always does, in the stead of actual observers, and you cannot help but move with the knowledge that you are being watched. The thing is to have them of your own choosing and to rid yourself of unwanted ghosts. (48)

Everyone becomes property insofar as everyone's actions become available for scrutiny and evaluation. Unlike the family, shrouded as it is in domestic privacy and tasked with the formation of moral conscience, the real thing is inescapably public. Moreover, as the uncle warns, practitioners do best when they internalize the practice of communal sexual-aesthetic judgment in the form of "ghostly witnesses." One is never alone with one's partner when one has sex; moreover, one would never want to be alone, as the ghostly witnesses, both inside and outside the subject, are crucial for the production of erotically intense and perfect actions.

However, as the reader soon learns, divorcing one's self from one's family is never so easy. As the plot to avenge the brother and former student begins to unfold, the lessons continue, further developing the uncle's theory of the real thing while foreshadowing the novel's bloody conclusion. For example, the uncle gives advice to his nephew on how to subdue and seduce the experienced man "J.," but the uncle warns that physical strength isn't enough. "You would do well to gag him immediately," advises the uncle, "since, frankly, I doubt that you will be able to withstand either the threats or the bargaining he is capable of—he is a most compelling and seductive person no matter the circumstances in which he finds himself" (128). The nephew's adversary is capable of literally talking his way out of any predicament in which the nephew places him. Such verbal seduction plays a crucial role in the final series of confrontations between the uncle and his nephew, wherein the latter manages to subdue the former and castrate him. However, despite the act's brutality, it acquires a new value within the framework of the Way, and several of the uncle's letters follow, begging and pleading with the nephew for a final meeting in which the younger man will finish the exquisite work that he has started.

The novel's ending reveals one more twist in the works. Addressed not to his nephew but to his sister, the final letter hints at the fact that the uncle's pleading for his nephew to return and finish the job was, in fact, his own calculated seduction. Having successfully lured back his now-former student, the uncle murders him. "Madam: he ought never to have come," the uncle begins, "J., it appears, had wisely warned him not to, and H., his other conspirator, already appalled at the results of what he had lent his consent if not his hand to, had clearly suggested to him what might happen if he gave in and came to see me. His mistake was not in cutting off my nuts, but in not cutting out my tongue" (157). Yet this final betrayal marks not a failure but an erotic culmination. The uncle's warning to his nephew that "[here] there is no privacy" remains true, as he completes his final betrayal of his protégé not only as an act of revenge but also as a means to distinguish himself among others as the most skillful practitioner of the real thing. As the uncle explains to his sister: "For I stood to win, no matter what he did. To have refused the challenge I flung at him would have meant that I was bested by one better than myself, and—most important—by one trained by myself and, so it would seem, for just this purpose" (158). The sexual aesthetics of the betrayal, its perfection, matter more than the personal motives of family strife that drive the betrayal in the first place.

The uncle warns against becoming too certain in one's beliefs about what the world is and what others think. Yet, the novel builds a world that is all the more immersive for its enigmatic qualities. First, the past events that have led to characters' current machinations are never fully explained, forcing readers to cobble together their own theories regarding what transpired between who and why. Second, the novel's one-sided epistolary form heightens the reader's sense of distance from the actions of its characters, news of which arrive secondhand via the uncle's vague and frequently euphemistic descriptions. That sense of distance calls attention to the ways that not only knowledge but also assumptions about what one knows provide the basis for many of the novel's power plays: it's the various characters' unshakable belief in their ability to ascertain the details of the others' state of mind that leads to their eventual downfall. In a novel that seems devoted to producing excellent students of the "Way," the story delivers a warning against sentimental reading. Thus, while the novel has all the trappings of an exposé, a tour of the ways and means of the real thing, it more appropriately serves as a late modernist example of the literary texts by queer writers who, as Scott Herring has shown, experimented with the conventions of urban slumming literature in order to thwart the genre's will to sexual knowledge.[37] The great irony of Carney's novel is that while it continuously teases an education in the real thing, the real thing itself never appears.

Nonetheless, the novel's ostensibly ethnographic qualities, and not its literary value, are what appealed to its publisher. After Carney completed the manuscript for *The Real Thing* in 1967, he managed to secure the attention of an agent at G. P. Putnam's Sons. However, the editor delayed the formal publication process in order to vet the manuscript with, in the editor's words, "an authority with greater knowledge than my own of the accuracy of the material contained herein."[38] By authority, the editor meant a psy-

chiatrist. The decision irritated Carney for a number of reasons. First, it put
the publication of the manuscript in question by linking its success to the
opinion of a mental health professional. Second, it challenged Carney's own
authority as a subcultural insider. In a letter that Carney drafted to his agent,
his anger on that point is palpable: "Does he mean that his psychiatrist goes
that route? Or does he mean that his 'authority' has handled some talkative
relapses from the discipline? My reaction to either of these is no more than
a shrug; if it is the first, then his man is an expert, if the latter, then he is, as
he states, merely an 'authority.'" Third, Carney objected to the implication
that the novel was anything other than a work of literary fiction. As his letter
continues: "what puzzles me is the suspicion that [the editor] may see this
work in the light of some kind of case history. [. . .] The point is that this
is first of all and above everything else a work of art. It is also, but on a sec-
ondary plain [sic] of importance, quite accurate in its details."[39] For Carney,
if the novel had redeeming value, then it was decidedly aesthetic.

Despite what appeared as a minor inconvenience, Carney remained
optimistic about the opportunities the novel's publication might bring.
For example, in November of 1967, he consulted with an agent regarding
the prospects for a film adaptation, yet decided that the novel's epistolary
form—rather than its content—would likely dampen any studio interest.
However, the psychiatric consultation proved to be a forewarning of additional difficulties, and Carney's success continued to be bittersweet as Putnam and subsequently critics continued to construe the novel in principally
sociological rather than literary terms. The Real Thing appeared on book-
shelves early in 1968 as a handsome hardcover edition with its title set in
gold lettering on a black dust jacket textured to resemble leather, yet it also
included an introduction by Alan Hull Walton, billed on the back cover as
an "internationally known literary critic and specialist in the field of erotol-
ogy," that asserted the novel's value for the fields of "psychology, sociology,
anthropology, and morals."[40] While the introduction recognized that the
novel had some literary merit, it subordinated the novel's literary qualities
to its sociological value. For example, Walton identified The Real Thing as
"French roman noir" yet concluded that it was "an honest document of a different morality."[41] The publisher's advertising lauded the novel in similarly
confused terms: "In the tradition of the Marquis de Sade, with the artistry
of D. H. Lawrence and Jean Genet, and with the authority of Krafft-Ebing
and Havelock Ellis—William Carney reveals the dark byways of the sadomasochistic psyche in The Real Thing."[42]

Notably, in invoking the names of Lawrence, Genet, and Sade, Putnam
implicitly associated Carney with the slate of vulgar modernists that Grove

Press had recently popularized. As Glass has shown, perhaps no other publisher profited more from depictions of sexual transgression, and male homosexuality specifically, than Grove, which sought to capitalize on the energies of the nascent counterculture by defending and publishing works that frequently blurred the line between male homosexuality and hetero-sexuality.[43] Like Putnam, Grove employed experts who could testify during obscenity trials to the redeeming aesthetic or social value of controver-sial works and tended to favor sociological arguments for its gay writers, thereby exploiting not only developments in obscenity law but also the will to knowledge about male homosexuality. For example, while *City of Night* never faced obscenity charges, Grove nonetheless marketed its author as a "chronicler of the homosexual world."[44] Critics followed that lead, dismiss-ing the novel's aesthetic value while praising it for its subcultural insights. Writing for the *New York Times*, Peter Buitenhuis remarked that "Mr. Rechy can hardly be called a novelist" yet nonetheless praised *City of Night* for its "unmistakable ring of candor and truth. It makes the reader see, without insistence, the awful compulsiveness of the homosexual act, the pathos of the transvestite, the loneliness beneath the callow toughness of the hustler. Perhaps, then, the book should be regarded more as sociology than as a novel."[45] While *City of Night* failed as a literary work, it was nonetheless worthy of readers' time for its ostensibly honest account of the nation's sexual underworld. If Rechy had been the "Kinsey of the homosexuals," as Buitenhuis had claimed, then Carney was to be Putnam's own lucrative cultural informant-cum-resident sexologist.[46]

Unfortunately for Carney, *The Real Thing* was largely panned by critics. Some, such as the book critic for the *Atlantic*, ridiculed its subject matter: "Correspondence school sadism is a promisingly funny notion. Unfortu-nately, Mr. Carney has approached it in all sobriety and produced preten-tious flapdoodle reminiscent of Monk Lewis."[47] Others, such as the critic at *Publishers Weekly*, complained that the novel's complex epistolary form failed to provide the slumming tour that its publisher had promised: "After all, when you take sex out of sexual perversion there isn't much left."[48] As one might expect, such reviews frustrated Carney, despite the fact that he found some support for his work among friends. In correspondence with Carney, the poet and fellow leatherman Thom Gunn praised *The Real Thing* and commiserated with its author over the inclusion of the Walton introduc-tion: "I can see why you find the introduction annoying, and I do too: it is irrelevant and could be misleading. The point is that the book should stand up even if the entire social background were completely out of your imag-ination. And it does stand up. The book is beautiful and terrifying, and the style is austere, lucid, and all that I most admire in prose."[49] However, more widespread recognition of *The Real Thing* as an unqualified work of literary fiction would largely elude the novel for the majority of Carney's lifetime.

While Carney struggled to gain the kinds of literary recognition he desired within the literary public sphere, his novel received a far warmer reception within the burgeoning gay press. Both the *Los Angeles Advocate* and New York's *Mattachine Newsletter* reviewed the novel favorably, although the latter valued the novel as both "a 'how to' book for the leather set" and a study of sadomasochism's role in forms of male homosociality, such as the Christian church or US Marines.[50] The novel received its most enthusiastic reception within the counterpublics of leather pornography. In addition to its own pornographic narratives and sections devoted to technical advice, Townsend's *Leatherman's Handbook* included a section devoted to "Literature," yet among the histories of flagellation, pamphlets on animal husbandry, pulp novels, and the "complete" and "unexpurgated" editions of Marquis de Sade that he recommended, he also directed readers to *The Real Thing* "for its literary merit; I would not suggest that a novice really take it to heart."[51] Himself no novice, Townsend *did* take the novel to heart insofar as *The Real Thing* provided a source of inspiration for his own pornographic fiction. His novel *Run, Little Leatherboy*, published in 1971, adopts the conceit of *The Real Thing* but dispenses with the epistolary form to tell a story about a far more congenial arrangement between an erotically talented gay uncle and his nephew. At one point, *The Real Thing* makes a cameo on the uncle's bookshelf; elsewhere, when the young protégé reveals his amorous feelings for his uncle-cum-mentor, the older man warns him that "[we] must not commit the foibles of Carney."[52]

Townsend was not the only one taken with the novel, either, and one can find references and favorable reviews of it peppered throughout the novels and subcultural publications that began to appear in greater frequency during the 1970s. The July 1976 issue of *Drummer* included a favorable review of *The Real Thing* by Ed Franklin, who praised the novel's form and quasi-mystical exploration of "S&M." "I recommend the book virtually without qualification," Franklin wrote.[53] However, the novel's popularity also led to some troubles, allegedly spurring *Drummer*'s publisher John Embry to blacklist Carney's writing from the magazine. According to Fritscher, the volatile Embry "had grown wary of the successful and challenging Bill Carney of San Francisco—which, Embry implied, was not a big enough town for the two of them."[54] The novel's subcultural popularity generated other kinds of headaches for Carney. In 1981, more than a decade after the novel's publication, Carney had written to David Lewis at the 15 Association, which is now one of the longest running organizations in the US dedicated to gay

BDSM, politely asking them to cease their unauthorized serialization of the novel in their newsletter. Carney had concerns both practical and aesthetic: serialization not only threatened his chances of publishing a new edition; it also spoiled the novel's form (*The Real Thing* was something to be read all at once, Carney elsewhere insisted).[55]

Carney worked for much of his life to republish *The Real Thing* and thereby rehabilitate its reputation, but he would not live to see Richard Kasak Books issue a trade paperback edition in 1995, replacing the Walton introduction with one by the gay cultural critic Michael Bronski. It also remains to be seen how Carney would have felt about such republication, which did little to shake the associations with pornography that troubled its original release. During the 1990s, Richard Kasak had made a name for itself as a publisher of gay erotic literature. In addition to publishing texts such as Oscar Wilde's *Teleny* and Samuel Delany's *The Mad Man*, the press also utilized its Bad Boy imprint to print new works of gay pornographic fiction and to reprint popular pulp novels from the 1970s, sometimes adjusting their content to match the taste of contemporary readers accustomed to a greater degree of sexual explicitness than the original texts had to offer.[56] Yet, in stark contrast to the novel's mainstream debut, the association of *The Real Thing* with pornography comprised an implicit recognition of some kind of value — if not also praise. It would also ensure that Carney's appeal for both BDSM practitioners and fans of its pornography extended into the new millennium. In the acknowledgments section of his pornographic anthology *Hard Men* (2004), the pornographer and public sex theorist Patrick Califia recognized Carney as one of the writers who "made me want to write about hard-ons, butt holes, and leather sex as well as they did and do."[57]

The kinds of BDSM pornography that Townsend, Preston, and Califia wrote sustained a memory of Carney's novel through their various acknowledgments, adaptations, and recirculations within gay pornographic counterpublics of the 1970s and 1980s. On the one hand, *The Real Thing* doesn't contain explicit depictions of sex, making Carney's inclusion within Califia's list of porn writers somewhat incongruous, and its characters seemed to feed into stereotypes of homosexuals as both antisocial and dangerous. On the other hand, these qualities may have been precisely why Carney's novel resonated so strongly with readers from the BDSM and leather subcultures. As reflected in the title of Califia's anthology, the characters in *The Real Thing* were hard men: they not only contrasted with the prevailing belief in the mutual exclusivity of homosexuality and conventional masculinity, but also organized themselves into a coherent form of sociality in which risk and danger seemed to be crucial sources of pleasure. They preceded and predicted the rise of other masculine gay social identities during the late

1970s, such as the gay clone for whom "hard-fought conformity to traditional norms of masculinity" and "detached, objectified, and phallocentric
sexual conduct" served as hallmarks.[58] While Carney's leathermen failed to
find much respect within the national culture, they would provide inspiration for the elaboration of men's leather identities and practice within the
pornographic counterpublics that began to proliferate in the next decade.
An interest in sexual risk would continue to feature within forms of leather
sexuality, and while the pornography would warn against the possible dangers of a print-mediated sexual sociability, it would also identify those risks
as integral, even vital, sources of intimacy and pleasure.

In this chapter, I've attempted to show how pornographic counterpublics depended on a kind of public objectification, for which fantasies of the
body's eroticized fragmentation mediated forms of gay male sociability.
While gay pornography certainly operated as a masturbatory aid, even the
acts of solitary pleasure it inspired could facilitate kinds of print-mediated
intimacy with other readers, a counterpublic of "ghostly witnesses" imagined to be present to one's pleasures. However, even writers who embraced
pornographic representation expressed some ambivalence about its take on
objectification. On the one hand, some pornographers understood porn's
traffic in stereotypes in terms of an idealized sociability. In the words of
Fritscher: "It is a curious 'compliment' within gay culture that the very eth-
nicity of a person, even a howdy white redneck, can be objectified by himself or others into a sexual fetish without prejudice. Page through all the
Drummer stories, and read the revealing Personal sex ads, lusting with equal
opportunity after Blacks, Latinos, Asians, Southern white trash, and the disabled during that taboo-busting heyday when Robert Mapplethorpe, Rex,
and Tom of Finland were fetishizing blond Nazis."[59] However, the reduction
of persons to stereotypes isn't arbitrary, but based on a history of White
supremacist or class oppression that has been responsible for producing
those traits in the first place. Whatever equality emerges does so at the cost
of disavowing historical violence and without redressing its effects. As Martha Nussbaum might ask: how can all objects be equal if the condition for
becoming an object in the first place is a history of one's violent dehumanization?[60]

On the one hand, scholars such as Darieck Scott and Ariane Cruz have
revealed the ways in which Black subjects have found empowering intimacies through both BDSM practices and pornographic representations
that conspicuously employ forms of racialized objectification, and so one
shouldn't dismiss these practices and representations outright because of
their social and political unseemliness.[61] Moreover, the leather counterpublics sometimes drew in unexpected participants. For example, Viola

Johnson, an important public figure in the history of Black lesbian BDSM practitioners, has described how the popular gay leather magazine *Drummer* was a favorite read among her lesbian friends.[62] On the other hand, the experiences of Black gay men and gay men of color with leather pornography confirm the fact that racialized fantasies were not simply fantasies, but in part responses to the White supremacist practices that shaped the publishing industry. For example, writers have pointed out the ways in which *Drummer* rarely featured either Black men or men of color in prestige positions including the magazine's cover. Similarly, Cain Berlinger reports that editors could be quite forthcoming about how the devaluation of Black bodies informed their editorial decisions: "we were told how whenever *The Leather Journal* featured a prominent member of the Black Leather Community on its cover, sales would drop."[63] As a consequence, a normative Whiteness constrained Black gay men's participation within the counterpublic. As Berlinger explained: "I am often hesitant to tell editors (not that I need to) that I am Black, afraid that I might lose favor, but I think that's just paranoia, although, I don't want to test it."[64] In some cases, publishers and other gay business owners engaged in practices that justified Berlinger's paranoia, such as when Embry permitted ads for the Gay National Socialists in *Drummer* magazine until his editorial staff publicly pressured him to stop doing so.[65]

In his memoir of his time working at *Drummer* magazine, Fritscher proffers two explanations for Embry's willingness to flirt with a fascist organization. The first reason had to do with Embry's vision that *Drummer* would become a "leather *Evergreen Review*."[66] Just as Grove had capitalized on the transgressive energies of its vulgar modernists, *Drummer* would do so in the service of promoting and elaborating leather's subcultural norms. The second reason pertained to Embry's ongoing animosity toward the Los Angeles Police Department. Through his experiences with HELP, Embry had become very familiar with police harassment of gay men, and he sought to use *Drummer* as a means to provoke the police with content that pushed the line of obscenity. According to Fritscher, "*Drummer* was a noble undertaking, but with the rebellious hubris of a bottom taunting a top, founding *Drummer* publisher Embry provoked the Los Angeles Police Department so relentlessly [. . .] that he nearly destroyed the magazine when he caused the LAPD to arrest him and forty-one other leatherfolk at the infamous Drummer Slave Auction in 1976."[67] In order to enrage the police as much as possible, Embry "stuffed *Drummer* with shady topics that drove [LAPD chief Ed Davis] crazy," including "bestiality themes and underage sex ads and Nazi display ads that Embry fancied made him and his petulant *Drummer* politically relevant in that first decade of gay liberation after Stonewall."

In ways that echo Carney's own dashed hopes for literary fame, *Drummer* magazine never became the avant-garde magazine that Embry apparently desired it to be. Moreover, after the police raid on the *Drummer* charity auction, Embry relocated the editorial offices for his magazine from Los Angeles to San Francisco and relinquished editorial control to others who would steer the magazine in a relatively less controversial direction.

For Fritscher, Embry's decision to run ads for the National Socialist League had little to do with Embry harboring sympathies for fascism. Instead, it had everything to do with his desire to transform *Drummer* into a publication that would regularly frustrate, offend, and provoke the true enemies: the LAPD and its ultraconservative chief. Fritscher evokes the power dynamics of gay sex to characterize Embry's relation to the police, yet it may be less of a metaphor than Fritscher suggests, as the macho, potentially violent cop was no stranger to gay pornographic writing. In the next chapter, I explore how two writers positioned on either side of the pornography-literature divide, Samuel Steward and John Rechy, explored that question in their fiction. On the face of things, they seemed to reach different answers. Growing up in the border town of El Paso, Rechy was both familiar with and outraged by the regular harassment that working-class sexual, gender, and ethnic-racial minorities faced from the police. Beginning with his reportage, continuing into *City of Night*, and extending into much of his midcareer work, he formulated a critique of policing that located homosocial eroticism at its core. In contrast, Steward's fiction actively embraces the cop in order to probe the top cop's seemingly irresistible appeal, but rather than pit one writer against the other, the next chapter considers how their respective takes were formulated in and through the genres in which they worked. In doing so, we begin to expand our understanding of, not only the kind of intimacies and subjectivities that gay men imagined in and through pornography, but also the kinds of political and ethical value they assigned to each.

CHAPTER 2

Police Cruisers

John Rechy and Samuel Steward Take on the Hot Cop

With the attenuation of US obscenity law, the spread of pornographic counter-publics provided an important foothold for gay writers who had struggled against the heteronormativity of the literary public sphere described in the previous chapter. These networks of discursive exchange self-consciously mediated gay subcultural identities and practices utilizing a repertoire of unseemly conventions, including scenarios of objectification and corporeal fragmentation, which reflected how the conditions of print publicity have shaped men's understanding of themselves and their relations to others since the mid-twentieth century. This chapter offers an extended investigation of gay pornographic writing's repertoire of conventions through a comparative analysis of two writers, John Rechy and Samuel Steward, each of whom explored the privileged place that gay men had accorded to the cop within their BDSM practices and pornography. As Steward would at one point put it: "why was it that so many gays wanted to make a cop more than anyone else in the world?"[1] In less humorous terms, Rechy also took up that question in a number of his early novels, and over the course of a decade developed a critique that linked the presence of cops in gay porn to both the criminalization of gay sex and its persecution by the police officers who patrolled the public spaces in which sexual and gender dissidents congregated. However, this chapter considers how Rechy's and Steward's respective genres enabled each to introduce questions of pleasure and desire into thinking about the risks that cops posed to public sex cultures, thereby highlighting dimensions of policing, its meaning, and its value otherwise neglected within cultural critiques focused on documenting cases of police violence and corruption.

It's difficult to exaggerate the extent to which the police officer is an overdetermined figure within the US cultural imaginary. In one form or another, the police are perhaps the most represented profession in popular culture, serving as the protagonists or antagonists within a variety of genres across different media, from reality television programs and radio dramas to Hollywood blockbusters and prestige films to pulp paperbacks and literary detective fiction. Moreover, as Christopher Wilson has shown, cops have also played an active role in the representation of their own work, such that modern policing entails a kind of "knowledge work" oriented toward producing "the first drafts of a great deal of our cultural knowledge about social disorder and criminality."[2] The rise of social media has further contributed to the glut of representations of cops while enabling creators to push back against the narratives that police agencies tell about themselves. However, the images of police violence circulated via mobile devices comprise only the most recent efforts by marginalized subjects to challenge the institution of policing, the structural inequities it preserves, and the sympathetic portrayals of itself that it often generates. The social turmoil of the late 1960s likewise occasioned a number of critical takes on cops, in many ways setting the language and tone for subsequent cultural critiques of policing. James Baldwin's "A Report from Occupied Territory," for example, famously invoked the language of embedded journalism in order to reflect on the urban protests sweeping the country in 1966, describing the police as an occupying army that protected White property at the cost of Black lives. Baldwin thus imagined a continuity between the police and the military, for which Black bodies became a dispensable tool to subdue and police populations abroad: "They are dying [in Vietnam] like flies," he concluded, "they are dying in the streets of our Harlems far more hideously than flies."[3]

In addition to their involvement in the deaths of those they are supposed to protect, cops also emerge as a flash point in US culture because police violence crystallizes a fundamental problem within modern democratic politics concerning the state's capacity to use coercive and potentially deadly force against its own citizenry. The conditions under which such force is appropriate, who may be empowered to use it, and by whom they may be so empowered are the subject of a vast body of historical, political, sociological, and philosophical writing, too vast to survey here in any coherent or easily digestible form. However, the theoretical problems inherent in the notion of police power and its frequent instantiation in documented instances of police violence have made it difficult to imagine the relation between cops and marginalized populations in anything but repressive terms. My point here is not that such analyses are wrong or deficient, but that such framing has rendered it difficult to understand the meaning that the cop acquires in gay pornographic representations in terms that do not situate violence or oppression as the primary terms of analysis. Thus, accounts of contemporary queer politics frequently frame themselves as an ongoing and heroic conflict with not just the state but also the police, from the raids on queer social spaces to the bedroom invasions at the heart of landmark legal cases, such as *Bowers v. Hardwick* (1986) and *Lawrence v. Texas* (2003). In the context of such historical narratives, the cops' pervasive presence within gay pornography might seem like evidence of gay men's questionable allegiances, their unconscious investment in oppressive political systems, or merely an embarrassing lack of seriousness.[4]

While politically expedient, such arguments reflect a lack of engagement with the object under critique, thus overlooking the ways in which gay men frequently debated the meaning that cops and other authority figures acquired in pornography, and that they did so within the same cultural contexts in which the offending representations themselves also circulated. For example, Rechy has made a name for himself in part for his unapologetic narratives of gay promiscuity, yet his early novels regularly explore the role that desire plays in the policing of dissident sexualities. Beginning with *City of Night* (1963), continuing through *This Day's Death* (1969), and culminating in his experimental novel *The Sexual Outlaw: A Documentary* (1977), Rechy developed a stark condemnation of the police that stalked the nation's urban sex publics by calling attention to the ways the cops themselves occasionally got in on the action. Rechy's fiction posited the existence of a universal homosexual desire whose repression stabilized the fraternal bonds among police officers and motivated their undercover vice operations. However, the instability of that repression also meant that cops provoked and at times participated in the action by soliciting gay men and having sex with them before subjecting them to arrest.[5] Critical of neither BDSM nor pornography per se, Rechy nonetheless posited that the eroticization of the police was merely a symptom of the ways in which the criminalization of homosexuality structured gay men's relations to each other by demanding punishment in exchange for the enactment of one's outlawed desire.[6] Thus, in a manner resonant with Baldwin's own use of reportage, Rechy turns away from cop porn and toward oppositional social documentary to expose the law at the center of gay men's fantasies.

In light of such a forceful critique, Steward's fascination with hot cops may seem like so much grist for Rechy's mill. As he would muse in his own autobiography: "The fondness I had for the police was an indication, I suppose, of the deeply buried residue of guilt from my childhood which accounted for my psychic masochism."[7] However, his pornography offers a very different take, perhaps one hinted at in the qualifying statement "I suppose." For example, in the 1964 short story "The Peachiest Fuzz," Steward's regular protagonist Phil Andros, an itinerant hustler who has landed a gig managing a small Chicago gym, is busy closing up shop for the night when a cop enters and makes a pass at him, triggering a series of anxious thoughts: "suppose I get so far and he says something like 'Come on, buddy—let's you and me go down to the station house.' Still—said another side—he can't do that, not with the Illinois law."[8] The story briefly instructs the reader on how the state of Illinois had decriminalized sodomy in the previous year, which Phil factors into his calculations of the risks and pleasures of bedding a cop.[9] Phil flirts; the cop flirts back, yet Phil remains unsure as to whether it will all end in sex, arrest, blackmail, or some combination thereof. The story's conclusion underscores that uncertainty while also identifying it as erotic in and of itself: naked except for a jockstrap and a few of his uniform's accessories, the cop turns to Phil and utters the story's last words: "and now what?"[10] The irony being that, no matter what, it's the cop's story that carries the day in court.

More than a decade before Michel Foucault would do so, Steward's story identifies both pleasure and the unsaid as integral to the operations of power. With *The History of Sexuality, Volume 1,* Foucault delivered his famous rejoinder to the repressive hypothesis that had motivated much of the sexual revolution's countercultural action. As Foucault argued, repressive models of power, especially those inspired by a particular strain of psychoanalytic theory, took patriarchal law as their model, and in so doing neglected power's productive operations at the nexus of pleasure and knowledge.[11] Steward's abrupt ending was, in part, a consequence of a legal climate in which sodomy laws prohibited homosexual acts and obscenity laws prohibited their explicit representation, yet the story works within those constraints by using the cop to imagine a productive mode of power, such that the story's eroticism lies in the sense of possibility that exists within the cop's concluding question. In other words, the story uses the cop to imagine not only the generativity of constraints but also the ways in which pleasure was integral to that process, each of which Steward also described in his biography only shortly after initially explaining his cop lust in terms of guilt and masochism: "the policeman—well, he was the single point at which the law touched the individual, the ultimate authority, and when he was young and handsome, he could hold me in his hands and shape me like clay."[12] In that formulation, contact with the cop entails contact with an impersonal agency, at once erotically intimate and opaquely transformational. The body molded as one molds clay suggests a remarkable vulnerability, yet it also suggests the reorganization of the body's sites and capacities for pleasure through the cop's touch.

Of course, as Rechy and others might point out, being touched by a cop also often results in violence and even death, depending upon whose body he takes in his grasp. Moreover, the association of the cop with creativity inadvertently speaks to Wilson's point regarding the significant influence that cops have had in the production of popular culture about themselves. Ann Marie Scott has identified a version of those problems in Steward's fiction, arguing that while Steward's pornography reflects his cultivation of a queer sexual ethics, it also fails to imagine durable same-sex intimacies in terms other than normative gender roles: in contrast to the cop's authoritative daddy, one man must play the submissive wife.[13] Those scenarios certainly play out in Steward's pornographic fiction, and in particular the collection of early short stories to which Schott confines her analysis, yet a broader survey of Steward's novels reveals that it is only one possible configuration among others, including ones in which the figure of the cop mediates forms of homosocial intimacy for which the logic of gender difference does not organize the action. In many cases, Phil's inability to enter into a form of couple-hood bespeaks an extensive network of intimate connections, a friend or fuck buddy in practically every city, who are willing to help Phil out when he gets in too deep with the police. Despite his general cynicism about politics, Steward's later novels have Phil side with his friends over his cop lovers, and in a final twist that seems positively Rechian, Phil captures the erotic actions of his former cop lover on film, thereby disciplining his authority while leaving him available for Phil and his friends' erotic use. Phil never abandons his masochistic cop lust, but it exists in tension with the cop as mediator of male homosocial intimacy and erotic and social mobility.

While this chapter concerns the meaning of the cop in Steward's pornographic fiction, it begins with an overview of Rechy's critique of cops and gay men's cop fantasies in order to provide an illuminating point of contrast. However, one of the things that will emerge from that comparison is the sense that Rechy and Steward were also operating with different forms of policing: Rechy's critiques were shaped in relation to his at times firsthand experiences with the Los Angeles police force, which became increasingly militarized in form and operation during the 1960s and 1970s, while Steward rarely encounters more than one cop at a time. Moreover, as I will explain, it is also possible to overstate the differences between these two writers, thereby positioning them as diametrically opposed. Perhaps the most significant similarity between them is their shared investments in promiscuity, not just as an erotic practice but also as a form of thinking. While Steward refuses to commit to any one way of relating to cops, Rechy's documentary culminates in a fantastic, mass-mediated orgy whose creative energy redraws the dividing lines between police and sexual outlaws in a manner that seems positively Stewardian. Yet Rechy only flirts with such an image of explicitly sexual revolution, and his documentary concludes with the sexual outlaw heading home again after another night out on the prowl. Such a conclusion hints at the pleasure that holds cops and sexual outlaws together in their own kind of oppositional intimacy. There has been no shortage of attempts to reclaim Rechy's writing on the side of progressive politics, yet, like Steward, his commitments to sex may prevent him from settling anywhere with anyone for too long.

CLOSING RANKS

While I will concentrate my analysis on *The Sexual Outlaw: A Documentary*, I'd like to enter into that discussion by way of *This Day's Death* because it is there that Rechy offers his first extended account of the male homosocial desire at the core of modern policing. The novel relates the legal troubles of Jim, a young man from El Paso, Texas, who is arrested while cruising for sex in Griffith Park during a trip to Los Angeles. The conditions of the arrest become crucial for the novel's critique of not only the police but also the California legal system, as the trial hinges on whether or not the two plainclothes officers, named Daniels and Jones, had an unobstructed view of what transpired between Jim and another man named Steve within a secluded area of the park. Both officers claimed to have witnessed the two men engaging in oral sex with each other. Rather than confirm or deny that claim outright, Jim instead insists that it was impossible for the officers to see what they claim to have seen for two reasons: first, Jim and Steve had been well hidden within a section of the park known as the bower, and, second, Jim had rejected Steve's advances—in fact, no sex had transpired between them. The outcome of the subsequent court trial thus appears to hinge on proving whether or not Officer Daniels's claim could possibly be true. The trial initially goes well for Jim, as Jim and his attorney regularly catch Daniels in his testimony's glaring inconsistencies. However, when Jim's lawyer explains that "[the judge] can't call the cop a liar—even if he knows he's one,'" Jim increasingly suspects that he is an outsider within a fraternal system that protects its own.[14]

As the trial progresses, Jim also soon realizes that Daniels's poor memory isn't the only open secret that the law is protecting, as Daniels cannot keep his story straight, not only muddling his account of the park but also betraying his own intensifying infatuation with Jim. When initially asked to point out Jim in the courtroom, Daniels identifies him as "the man in the blue eyes," before hastily correcting his statement to "the man wearing the blue *shirt*" (34). This interest in Jim's physical appearance reaches its climax toward the novel's end, when, in an unconventional move, the judge moves the location of the trial out of the courthouse and into Griffith Park in order to inspect the area where Jim and Steve's arrest took place. As Jim becomes more vocal and defiant in his criticism of Daniels, the officer loses his composure and attempts to force Jim and Steve into miming the alleged sex act. A fight nearly breaks out: "[the] cop raises both hands . . . he might as easily have been preparing to ward off Jim's blows as to strike back—or to embrace him" (207). Jim seizes on the ambiguity of the gesture in order to taunt Daniels: "You could get busted for reaching out for me like that!" (207). Jim says what the other representatives of the law, including his lawyers, refuse to acknowledge, thereby preventing the exposure of Daniels's desire and along with it the hypocrisy of a legal system that criminalizes homosexuality.

Through its combination of Jim's perspective and that of the omniscient narrator, the novel develops a critique of the law by exposing the male homosocial desire at its core. Coined by Eve Sedgwick, the term "male homosocial desire" refers to the affectively intense and potentially erotic force that permeates all same-gender relations, yet the existence of which has been disavowed through the polarization of desire into mutually exclusive hetero- and homo- forms during the early twentieth century.[15] Despite that polarization, Sedgwick argues, male homosocial desire nonetheless has found expression in narratives of erotic rivalry where two or more men compete for the affections and body of the same woman. In *This Day's Death*, Rechy offers his own instance of such mediation when Jim shamefully recalls his leading role in what is essentially a scene of gang rape, during which he and a group of his high school friends bond by watching each other have sex with their classmate Caroline. The only boy who does not participate is the effeminate Emory who instead of having sex with Caroline lays next to her and masturbates while pleading for Jim to take a second turn. On the one hand, Emory's actions imbue a homoerotic quality to the desire that bonds the boys together as they stand around with "their pants open, their hands grasping their own impatient cocks" (70). On the other hand, Emory occupies a socially inferior place with respect to the other boys, who only tolerate his presence in the group because of his access to a car. Instead, his relation to Jim and to the rest of the boys points to an alternative configuration of male homosocial desire, one organized not through women's bodies but through a hierarchy of differentiated masculinities.

Rechy had developed this idea in his earlier novel *Numbers* (1967). As Kevin Arnold has shown in his reading of that novel, Rechy's male characters desire one another, yet the polarization of desire, which not only produces homosexuality and heterosexuality as diametrically opposed but also construes homosexuality as mutually exclusive with masculinity, initially renders the enactment of that desire impossible. However, a workaround appears in the hierarchized arrangement of male subjectivities, according to which a man's relative masculinity determines which acts one can perform and with whom. Femininity is thus not the absence of masculinity; the two instead exist on separate axes. As Arnold puts it: "There are no gay or straight characters but rather all men are distributed around the same representational poles of masculinity that makes them more or less available."[16] This arrangement determines not only who has sex but also how they do it. The most normatively masculine men can fuck and receive blow jobs, but they cannot be penetrated sexually or initiate the sexual action themselves, as doing so compromises their status. In *This Day's Death*, the law provides the means for distributing men in a similar way. Despite and perhaps because of Daniels's outbursts, the judge finds Jim and Steve guilty, imposing fines and sex offender registration (237–38). While the judgment ruins Jim's dreams of a legal career, it positions him outside of the law's fraternal order. Jim isn't feminized so much as he is criminalized, a masculine status he finds erotically empowering: after the judgment, he returns to the park to engage in the act of which he has been found guilty: Jim permits another young man to blow him.

In contrast to the men of the law, Jim stands as a prototypical version of the sexual outlaw that would emerge later in Rechy's work. Unlike the men in *Numbers*, Jim also engages in a kind of unhierarchized intimacy with the man who he briefly meets in the park following his conviction. The details of that encounter become clear when Jim, having returned home to El Paso, seeks out his professional mentor in order to come clean about his arrest, the trial, and his subsequent return to the park. However, Jim remains suggestively elusive in his description of the latter: "I wanted to face myself at last . . . We kissed— . . ." (248). Initially, his mentor wants to protect Jim by mobilizing an appeal that would find a way to excuse Jim's behavior as anything other than what Jim claims it to be. When Jim refuses, accepting his fate, a heated argument ensues and their relationship comes to an end. Yet the syntax of his confession suggests that another form of social bond is possible, one that does not depend on the refusal to acknowledge Jim's desire for another man. Of course, Jim and the other man do more than just kiss, but Jim's confession secludes that act within its dash and ellipses. The contrast between what Jim says he did and what he doesn't say implies another contrast between the different physical configuration that each act entails: the symmetry of the kiss versus the asymmetry of the nonreciprocal blow job. Jim's mentor interprets his account of the kiss as an act of juvenile defiance, yet the novel proffers it to the reader as the untroubled reciprocity of gay desire, an expression achievable as a consequence of the men's outlaw status.

In its elaboration of a law that makes desire articulate and sex possible, *This Day's Death* serves as a significant precursor to Rechy's continued exploration of these matters in the next decade, when he increasingly formulates his critique of the law by way of a critique of gay "S&M."[17] As chapter 1 discussed, the abbreviation S&M stands for a diverse array of erotic practices that deliberately incorporate power differentials as a means to intensify the pleasures at stake and which had played a central role in the production masculine gay subjectivities during the 1970s, yet Rechy demonstrated a deep ambivalence regarding these practices as early as *City of Night*, when the novel's anonymous protagonist encounters Neil, a portly leatherman and self-declared leader of a masculinist social movement. While fascinated by the uniforms of cops and Nazis, Neil's masculinity is all pretense, which Rechy exposes with a description of how Neil's soft body strains the threads of his costume, causing his ample belly "to bulge out insistently over and under [his belt] in two sagging, lumpy old tires of flesh."[18] However, Rechy's most direct critique of S&M comes in *The Sexual Outlaw: A Documentary* (1977), where he identifies S&M as a symptom of the oppression that homosexuals face in the world. "Chilling proof," Rechy writes in *The Sexual Outlaw*, "of the self-hatred at the core of S&M is the existence of a gay bar— constructed to evoke a police headquarters station—which openly solicits gay patrons to dress in cop uniforms. [. . .] Thus the cop—the primary symbol of the straight world's repressive laws—is celebrated here in imitation by the victims themselves, wearing their oppressors' uniforms, replete with handcuffs!"[19] Police persecution of homosexuals was so severe that it had lodged itself in the very hearts, minds, and sexual fantasies of gay men.

It's important to note that Rechy was not uniformly opposed to S&M, and at certain points in *The Sexual Outlaw*, he differentiates between practices that "may range from the power-oriented to the loving, even gentle" from those dependent on "on pain or *gay-humiliation*" (254). While certain practices may produce a benign mobility of pleasure at the level of the body, Rechy argues, gay S&M entails a politically toxic form of psychological immobility. In fact, despite the pretense of role playing, S&M permits only one subjectivity: "Playing 'straight,' the 'S' humiliates and even tortures the 'M' for being 'queer.' But since the 'S' is himself a homosexual, too, he is transferring his feelings of self-contempt for his own homosexuality onto the cowering 'M,' who turns himself willingly into what gay-haters have called him" (261). Rechy concludes: "There is no 'S' in such gay relationships. The whimpering 'masochist' and the 'tough' posturing 'sadist' are, in reality, only two masochists groveling in self-hatred" (262). By masochist, Rechy means neither the particular role that the men involved in the S&M scene consciously adopt nor a pathological category of masochism. Instead, "masochist" refers to a structural position by which the law incorporates homosexual acts within itself. The masochist functions primarily as a subjectivity, rather than a psychological category or identity. Where the pro-

tagonist of *This Day's Death* required the law that punishes in order to speak
and enact his desire, the BDSM practitioners of *The Sexual Outlaw* have
managed to integrate this framework into the sexual act itself. BDSM serves
as a creative if conservative response to the law's discursive construction of
male homosexuality.

To illustrate these claims, Rechy provides a fictionalized account of the
April 10, 1976, raid on the Mark IV Health Club in Los Angeles, when officers from the Los Angeles Police Department deliberately targeted a charity
mock slave auction organized by the editorial staff of the popular leather-
and BDSM-themed *Drummer* magazine. Rechy's account of the event critiques both the police and the event itself, which it does by pointing to formal correspondences between the event's participants and the police, each
of whom shape their actions for a particular public. "Despite the carnival
hype of two 'masters' conducting it," Rechy observes of the auction, "the
thing kept pulling toward farce. Too loose, the shackles on a 'slave' slipped
off and he almost fell, helped solicitously by a 'master' or two. [. . .] Still,
they tried to keep it going, the strutting auctioneers puffily vaunting each
handcuffed-slave's capacity for pain" (270). Following the raid on the bar,
the police present the arrested men to the public in a manner that corre-
sponds with the mock auction: "The arrested men were paraded before representatives of the District and City attorneys offices (who had approved the
raid beforehand) and—important to the police design, indeed essential—
before television cameras alerted carefully in advance to create the desired
circus. One of the 'slaves' was brought out to be photographed semi-nude—
and then returned inside to put his clothes on" (272). If the fantasy version
of the slave auction failed to convince dubious spectators like Rechy, then
the police spectacle succeeds in broadcasting it onto "home screens as real,"
revealing the cops to be the true masters and authors of the "fantasy" scenario. Policing isn't just a matter of physical force; it also entails the symbolic
work of producing gay men in their positionally masochistic subjectivity.

COUNTERPUBLIC DOCUMENTARY

So, what to do? In his nonfiction writings, Rechy evinces a clear opposition to censorship, which explains why he refrains from arguing that gay
men should simply stop engaging in S&M, even as *The Sexual Outlaw*
forcefully decries its infiltration of gay popular culture, where, according
to one unnamed "gay filmmaker" cited in that text, "[every] porno flick,
no matter how lyrically it deals with gay love, has to have at least one S&M
scene" (255). Instead, *The Sexual Outlaw* sought to put its own counter-
fantasy into public circulation by drawing on another genre entirely, as

suggested by the novel's full title: *The Sexual Outlaw: A Documentary*. In the past, critics have interpreted the subtitle in terms of Rechy's derivation of the novel's content from his own public sex experiences, yet Manuel Betancourt has identified a more substantial connection between Rechy's nonfiction novel and documentary form by reading *The Sexual Outlaw* as a response to the period's lesbian and gay documentary films, such as Peter Adair's *Word Is Out: Stories from Some of Our Lives* (1977). However, where those films sought to normalize gay and lesbian experience for mainstream audiences, *The Sexual Outlaw* "[shed] light on the invisible and oft-forgotten outcast of the LGBT community, those young outlaws who cruise and define themselves against the white and affluent 'Mr. Middle of the Road' trope so exalted in the 1977 documentary."[20] In doing so, argues Betancourt, the goal was not just to offer a more expansive understanding of the gay underworld, which the audience might passively consume from the safety of their own homes, but to solicit the audience's participation, primarily through identification with the novel's protagonist as he puts his life at risk while cruising the streets of Los Angeles.

By tracing connections between the novel and a specific genre of documentary film, Betancourt's study of *The Sexual Outlaw* highlights its paraliterary orientation to the reader, yet Rechy's nonfiction novel and its effort to involve the reader in its action also draw crucial inspiration from the period's counterpublic documentaries. Those films foregrounded instances of intensified political struggle, and their ranks include such films as Cinda Firestone's *Attica* (1973), which recounted the prisoners' revolt against the inhumane conditions of their imprisonment at the New York State Attica Correctional Facility in 1971. As Jonathan Kahana explains in his study of these films, counterpublic documentaries called attention to the experiences of marginalized and oppressed subjects in the US and challenged the authoritative narratives of police agencies, politicians, and other authorities that often went unquestioned in popular news media. However, beyond providing those subjects with the means to document their own experiences, the counterpublic documentaries were also formally innovative, employing montage as well as visual and audio collage in order to issue "a filmic challenge to the supposed transparency of video, its effects on real time and self-evidence, and the notions of social commonality these qualities are thought to effect."[21] In doing so, counterpublic documentaries critiqued the conditions that shaped access to the public sphere by highlighting, not only its structurally determined exclusions, but also its dependence on the state and corporate media that it was meant to keep in check. In the process, they explored the means by which marginalized subjects constituted their own publics according to alternative discourse protocols. Put succinctly, counterpublic documentaries mediated publics of and for those marginalized and oppressed subjects while also rethinking "the rules and means by which a public can come into being."[22]

During the 1970s, argues Kahana, the aims of counterpublic documentaries were reflected in filmmakers' specific interest in prisons and prisoners, whose experience provided "a useful political allegory" to explore the formation of oppositional public spheres.[23] The visualization of prisoners speaking on their own behalf, contradicting state communications, and organizing with each other across cultural and subcultural differences transformed the prisoner from a figure deliberately isolated and excluded from society into a member of a potentially revolutionary collectivity, with whom viewers could align themselves. Proffered through forms that eschewed a linear logic, counterpublic documentaries challenged the seemingly transparent narratives that state and corporate media communicated to the public about prison dissidence, thereby indexing the real of social antagonism that escapes capture in representation. There are no prisoners in Rechy's nonfiction novel, yet an understanding of counterpublic documentaries helps to clarify how Rechy's own documentary outlaw operates. In short, Rechy has his sights set on, not only a newly visible gay middle class eager for respectability, but also those participants in the nation's sex publics caught up in the allure of cop-themed BDSM fantasies. To that end, *The Sexual Outlaw* is light on plot. Instead, it follows Jim, the gay biracial protagonist based loosely on Rechy himself, as he cruises for sex in Los Angeles over the course of a long weekend. The text breaks up that episodic narrative with reportage, short essays by the novel's narrator dubbed "voice overs," excerpts from police blotters, and other impressionistic "montages" of the city. Like the counterpublic documentaries, the novel cobbles together these various components, some of which come from the street and some of which come from supposedly authoritative sources, in order to create the liminal voice of the sexual outlaw and to formalize his position at the edge of social and political intelligibility.

Of course, Grove Press had originally promoted Rechy's debut novel *City of Night* to a national reading public precisely as an authoritative chronicle of homosexual underworlds, and the implication that Rechy's novels were sociologically valuable proved hard to shake. For example, Grove's original hardcover edition of *The Sexual Outlaw* identified Rechy as the author of *City of Night*, despite the fact that more than a decade separated the two novels and that Rechy had published many other books in that intervening period. However, rather than read Rechy's self-identified documentary as an embrace of his role as tour guide, its alignment with the period's counterpublic documentaries raises the question of its relation to different reading publics. Arguably, to the extent that films such as *Attica* sought to found counterpublics that might draw middle-class audiences in as participants, *The Sexual Outlaw* is a book with multiple publics, including the many gay men that allegedly inhabited the masochistic subjectivity propagated through cop-themed pornography. While alluring for the intimacy it enables, such masochism also lulled gay men into accepting their marginalized status. In response, Rechy's documentary proffers the sexual outlaw as an alternative subjectivity, defined by an unceasing practice of sex with strangers that places him at risk of arrest. Such public sex, what Rechy calls "the ultimate life-hunt, without object," constitutes the sexual outlaw as a self-consciously political subjectivity, for whom "[the] streets are the battleground, the revolution is the sexhunt, [and] a radical statement is made each time a man has sex with another on a street" (298–99). In this instance, the novel does not position promiscuity as inherently revolutionary; instead, it invites gay men to participate in its documentary counterpublic, where one's erotic practices become meaningful as "radical statements."

More than simply an essay about the sexual outlaw, Rechy's prose documentary pairs its theoretical elaborations with narrative examples detailing Jim's movements through various public scenes populated with sexual and gender dissidents. Some of those scenes include the leather bars and S&M dungeons where Jim confronts both the eroticism and shame that the text imputes to such spaces, but in other instances the narrator evaluates other forms of participation, including the less controversial public sphere displays of gay and lesbian Pride celebrations. For example, in the chapter "Voice Over: 'The Gay Parade,'" the narrator describes the Los Angeles Pride Parade and confesses to the bond that such publicly sanctioned protests produce: "man—I felt the itchy sentiment that signals real pride. Here you are, and here they are, and here we are" (179). However, when the cops employed as the parade's reluctant escorts begin to harass a group of hustlers, the feeling of the parade changes, nearly leading to a physical confrontation between the parade's participants and the police. The incident sends the narrator off into a speculative daydream of "the inevitable gay apocalypse—of thousands of homosexuals rushing against the helmets and the sticks, the guns—thousands of gay men and women riding a tide of pent-up rage released at last." The vision then shifts as the narrator questions whether the gay apocalypse might be not an orgy of violence, but "instead, the ultimate, the liberating, public sex orgy?" (183). The scene acknowledges the sentimental force that attends the inclusion of sexual minorities within the public sphere: there is a nullifying pleasure in identification. However, it quickly points to the limitations of intervening within a public sphere where police dictate both who participates and under what terms: no hustlers allowed. In contrast, the "gay apocalypse" as orgy teases the promise of something far more transformative.

While the parade chapter only flirts with the idea of an apocalyptic orgy, it returns in the chapter that provides the theoretical elaboration of the sexual outlaw. After describing how the practice of public sex, rather than the act of getting off itself, is what defines the sexual outlaw, the narrator's thoughts turn toward the challenge such searching poses to the social forces that seek to stop it, either through arrest or through closing down the public places where outlaws congregate. The tension between collectivized sexual outlaws and the police works dialectically toward a massive and remarkably mass-mediated orgy:

> Sex in the streets.
>
> Reality or shock proposal?
>
> On Hollywood Boulevard, Times Square, in the French Quarter, San Jacinto Plaza, Newberry Square, Market Street, throughout the country, throughout the world, at an appointed sun bright time—let it be high noon—mass orgies! Televise it all, the kissing, the fucking, masturbating, sucking, rubbing, rimming, touching, licking, loving. Thousands of bodies stripped naked joined in a massive, *loving* orgy—and in Los Angeles, let it be on *our* boulevard, Hollywood Boulevard. Yes, and let it happen before the cops, right in front of them we would fuck, with *joy*.
>
> Would the cops break ranks? Flee? Join?
>
> Not an outrageous suggestion—we have seen filmed orgies before. Dachau. My Lai. Others. (300–301)

The references to the documentary capture of well-known atrocities, specifically the Holocaust and the mass murder of unarmed South Vietnamese villagers by US soldiers, bears a resemblance to Baldwin's own suggestion of a continuity between US police forces and the military then occupying Vietnam. The proposed metonymy, jarring as it may be, posits solidarity among sexual outlaws and other subaltern subjects, yet it also extends potentially beyond those groups by hinting at the ways that news coverage of Vietnam helped to drive public opinion in opposition to the war. The narrator's call to televise the orgy functions as a summons to mass participation, reaching out beyond gay men to imagine a world transformed in and through the operations of a mass public of not just desire but also love—an uncommon word in Rechy's novels. The new world hinted at is one in which the cops "join in," ceasing to be cops in part because the public sphere they are assigned to police no longer exists. Yet, so too does the sexual revolution herald the sexual outlaw's end. As the narrator observes: "Doesn't a won revolution end the life of the revolutionary? What of the sexual outlaw? One will mourn his passing" (301).

Despite the potential to collectivize in such dramatic ways, *The Sexual Outlaw* ends on a much more lonesome note. In the early predawn hours of the last day of his sex hunt, Jim cruises one last man only to turn him down when he expresses an interest in the "heavy stuff," meaning heavy S&M (307). The sexual outlaw stands alone at the novel's end, which closes with the final image of Jim standing on an empty street at dawn: "still shirtless from the night's hunt, Jim stares at the garage. At the crumbling walls, the peeling boards, the discarded cans, the broken bottles, the cluttered dry weeds, the tangled barbed wire" (307). The sense of violence and urban decay enhances the sexual outlaw's edgy appeal, yet it also suggests a dissatisfaction with the crumbling infrastructure of contemporary public life, whose cracks and fissures provide the liminal spaces for outlaw counterpublics. A number of critics have noted the particular challenges that Rechy's novels pose for readers in search of political value.[24] Others suggest that Rechy's novels express a dissatisfaction with the kinds of political categories made available within liberal political thought and thus seek something beyond it.[25] Given its public-sphere-busting orgy and dystopic final image, *The Sexual Outlaw* invites the latter reading: the mass orgy itself suggests not only a radical transformation of "the rules and means by which a public can come into being," but also a dissolution of the identity categories that condition erotic practices and seemingly speak to a truth of the subject's desire. The outlaw counterpublic thus emerges as a transitional formation necessary for the de-repression of the "living, *defiant* body" and consequently a shattering of the mass-mediated fantasies that keep gay men in their place.

"A BATTALION OF COPS, ALL READY TO MOUNT ME"

In much the same way that the counterpublic documentaries of the 1970s responded to a public sphere irreparably compromised by state and commercial interests, Rechy's outlaw documentary similarly targets the police who co-opted the public sphere to justify their attacks on sexual and gender dissidents.[26] *The Sexual Outlaw* sought to up open a position from which to imagine alternatives that might appeal to those subjects criminalized by the law and seduced into compliance through S&M and its associated pornography. In doing so, Rechy's nonfiction novel both stands as a document of the period's radical sexual politics and, with its emphasis on the relations among power, desire, and fantasy, continues to offer important insights for current critiques of policing, including those that seek not reform but abolition. Still, like many of critiques that equate the enjoyment of gay porn's unseemly fantasies with false consciousness, it's difficult to find moments when Rechy engages with the erotic practices and porn that he criticizes. In fact, just as the police seek to move public opinion against sexual dissidents by the exposure of their fantasies and practices to a mass audience, Rechy's own derisive account of the Mark IV Health Club adopts a similar tactic: even if it attempts to sway readers against the police, it still treats the counterpublic convened around the slave auction as a haplessly unsexy pantomime. In what remains of this chapter, I take a closer look at Samuel Steward's pornographic novels, which epitomize the kind of cop lust that in part motivated Rechy's critique. In doing so, my goal is to open up thinking about the cop as pornographic trope to show how even his adoration in porn could generate meanings that were not entirely at odds with those articulated in *The Sexual Outlaw.*

To state that point another way, while I put Rechy and Steward in conversation here, my aim is not to determine which has the greater social or political value, but to characterize their differences in terms of what their respective genres make available for thinking. If Rechy's documentary presents a politicizing call to action, then Steward's pornography explores a gay ethics of pleasure that is best apprehended through a survey of his work. However, my interest in reading these writers in this way also stems from a desire to counter a trend in Steward's recovery that pits him against Rechy, counterintuitively contrasting Rechy's mopey gay fiction against Steward's happier, friendlier takes on gay life. For example, when Alyson Publications reissued Steward's early short story collection $tud (1982), it included an introduction by John Preston who claimed that Steward had "[returned] to writing by the waffling stance of the narrator in John Rechy's *City of Night.* There wasn't enough honesty in that book to satisfy Steward, no matter how many barriers it broke down in American thinking and publishing. He realized that if he wanted more from writing about homosexuality, he would have to produce it himself."[27] In the acclaimed biography of Steward, Justin Spring reveals the semi-apocryphal status of Preston's introduction, yet he ends up doing so in a manner that more or less rehearses Preston's position: "[*City of Night*] was hardly prohomosexual," writes Spring, "for Rechy was coy about the 'true' sexuality of his hustler-protagonist, and disparaged the majority of 'youngman''s [sic] homosexual patrons, drawing them instead as pathetic, predatory grotesques." Unlike Rechy, Steward took "a much less angst-ridden approach to hustling, and [. . .] portrayed the men on both sides of the hustling equation as basically friendly, attractive, and human characters simply seeking sexual release."[28]

The image that one gets is of Steward tossing his copy of *City of Night* on his desk, rolling up his sleeves, and sitting down before his typewriter in order to dispel the juvenile pessimism of Rechy's novel with wholesome, sex-positive representations of gay sexuality. Both Preston and Spring are correct in that Steward had expressed reservations about *City of Night*'s protagonist, yet Steward also had been an important and early advocate of Rechy, who had written to Steward asking him to review the novel for the trilingual European homophile magazine *Der Kreis*, which Steward agreed to do.[29] A review had already appeared in the magazine, so Steward donned a pseudonym and penned a favorable report in a letter to the editor, praising *City of Night* in detail for its daring content and innovative form. After his disappointing debut in the straight press, Rechy was so touched by Steward's recognition of his novel's literary value that he considered asking him to review *Numbers* following its publication.[30] Thus, Steward and *Der Kreis* served for Rechy in a manner similar to the ways that *Drummer* magazine and leather pornography provided a counterpublic for Carney's novel following its dismissal within the US literary public sphere. Spring's biography recounts some of that exchange, but filling in a few more of the details points to a more congenial relation between Rechy and Steward than Spring acknowledged. Preston and Spring are correct that there are noticeable differences between the two writers, particularly in tone, but Steward's fiction was not as sunny as either claimed it to be. Yet, for that reason, it ends up also bearing some significant similarities to Rechy's fiction, including his take on cops, despite perhaps being an exemplar of the kind of pornography that Rechy derided.

The most obvious similarity between the two writers is that Steward and Rechy both favored characters modeled after hustlers and rough trade: young, working-class men who identified as straight but engaged in sex with other men for money or other favors. If "trade" referred to the exchange, then "rough" denoted the fact that such men were emotionally unavailable and potentially belligerent partners, who might blackmail, rob, or otherwise treat violently the older middle-class men who hired them for their sexual services. In keeping with their tough persona, hustlers and trade typically avoided acts or positions that might compromise their masculinity and thus tended to perform only the dominant, penetrative role during sex. As Phil Andros, Steward's regular hustler protagonist put it: "A hustler, a gen-you-wine platinum-plated hustler, always stuck his cock in somebody's mouth or ass. He never sucked a cock or got screwed."[31] In many ways Phil typified the many working-class men that Steward enjoyed and with whom he would align himself during his middle age by renouncing his position as a university lecturer to become a tattoo artist. However, Phil was also a vehicle to explore the particular ways in which sex with trade often provided fertile grounds for vulnerability and emotional attachment that befuddled the seemingly well-defined roles that structured the relation. As Phil continues:

And yet, while naked on the bed, feeling the hot mouth licking and sucking at him, he always sensed that his customer must have liked him a little or he would not have been there—that the client desired or wanted him. [. . .] And yet were not most hustlers—at least when they were being blown— showing a curious kind of passivity, lying there outstretched, arms behind the head so as not to touch the "fuckin' fruit" who was at work on them? Where was the hustler's "aggression" when the fruit did all the work? Paradox. . . ." (S, 105)

Scenes such as these hint at the ways in which the relation between rough trade and scores or fruits, despite its impersonally transactional qualities, was also potentially a mode of intimacy. Rigid roles are necessary for the sex to occur, but while explicit sexual desire may only flow in one direction, the conditions of the erotic practice suggest that identity-confounding pleasures and attachments were also present on the hustler's side, albeit in a more amorphous form.

While the above example finds Phil pondering a hypothetical hustler and score, Steward more often than not embeds those mediations in Phil's own interactions with other men and, in particular, in scenarios where Phil relinquishes his role as dominant top. In fact, while Rechy's protagonists rarely—if ever—get fucked or perform blow jobs without reciprocation, Steward's novels frequently track Phil as he anticipates, engages in, and then reflects on the pleasures that such practices can bring. This deviation from type provides a solution to a practical problem introduced by Phil's hustler identity, as Phil's willingness to explore such variety helps to satisfy the genre's demand for sexual novelty as well as the publishers' quota regarding the number and length of sex scenes in their pornographic novels. Being a hustler with a limited erotic repertoire is in and of itself a recipe for monotony and potentially a sexually boring novel, as Phil intimates: "When you're a hustler, you get mighty tired sometimes of having to do the same things all the time."[32] However, Phil's willingness to explore the pleasures of submission, penetration, and passivity nonetheless brings his erotic practices in conflict with his hustler masculinity, potentially revealing him to be a fruit after all. As Schott has shown, Steward often had trouble imagining such erotic arrangements in terms that did not reduce to normative gender terms, yet while Steward had difficulty abandoning his investments in that model of erotic relationality, his novels do reveal him experimenting with other forms, including those that bring Phil into contact with other masculine figures. Throughout his fiction, the masculine cop frequently provides the counterpoint to Steward's macho hustler.

Originally published in 1970 as *San Francisco Hustler*, Steward's *The Boys in Blue* (1984) begins with Phil cruising a cop he meets on the streets of Los Angeles. Once the two are alone, Phil finds himself playing the bottom. The encounter provides an occasion for reflection during which Phil explains his sudden change of heart and position in terms that end up sounding suspiciously Rechian: "[This] was different—he was the symbol and active agent of authority, punisher of my own guilt feelings (if there were any left)—and in addition to that, a handsome stud with an enormous cock" (*B*, 14). In addition to the normative scheme of gender difference that Schott identifies in Steward's early short stories, the relation between masochist and sadist becomes another frequent model to explain Phil's interest in not only cops but also bottomhood. In doing so, Steward's *The Boys in Blue* sets up a theme that he will vary across his subsequent short fiction and novels. For example, among the twelve stories collected in the anthology *Below the Belt and Other Stories* (1982), five deal specifically with the police. In *Shuttlecock,* Phil attempts to transform a wayward Berkeley college student, Larry, into a version of the macho top cop he meets in *The Boys in Blue*. After a nasty falling out, Larry returns in Steward's last novel, *Greek Ways* (1984), originally published as *The Greek Way* (1975), as an undercover vice cop who attempts to bust up the combination escort agency and pornography studio that employs Phil as its star stud. In a dramatic turn, although one perhaps in line with Phil's status as rough trade, he documents Larry having sex with another man and uses the evidence to blackmail the cop into serving as his sex slave. In *Roman Conquests* (1983), originally published as *When in Rome, Do . . .* (1971), Phil's interactions with the *carabinieri*, or Roman police, reach epic proportions, as in the midst of being fucked by one handsome member of the force Phil suddenly envisions "a battalion of cops, all ready to mount me."[33]

While it's perhaps tempting to read that scene as one of abject masochism, Phil's fantasy gang bang also entails a remarkable homosocial intimacy, in which erotic receptivity provides the means to organize a group of men in their desire. Unlike Steward, Rechy's turn to counterpublic documentary was an attempt invite readers into an alternative practice by clarifying the masochistic relation that defined gay subjectivity generally. Rechy reimagined the relation between cops and queers in starkly oppositional terms, thereby intimating that cops could participate in gay erotic practices only if they did so on gay men's terms, by throwing down their badges and joining the outlaws' ranks. However, working within a genre beholden less to the mandates of liberationist politics than an ethics of serialized pleasures, Steward's pornographic fiction becomes a laboratory of sorts in which to experiment with bodies and the erotic possibilities that their various configurations may entail. In some cases, they end up resembling highly gendered arrangements or the psychologized language of masochism, but when viewed across

Steward's novels, a somewhat different picture emerges. By the time of *Greek Ways*, the practice of getting fucked by cops turns into one of fucking with cops and leads to a kind of promiscuity-based homo-intimacy that bears surprising similarities to Rechy's counterpublic of sexual outlaws.

"NO ENTRAPMENT OF THE HEART"

One can best apprehend that conceptual movement by attending to the various ways that Steward's fiction regularly thematizes mobility itself. In addition to hustling, sucking, and fucking his way through various locales, including Los Angeles, San Francisco, Dallas, New York, Chicago, and Rome, Phil also rotates through a number of odd jobs, including police officer, hotel page, pornographic actor, and gym owner. Finally, Phil's mobility not only encompasses the movement between erotic roles, as evident in his frequent switching from macho top hustler to submissive bottom and back again, but also the "desexualization" of his pleasures through the cultivation and redistribution of erotogenic zones across his body.[34] The plot of *The Boys in Blue* brings these different thematic threads together. After his initial encounter with Greg, the cop whom he cruises on the streets of LA, Phil enlists with the San Francisco Police Department and convinces Greg to join him so the two may cohabitate, shielding their illicit sex under the guise of bachelor cops rooming together. Soon, they are joined by Pete, a youthful rookie whom Phil encounters in the station's bathroom. Consequently, their respective ages and ranks comprise an erotic hierarchy with Greg on top. As he explains to his new live-in subordinates: "You see . . . I've been a cop a lot longer than either of you guys, and it's me who's going to be calling the shots around here" (*B*, 37).

As in Rechy's novels, each man's position in the hierarchy determines what actions he may perform with his housemates, yet that structure proves crucial for the kinds of erotic mobility that Phil and Pete experience at the level of their bodies. In one memorable set of scenes, the men respond to a suicide where a young man has hanged himself while wearing a dress and a set of clamps on his nipples. The trio speculate about the young man's motivations for approximately two pages until Greg cuts their discussion short and redirects their attention back toward the sex: "I suggest we all go home, have a coupla stiff ones — drinks, I mean — and then fuck ourselves silly" (*B*, 54). Greg's punning on cocktails foreshadows how elements of the suicide will carry over into the next scene: back at home, Greg engineers a set of clamps similar to those found on the dead body, which he then puts to use on Phil and Pete. However, the scene's take on the suicide entails a repurposing of not only found objects, but also conventions.[35] The scene of the young man's death initially recalls the period's sociological exposés of gay life in which the seasoned cop serves as tour guide through the nation's underworld, introducing the reader to various examples of vice and tragedy, including the feminized queer undone by his deviant desires.[36] However, Steward's text redeploys these conventions so that they acquire a very different function within the pornographic novel: the goal is not to explain the cause of the suicide, but to explore how it can lead to the discovery of strange pleasures through unusual uses of the body. Far from being an object of lurid fascination or pity, perversity instead becomes a source of inspiration.

Reflecting back on his work at the end of his life, Steward seemed almost surprised that his novels contained pedagogical themes. "One can hardly find credible the idea of 'educational pornography' or erotica written with a humanitarian purpose," Steward wrote, "but I think that I honestly tied to produce such material."[37] One of the reasons why Steward balks, at least initially, at the claim that pornography could be educational concerns his own theory that pornography requires no reflection and thus circumvents the mechanisms of subjectivity presumed responsible for learning. Unlike music or painting, which engage the critical faculties of the listener or viewer, the pornographer "communicates without frills with the nervous system of the reader; he stimulates the reader's juices, makes his eye sparkle, sets the adrenalin flowing, activates the sweat glands, and finally creates the tumescence . . . or in the classic example, ejaculation."[38] However, Steward's tongue-in-cheek behaviorism contrasts with his narratives, which link Phil's practices, such as wearing a pair of painful nipple clamps, precisely to the kinds of reflection that Steward elsewhere denies to pornography. On his way home with Pete and Greg from the suicide scene, Phil is uneasy about what lies in store: "I found myself shivering a little in anticipation. But that's part of it all. Anticipation and retrospect. You look forward to something, you don't particularly like going through with it, but the memory of it can give you a hardon for years" (B, 53). As Tim Dean might argue, Steward's fiction recognizes the crucial role that fantasy plays in the mobility of the body's pleasures, yet it also suggests the need for an external motivating force, a top cop like Greg, who can push Phil over the mental barrier that the prospect of such practices pose before fantasy can do its work.[39]

Configured in this way, it's tempting to construe Greg as the cool and dispassionate sadist who retains control of his subjects precisely by shattering them into various kinds of pleasures. However, as Steward reveals, Greg has his own ego to get over, yet when he does, he is able to participate within the same practices he foists on Pete and Phil, suggesting that in the novel's erotic arrangement no one gets to be top cop for too long. The novel explores that possibility within a subplot that concerns Phil's increasingly intense desire to top Greg. He gets his chance one evening when he returns home from work to find Greg passed out drunk on their bed. As Phil moves Greg into position and prepares to penetrate him, he awakens Greg from his stupor. However, rather than fly into a rage, Greg drunkenly confesses that he had wanted Phil to fuck him, but couldn't verbalize his desire because of an "[idea] . . . about my image" (B, 104). With Greg unable to top himself, Phil assumes command. After Greg quickly recovers from his drunkenness (suggesting that his inebriation was partly a ruse), he confesses to his enjoyment: "I guess I liked it as much as you did. It felt good," and Phil responds: "Nothing really matters [. . .] You learn that after a few years, don't you?" (B, 110). On the one hand, the statement reflects Steward's own cynicism about politics; on the other hand, what doesn't matter is the pleasure-inhibiting image that Greg has of himself, but crucially in this scene pleasure does matter, as does Greg's seemingly newfound capacity to reflect on and make judgments about the pleasures of which his body is capable.

While the figure of the cop in Steward's fiction helps to satisfy the genre's demand for erotic variety, it also has its limits. For example, in the chapter titled "The Copnap," Phil is out walking his beat when a racially mixed gang of three Black men led by Al, a White man who identifies himself as one of Phil's former scores, abducts Phil, mocks him for becoming a cop, and then secures him in a secret location with the intention of raping him. Much as the earlier suicide scene redeployed the figure of the tragic queer in service to the cultivation of new pleasures, the abduction scene traffics in racist stereotypes to compose a racialized revenge fantasy; as Al commands his subordinates: "Undress him and get to work. [. . .] You always wanted to fuck a pig, dintcha?" (B, 74). The scene offers an example of the ambivalent racial fetishism that Martin J. Ponce has examined in other examples of Steward's fiction, which utilize racist tropes to intensify the scene's eroticism yet exhibit an awareness of racist oppression "irreducible to the black abjection/white mastery binary."[40] In this scene, the characteristic ambivalence of Steward's fiction plays out through a public health lesson: when one of the Black men reveals that he is "under treatment" for syphilis, he volunteers to go last to keep from spreading the disease to his buddies, and so Al goes first (B, 71). However, once Al finishes fucking Phil, the cops arrive and end the scene. This moment is one of very few where cops stop rather than initiate sex acts, and in this case, they arrest both the rape and the potential transmission of disease from Al to the gang's members: as it turns out, Al had syphilis too. However, since Al may have infected Phil, he is later excluded from Greg and Pete's nightly sex until he completes his treatment, yet he isn't entirely left out of the action. In the next scene, Phil offers himself up as an erotic spectacle for his two lovers by masturbating while they fuck each other senseless.

The men of *The Boys in Blue* live in a world apart from the one whose laws and norms they're hired to uphold and protect. In ways that resemble the male homosocial communities that were incubators for poetic innovation during the mid-twentieth century, Phil and his live-in lovers redirect that creativity onto the body and its pleasures.[41] As such, it provides a contrasting example of the masochistic structure that Rechy attributed to cop-themed pornography, yet Steward also used the cop to explore other configurations of gay intimacy that seem to be exactly what Rechy had in mind. For example, *Shuttlecock* (1984), originally published as *Renegade Hustler* in 1972, maps the relation between Phil and his new cop lover onto a gendered sadomasochistic relation. Having relocated to Berkeley, Phil encounters Larry, a handsome yet aimless flower child whom Phil aims to transform into a version of Greg. Initially, the plan works; Phil convinces Larry to join the San Francisco police force, where the training melts away the effeminizing effects of the counterculture and returns Larry's "cock to him in the shape of a billyclub" (*S*, 121). However, the arrangement goes wrong insofar as it positions Phil and Larry on opposite sides of the law, and the novel's central conflict entails how Larry's growing allegiance to his fellow officers and increasingly sadistic tendencies have Phil adopting an increasingly feminized and masochistic role, forsaking hustling by spending his days in their home, cooking, cleaning, and waiting for Larry to return. The novel reaches its climax when Phil learns of Larry's plot to turn both Phil and another one of his young hippy friends into the police. Phil decides to flee town, but not before double-crossing Larry, disgracing him in the eyes of his fellow officers.

The *Boys in Blue* and *Shuttlecock* contrast markedly in terms of their depiction of cops. If in the first instance, the cop serves as the mediator of erotic creativity, then in the second instance, the cop poses a risk of trapping Phil within an identity. In both novels, the solution lies in Phil's ability to keep moving. Of course, this movement ensures that Phil continues to have new adventures and new kinds of sex, thus meeting the expectation for erotic variety that characterizes the genre, yet it also points to the ways in which Steward was deeply suspicious of the idea that homosexual men could ever form lasting intimate attachments with one another. One of the earliest and most explicit formulations of that belief appears in Steward's 1958 essay for *Der Kreis* entitled "Detachment: A Way of Life." Promiscuity, he observed, was "an almost universally recognized trait of the homosexual": "Momentarily with one, for five dirty minutes, we pass from him to the next, [always] with starry eyes raised to the impossible and unattainable ideal—a permanent 'arrangement' with the man of our romantic dreams."[42] For that reason, it was impossible for homosexuals to remain satisfied and fulfilled with another homosexual. Instead, their only hope was to cultivate an "attitude [of] detachment": "settle yourself into a pattern which will enable you to observe, even participate, and still remain detached—to protect yourself completely, surrounded—but not touched in the deeply emotional sense—so that no person or situation will ever have the power to wound you again."[43] It's a depressingly cold vision, and Steward would continue to profess a version of it throughout his life. However, I want to conclude this chapter by suggesting that Steward's fiction flirted with an alternative, according to which Phil's refusal to settle down with any one man becomes the condition for a kind of promiscuous intimacy.

Greek Ways, which rounds out the unofficial cop trilogy along with *The Boys in Blue* and *Shuttlecock*, provides one of the more explicit articulations of that alternative intimacy. *Greek Ways* finds Phil once more in San Francisco, this time securing work as a writer and performer for a local gay porn studio. Phil discovers that his former cop lover Larry is now employed as a vice cop who has plans to infiltrate the studio and arrest its owner, Phil, and the other men employed there. In consultation with his director, Phil hatches a plot to catch Larry on film having sex with a friend from Phil's past, Art Kain, whom Phil hires to give the new performer a "tryout" (*G*, 81). The plot reverses the conditions of the typical entrapment scheme, according to which cops solicit gay men into committing acts for which they are then arrested. Instead, Phil documents Larry having sex with Art, which he then uses to blackmail Larry into serving as his regular sex slave. The fantasy scenario inverts the masochistic structure that Rechy located in cop-themed pornography: in this case, it's the cop who is trapped within the submissive role mediated by the very pornography he helped to produce. From Larry's perspective, only one form of escape is possible: suicide. In a later scene, Phil shows up at Larry's apartment with the incriminating film in his pocket and a can of Crisco grease under his arm, intending to introduce Larry to the pleasures of fisting, yet he discovers that Larry has deliberately overdosed, leaving behind a note that declares the act "nobody's fault but my own" (*G*, 155). While Phil and his former cop lover Greg were able to surmount the arresting power of their self-images to engage in forms of erotic experimentation, Larry remains too invested in his macho cop identity, dying into it at the novel's end. Sparing Larry one final and lasting humiliation, Phil pockets the suicide note, notifies the police, and then quickly skips town once more.

The novel's epilogue finds Phil concluding a long, sex-filled vacation with Art at his residence in the rural town of Indiana, Pennsylvania. As the two discuss where Phil plans to head next, Phil has difficulty keeping Larry out of his mind: *"There'll be no entrapment of the heart,* I thought. I'd never realized how close I'd come until I looked into that bedroom on 20th Street in San Francisco. And even after that, it had taken weeks to understand that the hate I felt for him and what he'd done had spread like ink on a blotter, overrunning the line between hate and love, spreading, diffusing, until the two areas were joined" (*G,* 158). Durable attachment between two men *is* possible, but it carries significant risks. That observation contrasts with Phil's relation to Art, with whom he has spent the past two weeks doing "everything in the book and then some, both of us caught and held in the net of sensation—pure sensation, pure sexual activity, the spiraling helix of orgasm after orgasm" (*G,* 158). The scene posits the impersonal intimacy of "pure sex" as preferable to the emotionally intense attachment that bound Phil to his former cop lover-cum-nemesis. Phil then cuts the last of his ties to Larry when he destroys the suicide note that he has been carrying with him since leaving San Francisco.

Phil's reflections on Larry and the destruction of the note seem to posit the impersonal intimacy of causal connections and pure sex over and above romantic attachment. However, in reading Steward's fiction, one gets the sense that an index would be helpful to keep track of the many reoccurring characters who often provide Phil with assistance whenever he needs to escape his current predicament. Even if Phil is unattached, he remains surprisingly and enduringly well connected. The conclusion to *Greek Ways* also suggests that pornography may be one way to mediate these kinds of promiscuous ties. As Phil explains, he and Art spend their time together "doing everything in the book and then some" (*G,* 158), which picks up on the generic self-reflexivity initiated by the novel's setting within a pornographic studio. Just as the phrase evokes the legal practice of bringing every criminal charge possible against a defendant ("throw the book at 'em"), it also alludes to the range of acts detailed in a pornographic text. The reference becomes a bit more explicit in the conclusion, when Phil, on his way out the door to his next yet unknown destination, gifts Art the film used to blackmail Larry, calling it a "souvenir": "Be sure you're with friends when you watch it" (*G,* 159). Far from being a solitary pleasure to be enjoyed in one's detached repose, the pornographic text in which Art literally and figuratively fucks the police facilitates a specific kind of intimacy gained through communal consumption. Steward's comment is as much a warning as it is a recommendation; just as one wants to be with friends when one watches porn, perhaps one is also always with friends when one reads it.

Rechy and Steward likely would have agreed on the point that the police posed a significant threat to gay men's public sex practices, but each differs on the kinds of relational possibilities that one could imagine taking place between cops and queers. In Steward's case, his pornography offers a means to understand the police encounter as saturated by power and pleasure such that the cop could promote—rather than arrest—an erotic mobility whose various modes included the shifting of roles, the changing of positions, and the experience of new acts and pleasures, not to mention pains. While Rechy was somewhat sensitive to the cop's function in gay fantasy life, he was more concerned with the way in which such fantasies seemed to emanate from the police themselves. With censorship not an option, Rechy turned to a form of prose documentary to envision a counterpublic of sexual outlaws defined in terms of their oppositional stance toward the police and state-sponsored repressions of public sex. However, as the conclusion to *Greek Ways* suggests, the line between documentary and pornography may not have been all that easy to maintain insofar as the power that Phil obtains over Larry lies in the pornographic film's capacity to serve as evidence of a vice cop participating in the act he's supposed to prevent. In that sense, Phil's pornography functions like Rechy's outlaw documentary, insofar as the exposure of a suppressed homosexual desire within the police force serves as a means to connect Phil to Art and the friends with whom Art may watch the film. Unlike Rechian documentary, however, the collective spectatorship in Steward's fiction seems less public given that only one's "friends" should participate.

Despite the relative success and interest in his novels, Steward's porn production diminished considerably after the publication of *Greek Ways*. Spring attributes this slowdown to a decline in reader interest caused by the emerging HIV/AIDS epidemic, which led many to question the kinds of sexual license that feature so prominently in Steward's fiction.[44] According to Steven Saylor, who served as editor of *Drummer* magazine during the 1980s, Steward was uninterested in writing more pornography as the epidemic led to new restrictions on writers—chiefly, that representations of anal sex emphasize condom use.[45] Considering the ways that the sexual transmission of disease functioned as a significant limit on action in Steward's narrative, there may be something to Saylor's claims. If the vice cop was hard to identify, then HIV was infinitely more so, shrinking risk to the microbial scale and delaying signs of infection well after the moment of transmission. As a result, the anxiety that Phil has during his run-ins with the police would acquire terrifying new proportions. In the next chapter, I consider more broadly how themes of risk and creativity shifted in the shadow of the HIV/AIDS epidemic, when the terror of HIV transmission was more effective at arresting men's desire than the police could ever hope to be.

CHAPTER 3

Samuel Delany, Scott O'Hara, and the Counterpublic of Sleazehounds

On the Risks of Public Sex in AIDS-Era Pornography

The period roughly between the late 1970s and the early 1990s was an important moment for the history of gay pornographic writing in at least three interrelated ways. First, the rapid proliferation and diversification of pornographic writing that began a decade prior helped to drive shifts in the formation of markets for other pornographic media. With the advent of inexpensive recording and playback technologies, pornographic writing increasingly shared space with publicity for pornographic film and videos on the pages of magazines, zines, and newsletters; as video producers could now market their products directly to consumers, pornographic publications helped to shift the primary site for exhibiting porn from public spaces to the home.[1] Second, the ongoing proliferation and diversification of pornography rendered it an appealing target for antiporn feminists and an empowered neoconservative movement, backed by White evangelical Christians, who cast porn as a symptom of the moral decay unleashed by the social and economic policies of the previous decades.[2] As a result, porn came to play a significant role not only in the period's sex panics but also in calls for private developers to revitalize so-called blighted commercial districts where sexual and gender dissidents regularly congregated. Third, the outbreak of the HIV/AIDS epidemic and the subsequent mass deaths of gay men ostensibly provided further justification for the redevelopment of queer sex publics into family-friendly destinations. However, as a growing contingent of activists called on gay men to exchange promiscuity for respectability, others considered how pornography itself might meet a moment when perversion, danger, and death once more were associated with homosexuality in the public imagination.

Both this chapter and the next will explore what such developments meant for gay pornographic writing and its counterpublics. While chapter 4 considers gay pornographic writing in relation to the period's pedophile porn panics, the present chapter reckons with the impacts of HIV/AIDS on gay pornographic writing during the 1980s and early 1990s. It does so in part to fill a gap in accounts of AIDS-era literature, which often acknowledge the variety of genres that writers deployed in response to the epidemic while neglecting the contributions of the period's pornographers. Similarly, histories of pornography have identified the epidemic's impact on pornographic film and video but have paid less attention to its effects on novels and short fiction. Of course, those histories are interrelated, yet the pornographic counterpublics provided an important site through which pornographers, regardless of the media they employed, developed one of two general responses to the epidemic. Facing calls for men to give up their promiscuous "lifestyles," pedagogically minded activists argued that gay men need not abandon public sex if they engaged in safer-sex practices. Porn could play an active role in that work by helping gay men to imagine, not only new ways of having sex, but also how pleasurable that sex could be. In contrast, others balked at the idea that pornography should have to change, believing that to include safe-sex information in pornography would compromise the genre's capacity to arouse. Such arguments often reflected publishers' concerns for the bottom line, but they also derived from an important line of thinking developed within the pornographic counterpublics of the previous decade, which held that gay men's enjoyment of fantasies featuring high-risk practices did not necessarily mean that men would engage in those practices: the ability to fantasize about something dangerous or risky was often all readers and audiences wanted.

The recovery of these developments in gay pornographic writing will help fill out our understanding of AIDS literatures as well as serve as a provocation for scholars to include pornography in their examinations of cultural responses to traumatic events. However, the history of gay pornographic writing also reveals how the HIV/AIDS epidemic caused both representations of risk in gay pornography as well as discussions of those risks to narrow considerably across the period in question. As I argued in previous chapters, the gay pornographic writing of the 1970s and early 1980s engaged a range of risks associated with public sex, from encountering strangers who were dishonest about their appearance or technical skills to the risks of violence from cops or other homophobic vigilantes. However, by the end of the 1980s, sexual risk became increasingly associated with the risk of HIV transmission. Consequently, studies of risk in gay pornography produced after the advent of combination drug therapy have focused on the archive of bareback pornography.[3] Following the publication of Tim Dean's

Unlimited Intimacy: Reflections on the Subculture of Barebacking (2009), scholars have devoted much of their time and effort to illuminating pornography's significance for subcultures that deliberately abstain from condom use and, in some cases, intentionally orchestrate the transmission of HIV among sex partners. In doing so, they have effectively countered efforts to stigmatize barebackers, yet the transgressive allure of barebacking, itself a result of the ways that the meaning of risk changed during the late 1980s, has led to a general neglect of the other ways that gay porn has imagined not only sexual risk, but also the relation between risk and HIV.

One of the few novels to recognize that change as it was occurring was Samuel Delany's self-described work of "pornotopic fantasy" *The Mad Man* (1994).[4] The novel follows approximately fourteen years in the life and education of John Marr, a young Black gay man from a middle-class home pursuing a doctorate in philosophy in New York City. John's research focuses on the life, work, and mysterious murder of the gay Korean American philosopher, Timothy Hasler, but as he conducts his investigation, he is pulled into a variety of erotic encounters throughout the city with various men, many of them homeless, who are somehow connected to Hasler's death. Crucially, the novel excludes the one sex act from its characters' erotic repertories that by the time of the novel's publication had become the narrative focal point in gay porn: penetrative anal sex. With only fleeting references to butt fucking, either with or without condoms, the novel's characters explore a wide variety of other erotic practices, from oral sex to foot fetishism, as they occur in a variety of public and private venues, from adult theaters, bars, and parks to a particularly messy orgy held in the living room of John's apartment. Noting this variety, at least one contemporary critic has argued that the novel's eschewal of be-condomed butt fucking comprises a form of safe-sex activism in and of itself.[5] However, this chapter takes seriously the novel's opening "disclaimer" that it is "not a book about 'safe sex,'" but instead "a book about various sexual acts whose status as vectors of HIV contagion we have no hard-edged knowledge" (xiii). By shifting attention away from the one practice for which reliable information regarding HIV contagion did exist, *The Mad Man* highlighted the often-terrifying uncertainty that pervaded gay men's efforts to determine the risks of their public sex practices.

To put that point differently, Delany's *The Mad Man* bares traces of both the pedagogical and escapist approaches to porn, yet it takes a more expansive approach to the theme of sexual risk by exploring the varieties of risk its characters face during a period of profound and lasting changes. If AIDS-era pornographers sought either to protect gay men through the promotion of low-risk practices and condom use or to insulate them from harm via the privatized consumption of transgressive fantasies, then *The Mad Man* exposed the limitations of those approaches by questioning the mastery over risk that each seemed to promise. To be clear, *The Mad Man* is not an example of proto-bareback pornography: it repeatedly acknowledges the need for activist responses to the epidemic and at times delivers a forceful critique of the political forces that eliminated gay men's spaces for public sex in the name of health and safety. At the same time, it also explores how efforts to reduce or even eliminate risk comprised an inhibiting denial of the subject's constitutive vulnerabilities, a state of precarious existence consistently exacerbated by politically engineered structural inequities. For John Marr and many of the men he meets, fantasy-fueled erotic practices become one means to engage with that condition of vulnerability in a manner that neither denies its reality nor seeks to eliminate it through a comprehensive knowledge of the risks involved in cruising. Instead, the novel proffers an account of public sex according to which fantasies comprise an engagement with that vulnerability, a means of sitting or working with it, that becomes the basis for an empowering creativity.

Only recently have scholars turned their attentions toward illuminating those aspects of the novel. Darieck Scott, for example, takes on its pornographic framing by discussing how John's eagerness to adopt submissive roles in sadomasochistic arrangements with White partners illuminates the powers of Black abjection. Reenacted in fantasy, John does not transcend the historical abjection of Blackness but instead activates its creative power, which fuels both his intellectual production and his intimate engagements with other men.[6] Similarly, Tyler Bradway situates the novel as an example of queer experimental literature that cultivates "new economies of relation through the forces of affect" by intervening in the epistemological confusion unleashed by the HIV/AIDS epidemic.[7] In a process that Bradway terms "bad reading," the novel utilizes eroticism in order to counter the emotional habitus informing heteronormative reading practices by helping readers to feel their "way toward more radical modes of erotic and social belonging in historical moments when these possibilities are increasingly foreclosed, stigmatized, and forgotten."[8] However, neither Scott nor Bradway considers how Delany's novel was situated in relation to broader trends in gay pornography taking place during the 1980s and early 1990s. Instead, Bradway helpfully contextualizes the novel within gay writers' stark preference for realism versus experimental writing during this period, especially as the need to communicate to readers about the epidemic's traumatic effects became increasingly acute, yet his neglect of the era's pornographic writing and its counterpublics leads to a mischaracterization of the novel's emotional stakes by treating fear, anxiety, and shame as more germane to Delany's earlier, nonpornographic writings about HIV/AIDS than to *The Mad Man*'s eroticism. Expanding one's reading to consider the novel's relation AIDS-era pornography clarifies not only its significance but also what about Delany's novel rendered it experimental.

This chapter concludes by connecting Delany's novel to the emergence of a new wave of print-mediated counterpublics at the moment when, as historian Deborah Gould has argued, the emotional habitus undergirding many activists' responses to AIDS had change from one of shame and self-recrimination to one of anger.[9] While *The Mad Man* first appeared as a full-length text in 1994, a passage had previously appeared the year prior in *Steam*, an alternative journal dedicated to public sex and edited by the famously HIV-positive gay porn star Scott O'Hara.[10] *Steam* was one of a handful of public sex zines and journals that appeared for a brief moment during the early 1990s that, as John Paul Ricco has argued, "[exemplified] a short-lived political movement in the early-to-mid-'90s (did any of us really think that it would endure?), a historical moment marked by the early years of the second decade of the AIDS pandemic and intense sexual persistence and invention."[11] The pornographic counterpublics of the early 1990s thus marked a break from those of the preceding decade that focused so intently on the rhetoric of safety and private consumption and gave expression to the exhaustion and anger fueling the period's more militant AIDS activism. Delany's novel contains no mention of ACT UP New York or the many protests taking place in that city during that period. However, by noting the particular way it appeared in *Steam*, we can apprehend the novel's contributions to the period's counterpublics even as its subsequent full publication echoes a by now familiar story, according to which a book's underground associations help its publisher to stake out a new market territory.

AIDS LITERATURES, AIDS PORNOGRAPHIES

The HIV/AIDS epidemic placed significant pressure on writing by gay men about gay sexuality, and over the course of the 1980s, AIDS literature itself took shape through the question of what writing could do in response to epidemic. Many critics described the genre in terms of its activist function. For example, in the early anthology *Confronting AIDS through Literature* (1993), Judith Laurence Pastore observed that "[one] of the earliest tasks literary AIDS took on was combating the multiple untruths and prejudices surrounding the disease."[12] One of the clearest ways that writers did so was by showing the diversity of experiences that characterized living with HIV. Specifically, writers sought to counter a pervasive cultural narrative that understood AIDS experience in terms of what Steven Kruger called the invariable trajectory of "irreversible decline."[13] Such narratives followed a predictable set of plot points, beginning with a character who comes into contact with HIV either accidentally or through an "irresponsible" behavior, tests positive for antibodies to the virus, develops symptoms, receives a diagnosis, and then dies; "passivity," Kruger explains, "is imputed at all stages in this narrative, except the initial stage where too often a certain 'culpable' activity is associated with exposure to HIV."[14] Insofar as an act of sex with strangers provided the means of infection, irreversible decline narratives provided a new way to tell a familiar story about, not only the imaginary link between feminine sexuality and disease, but also the presumed pathology of gay men's desire to be sexually penetrated.[15]

Narratives of irreversible decline gained traction in part because the AIDS epidemic itself was also, as Paula Treichler demonstrated, an "epidemic of signification," a hyperactive confluence of biomedical, legal, and popular discourses that sought to contain the troubling emotions AIDS generated within easy-to-understand narratives about who was most at risk and why.[16] In the years prior to the advent of effective drug treatment when a diagnosis of AIDS often proved fatal, irreversible decline narratives provided a sense of reassuring coherence by oversimplifying the realities of the AIDS experience and by occluding the various kinds of people who acquired the virus. As Douglas Crimp has shown in his critique of gay journalist Randy Shilts's *And the Band Played On: Politics, People, and the AIDS Epidemic* (1987), irreversible decline narratives also often indulged in self-righteous moralizing according to which promiscuous HIV-positive gay men served as unambiguous villains while their unsuspecting "victims" became objects of pity.[17] In addition to its melodramatic dimensions, the irreversible decline narrative also took ready shape in popular novel forms that tracked a unidirectional trajectory from life to death. As a consequence, many writers went in search of other genres and narrative forms to convey not only the more complex temporalities that shaped AIDS experience, but also the wide range of people affected by the epidemic and the government's negligent response to it. Thus, as Richard Canning notes: "[the] cultural responses to AIDS constitute a 'local epidemic' in themselves. The huge quantity of novels, memoirs, films, dramas, and collections of verse has never come close to reflecting the diversity of the epidemic's affected populations, in respect of geography, race, gender, age, class or sexuality."[18]

While often not included in the range of genres surveyed by scholars of AIDS literatures such as Canning, pornography provided yet another means for writers, filmmakers, and videographers to intervene within the course of the epidemic. For example, as Cindy Patton has recounted, the "dissident safe sex educators" of the Boston-based Safe Company believed that porn could recontextualize risky sexual practices among a menu of "already and always safe" sexual activities that had served in the previous decade as "core elements of queer erotic life."[19] Porn writers adopted similar strategies. For example, John Preston's edited collection *Hot Living* and Max Exander's *Safestud*, both published by Alyson Publications in 1985, provide two early examples of what safe-sex strategies looked like in pornographic terms. Exander's *Safestud* is a fictional sex journal in which the novel's protagonist documents his various exploits between 1982 and 1984. The perceived incompatibility of "safe sex" and "good sex" provides the novel's conflict. While it begins with the protagonist's reservations about "the kinds of fantasies that might make somebody get sick," by the end he concludes that hot sex and self-preservation are not mutually exclusive. "I *could* live," he writes, "that I *could* have hot sex with precautions only, that I *could* form any kind of relationship with anybody I wanted to . . . well, when I figured that out, I was home free."[20] As Exander's experience suggests, safe sex wasn't simply about overcoming the shame associated with gay promiscuity. It was also attuned to gay men's fears of about their ability to be both promiscuous and to survive the epidemic.

Like *Safestud*, the stories collected in *Hot Living* aim to minimize fears of promiscuity's riskiness through the promotion of no-to-low-risk practices as determined according to the available information at the time. In his introduction, Preston describes how, after consultation with a number of AIDS service organizations, he derived a set of constraints for the volume's contributors that doubled as safe-sex guidelines. These constraints included four basic tenants: "Do not ingest semen in any form," "There can be no oral-anal contact," "Don't fuck without a condom," and "Do not swallow urine."[21] In addition, Preston also included recommendations that men reduce their number of sexual partners and limit sexual contact to friends and known acquaintances. The volume's contributors produced a surprisingly diverse array of sexual configurations. While for some stories the move toward a more or less committed sexual relationship with a friend or lover provides the narrative climax, others foregrounded public sex as a still-viable erotic outlet. George Whitmore's "No One Gets Hurt," for example, follows a man at once depressed and terrified to have sex after the recent death of his childhood friend and lover, Eddie. The ritualistic play of BDSM becomes the narrator's route to a new sex life, and the story concludes when a group of leathermen "breaks" into his apartment and spirits him away for a scene at a local leather bar.

Other stories in the collection emphasized the value of unconventional erotic practices in ways only tangentially related to the epidemic. Samuel Steward's "The Broken Vessel" minimizes mention of AIDS and instead explores the body's capacity for pleasure following severe bodily trauma. The story opens as Phil receives word that a longtime friend has recently suffered a motorcycle accident that has left him paralyzed from the waist down. Perhaps worse: his friend has also lost all sensation in his genitals. Phil then confesses his passion for "'broken vessels' — guys who were incomplete, who had lost something or other . . . an eye, an arm, a leg."[22] Such men fascinate Phil because their ostensible disabilities function as enhancements during sex. Phil recalls a lover whose missing right hand transformed his forearm into a "lengthy tapered cock, very good for fisting" and another man whose missing limb made "screwing him easier—no leg in the way."[23] At the end of the story, Phil gives his disabled friend his first postaccident orgasm by masturbating in front of him as he plays with his buddy's highly sensitive nipples. The story presents an argument for the "desexualization of pleasure," according to which the genitals no longer serve as the organizing point for one's erotic practices.[24] However, the sex theorist most responsible for Steward's account of erotic mobility is neither Michel Foucault nor Freud but Alfred Kinsey, whose research on "phantom feelings" leads Phil to try his nipple tactic in the first place. In addition to providing an example of how sexological knowledge filtered into pornographic works, "The Broken Vessel" suggests the variety of sources on which pornographers drew for inspiration in inventing creative solutions to the perceived risks of HIV transmission.[25]

In some cases, activists found it necessary to testify to the life-saving value of pornography not only to alleviate gay men's discomforting emotions through the eroticization of safe-sex practices, but also to defend the efforts of AIDS activists from political fear-mongering. Senator Jesse Helms's proposed amendment to the 1988 fiscal appropriations bill provides one well-known example. What came to be known as the Helms amendment sought to curtail funding to any organization believed to "promote" homosexuality, a change that would withhold federal support from a number of AIDS service organizations.[26] In order to drum up congressional support for his amendment, Helms began his floor speech by denouncing the New York–based Gay Men's Health Crisis's *Safer Sex Comix,* which depicted hunky, cartoon men demonstrating the proper application and use of condoms for anal sex in porn's characteristic vulgar lingo. While the comics' value lay in their ability to spread information about low-risk practices to gay men who engaged in casual sex, Helms received near unanimous support in the Senate for his amendment. Attacks on safe-sex pornography were also often explicitly racialized. As Dan Royles recounts, the National Task Force on AIDS Prevention relied on live demonstrations and pornographic publicity to promote safer-sex practices among gay and bisexual men of color, yet after receiving federal funding in 1988, the NTFAP came under fire from the conservative syndicated columnist Cal Thomas. In his popular columns, Thomas assailed the program in various and often contradictory ways, from denying the existence of the Black gay and bisexual men the organization served to construing its methods as a threat to American moral decency.[27] Despite the NTFAP's efforts to counter Thomas's attacks, he proved successful at stirring up enough public outrage such that, in 1991, the NTFAP and a number of other AIDS service organizations focused on ethnic and racial minority groups experienced drastic cuts in their federal funding.[28]

As those examples show, pornographers' efforts to reduce the spread of HIV by targeting high-risk practices could be risky in and of themselves. Yet some pornographers were reticent to address the epidemic in their work for reasons other than the threat of political backlash. During the 1980s, the industry experienced a boom in profits when existing pornographic print cultures provided a means to open up new markets and distribution patterns for newly available pornographic videocassettes.[29] While US studios collectively released only a few hundred videos per year during the early 1980s, that number soon shot up to approximately eleven thousand videos annually, and advertisements for video features comprised a growing share of a magazine's revenue.[30] Pornography was once again proving to be a lucrative business, yet publishers and video producers worried about the impacts that any effort to address the epidemic might have on porn's production and sale. In turn, they devised creative solutions. Some required performers to wear condoms during the filming of a sex scene yet edited any visible evidence of condom use out of both the feature and its publicity materials. The attentive consumer might only know that safe-sex protocols had been employed from the notice provided on title screens or as a part of the occasional educational trailers that bookended the feature. Producers also argued that the consumption of porno videos, regardless of the kinds of sex the video featured, was the safest form of sex possible because home viewing eliminated the need to venture into public spaces, such as theaters and adult bookstores, where viewers might be tempted to live out their fantasies with strangers. Instead, the argument went, men could simply order a videocassette through the mail or purchase it from the local video store and view it within the privacy, solitude, and thus safety of their own homes.[31]

While the use of live performers made the problem of HIV especially salient to video pornographers, writers also faced the questions of what to represent and how. Some similarly affirmed that pornographic representations of risky sex were inherently safe because they allowed men not only to live vicariously through the lives of their characters but also to do so in solitary acts of reading. As T. R. Witomski argued: "Reading and looking at porno is just about the safest sexual action that you can do. Most regular readers and viewers of porno do not lead the adventurous sex lives that are the rule in porno; that's partially *why* they are buying the stuff—and, if the

whole truth be known, that's a good part of the reason why writers and illus-
trators are making the stuff."[32] Perhaps anxious regarding the liabilities that
risky representations might expose them to, publishers sought to mitigate
any potential risks that depictions of "unsafe" sex might cause in a number
of ways. In 1986, when Anthony DeBlase and Andrew Charles replaced John
Embry as the publishers for *Drummer*, the magazine's new owners included
a disclaimer in the table of contents that served as an explicit defense of the
magazine's content:

> While *Drummer* hopes to educate its readers on a wide variety of topics, its
> main purpose is to entertain! Works of fiction presented in this magazine are
> just that—fiction! They are not in any way intended to suggest or describe
> activities that anyone should—or often could—actually do. They are meant
> for entertainment only. In other than fictional pieces we will emphasize safe
> sex with respect to contagious diseases and safe and sane behavior with
> respect to all activities, and will try to point out all activities which deviate
> from generally recognized safe-sex and safe-and-sane play activities.[33]

The decision (and thus the responsibility) to engage in safe sex lay with the
reader, and the editors fulfilled any perceived responsibility on their end
by publishing all the information necessary for readers to make informed
choices. For the magazine's publishers, the readers' understanding of the
difference between fiction and nonfiction, fantasy and information, shielded
the magazine's pornographic content from critique.

The readers' presumed capacity to tell the difference between fantasy and
reality also informed the editorial policies of other publications. Discussing his editorial work for *Inches* magazine, Steven Saylor describes how the
decision to change stories to conform to prevailing safer-sex advice often
occurred on a case-by-case basis: "if I got a story that was clearly fantasy
material—typical fantasy stuff, like the college coach and the football player,
firemen having sex with each other—the things none of us think are realistic,
but just accept as typical fantasies, I wouldn't be that careful about wanting
the author to introduce safe sex into the story."[34] Sometimes publishers also
required extensive revisions. When Alyson Publications collected together
previously published material for Patrick Califia's *Macho Sluts* (1988), the
publisher required that he update the stories to comply with the publisher's
"policy against eroticizing high-risk sex."[35] In the anthology's introduction,
Califia noted his ambivalence about the changes: "Porn can be a valuable way
to teach people how to have hot and satisfying 'safer sex.' But I don't believe
'unsafe' porn causes AIDS any more than I think 'violent' porn causes rape."
Califia's statement contains a faint challenge to the publisher's policy, suggest-

ing that the excision of "high-risk sex" itself risks the phobic identification of porn as a cause of AIDS. "Keeping these stories in this book was so important to me that I was willing to rewrite them," Califia explains, "but I also need to say that it feels like a form of bowdlerization, even censorship, and if it were my choice, I would have left them in their original, sleazy form."[36]

Califia's comments here suggest a somewhat different position on pornography than that proffered by either Witomski or the publishers of *Drummer* magazine. A vocal proponent and theorist of public sex, Califia's irritation with the publishers' edits reflects his awareness of the complex relation between erotic practice and pornographic fantasy that writers of pornography had developed over the preceding decade. The republication and thus cultural elevation of Califia's fiction from the pages of subcultural magazines to a trade paperback, published through one of the few presses devoted to gay and lesbian books, necessitated an alteration of their "original, sleazy form" to comply with a prevailing safer-sex orthodoxy. However, the move entails not an active promotion of safer-sex practices, as done by the pedagogical pornographers, but a kind of prophylactic editing, according to which the revised manuscript is presumed to prevent the accidental transmission of risky practices themselves. In ways that recall the efforts of video producers who promoted their stock in terms of the convenience and safety of home viewing, the mode of passive intervention at stake in the edits required by Califia's publisher bespeak an attenuation of pornographic writing's association with public sex and its growing association with reading as a private act of solitary masturbation. My point here is not that print and video were inherently privatizing, but that the epidemiological pressures of HIV/AIDS, combined with a broader social and political response that imagined a causal link between gay promiscuity and AIDS-related deaths, activated the potentials inherent in both print and video media to drive the privatization of public sex practices. If previously pornography had linked together imagined and embodied intimacy with others via its mediation of public sex, then with the epidemic, that link weakened as solitary consumption became the presumed principal mode of engaging with porn.

THE MAD MAN: ACCEPT NO SUBSTITUTIONS

While many forms of pornographic writing would continue to follow the path laid out by escapist pornographers, by the late 1980s some writing and the vast majority of moving-image porn tracked with the efforts of safe-sex pornographers. The content of safe-sex messaging in gay pornography would begin to shift as well during that period, narrowing from the promotion of a broad menu of low-to-no risk practices to the conspicuous use of condoms for penetrative anal sex and a prohibition on depictions of fluid exchange. These changes followed from the introduction of new knowledge about the particular risks associated with receptive anal sex between sero-discordant partners, but the promotion of condoms was also part of an effort to counter the stigma that penetrative anal sex had accrued within AIDS discourse. When Leo Bersani polemically argued that popular depictions of gay men dying from AIDS screened the "the infinitely more seductive and intolerable image of a grown man, legs high in the air, unable to refuse the suicidal ecstasy of being a woman," he was in part emphasizing the degree to which anal sex itself had been invested with a variety of meanings.[37] Calls to forgo anal sex seemed to be an implicit capitulation to the anxieties of AIDS discourse and generated suspicion among some gay men for whom the practice had become an important part of their identities in the preceding decade. The Gay Men's Health Crisis's *Safer Sex Comix* depiction of working-class men with big, rubber-wrapped dicks thus sought not only to save lives but also to counter the fantasy of anal sex as lethally emasculating.

Those developments provide crucial context for understanding Delany's *The Mad Man*, a pornographic text whose approach to representing the risks of HIV/AIDS remains anomalous with respect to both the escapist and pedagogical positions, even as it seems to exhibit features of both. On the one hand, it seems possible to locate Delany's novel on the side of safe-sex discourse because the novel excludes the act considered most likely to transmit HIV: receptive anal sex without a condom. In fact, the novel depicts a range of sexual acts, including ones that treat the anus as a locus of pleasure, but penetrative anal-genital sex is not one of them. For that reason, Jeffery Allan Tucker argues that *The Mad Man* contributes to the efforts to promote safer sex by "representing sex as pleasurable, redemptive contact between bodies, militating against an anti-sex conservatism that is both unrealistic and ultimately unhealthy," as well as "[representing] gay sex—and sex in general—as a remarkably varied spectrum of possibilities, highlighting safer sex options than protected anal sex."[38] One of the acts the novel highlights is oral sex. As one of John's friends describes him, John is a "stoned cocksucker," whose primary means of sexual gratification comes through receptive oral sex practices that include the consumption of his partners' various bodily fluids (403). While John's actions would not necessarily qualify as "safe sex" according to the guidelines that Preston delineates in the introduction to *Hot Living*, the strategy of oral substitution, or the replacement of one's anal sex practices with oral sex practices, had become a recognized safer-sex strategy by the early 1990s.[39]

In addition to John's disinterest in anal sex, the novel suggests a safe-sex reading in a few other ways. One is the inclusion of a research study originally published in 1987 in the British medical journal the *Lancet* as an appendix to the novel. Entitled "Risk Factors for Seroconversion to Human Immunodeficiency Virus among Male Homosexuals," the appendix describes a longitudinal study, conducted over a yearlong period with a cohort of 2,507 homosexual men, which found that of the many sexual behaviors surveyed, "receptive anal intercourse accounted for nearly all new HIV infections." The novel also includes the study within its narrative as a topic of conversation in an epistolary exchange between John and Sam Mossman, the soon-to-be ex-wife of his PhD adviser, Irving Mossman. In response to what John feels is Sam's ignorance of his erotic practices, John provides a lengthy description of his various cruising venues and the particular precautions he takes before seeking out sex (175). The letter details a great deal of personal information from John's sex life, much more than has ever passed between the two characters before, and his sudden candor is one of the reasons why Sam's response does not come until 1989, roughly five years after John's initial letter. Sam's letter includes a copy of the *Lancet* study with the following note: "Although the medical stuff in your '84 letter is really out of cloud-cuckoo land, my friend, the article [. . .] may suggest some of the reasons why you're still HIV-negative—assuming you still are" (242). The letter exchange comprises an instance of mutual education: John schools Sam on sexual variation; Sam teaches John about sexual risk. In that way, it resembles the porn of the safer-sex educators as the reader vicariously participates in the exchange, coming to learn along with John that oral sex offers a safer and highly pleasurable alternative to penetrative anal sex.

The problem with reading *The Mad Man* in this way is that neither John nor any of the other characters deliberately make the choice to adopt oral sex over anal sex. Moreover, in his letter to Sam, John acknowledges the efforts of the safe-sex activists providing information and live demonstrations in the city's gay bars and clubs but ultimately rejects them: "For all my sympathy with them, however, let me note that their particular option—condoms, no fluid exchanges—while I feel it is just as valid as mine, still, is *not* mine; indeed, it's not lots of people's. I've never yet sucked off a dick with a condom on it, and I'm not particularly anxious to start!" (180). Instead of indicating a deliberate choice to engage in lower-risk practices, John's lack of interest in adopting condoms instead reflects a kind of fundamental incompatibility between his desire and what David Chambers has termed the "hegemony of anal intercourse."[40] By the late 1980s, the small amount of epidemiological evidence regarding the risks of anal sex caused a shift in AIDS prevention efforts, and "the most insistent message was that men engaging in anal intercourse must always use a condom."[41] While the demand to always use a condom might apply as readily to oral sex as to anal sex, Chambers goes on to argue, "most gay men who see a condom poster probably do not understand it to mean oral sex."[42] Framed in terms of a miscommunication, John's unwillingness to take the advice of the safe-sex poster thus suggest the need for more targeted forms of messaging. While that may have helped other men like John, the novel heads in a different direction, exploring the ways that the specificity of one's preferred practices were always already conditioned by a number of other factors beyond the quantities of pleasures that could be produced.

Put differently, the specificity of an erotic practice is as much about fantasy as it is about the actions and locations in which men enact them. This theme is introduced early in the novel when John cruises a homeless White man in the park who goes by the nickname "Piece o' Shit." In response to John's forthright offer for a blow job, Piece o' Shit responds: "I'm straight, man. I really like women! 'Specially black ones—older ones. But I always had me a good imagination. So if a cocksucker don't mind me doin' a little thinkin', a little imaginin', I sure don't mind no cocksucker [...] nurisin' on my fuckin' peter. I don't need me no picture magazines" (30). Piece o' Shit then introduces John to the erotic game of "pussy-face," according to which John must contort his face, lips, and so that in Piece o' Shit's mind it resembles a "funky black pussy" (33). As a straight man, Piece o' Shit cannot bring himself to have sex with John unless he can approach his body through a fantasy that is at once racializing and feminizing, yet the fantasy at stake should not be understood in terms of a simple escapism. As Scott has shown, the Piece o' Shit scene in fact reverses a common scenario in gay pornography in which well-endowed and hyper-virile Black men sexually dominate White men in revenge for the history of White supremacy. Such fantasies comprise a disavowal of the history that motivates them insofar as the erotic punishment redeems and preserves Whiteness by situating White supremacy as a relic of the past. In contrast, the Piece o' Shit scene instead enacts White supremacist relations, repeating in fantasy the forms of oral rape visited upon Black male bodies that historically constituted them as racialized others.

In a manner that foreshadows John's future engagements with other White men in racialized BDSM scenes, his willingness to inhabit the Black abject with Piece o' Shit entails a risk that would invalidate the good-natured and consensual conditions under which the two men have sex together. Put differently, John faces an uncertainty similar to what characters in leather pornography often faced when sex began under consensual terms but then escalated excitingly beyond those terms of agreement, such as when the protagonist of Aaron Travis's "Blue Light" finds himself magically but thrillingly dismembered. Perhaps more pointedly, John's eroticization of his abject state affords access to a power in powerlessness: John must be degraded for it to work, yet the pleasure found in such degradation marks an alternative relation to the traumas that mark him as a Black subject. As Scott explains, John does not transcend the conditions of his abjection as the White revenge fantasy would have him do. Instead, he revels in that history: "This is his *black* power, a power of blackness-in/as-abjection."[43] John's "feeling good" is not some kind of unconventional personal therapy, even as the most dramatic effects of abjection entail changes that one might be tempted, however incorrectly, to call personal. John's power manifests itself specifically as a potent creative energy, a "prolific cultural and intellectual production," that results in the completion of *The Mad Man* as a text that John himself has authored.[44] This creative power follows not from the reinforcement of his ego through rhetorics of respectability or pride, but from John's openness to the otherness of history, which allows him to return himself to the world in terms of both his erotic practices and his intellectual work.

Scott's reading of *The Mad Man* highlights the interrelation between fantasy and erotic practices, but it also explains that interrelation in terms of what such fantasies do for men like John. In other words, John gets something important from his participation in racialized BDSM, conducted according to a specific configuration of White and Black bodies, that he cannot get through other modes of erotic practice. One cannot fully account for that specificity entirely as the consequence of a rational calculus meant to determine what acts will produce the maximal quantity of pleasure. Instead, pleasure indicates a potentiality that the novel depicts in terms of both John's intellectual production and the erotic friendships he generates with other men, many of whom differ markedly in terms of their social status.[45] Yet, in a manner that Scott does not quite account for, the power John experiences through the Black abject also entails his embeddedness within HIV's epidemic of signification. John comes to believe that he has acquired the virus following his final encounter with Piece o' Shit, during which John performs oral sex on his friend and swallows his cum. After Piece o' Shit falls into a deep, postorgasmic slumber, John discovers that what he first took for smudges of dirt on Piece o' Shit's body may in fact be Kaposi's sarcoma lesions. When John develops a rash, he believes he is infected with HIV and thus will soon die, yet this experience points to another source of power in powerlessness that works in tandem with his Black bottomhood: it marks the start of an erotically and intellectually productive period in John's life, during which he engages in sex with other men while completing a number of research essays on the subject of Timothy Hasler's writing.

In the period before the introduction of combination drug therapy, which transformed the meaning of HIV infection from a death sentence to a manageable chronic illness, the belief one had or would inevitably acquire a life-ending illness caused significant emotional turmoil for many gay men. However, this is not the case for John. In his letter to Sam, John explains that any mental and emotional suffering he has endured as a consequence of the epidemic actually resolved itself well before his fateful encounter with Piece o' Shit. The uncertainty the epidemic cast over men's public sex practices *had* transformed the pleasurable rhythms of cruising into an experience of "vast stasis" and "psychic immobility" (148), yet his continued commitment to cruising in public also enabled a significant transformation of that emotional habitus, which he describes using a pair of biological and architectural metaphors:

> At any rate, the experience itself in the Variety felt, through the course of its two hours and the hour right after, as though my whole brain were untying itself, neuron by neuron, thought fragment by thought fragment, if not synapse by synapse—and reweaving itself into a new pattern, in which the heavy, nervous, and interminably obsessive, wheedling *fear* of AIDS that has been a part of my life in one form or another since a year before it was *called* AIDS—over three years now, I realize!—was simply no longer there, the way an ugly, unfunctional, and depressing room, with its shredding wallpaper, broken light fixtures, and cracked molding, vanishes when the house that contained it is at last pulled down. (178)

John's description of his emotional transformation calls into question any clear distinction between inside and outside, interior and exterior, as cruising for sex forces, first, a fantastic rewiring of John's brain and then, second, the demolition of a derelict structure whose previously enclosed spaces becomes open to the outside world. As a consequence, the terror that led to a state of physical, mental, and emotional petrification transforms into what he calls his "New Feeling of Power and Strength" (177).

Crucially, and in stark contrast to other examples of AIDS-era pornography, this feeling derives from neither a rational adoption of low-risk practices nor an escape from the realities of the epidemic into the safety of fantasy. In a sense, both of those positions, even as the novel acknowledges their necessity as responses to the epidemic, express a denial of the subject's limited being via efforts to exert epistemological mastery over the risks of HIV transmission. In contrast, John's public cruising does not entail an effort to overcome risk, even as he elsewhere engages in various rituals to do so, but instead reflects an effort to become intimate with it. As he explains to Sam: "The thing I am terribly aware of [. . .] is that, until much more is known, there is no earthly way I can, with any degree of responsibility, recommend the logic of these precautions to anyone else with any sort of suggestion of even probable safety. They are all entirely a blind gamble. [. . .] Yet it is the realization that one is gambling, and gambling on one's own—rather than seeking some possible certain knowledge, some knowable belief in how intelligent or in how idiotic the chances are—that obliterates the terror" (176). Both John's and the novel's disclaimer have established that there is no way to determine the probabilities of HIV transmission and thereby obtain a clear-eyed calculation of the risks. Instead, John understands his continued cruising as a gamble that verges on madness: "What I must live with—and quite possibly die with—is a certain sense of its reasonableness, a certain sense of its risk, knowing my 'sense' of both are absolutely without experimental foundation; and somehow because of it [. . .] I can now live without basic terror or basic hope" (177).

In his account of the transformation enacted during his cruising of the Variety Theatre, John emphasizes not knowing the risks his practices entail but a "sense" of "reasonableness" and "risk." In doing so, he describes a different form of engagement than those based in acts of knowing that might falsely promise "basic hope" or drive the subject into an immobilizing "basic terror." Hence his confrontation with risk does not resemble the kinds of heroic or sacrificial masculinity that characterize some men's orientation toward HIV within bareback subcultures.[46] Instead, John's transformative sensing is more in line with the pleasurable and empowering engagement he obtains with the Black abject through scenes of racialized BDSM. In both cases, and despite the fact that John describes his gamble as something he makes "on [his] own," the unintelligible thing that is unknowable yet sensible occurs through a collective practice. John's cruising in the Variety Theatre thus also bears more than a passing resemblance to the orgy that John subsequently holds in his apartment, which plays out according to a game devised by one of the participants. As Mad Man Mike explains, the principal rule of the game is that each man may purchase any other man in the room for a penny and then "do whatever he wanted with the guy" (441). While the sale and exchange of Black bodies evokes the history of the trans-atlantic slave trade, John explicitly compares the game and its seemingly endless permutations of bodies and pleasures to the writings of Sade—yet with a key difference: "Call it structure. Call it whatever. The same thing that seems so abhorrent in Sade, when it actually occurs among people of good will [. . .] is as reassuring as a smile or a warm hand on a shoulder or a sharp, friendly smack on the ass" (442).

The men convening for the penny game comprise a more deliberately organized group than the sex public of the Variety Theatre, which takes shape as an unintended consequence of the broader political forces shaping the life of the city. However, the novel posits both as mediating their respective participants' relation to affect in a manner that resolves what could be a debilitating terror or anxiety into a source of pleasure. As John explains to Sam in his letter, the men in the Variety Theatre are also, in a sense, playing a game: "At this period, people who cruise with any frequency are not gambling on the possibility of avoiding it. Largely, they are gambling on what strikes them as the much higher probability that they already have it—so that, in terms of their *own* eventual health, their activity makes no difference" (172). This orientation toward the virus predicts the arguments that the gay porn star Scott O'Hara began to make in the mid-1990s about the advantages of a positive sero-status: "AIDS has been an undeniable blessing. [. . .] I look at the HIV-negative people around me, and I pity them. They live their lives in constant fear of infection: mustn't do this, mustn't do that, mustn't take risks."[47] While John's decision to "gamble" is his own, the gamble as enacted in cruising the theater puts him in relation to a group itself constituted by similarly enacted gambles. The game doesn't offer a minimization or escape from risk, but it does offer an oblique relationship to it, rendering it into a source of empowerment that is at once conditioned on its being in relation to strangers and a means by which one is put into relation with them. The novel is not proposing a social policy; instead, it explores how the subject's engagement with finitude can paradoxically provide an escape from a life so racked with terror that it is otherwise unlivable.

In order to clarify the contours of these empowering relations, the novel occasionally contrasts them against forms of public sex in which the demand for safety comprises, in the language of the novel, another kind of madness. In a later scene, John's friend Tony, a self-identified "stone shit eater," ends up in the hospital with symptoms that resemble AIDS-related illness. John and his friends begin the process of mourning Tony, yet they soon discover that Tony is not HIV positive but is instead suffering from "a serious case of intestinal parasites" (495). As John explains: "Apparently, Tony said, the parasite business had happened to him at least twice before. From now on, he explained to us as though it were the most ordinary of seasonal resolutions, no more dog shit—" (495). The scene dislodges risk from the narrow framework of disease transmission: sex can be risky for a number of reasons, including the demand to be free of risk itself. The novel raises this possibility in another brief but notable scene in which John picks up a young man who insists on wearing a condom while John blows him. The experience, as John reports it, is unsatisfactory both for its brevity and for the condom, but it then becomes violent as afterward the teen aggressively demands payment. If the point of the condom is to keep both John and the teen safe from possible infection, then the risk it represents recedes behind the very present danger that the young man poses to John, who manages to escape his attacker by boarding a crowded city bus that whisks him away from the encounter.

John and the young man that he encounters reflect two different orientations toward the world of risks that characterize cruising for sex in New York City. Neither one is "safe," even as the young man's insistence on using condoms during oral sex may offer a degree of protection from HIV infection that John forgoes. Thus, it's not simply a matter of engaging in public sex, but of adopting a specific ethic of public sex. While the intimacy that John acquires allows an empowering relation to that world of risk, the young man's attitude entails a destructive drive to self-protection that simultaneously redistributes the dangers of public sex onto men such as John. As a result, their brief encounter evokes another significant theme in the novel regarding the broader political forces remaking the city itself, as it becomes increasingly inhospitable to the erotic subcultures that had emerged within it prior to the start of the epidemic. John mentions those developments in his letter to Sam, describing the ways in which city officials used the epidemic as an excuse to force the closure of the bars and sex clubs: "The closing of these places is a murderous act by the city—not because of anything necessarily to be learned from the 'safe sex' demonstrations about AIDS," John writes, "but because it drives thousands of gay men from fairly protected environments out into far more dangerous venues, where robbery, murder, and general queer-bashings are far more common" (180). Rather than reducing risk, city officials have intensified it in the way that John describes, yet given the manner in which those public venues remain crucial for mediating John's empowering erotic ethics, the damage may be even more far reaching. "[Instead] of writing those articles," he confesses, "likely I would have committed suicide" (234).

SCOTT O'HARA'S COUNTERPUBLIC OF SLEAZEHOUNDS

Following the initial publication of *The Mad Man*, the novel's approach to public sex and the risks of HIV/AIDS caused trouble for some critics, which they expressed through a suspicion of the novel's self-designation as a "pornotopic fantasy." For example, Ray Davis lauded Delany's other pornographic writing, yet he argued that *The Mad Man* was different: the world of the novel wasn't pornographic but "unmistakably that of mainstream realism."[48] Reed Woodhouse likewise took "the disclamatory word *fantasy* with a grain of salt," and instead elaborated a reading of the novel that sought to redeem John's risky behavior.[49] According to Woodhouse, *The Mad Man* was an important intervention into the AIDS epidemic because it challenged the popular belief that promiscuous sex was itself a cause of disease: "The book implicitly asks

'Why not?' Why not satisfy every appetite that is not violent or destructive? [. . .] *The Mad Man* is, in this respect, a surprisingly old-fashioned justification of seeking your own pleasure and development, provided they do not harm others."[50] Both of those readings reflect the pressures that the epidemic had placed on, not only gay sexuality, but also its representation and criticism: a sexually explicit novel that offered an unapologetic depiction of gay promiscuity in one of the US spots for HIV infections needed to be brought into alignment with the period's antihomophobic politics, a critical move that required distancing the novel from pornography. However, Delany would eventually rebuff these readings, rejecting efforts to associate the novel with realism. "*The Mad Man* is a serious work of pornography," he explained in a 1999 interview. "I suppose I ought to be flattered by some readers' confusing it with realism. But, finally, it *is* a pornographic work."[51]

To be fair to Davis and Woodhouse, aside from its sexual explicitness, *The Mad Man* didn't exactly resemble the gay pornographic writing that many had come to know. The novel ran over four hundred pages in length and was as much about philosophy and the university as it was about public sex; moreover, the first edition appeared in hardcover, and the author blurb noted the critical acclaim of Delany's genre-busting science-fiction novels as well as his then recent appointment to a position at the University of Massachusetts, Amherst. The original edition was also published by Richard Kasak Books. An acquaintance of Grove Press founder Barney Rosset, Kasak had started his New York–based publishing house in 1990 as a press dedicated to "erotic literature."[52] The category was far from being a euphemism. Instead, it reflected Kasak's efforts to carve out market territory by publishing sexually explicit novels by writers such as Delany, William Carney, and Oscar Wilde alongside reprints of midcentury pulp novels with their sex scenes updated to meet the expectations of contemporary readers.[53] Kasak did not focus exclusively on gay writers, yet his promotion of their work aligned him with a handful of other publishers, including Alyson Books and Cleis Press, that began publishing "erotica" for gay and lesbian readers during the 1990s. Of those Cleis stands out as a notable example for its enduring *Best Gay Erotica* anthologies, the first of which appeared in 1996. In ways that mirrored Kasak's own blending of the literary and the pornographic, the *Best Gay Erotica* series featured short fiction by known pornographers, including Larry Townsend and Jack Fritscher, as well as work by writers better known for their literary output, including Alexander Chee, Justin Chin, Dennis Cooper, Scott Heim, Kevin Killian, R. Zamora Linmark, and of course, Delany.

Like Richard Kasak Books, Cleis's *Best Gay Erotica* series helped to establish gay erotica as a semi-legitimate genre of fiction in part through its deliberate mixing of literary and pornographic writing. However, unlike Cleis,

Richard Kasak Books actively differentiated between its erotic literature and its pornographic fiction. While titles of the former variety appeared under the name Richard Kasak Books, those of the latter appeared under various imprints that targeted different identity-based reading publics, including Badboy (gay), Masquerade (straight), Hard Candy (lesbian), and Rosebud (lesbian). By publishing *The Mad Man* as a Richard Kasak book, the publisher positioned Delany's novel in the market differently from the pornographic novels and short story collections it released under its imprints, thereby seeking to capitalize on the paraliterary reputation of its author while underscoring the novel's sexually transgressive dimensions. To that end, the publisher included a quote from the novel on the book cover, in which John confesses: "I do not have AIDS. I am surprised that I don't. I have actively had sex with other men weekly, sometimes daily—without condoms—for the last decade and a half." Arguably, Richard Kasak Books' presentation of *The Mad Man* bears more than a passing resemblance to the successful marketing strategies developed by Rosset's Grove Press more than twenty years prior. However, Richard Kasak Books appeared less interested in leveraging the heteronormativity of the nation's reading public than in realizing a kind of pluralized and gay-friendly version of the vision that Steven Marcus elaborated in his conclusion to *The Other Victorians*, according to which eroticism becomes a legitimate function of literature. As such, it suggests the role that pornographic writing may have played in the neoliberal pluralization and diversification of reading publics at a moment when some sexual and gender minorities were gaining increased access to the rights and privileges of citizenship.

At the same time, the Richard Kasak Books edition of *The Mad Man* was not the first instance in which at least some readers would have encountered John. A few months prior to the novel's full publication, an excerpt from *The Mad Man* appeared on the pages of Scott O'Hara's public sex journal *Steam: A Quarterly Journal for Men*. *Steam* was just one example of the queer print culture that emerged in the US during the late 1980s and early 1990s, when the US Supreme Court's ruling on *Bowers v. Hardwick* (1987) instigated a shift in the emotional habitus for queer politics.[54] As Gould has shown, the shift from shame to anger coincided with the rise of militant queer politics of activist groups such as ACT UP New York, yet it also fostered a queer print culture whose titles, such as *Diseased Pariah News*, likewise reflected that emotional turn. Billed as "The Literate Queer's Guide to Sex and Controversy," the title of *Steam* also captured something of the political edge that characterized the period's queer print culture. During its relatively short run, from the spring of 1993 to the winter of 1995, *Steam* not only offered forceful defenses of public sex but also promoted it among its readership. In fact, the vast majority of its content was directed in some way toward theorizing and facilitating public sex: the journal's primary feature consisted of listings of public and semipublic spaces where readers could go to find anonymous sex. Submitted and sometimes reviewed by readers themselves, the listings provided information on both urban and rural spaces in both the United States and abroad. O'Hara supplemented these listings with more in-depth reviews of bars and sex clubs, histories of cruising, critical journalism on efforts to regulate public sex, and reader-service articles assessing, for example, the potential of a newly accessible internet for arranging sexual encounters.

Despite its orientation toward public sex, O'Hara resisted publishing pornographic content in *Steam*. It was, he insisted, neither a "contact mag" intended to help men find dates or arrange sex in secluded bedrooms nor a porno mag that might facilitate solitary acts of masturbation.[55] As if to emphasize this distinction, O'Hara released a companion publication called *wilde* in 1995 dedicated to pornographic fiction, yet it would fold within a year due to the costs and demands of managing both journals.[56] In some ways, O'Hara's publication of *The Mad Man* excerpt marks an exception to his policy of not publishing pornographic fiction, even as the excerpt itself contained very little in the way of graphic depictions of sex. Instead, it consisted of different sections from the novel, including one pulled from the disclaimer emphasizing the lack of studies needed to better understand the risks of transmitting HIV via erotic practices other than penetrative anal sex and a section detailing an encounter between John and a friend in one of the city's parks. However, the largest section consisted of a passage from John's letter to Sam about the various people whom he interacted with in the Variety Theatre, including Mark, a homeless White teenager who volunteers with the Guardian Angels; a "young, Spanish queen" and his abusive pimp; a man named "Little Black Joe"; and one of the many Black trans women who quietly dish gossip in the theater's darkened back corners.

While offering readers little in the way of sex, the excerpt provided an extended reflection on what it often felt like to cruise for sex in public spaces. John describes his mixed feelings of unease and attachment to those with whom he shares the space of the Variety, but he suggests that such ambivalence is a necessary condition of public sex itself, contrasting starkly with the intense terror and hatred directed at them all by "the boys for whom society is made":

> We are guilty that we are not them—are not those boys destined to run the systems and cities of the world: that puts a rift between us. They, however, are terrified, lest through some inexplicable accident some magic happenstance of sympathy or contagion they might become us. In most of them, we know, that terror can be repressed before adolescent curios-

ity. But we also know that that terror, given the license of adult exercise in the darkness of unquestioned moral right, can assume murderous proportions: our deviance, our abnormalities, our perversion are needed to define, to create, to constitute them and make them visible to each other and to themselves.[57]

John's statement exemplifies the manner in which his "New Feeling of Power and Strength" is as much social and inchoately political as it is erotic and intellectual. While "the boys for whom society is made" view the Variety's gender and sexual dissidents in terms of terror and disgust, John's uneasy yet generally pleasant, and at times erotic, relation to the other denizens of that space comprises a form of solidarity grounded in their limited and imperiled being. Importantly, this process includes generating ties across both identity categories and class positions, as John's middle-class status often affords him a degree of safety and security not available to the many working-class and homeless men that he takes for sexual partners. To borrow from Bradway, John's particular practice of cruising, which differs from that of the young man who demands that John use a condom, thus entails a mode of "feeling [his] way toward more radical modes of erotic and social belonging in historical moments when these possibilities are increasingly foreclosed, stigmatized, and forgotten" (193).

The affective politics that Bradway has in mind pertains not necessarily to cruising, but to a particular practice of "bad reading" that readers cultivate in and through their eroticized engagements with Delany's novel. It's a similar kind of process that Scott likewise describes in his account of the novel's evocations of feelings of lust, stress, and disgust for readers, particularly in its scenes of John's enthusiastic embrace of the Black abject, which entail a potentially empowering (if not transformative) relation to the discursive inheritance of contemporary subjects. While they do so to different degrees, both Bradway and Scott place emphasis on the importance of reading and textual engagement, but by highlighting the passage from Delany's novel published in *Steam*, we get a clearer sense of how that reading practice may have been enacted through the counterpublics of the early 1990s. O'Hara's refusal to publish pornography in *Steam* reflected not his distaste for the genre but a desire that the journal might help revitalize the public sex cultures that had been devastated by both the epidemic and the assault on queer public spaces that it had precipitated. If pornography was increasingly understood as a solitary pleasure to be enjoyed in the private space of the home, then *Steam* was intended to drive readers back out into public. In that way, it was pornographic in the sense that *Steam* and the many other publications that began to appear during this period carried on

FIGURE 3.1. "Uptown Manhattan for Sleazehounds." From *Steam* 2, no. 2 (1994): 174. Scott O'Hara Papers, Literary and Popular Culture Collections, John Hay Library. Reproduced with the permission of Brown University. Photograph: Leather Archives and Museum, Chicago.

the legacy of the pornographic print cultures and the counterpublics they had mediated in the previous decades.

To that end, O'Hara punctuated the excerpt with a pair of street maps that indicated a number of viable cruising grounds in New York City (figures 3.1 and 3.2). At first glance, the maps are indistinguishable from the kind that a tourist might use to locate a city's iconic attractions. However, specific details, including the title "Manhattan for Sleazehounds" and the key

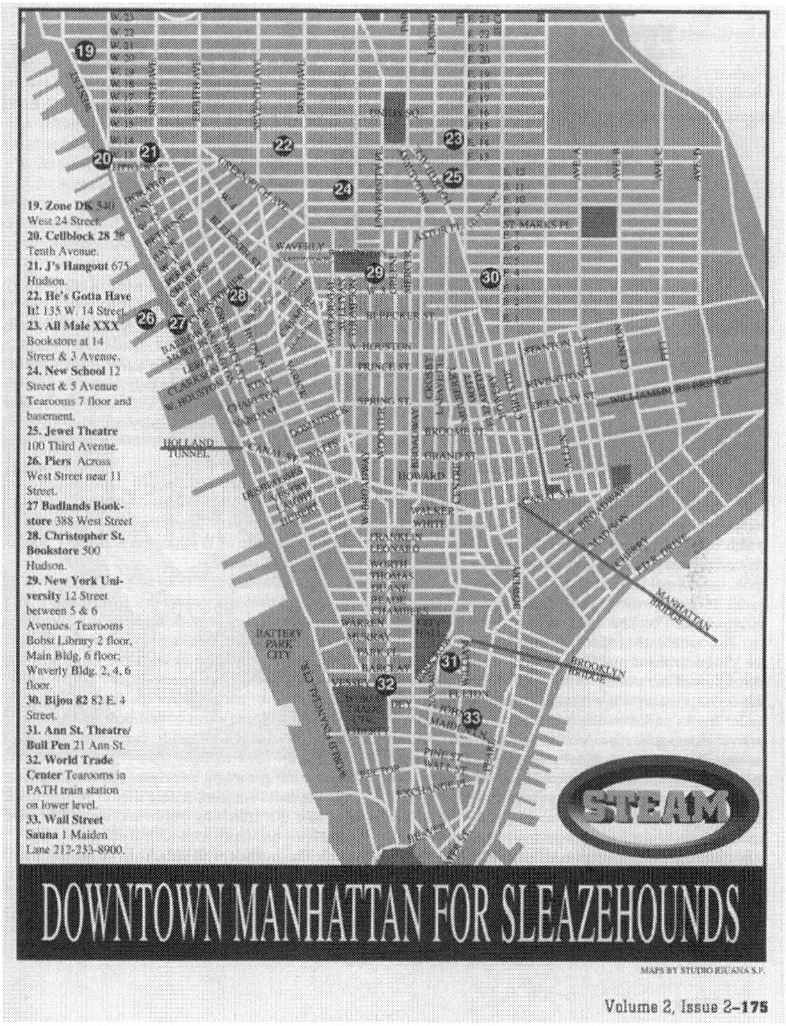

FIGURE 3.2. "Downtown Manhattan for Sleazehounds." From *Steam* 2, no. 2 (1994): 175. Scott O'Hara Papers, Literary and Popular Culture Collections, John Hay Library. Reproduced by permission of Brown University. Photograph: Leather Archives and Museum, Chicago.

directing readers to bookstores, tearooms, and parks, imagine a queer rela-tion to urban space, one implicitly at odds with the various forces seeking to render the city "safe" for specific classes of tourists and inhabitants through urban revitalization projects. The conjunction of the "Sleazehound" maps with Delany's excerpt functions as a call to readers, not only to participate in public sex, but also to understand that practice in terms of something other than leisure, a kind of recreational ethos that O'Hara at other times explicitly opposed. "*Just sex*. I've heard that phrase in many contexts; it always grates on my ears," O'Hara wrote in an editorial: "Sex is never isolated. There is no such thing as sex 'taken out of context'—except perhaps in a court of law, in a case involving 'public lewdness' or some such farce."[58] Pairing the maps with Delany's excerpt contextualizes erotic practice within the political forces that apportion its subjects into those "for whom society is made" and those for whom it is not. The fantastic invitation to participate in a city alive with sex sought to induce an enactment of the empowering practice of cruising despite an epidemic and despite the hostility, to borrow from Delany's protagonist, of those for whom the world is made. While neither revolutionary nor utopian, cruising in spite of the risk (and not because of it) presents an alternative to a fate worse than death and in turn enables a way of feeling toward the other denizens of the Variety Theatre.

While mediated through print, *Steam* explicitly distanced its account of that cruising practice from pornography. However, Delany continued to develop this idea beyond *The Mad Man*, culminating in the text that has become something of a touchstone for queer theory's engagements with public space and public sex: *Times Square Red, Times Square Blue*. Published in 1999, Delany's pair of extended essays describes how the Times Square porno theaters largely eradicated by urban renewal projects mediated subcultures of anonymous sex between men much in the manner that John describes the action taking place within the Variety Theatre. However, unlike *The Mad Man*, Delany explicitly suggests in the later text that what made such cruising possible was the heterosexual pornography that appeared on screen: "The movies presented a world in which a variety of heterosexual and lesbian acts were depicted regularly, even endlessly, in close-up detail. The only perversion that did not exist in their particular version of pornotopia, save for the *most* occasional comic touches [. . .] was male homosexuality. But its absence from the narrative space on the screen proper is what allowed it to go on rampantly among the observing audience, now in this theater, now in that one."[59] Delany's description of the heterosexual films' generic exclusion of male homosexuality resonates with the exclusion of butt fucking in *The Mad Man*, and there are other similarities too, including Delany's anecdote about Larry, a heterosexual man he encounters while cruising one of the theaters, whose interactions with Delany recall those between John and Piece o' Shit. Larry rejects Delany's offer for sex: "My fuckin' luck—I pick some gay guy! Well, you see, *I'm* not gay," yet then happily accepts Delany's offer of a hand job.[60] In the words of Piece o' Shit, the films on screen help Larry do "a little thinkin', a little imaginin'," which suspends the identity-based conflict motivating his initial refusal of John's offer.

The production of such goodwill between strangers is a central theme in Delany's *Times Square Red, Times Square Blue*. While readers often focus on the public sex that Delany describes in the first essay, it's important to note that he does not romanticize it. As he states in the second essay, he is interested in thinking about the challenges for producing the kinds of cross-class contact that the porno theaters enabled at a moment when the conditions of the ongoing "class war" of late capitalism "perpetually [work] for the erosion of social practices through which interclass communication takes place and of the institutions holding those practices stable, so that new institutions must always be conceived and set in place to take over the jobs of those that are battered again and again till they are destroyed" (111). Time and space prevent me from elaborating on this point, but *Times Square Red, Times Square Blue* is in some ways a statement on the social and political importance of what one might call pornographic institutions, spaces or other public registers in which different participants can collectively engage in the kinds of "thinkin'" and "imaginin'" that help promote contact across identity categories and class positions. These are not sites that cultivate empathy or sympathy, but ones in which fantasy can do its work, mediating participants' relation to each other by way of an affect that cannot be symbolized but can be sensed. In other words, Delany's account of pornographic film in *Times Square Red, Times Square Blue* reflects a continued working through of the ideas previously raised in *The Mad Man*, and which O'Hara sought to realize through his journal *Steam* and its imagined counterpublic of Sleazehounds. While there are significant differences among them, together they participate in the generic legacy of gay pornographic writing as it took shape in and across the preceding decades.

Importantly, Delany's account of the Times Square theaters acknowledges that the incipient solidarity they fostered occurred within and as a result of the material relations that have shaped, not only the adult film industry, but also the dereliction of the Times Square neighborhood. It provides a way to understand Richard Kasak Books' publication of Delany's *The Mad Man* as an example of capture within the material relations informing the production of genre categories such as "erotic literature" even as those texts promote social relations that may call that process into question. O'Hara's *Steam* provided an opportunity to market the book to the journal's readers, yet the excerpts' appearance within the journal, their contextualization next to the Sleazehound maps, was at the very least an attempt to promote the kinds of relation that characterized John's interactions with many of the other characters he encounters in the novel. Just as various antagonisms shaped the publication of *The Mad Man* and *Steam*, the journal hosted counterpublic debates in which readers complained about O'Hara's principled rejection of condoms or his toleration of sex clubs that vetted patrons based on their looks. O'Hara also generated controversy for publishing essays devoted to erotic and relational practices that raised serious ethical and political questions. For example, the same issue that contained the excerpt of Delany's novel included an essay by Bill Andriette, then editor of the North American Man/Boy Love Association's newsletter. The essay located the origin of NAMBLA in the gay liberation and pro-porn/anticensorship activism of the previous decades, but it also lambasted "the cowardice of our intellectuals and writers, who stand by mute as the possession of our art, our pornography, and our writing becomes felonious, who never question why taking a photo of a sixteen-year-old—or an eight-year-old!—with a hard-on should be punished worse than killing that same sixteen-year-old. It is the failure of nerve, of belief, of memory as a campaign takes hold for the systematic liquidation of boy-lovers from society."[61]

O'Hara's willingness to publish Andriette's defense on the pages of *Steam* manifests less as an endorsement of man-boy love than a commitment to experimental thinking about gay sexuality in its various forms. Moreover, Andriette was not entirely incorrect when he claimed that gay "intellectuals and writers" exhibited a failure of memory when they refused to defend art and pornography featuring boys from moral condemnation and legal prohibition. Such intimacies have been a persistent feature of gay pornographic writing since at least the 1970s, in addition to being a major topos within forms of gay male culture throughout the twentieth century, but the same political turmoil that set the conditions for AIDS-era pornography and Delany's *The Mad Man* would help drive a wedge between an emergent gay and lesbian civil rights movement and those who sought to defend intimacies that crossed the age of consent. An important development during that period would be the invention and evolution of child pornography law, which would establish the representation of children, including boys, in particular images as evidence of a pathological intention in the viewer. The counterpublics of gay pornographic writing thus seized on the boy as an emblem of sexual revolution in the face of a repressive society, yet one whose potential force was undermined by the structural exclusion of children as consumers of "adult materials" that enabled gay pornography's initial efflorescence. In keeping with the present chapter's efforts to rethink risk, pornography, and gay sexuality outside the framework of barebacking, the next two chapters will shift attention away from HIV and toward intergenerationality as an alternative framework for approaching these themes. In different ways, each will consider how the question of gay youth has been elided in accounts of gay pornography in ways that are becoming increasingly untenable in the digital age.

CHAPTER 4

Boy Problems

Boyd McDonald's Straight to Hell, *Matthew Stadler's* Allan Stein,
and the Becoming Historical of Intergenerational Intimacy

Near the beginning of Matthew Stadler's *Allan Stein* (1999), the novel's narrator delivers an impassioned plea to readers regarding how to take what follows: "Though my account will lapse into coarseness, flippancy, lies, and pure pornography, you must never forget that I truly and impossibly did love him."[1] The narrator's request raises the challenging suggestion that even those things the reader might find to be dishonest, off-putting, and repugnant may nonetheless contain a kernel of truth in them, in this case the possibility of an impossible love. But what could warrant such a plea? *Allan Stein* recounts the travails of its narrator, a young high school teacher from the Pacific Northwest, who loses his job following allegations that he slept with one of his students. In order to escape his disgrace, he assumes the identity of his travel-weary friend Herbert Widener, the art curator of a local museum, and journeys to Paris in order to investigate and potentially procure a set of Picasso's sketches on Herbert's behalf. Herbert suspects that the sketches may prove that the model for Picasso's *Boy Leading a Horse* (1905–6) was Gertrude Stein's nephew, Allan Stein, yet during his investigation, the impostor Herbert is sidetracked by the impudent charms of his Parisian hosts' fifteen-year-old son, Stéphane Dupaignes. The narrator eventually flees with Stéphane to the South of France, but the boy falls sick when the narrator's indulgent attitude toward Stéphane's diet aggravates a preexisting health condition. Their relationship, such as it is, falls apart, and the narrator's sundry deceptions are exposed, leaving him by the novel's conclusion stranded within his own reveries.

In short, *Allan Stein* is a novel about intergenerational intimacy told from the point of view of an adult who remains both remarkably forthright about his desire for adolescent boys and largely unapologetic about his willingness to act on those feelings. That is, in one loose sense, what makes the novel pornographic, yet the narrator also fulfills the implicit promise of explicit sexual details, going so far as to give readers directions to which page they might skip ahead should they wish to avoid the offending sections. Despite reveling in explicit descriptions of transgressive sex, the novel's influences are decidedly literary, its plot and self-referential narration style giving *Allan Stein* queer echoes of Nabokov's *Lolita*, which like other modernist bildungsromans employed figures of unseasonable youth to allegorize the frame-disrupting effects of modernity.[2] As Jed Esty observes: "Nabokov's playful work refracts and transcodes the historical traumas of Europe (revolution, world war, holocaust, totalitarianism, and the dawn of the nuclear age) into a plot of stalled subject formation."[3] While less concerned with such world-scale events, *Allan Stein* nonetheless bears significant similarities to both *Lolita* and the body of modernist antidevelopmental novels that Esty describes: the narrator punctuates his story with scenes drawn from his youth as well as accounts of Stein's own tumultuous childhood, and the various narrative strands dead-end in a timeless and placeless present from which the story itself unfolds. By the end of things, the narrator is a homeless, friendless, and jobless loner adrift in the world, his opening plea marking him as an anachronistically queer subject without a public to hear him.

Despite the bleakness of its ending, *Allan Stein* offers neither a stark condemnation of pederasty nor an elevation of its relations into a radically transgressive politics. Instead, the novel provides an extended reflection on fantasies of intergenerational intimacy while underscoring how they have become queerly out of time and place by the end of the twentieth century. In doing so, *Allan Stein* predicts the claims that Kadji Amin has made regarding queer scholars' reticence to engage with the subject of modern pederasty, which Amin defines as relations that eroticize social inequalities along an age differential.[4] As Amin observes, pederasty has posed a conceptual stumbling block for the field of queer studies insofar as its efforts to identify stigmatized erotic practices as the basis for a radical sexual politics has generally favored those whose "badness" is easily aligned with liberal norms of egalitarianism, consent, and mutualistic pleasure. The field has thus been locked into an endless cycle of enthusiasm and disappointment as the idealized erotic practice du jour inevitably fails to sustain the political hopes invested in it. Meanwhile, unredeemable practices that traffic in the eroticism of structurally determined power differentials—such as pederasty—become embarrassing relics of a benighted past.[5] As Stadler's writing highlights, what's true for queer studies has also been true for contemporary gay politics; at the same time, this chapter is more centrally concerned with showing how the antidevelopmental force of the novel's critique draws on a tradition of gay pornographic representation that actively engaged with themes of youth sexuality and intergenerational desire. Thus, when the narrator describes his tale "as pure pornography," he is not only invoking that genre's vulgar associations but also implicitly situating his narrative in relation to a history of intergenerational intimacies imagined in and through the pornographic counterpublics of the 1970s.

To illuminate those connections, this chapter places Stadler's novel in conversation with Boyd McDonald's *Straight to Hell*, an underground zine that got its start in the early 1970s and that consisted of reader-submitted "true tales" documenting their various homosexual experiences. Crucially, *Straight to Hell* was not dedicated to intergenerational sex; instead, as John Heywood has argued, the zine "functioned as an informal catalogue of male/ male sexual practices transacted across the 'border' between 'straight' and 'gay.'"[6] To that end, its letters imagined a world of masculine desire in which a fantastic scene of public sex could happen anywhere and at any time. In the world of *Straight to Hell*, observes Bernard Welt, "every barracks shower is an orgy room; every Boy Scout jamboree is a festival of sexual initiation; every conservative politician and clergyman pays male hustlers for sex. Everything men do to bond or compete in sports, war and politics is a sublimation of, if not a substitute for, homosexual desire."[7] In other words, McDonald was not interested in simply providing readers with titillating stories; instead, he understood his porno-documentary project as a form of critique directed at the sexual hypocrisy of the nation's political leadership, which he lambasted in the many acerbic editorials, essays, and photo collages that filled out the pages of his zine. However, while the aforementioned critics have paid some attention to the relation between the zine's erotic imaginary and its political projects, they have tended to downplay or otherwise ignore the ways in which the world of *Straight to Hell* paid little heed to age-of-consent laws and instead identified male youth as frequent participants in the scenes of public sex described by the zine's contributors.

Understandably, scholars' reticence to engage with the zine's representations of male youth and intergenerational sex may have to do with the ways in which the sexuality of minors became intensely politicized during the late twentieth century. Between the late 1970s and the late 1990s, the US endured wave after wave of moral panics over the predatory pedophile, who not only abused children but also documented his crimes and shared the results with other pedophiles via clandestine child pornography rings.[8] The pedophile panics thus offered their own kind of perverse developmental plot, according to which porn-fueled acts of child sexual abuse begot a new generation of predatory pedophiles. Over the past twenty years, a variety of scholars working across various fields have subjected those developments to intense scrutiny, highlighting not only their deeply problematic conceptualization of the child as an erotic innocent but also how fears of pedophiles have driven the rapid expansion of a security state and a medico-juridical complex tasked with tracking, confining, and managing sex offenders. Similarly, Gillian Harkins and Joseph Fischel have conceptualized the problems inherent in discursive constructions of erotic innocents and sexual predators while also correcting for a tendency in those critiques that either understates the problem of child sexual abuse or overlooks the significant part that race and class each play in discourses of sexual predation and childhood innocence.[9] In the wake of that history, scholars interested in McDonald's work have been careful to distance themselves from the zine's pornographic depictions of youth and intergenerational sex. As McDonald's biographer William E. Jones succinctly sums it up: "Amid the shifting boundaries between art and pornography and waves of child abuse hysteria, this attitude seems reckless today, but Boyd did his work in different times."[10]

While I don't fault such reticence, the tendency to construe the zine's fantasies as "of another era" suggests the same kind of disavowal that Amin traces out in efforts to uphold writers such as Jean Genet as emblems for radical contemporary queer politics. Genet proffered a far stronger and far more specific commitment to pederasty than McDonald ever gave expression to in *Straight to Hell*, for which the adolescent boy was simply one among a range of participants in the pervasive public sex that the zine imaginatively documented. Still, careful analysis of those fantasies of intergenerational public sex suggests some of the ways in which the adolescent boy was hardly incidental to McDonald's understanding of gay sexual sociability. While some narratives incorporated boys into more or less conventional pornographic scenarios, others detailed the writers' own childhood experiences of sexual abuse, whose reworking as a pornographic text provided the basis for modes of counterpublic witnessing. In short, the eroticization of past trauma facilitated modes of growth for the zine's contributors and readers. However, aside from serving as a regular character of sorts, the boy was also crucial for the zine's understanding of gay sexual sociability insofar as he, like the male homosexual, was imagined as retaining a privileged relation to the anus as a sexual, and not merely excretory, organ. Boys were thus crucial to the magazine's political critique: by centering the anus, the boy decentered the phallus and scrambled the normative plot of psychosexual development that installed the normative family at the core of both capitalist relations and US national culture. While the boy took on a variety of means and functions in McDonald's zine, these various instances share in common a fascination with the boy as a means to formalize the erotic and, according to some of the zine's readers, potentially world-transformative force of queerly antidevelopmental temporalities.

Stadler's novel does not engage directly with McDonald's zine, and there are significant differences between them. However, reading *Allan Stein* against the backdrop of *Straight to Hell* helps to mark the distance between the fantasies of intergenerational intimacy elaborated within the pornographic counterpublics of the 1970s and their status at the end of the twentieth century: excluded from the discourse of gay civil rights, sequestered within the pathological subjectivity of the predatory pedophile, and confined to hapless organizations such as NAMBLA. However, Stadler's novel does not offer a categorical repudiation of fantasies involving youth; instead, its allegory employs antidevelopmental temporalities similar to those imagined in *Straight to Hell* in order to mark the significant attenuation of those fantasies' public-convening power during the 1980s and 1990s. Thus, while the two might now be in direct reference to each other, *Allan Stein* and *Straight to Hell* are, in some sense, kindred spirit texts. Before I get there, and given the controversial subject matter at stake, this chapter begins by historicizing the figures of the erotic innocent, the imperiled adolescent, and the pedophile pornographer that have become staples of the fortifying developmental plots that have played a key role in producing intergenerational intimacy's image problem. To be sure, as I write this, yet another sex panic has swept the US with the mainstreaming of conspiracy theories regarding clandestine pedophile networks supposedly run by leftists, Jewish people, and gay men, highlighting how fantasies of childhood innocence have become an endlessly renewable resource for high-powered political attacks that fail to improve the actual material circumstances of youth in the US.[11] We've been here before, and we will likely continue to return here until we develop a better sense of where we have been.

EROTIC INNOCENTS, IMPERILED ADOLESCENTS, AND PEDOPHILE PORNOGRAPHERS

The meaning and implications of adult-youth sexual contact have fluctuated throughout the twentieth century. During the 1960s and early 1970s, psychologists generally viewed sexual contact across the age of majority as something akin to a nuisance resolvable with appropriate social and psychological treatment, but by the early 1980s a new understanding had emerged that understood sexual contact between adults and youth of any age as the consequence of a moralized and incurable pathology that inflicted permanent damage on the young. A number of contemporaneous developments helped to drive that change in thinking. First, feminist political activism and cultural production, including a raft of women's memoirs detailing experiences of intrafamilial rape, helped to shift public understandings of sexual violence by challenging the belief that rape was an act committed primarily by strangers.[12] Second, the particular ways that such critiques helped to reconceptualize the domestic space as a set of power relations drew additional support from the advent of new medical imaging technologies, which allowed doctors to detect previously invisible injuries, such as bone fractures and internal bruising, in the bodies of children who may not respond truthfully or accurately during a routine medical exam.[13] Without any clear explanation for such injuries, their documentation further intensified interest in the many dangers that children faced at home, from physical violence to malnutrition and neglect, which were all collated together under the term "child abuse." Third, in light of renewed interest in posttraumatic stress disorder, child abuse expanded to describe both physical and psychological injuries. In particular, children's advocates relied on the notion of trauma to argue that even nonviolent sexual contact was still harmful to children: like soldiers experiencing the shock of war, children lacked the capacity to integrate the experience of sexual contact into their still-developing egos, thereby leaving everlasting psychic wounds.[14]

The attention that such investigations of child abuse brought to the lives of children effected significant improvements in the well-being of young people, not the least of which being the revelation that the patriarchal culture of home and family was one of the biggest dangers that children faced on a day-to-day basis. At the same time, efforts to safeguard children also drew rhetorical force from the figure of the child as erotic innocent, which helped to explain why sexual abuse was so psychologically harmful. The terms "childhood" and "sexuality" became mutually exclusive in the public imagination, helping to drive a number of subsequent legal changes during the period, including the reformation of statutory rape laws. For much of the earlier half of the twentieth century, statutory rape laws in the US were both raced and classed insofar as the laws were designed to protect the chastity of White girls prior to marriage. However, as Carolyn E. Cocca has shown, midcentury reforms entailed a neutralization of the child's gender in order to recognize, not only that male children were victims of abuse, but also that adult women committed acts of abuse against minors.[15] Again, that change came with mixed consequences. On the one hand, it helped to highlight forms of violence against particular youthful subjects that had either been neglected or simply dismissed as unserious, owing to the child's perceived culpability by signaling some form of interest in the erotic act. On the other hand, the figure of the child installed within statutory rape law and elsewhere became an ill-defined figure, genderless yet implicitly White, of an amorphous age and lacking in erotic self-awareness, autonomy, or agency.[16]

The child as erotic innocent thus also facilitated a number of far more problematic outcomes. Specifically, fears of child sexual abuse provided a rhetorically powerful weapon in the hands of conservative critics eager to push back against the gains of both the sexual liberationists and those sexual minorities who were becoming an increasingly visible presence in the nation's public life. While feminist critics had emphasized the fact that rape and other forms of sexual violence were most likely to occur between family members, popular conservative activists such as Anita Bryant, Phyllis Schlafly, and Jerry Falwell bemoaned the dangerous stranger, for which gay men served as a ready-to-hand figure, as preying on children in order to initiate them into a life of perversity and depravity. While such claims frequently depended on the erotic innocent, they also often framed the child specifically in terms of the imperiled White adolescent boy. As Roger Lancaster has shown, during the late 1960s, the rise of the counterculture had generated middle-class concern for White adolescent boys, who were abandoning the suburbs for the cities where they experimented with drugs and sex, explored various forms of religious mysticism, and came in contact with other youth from other class positions as well as with other ethnic and racial identities; in turn, those developments sparked a wave of panics regarding an epidemic of teenage hustling, according to which once-wholesome boys were now selling themselves in order to fuel drug habits or simply to survive on the street.[17] As a consequence, the child as erotic innocent and the imperiled adolescent White boy "inaugurated many current conversations for talking about teen sexuality, child sex abuse, and irreparable harm to the person."[18]

The panicked discourse about erotic innocents and imperiled adolescents drove subsequent efforts to "fortify and purify" the White middle-class family by purging it of any trace of perversity, thus proffering a consoling image of stability to the public otherwise deeply shaken by the economic and political turmoil of the 1970s.[19] That process facilitated the transformation of the adult who had sex with youth of any age from a misguided loner who could be reformed into a pathological actor who invaded the home and family and so needed to be rooted out. The construction of child pornography as a category within US jurisprudence provides one way to track that process, yet it also reveals how pornography was caught up within evolving notions of child abuse and the sex predator panics of the 1970s and 1980s, which further stoked anxieties about predatory gay men and helped to suppress discussions of youth sexuality and intergenerational desire within gay political groups.[20] Early legislation sought to prohibit the use of minors, at this point persons under the age of sixteen, from participating in the production of pornographic images, a prohibition it framed in terms of preventing exploitation.[21] However in 1982, the Supreme Court's decision on *New York v. Ferber* (1982) reflected a move away from conceptualizing child pornography as a matter of unfair labor practices to constructing it as a category of speech "intrinsically related to the sexual abuse of children."[22] Understood in terms of not only abuse but also an intrinsic relation, the child pornographic image acquired a new kind of destructive power that lasted well beyond the moment of production and thus necessitated strict prohibitions. As a consequence, it subsequently became illegal, not only to produce child pornographic images, but also to distribute, possess, and consume them.

In the wake of *Ferber*, courts continued to define, debate, and redefine the definition of child pornography in ways that not only intensified the sense of an intrinsic linkage between pornographic representations of minors and traumatic abuse but also located the source of such representations in a pathological subjectivity. First, it increased the legal age for appearing in pornography from sixteen to eighteen.[23] Second, the courts gradually broadened the scope of what visual contents met the definition of child pornography. In 1994, for example, the lower court decision on *United States v. Knox* determined that an image could meet the law's criteria regarding the "lascivious exhibition of the genitals" even if the child were fully clothed.[24] As a result, a wide range of images, including family photographs of children in the nude, bathing, or dressed in costumes, potentially qualified as child pornography. This notion of child pornography furnished suspect images with a hyper-documentary quality: child pornography constituted evidence of a crime even if the image did not unambiguously depict a "sexual" act.[25] However, the possibility that some seemingly innocuous images could comprise child pornography required investigators to scrutinize such images in order to locate the pathological desire that created it. As Amy Adler has shown in her analysis of child pornography law in general and of *United States v. Dost* (1989), the courts developed a series of procedures, such as the so-called Dost test, which guided investigators in the act of determining whether or not an image was in fact evidence of sexual abuse. To that end, the various guidelines of the Dost test required one to consider, not only the child's pose, state of undress, or perceived "willingness to engage in sexual activity," but also "whether the visual depiction is intended or designed to elicit a sexual response in the viewer."[26] "The law requires us to study pictures of children to uncover their potential sexual meanings," explains Adler, "and in doing so it explicitly exhorts us to take on the perspective of the pedophile."[27]

An important implication of developments like the Dost test was that even as the law sought to localize the source of child pornography in a specific and pathological subjectivity, it retained a tacit recognition that anyone could not only access that desire but also do so without becoming a pedophile oneself. By the 1990s, this particular way of approaching the matters of child pornography, erotic innocents, and imperiled adolescents had filtered out into popular culture, where it informed the plots of numerous television series, films, and novels. For example, as Jenkins has described at length, paperbacks such as "[Jonathan] Kellerman's *When the Bough Breaks* featured the Gentlemen's Brigade, a voluntary social work group that concealed a network of elite child molesters and 'closet sickos.' Ron Handberg's *Savage Justice* had as its villain a judge who used pornographic videos to seduce pubescent boys and whose extensive connections enabled him to escape detection and to silence critics, by murder if necessary."[28] Televisual melodramas such as *Law and Order: Special Victims Unit* (1999–) and the controversial *To Catch a Predator* (2004–7) followed suit by allowing audiences to enjoy the sensational thrills of pedophile characters while judging their actions from the comfort and safety of their own homes. During this period, both Hollywood and independent studios also released a cluster of films about pedophilia that deployed a number of formal techniques to compensate for the impossibility of depicting adult-child contact on screen, giving rise to what Jon Davis has termed "the black hole of representation that is arguably at the center of every pedophile movie."[29] Such enigmatic "black holes" solicited the spectator's imagination to fill in the gaps, provoking viewers' erotic imaginations while simultaneously sequestering the implications of having such thoughts through their projection onto the film's morally condemnable pedophile characters.

As I've outlined in this section, the discourses of child pornography and predatory pedophiles derived much of their force from conceptualizing both childhood and adolescence in terms of a discreet periods of developmental vulnerability that, if correctly managed, would result in the normal adult. As Kathryn Bond Stockton has put it, the normal child of the twentieth century was "a creature of *gradual growth* and *managed delay*," who required protection so that its childhood innocence can be shed so as not to impinge on its natural and normal movement toward adulthood.[30] However, if these developmental periods were disturbed in some way, such as through premature sexual contact with others or via access to pornography, they would eventuate in adult pathologies. By the turn the millennium, the predatory pedophile seemed so incurable that he warranted securitizing measures such as indefinite confinement, which linked a convicted subject's release from the detention facility not to the specifications of a legal sentence but to the judgment of medical-forensic experts. As a consequence of that history, it's become harder to recognize or discuss the sexuality of either children or adolescents in terms that are not immediately framed by moral, physical, or psychological violence. This problem becomes all the more evident when the conversation shifts to an adult's own erotic fantasies about youthful subjects or their depiction in pornographic representations.

While the Supreme Court has acknowledged that pornographic representations featuring imaginary youth, such as adult performers acting as minors or featuring computer-generated images of children or adolescents, are protected forms of speech, such images remain controversial, and likely will raise suspicions and potentially accusations regarding anyone who creates them, possesses them, or draws pleasure from them.[31]

In briefly tracing out some of this historical context, my point here is not that we should do away with child pornography law, although like a number of the scholars whose work I have discussed above I agree that this remains an important area where reform is needed, especially in light of how child pornography laws are now used to prosecute youth's sexual media practices. Instead, my goal has been to highlight some of the significant constraints, desires, and fantasies that impinge on discussions of pornographic representations of youth, including those that consist of adult reflections on youthful experiences or in which the youth may be entirely fictional. In the next section, I find another way into these subjects by way of Boyd McDonald's *Straight to Hell*. Working from within not porn studies but literary studies, Stockton has already shown how imaginative texts produced during the twentieth century have queered the child as conceptualized within the normative framework of childhood studies. As Stockton writes of her literary and cinematic archive: "These [works] are fictions that imagine and present what sociology, Law, and History cannot pierce, given established taboos surrounding children. Novels and films, in their inventive forms, are rich stimulators of questions public cultures seem to have no language for encountering."[32] Stockton's wide-ranging study of queer children does not consider pornography—and understandably so, given the legal and ethical problems inherent in examining photographic representations. However, written representations such as those found in Boyd McDonald's *Straight to Hell* may not only serve as another "rich stimulator" of conversation about both youth sexuality, modern pederasty, and intergenerational intimacy but may also provide insight into the ways in which the pornographic counterpublics of the 1970s facilitated their own kinds of conversations, even as the national public was itself coalescing around fortifying narratives of erotic innocents, imperiled adolescents, and predatory pedophile pornographers.

MCDONALD'S BOYS AND THE COUNTERPUBLICS OF *STRAIGHT TO HELL*

Owing to the spotty nature of the publication, it is difficult to date precisely the first issue of *Straight to Hell*, yet it likely appeared in 1973, when McDonald would have been forty-eight years old.[33] The publication's launch followed a significant turning point for its founder and editor, whose earlier life more or less conformed to the normal developmental plot set out for middle-class White youth in the US during the midcentury. Originally from South Dakota, McDonald had served in the US military during World War II and graduated from Harvard in 1949 with a concentration in American literature and history; after completing his education, he went to work as a reporter for a number of reputable news and literary magazines including *Time* and the *New Yorker*. While McDonald displayed a talent for his work in journalism, he also struggled with alcoholism, which led to significant disruptions in his life. As McDonald's biographer William E. Jones reports, there are few clear records regarding McDonald's life between 1958 and 1968, other than that he had voluntarily committed himself to the Central Islip Psychiatric Hospital. Following his release, the newly sober McDonald abandoned what little remained of his previous life, settled into a small studio apartment on New York's West Side, and committed himself to the kinds of gay public sex encounters he had infrequently and surreptitiously enjoyed as a youth. According to Jones, "When he left a corporate environment, the flood gates opened. His literary skills did not abandon him, but his sense of shame certainly did."[34] Drawing on his talent and experience with journalism, McDonald's renewed dedication to pursuing a life of public sex included the founding of a number of mimeographed publications, beginning with *Skinheads* (dedicated to uncircumcised cocks), which he soon abandoned in order to launch *Straight to Hell*.

The zine was promiscuous in both form and content. Specifically, McDonald employed a collage technique that combined readers' letters detailing their own public sex encounters, interviews with various men about their sex lives (including one interview with an anonymized Samuel Steward), and his own acerbic attacks on homophobic politicians and religious leaders.[35] In keeping with the spirit of McDonald's editorials, the zine's masthead included a proclamation declaring *Straight to Hell* "pro homosexual. pro women. pro children. anti 'straight' male. Libertarian and libertine; left of communism," yet McDonald also regularly took aim at gay activists any time he believed they either sought to make sex respectable or to subject it to undue moral or ethical strictures.[36] McDonald mixed such original writing with texts appropriated from other sources, including passages from sexological tracts and Bible quotations, which provided "evidence" for the existence of a pervasive and transhistorical mode of male homosexuality. However, despite the relentless focus on sex, McDonald rejected describing *Straight to Hell* as "pornography," a genre he aligned with the escapist fantasies and patriarchal ideologies of mass media. Rather, McDonald argued that *Straight to Hell* was documentary. As he explained in a 1976 editorial statement titled "Memories and Desires": "Fiction invented to please can be pornographic. The lies about homosexuality on TV and in the mass magazines and newspapers are pornographic. They are designed to make the 'straights' feel big." Unlike mass publications such as *Playboy* and *Time*, which unidirectionally dictated desires and ideas to their readers, McDonald argued, *Straight to Hell* was "so good because of its readers, who also write it. It's more fun, but more dangerous to publish a magazine that is so good because of its readers than a magazine that is so bad because of them."[37]

Given both the anonymity of the letters and McDonald's apparent indifference to record keeping, it's difficult to tell in what sense the letters in *Straight to Hell* described "real" experiences. According to Jones, McDonald claimed to heavily edit the letters he received but never added to them or altered any details.[38] Regardless, the letters frequently followed the conventions of gay pornographic writing, including the ways that McDonald favored letters about working-class masculine types and was occasionally scornful of male effeminacy.[39] Those attitudes helped to create distance between not only *Straight to Hell* and the gender-fuck politics espoused by a younger cohort of gay liberationists but also between McDonald and many other gay men of his age, for whom gay effeminacy had been a celebrated feature of the gay publics assembled in bars and nightclubs of the 1950s and 1960s. At the same time, such spaces may not have appealed to a recovered alcoholic, who was also deeply agoraphobic and thus relied on his print networks as a crucial source of contact with other men.[40] In any case, McDonald's preference for public sex and print culture puts him more in line with the masculinist physique magazines of the previous decade with two key differences. First, the zine rejected any pretense to middle-class respectability, and, second, it understood homosexual desire as not a property of a distinct minority but one common to all male subjects — regardless of age. On that point, many letters recounted the writer's past experiences with other boys during his own youth. In the letter "4 Boys Raped Me — Thank God," the writer relates his first same-sex sexual encounter as "a shy, slightly-built" White teenager forcibly gangbanged by four Black students in the high school locker room.[41] "4 Boys" thus offered readers a familiar fantasy of Black revenge, culminating in a form of erotic reconciliation: after the initial gang bang the narrator and one of the Black boys become friends who periodically get together to "[fuck] in every position and location imaginable."[42]

As with "4 Boys," racial difference likewise informs the action of the letter titled "In the Park," which featured an encounter between the adult letter writer and "a brace of Japanese chickens, brothers 12 ½ and 14, in one of the rustic tearooms. The elder had five slender uncut inches, no hair, and the clearest and softest skin you can imagine (even nicer than his kid brother).

They were both very cute and very willing."[43] The letter's description of the boys grounds their eroticism in a presumed proximity to the natural world. Originally deriving from midcentury nautical contexts to describe new and inexperienced recruits, the term "chicken" soon migrated into gay slang to describe any attractive boy under the legal age of consent. However, the boys' association with the natural world also carries through in other elements of the letter, including its mock-bucolic setting of the "rustic" tearoom and in the attention the writer pays to the boys' uncircumcised penises.[44] In a similar vein, the boys' encounter with the narrator recalls the plot of the White man/native boy dyad according to which the undisciplined youth inspires and rejuvenates his flagging White admirer.[45] The park of the letter's title thus takes on a familiar role as a public space to mediate forms of revitalizing contact between, not only men and boys, but also civilization and nature. Unlike "4 Boys," the tone of "In the Park" is gushing and conspiratorial, and each presents a different scene: the former details the experiences of youth among themselves while the latter describes a series of interactions between an adult and two boys. However, both seem to be shaped as much by the conventions of gay pornographic writing as by the writers' memories of their experiences.

At the same time as many of *Straight to Hell*'s boys seemed pulled from the fantasy life of McDonald and his contributors, some of the letters suggest that they were more than simply escapist pleasures, providing instead reflective takes on youth sexuality and intergenerational intimacy, including both its benign and abusive forms. For example, one letter recounts the experience of its writer, identified only as Bart, during one summer of his childhood spent in a Wisconsin lake town where he encountered a young man that lured him into the woods and then overpowered him. Like the previous stories, Bart's narrative recounts the actions of the encounter in the language of gay pornographic writing: "I felt his cock trying to get into my hole. The pain was immense. 'Oh, please, mister, please.' I begged. I felt as though I was going to faint. My asshole felt as if it were on fire."[46] In fact, the pain's cause resides in the considerable size of the man's member, which Bart describes in hypnotic detail: "I can still recall the sight of him over me when he raised himself up on his knees and jerked his undershorts down, exposing his thick black cock hair and enormous cock, all of which I had never seen before. His cock seemed gigantic, his balls huge. The tip of his cock glistened with a substance that reminded me of honey."[47] According to Bart, after the sex concluded, he ran down to the river to wash himself while the man dressed; when he returned to the clearing, the man had gone. The letter then concludes with a final confession: "Even now, after 15 years, I still think of it. Ten years after it happened, I did come out into gay life."[48]

The example of Bart's story provides some sense of how *Straight to Hell* may have been documentary, insofar as it operates as a form of testimonial writing in which traumatic events from the past become accessible to consciousness through their eroticization. As Darieck Scott has argued regarding pornography that engages histories of racialized abjection, fantasies about violence have provided Black readers and writers with "a method for effecting abilities or powers of that otherwise seemingly powerless state of being."[49] The pornographic representation of a "terrible history" generates an erotic effect that "immerses you *in* [history] rather than necessarily working you *through* it—which is potentially to effect a metamorphosis, an evolution, a transformation, but not a recovery or a remission."[50] Similarly, Bart's narrative eroticizes the difference between adults and adolescents as historically contingent positions generated through discursively mediated relations of power. Its narration becomes the basis for the writer to convene a pornographic counterpublic through the zine itself, for which Bart holds out the promise of additional stories: "Should your readers give a good response, I have another story which took place in Vietnam that I can write about."[51] As a public-producing testimonial, Bart's story also conveys a judgment about the sex it describes. In addition to titling the letter simply as "Raped," McDonald paired it with a photo supposedly submitted by Bart of himself as a boy and published it just opposite the masthead containing the zine's declaration of its commitment to various radical causes (figure 4.1). In doing so, McDonald convenes a counterpublic around the shared recognition of the violence at the core of Bart's experience.

More specifically, the man's actions were likely offensive to McDonald, not only for their violation of the boy's autonomy, but also for their brutish disregard for the boy's anal pleasure. The boy's capacity to use his anus as an erotic organ was a persistent theme throughout *Straight to Hell*, evident both in readers' letters and in the various collages with which McDonald illustrated his zine. For example, the cover of issue number 24, published in 1975, depicts the lower half of a youthful body, his ass cheeks spread by a pair of disembodied hands exposing his anus and testicles (figure 4.2). The caption, "pink is the color of my true love's hole," riffs on the popular folk song "Black Is the Colour (of My True Love's Hair)" to emphasize the loveliness of the organ, rendering the anus as a source of both one's physical pleasure and visual pleasure for others. For the activist Charley Shively, the zine's lauding of the anus was both erotic and pedagogical: "Many faggots now accept cocksucking as clean and are relatively comfortable with it, but they hesitate running their tongues another two inches or so along the perineum [. . .] into the asshole. [*Straight to Hell*] might help us all along this trail more easily."[52] McDonald himself visualized that process through

Raped.

STRAIGHT TO HELL.
THE MANHATTAN REVIEW
OF UNNATURAL ACTS.
No. 27. MCMLXXV.

"Love and hate for
the American straight."
PRO HOMOSEXUAL.
PRO WOMEN.
PRO CHILDREN.
ANTI "STRAIGHT" MALE.

Libertarian and libertine;
Left of Communism.

BACK ISSUES: Nos. 15, 16,
17, 20, 21, 22, 23, 24,
25, and 26   80¢ a copy.
SUBSCRIPTION: 12 issues, $8
                Foreign, $9
Please make checks payable
to cash and send to:
Box 982
Radio City Station
New York, N. Y. 10019.

Published by
HI KLASS PRESS.
PÈRE ANNOYED, Director.

In journalism, the
only things that have
any real class are
white space and the
truth.

--PÈRE ANNOYED.

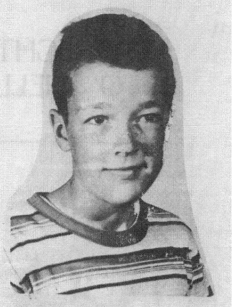

MINNEAPOLIS. My name is Bart--a name that I
took after the guys in Vietnam started using
it.
    The picture was taken when I was 11. I was
12 when I had my first experience. Fifteen
years have passed since then.
    This is the first time I have told this to
anyone, even my gay friends. Should your readers give a good response, I have another story
which took place in Vietnam that I can write
about.
    In the meantime, I do hope your paper be-
comes a great success.
              +   +   +
I am originally from Rice Lake, Wisconsin. It
is a beautiful tourist town of about 12,000
people. It was there that I had my first experience.
    It was a bright summer day. Carefree. I
was a boy of 12. I was on a familiar country
dirt road that wound along the lake. I had
traveled that road many times before.
    I saw him emerge from a wooded thicket along
the road that many fishermen parked their cars
along. (Then they walk down to the lake to
catch sunfish.)
    He called out, "Hey, kid." I pulled my bi-
cycle off the road and laid it down. He asked
if I could make change for a dollar.
    When he reached for his money, he said,
"Shit, I must have dropped my billfold over
there in the brush." He said if I would help
him find it he would give me a dollar.
    I said, "Wow, really?"
    He was around 5' 11" and quite slim. He

FIGURE 4.1. "Raped" testimonial. From *Straight to Hell* 1, no. 27 (1975): 2. Reproduced
with the permission of Billy Miller. Photograph: Leather Archives and Museum, Chicago.

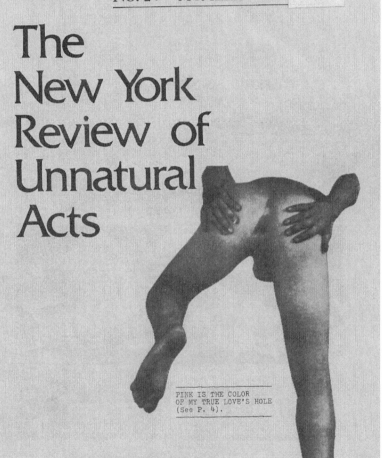

STRAIGHT
TO   HELL

NO. 24   MCMLXXV $1

The
New York
Review of
Unnatural
Acts

PINK IS THE COLOR
OF MY TRUE LOVE'S HOLE
(See P. 4).

FIGURE 4.2. Cover for *Straight to Hell* 1, no. 24 (1975). Reproduced with the permission of Billy Miller. Photograph: Leather Archives and Museum, Chicago.

the zine's collages. In another example, McDonald stitched together two images taken from different moments in the history of physique magazines, which the caption narrates as a shift from a pre- to post-posing strap era (figure 4.3). The collage creates a third era by configuring the youths in the act of rimming, which, like the exposed anus itself, would have been prohibited under the previous era's obscenity laws. While Bart's narrative conveyed its narrator's fascination with the man's "gigantic" cock, which is partly the source of Bart's rough treatment, *Straight to Hell* demonstrated a greater attachment to other, less visually compelling parts of the body.

The zine's approach to anal pleasure was not unique, and it reflects some of the more radical theories about homosexuality formulated by those gay liberationists who linked the repression of desire to various structural inequalities. As Shively argued in his introduction to the first anthologized edition of *Straight to Hell*, "the ass is indeed fundamental to our sexuality (in early English 'fundament' and 'butt' are synonymous)—here is the 'foundation' of our sexuality—terrifying and threatening to middle-class values."[53] Such claims had received a much fuller elaboration in the prior work of the French activist and Deleuzean philosopher Guy Hocquenghem, about whom Shively had authored the entry for William Percy's *The Encyclopedia of Homosexuality* (1990). Like Shively, Hocquenghem identified anal pleasure as a potentially potent counterforce against the laws and norms of Western capitalist societies, which had come to ensure their dominance during the late twentieth century through the normative idealization of the Oedipal family. Organized according to a phallocentric logic of possession and lack, the family not only dispensed identity through the production of gendered subjects, but also entailed a disciplining of the drives active across the various surfaces and orifices of the child's body. The result was a genitally organized sexuality that set the penis-cum-phallus as the bearer of social meaning. As a consequence, normal desire became a matter of sexual difference, and the anus was reduced to the status of a functional organ where it provided the developing subject's first lesson in possessive individualism. "Control of the anus," Hocquenghem argued, "is the precondition for taking responsibility for property. The ability to hold back or to evacuate the faeces is the necessary moment in the constitution of the self. 'To forget oneself' is the most ridiculous and distressing kind of social accident there is, the ultimate outrage to the human person."[54]

While capitalist societies depended on the reproduction of the Oedipal family, resistance lay in disruption of that developmental plot via recovery of the sociogenic potential of the anus, whose full desublimation would lead to the nonphallic modes of relation that Hocquenghem associated with the group.[55] Unlike the hierarchical structure of the family and its instantiation

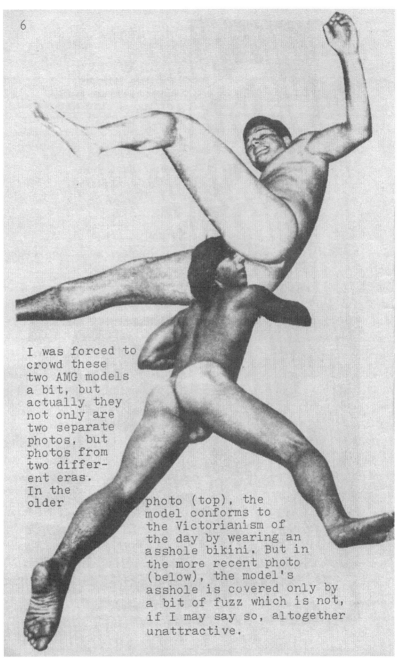

I was forced to crowd these two AMG models a bit, but actually they not only are two separate photos, but photos from two different eras. In the older photo (top), the model conforms to the Victorianism of the day by wearing an asshole bikini. But in the more recent photo (below), the model's asshole is covered only by a bit of fuzz which is not, if I may say so, altogether unattractive.

FIGURE 4.3. Collage from *Straight to Hell* 1, no. 27 (1975): 6. Reproduced with the permission of Billy Miller. Photograph: Leather Archives and Museum, Chicago.

in various institutional forms such as the military or the school, a group resembled a "circle which is open to an infinity of directions and possibilities for plugging in with no set places. The group annular mode (one is tempted to spell it 'anular') causes the 'social' of the phallic hierarchy, the whole house of cards of the 'imaginary,' to collapse."[56] Hocquenghem argued that gay men who engaged in forms of anonymized and promiscuous anal sex exemplified the open and communalizing network form of the group, yet he also acknowledged that it was not exclusive to gay men owing to the universal status of the anus: everybody's got one. In any case, neither McDonald nor Shively explicitly linked the depiction of anal pleasure in *Straight to Hell* to Hocquenghem's theory of grouping, yet it helps to explain both why Shively identified the zine's fascination with anal sexuality as a threat to middle-class values and why the boy so frequently appeared within the zine's depictions of promiscuous sex. As with Bart's narrative of childhood sexual trauma or the collages composed of older physique magazines, the zine's investment in depicting boys as anal virtuosos reflected a similar reworking of a previous stage in the developmental life of the subject to imagine a form of gay collectivity founded in the pleasures of the anus.[57] While *Straight to Hell* frequently featured narratives about "real" boys, the boy himself emerged as a model subjectivity defined less by chronological age than by the desublimation of his anal desire.

McDonald's zine thus remains a remarkable example of gay pornographic writing in that it imagined erotic contact between men and adolescent boys in terms of neither narratives of traumatic abuse nor of idealized youth who function more or less as miniaturized, consenting adults. Thus, it cannot be so swiftly dismissed as simply a rehash of the naive sexual libertarianism that seeks to enable freedom through the elimination of age-of-consent laws.[58] Instead, the reworking of the teenaged boy in present-day fantasy became the basis for imagining nonphallic modes of relation, which were only ever partially realized in and through the zine's print-mediated counterpublic. To that end, it bears significant similarities to the approaches of other texts I have so far examined, including John Rechy's own *The Sexual Outlaw: A Documentary* (1977). While framed as prose documentary, Rechy's nonfiction novel was not engaged in the act of producing objective knowledge about gay sex practices but in deploying its eroticism to convene a counterpublic of sexual outlaws whose radical commitments to public sex positioned them against the repressive actions of the police. Similarly, stories like "Raped" eroticized the violent past experiences of their writers in order to convene the zine's own brash counterpublic, in which youth sexuality and intergenerational sex were not defining features but unremarkable possibilities within a masculine world operating according to the logic of anal desire. At the same time, the zine's vision of queer sociability comes with significant limitations, not least of which being the fact that the zine's free and largely untroubled publication depended on the restriction of minors' access to "adult" materials. In *Ginsberg v. New York* (1968), the Supreme Court had established age as an important factor in determining obscenity, such that sexually explicit texts that enjoyed First Amendment protections became obscene when they fell into the hands of minors. In addition to other limiting factors, the law ensured that while boys might frequently appear on the pages of *Straight to Hell*, they were far less likely to serve as participants in its counterpublic.

To be clear, my point here is not that the ethical and political questions raised by McDonald's zine would simply be solved by revising obscenity laws in a manner that permits such participation. As I will explore at greater length in the final chapter, the question of access is presently moot insofar as the advent of digital technologies has revealed that the previous modes adults have devised for restricting minors' access to pornography are now largely ineffective. Instead, the questions of access and participation bring into focus the larger problems surrounding the zine's boy fantasies, namely, the relations of power that constitute adults and minors in their difference from one another. While McDonald's framing of narratives such as "Raped" reflect a conscious awareness of such relations, narratives such as "In the Park" obfuscate matters of power by construing the boys as sexual agents more or less equivalent to the letter's adult writer. In short, even though *Straight to Hell* offers a counterexample to the panic-inducing triad of erotic innocent, imperiled adolescent, and predatory pedophile, the far more congenial fantasies it offers as an alternative come with their own set of problems, including the matter of how age-differentiated subjects may relate to one another in a world defined by various structural inequalities. As Kate Millet argued in her contribution to the 1980 special edition of *Semiotext(e)* devoted to the subject of age-differentiated intimacy: "But what is our freedom fight about? Is it about the liberation of children or just having sex with them? I would like to see a broader movement involving young people who would be making the decision because it's *their* issue and *their* fight. *Theirs* is the authentic voice."[59]

Millet's posing of such questions bespeaks the difficulty that adheres within them. On the one hand, she registers the possibility of age-differentiated intimacies; on the other, she codes those possibilities in the language of children with the ability to express their "authentic voice" in a clear and uncomplicated way, revealing an attachment to the kinds of values that, as Amin has argued, have locked queer thinkers into a perpetual cycle of excitement and disappointment regarding the radical political potential of their erotic practices.[60] Such questions have also become simply harder to ask and explore in the wake of the pedophile panics that cast particular suspicion over gay men's efforts to engage publicly with the ways in which intergenerational intimacies comprise an open secret within gay subcultures. As a consequence, such intimacies become a past histori- cal moment in the development of self-possessed gay adults, an artifact of the past that reasserts itself in the lobbying of cringe-inducing groups such as NAMBLA. With these problems mind, the final section of this chap- ter returns to Stadler's *Allan Stein* in order to consider how the novel both indulges in and responds to the fantasies exemplified in McDonald's *Straight to Hell*. In Stadler's novel, the ethical problems of all age-differentiated rela- tions, and not simply pederasty, pertain as much to materialized relations of power as to the boy's broader status with US national culture as a tantalizing impossibility, something only ever glimpsed through the fantasies of one's own ever-changing childhood.

GROWING NOWHERE, OR *ALLAN STEIN*

Stadler's *Allan Stein* is not a direct response to McDonald's *Straight to Hell*, yet it engages with the legacy of the zine's antidevelopmental fantasies. That engagement becomes easier to apprehend in light of the context inform- ing the novel's publication, which includes Stadler's participation within NAMBLA's 1995 conference held in his hometown of Seattle. While not a member of NAMBLA, Stadler had received an invitation to speak at the conference from an organizer who had read his then recently published novel *The Sex Offender* (1994), a work of dystopian speculative fiction in which a man convicted of having sex with an adolescent boy must undergo a series of rehabilitative treatments that include the forced viewing of por- nographic films featuring children. Intrigued by the unusual invitation, Stadler accepted and then documented his experience in a feature story for the *Stranger*, Seattle's alternative newspaper, entitled "Keeping Secrets: NAMBLA, the Idealization of Children, and the Contradictions of Gay Pol- itics." Describing a series of low-energy meetings and discussions occasion- ally punctuated by catered meals, Stadler's account of the conference works to cut through the image of NAMBLA that both law enforcement and pop- ular media have created for the organization, construing it not as a clandes- tine society of murderous pedophiles but as "a hobby club like any other, with all the fanaticism, petty internecine wars, and peculiar organization trivia of the stamp collectors or Civil War buffs who were meeting in other dreary halls, eating the same donuts, drinking the same awful coffee, and achieving the same strange private results."[61]

While the feature takes pleasure in documenting the weird banality of the event, the conference itself provides the basis for a pair of extended reflections, the first of which concerns the history of gay and lesbian activism and its exclusion of NAMBLA in fealty to what one member termed "gay enlightenment politics."[62] According to Stadler, NAMBLA's controversial status bespeaks a long-standing tension that arose serval decades earlier between, on the one hand, a tradition of the transformative gay sex-radicalism of the leftist homophiles and the Gay Liberation Front, and, on the other, the assimilationist activism of the Gay Activists' Alliance, which consisted primarily of well-resourced gay men demanding entrance into positions of institutional power.[63] In 1977, the bust of an alleged gay pedophile ring in Revere, Massachusetts, energized the members of the Boston-based radical gay newspaper *Fag Rag* (whose ranks included Shively) to form the Boston-Boise Committee, which organized against the subsequent increase in police pressure on gay men's public sex practices.[64] The work of the Boston-Boise Committee led in turn to the formation of NAMBLA, which extended the committee's legacy of sex-radicalism by militating on behalf of a range of progressive issues, from expanding women's reproductive rights to the abolition of age-of-consent laws; however, its defining endorsement of man-boy love rendered it both an unwanted ally among other gay and lesbian civil rights organizations as well as an easy target for conservative critics eager to cast gay men as child predators. Following a series of sensational media campaigns that spuriously tied NAMBLA to a number of high-profile child murders and sex abuse scandals, critics succeeded in disarming whatever political force the organization may have had.[65]

Effectively marginalized, Stadler argues, "NAMBLA remains a troubling reminder of [the gay community's] own past, an anachronistic trace of the shadowy homophile sex-radicals, condemned to their peculiar utopian visions by the impossibility of assimilation."[66] Yet beyond linking NAMBLA to the history of gay sex-radicalism, Stadler's second extended reflection links the organization to the broader cultural construction of children, and young White boys in particular, as idealized erotic innocents, at once devoid of Eros yet also positively bursting with it. "In the rhetoric of NAMBLA and of family values," Stadler writes, "the child is angelic, otherworldly, and burdened with the task of spiritually redeeming his protectors. For a boy-lover, the redemption becomes erotic precisely because the eroticism of boys has been made 'unthinkable.' The Eros of children takes the boy-lover outside the grid of social realities within which adults are usually trapped. Man-boy relationships unfold like dreams: silent, uncontained, and unreachable."[67] To that end, NAMBLA isn't just the anachronistic trace of contemporary gay politics but also a product of the modern developmental plot that construes the child as an unmarked potential that grows linearly into adulthood. NAMBLA did not create its fantasies but adapted them from the images and

narratives of boyhood that proliferate in contemporary popular culture, sus-
pending boyhood in a state of unactualized potential. As Stadler observes
of the organization's publicity and literature arranged on display tables at
the back of the conference rooms: "I had found NAMBLA's 'porn,' and it
was Hollywood. It was network television, Sunday ad supplements, Nick-
elodeon, and the Disney channel. NAMBLA doesn't need to manufacture
porn, because America manufactures it for them."[68]

NAMBLA's eroticization of the boy becomes clear in Stadler's remarkably candid conversation with one conference participant identified pseud-
onymously as John. When Stadler queries John about his interest in "real
porn," John replies: "Real porn has nothing to do with boys — that's what's
so strange about, you know, 'boy porn.' I mean, what boy would ever make
boy porn? It's just sexy to gay men. It's *gay* porn, and the boys just happen
to be in it. Sometimes I like the boys, but in a porn movie they're not doing
anything sexy, you know, like just being boys. Now, if some boys actually
got together with a video camera and made their *own* porn, that could be
sexy."[69] As heavily sanitized and severely attenuated versions of McDonald's
boys, the boys of John's imaginary pornography reveal a series of assumptions about the formal features of the image and its content, as well as who
would use it and why. What distinguishes one genre from another, boy porn
from gay porn, is an absence of sex structured according to pornographic
conventions as imagined by gay adults. In a sense, it resembles what Mc-
Donald claimed to capture more generally with his zine: true tales of male
homosexual experience organized according to the nonphallic logic of anal
desire, according to which boyhood is not a stage one passes through on the
way to adulthood but a subjectivity defined by spatialized sideways group-
ings. Yet where *Straight to Hell* imagined this boy in concert with a radical,
anticapitalist politics, NAMBLA's boy porn feels Arcadian and thoroughly
severed from any political context. Devoid of the conventions that make gay
porn unappealing, boy porn is an impossible genre with neither a history
nor a future into which to grow.

The boy porn as defined by the eroticism of its potential, whether in the
more overtly radical form promoted by McDonald and Shively or in the
attenuated version proffered by NAMBLA's members, provides another
way to understand the plea of *Allan Stein*'s narrator, whose confession both
comprises a rapturous profession of impossible love and exemplifies that
genre of stunted aesthetic development: "pure pornography." However,
beyond the scenes detailing the narrator's fantasies and engagements with
Stéphane and Dogon, the students whom he is accused of molesting, *Allan
Stein* challenges conventional forms of linear, developmental plotting at the
structural level. The various sources of conflict in the novel feel familiar:

first, there is quest to find the alleged Picasso sketches that drive the narrator from the Pacific Northwest to Paris; second, there is a historical mystery,
according to which the narrator investigates both Allan Stein's connection
to the Picasso painting and the reason for the lad's transformation from
robust boy into a despondent and overweight adult; third, but perhaps not
finally, there is the psychological mystery wherein the narrator explores
his own childhood to explain his own infatuations with the various boys
he encounters. Yet these plots all have nonresolutions: the sketches remain
unfound, the historical record fails to yield anything of use regarding the
Stein boy's life, and the reader finds no singular event in the narrator's past
to explain his unseemly desires. Even his clandestine affair with Stéphane
resolves anticlimactically: a pair of letters from Stéphane's mother arrive
at the cabin where he and Stéphane are staying, chastising the narrator for
his lies and requesting that Stéphane return home immediately, which he
then does, leaving the narrator stranded at the novel's end near Agay, Allan
Stein's childhood summer vacation spot.

While the novel's plots fade out without a strong sense of resolution,
they nonetheless open up space for various sideways movements, which
the novel initially sets up in the narrator's recounting of his sexual relationship with Dogon. The accusation of the relationship leads to the narrator's
suspension from his job, but, as he explains, "I had never imagined molesting him until the principal suggested it by notifying me of the charges" (9).
The narrator thus scrambles the normative sequence of crime and punishment, initiating an affair with Dogon that only concludes because of the
narrator's departure for Paris. The novel's antidevelopmental thrust also
reappears in the lead-up to the narrator's account of the night that Dogon,
having successfully deceived his parents as to his whereabouts, spends at his
apartment. Aware that what follows may be distasteful to some readers, the
narrator directs those "who can't stomach any more of this sort of thing" to
skip ahead while also warning of the roughness of what follows: "Since the
narrative hounds have all skipped forward anyway, I'll just dispense with
the clumsy linkages and survey some of the highlights of that night" (41).
What follows is a series of loosely connected moments from a night of sex,
pillow talk, and midnight snacks that the narrator enjoys with Dogon, yet
the warning about the coming disjointedness resonates with the previous
warning about the potential unpleasantness of what follows, creating an
association between sexual propriety and the desire for narrative coherence.
While seemingly inconsequential to the plot, this passage points to the pleasures of getting sidetracked into the dilated and disjointed temporalities of
pure pornography.

The tension between narrative development and pornographic delay parallel a number of other tensions in the novel, including a tension between the actual and potential that is formalized in the transitory figure of the boy. This tension is summarized most clearly not by the narrator but by Miriam, the mother of Stéphane, during a conversation between her and the narrator regarding the adolescent figure in Picasso's painting: "This is one of the features of the Picasso Herbert speaks of, the most erotic and moving aspect of it—that it is a boy. He has tremendous power because he is nothing yet, no one, and so he has the power in him to be a god, like all children do, you see? If Picasso had painted a man leading the horse, just imagine it. This man would be someone, some man who will never be a god at all, just a man, without the limitless power this boy has" (82). While it may be easy to recognize the eroticism in an anonymous nude portrait of a boy, it's much more difficult to understand in what way a boy can be said to be powerful. Children are usually construed as vulnerable and in need of protection, yet according to Miriam, a boy retains a degree of power unparalleled by any man. To further complicate matters, while a man is "someone," a boy is not only "no one," he is also "nothing," a depersonalized entity that draws its power from an unactualized potential. The indefinite article emphasizes this point; Miriam speaks of "a boy" versus "the boy," thus underscoring the boy's indefinite nature while reserving this quality for the boy alone. The eroticism of a boy appears linked to the power he keeps in reserve, the potential power he retains but loses in the moment he grows into the form of a man.

The narrator's relation to the boy in the image replicates his relation to Stéphane, who both acts as an informal guide to the narrator as he halfheartedly conducts his errands across the city and leads the narrator on various other unrelated tours. In turn, these shared journeys yield opportunities for the narrator to reflect on his own fascination with the boy:

> Language was the least of our barriers, Stéphane hovered behind a scrim, trapped inside a body whose proportions and angularity perfectly expressed something to me . . . "becoming," I'd like to say, but it might have been nostalgia. His posture as he led me, the narrowing shoulders, the lilt of his arms and bounce of his blue knapsack that kept disappearing into the crowd, enthralled me by pointing elsewhere—away from him. The hollow of his back and then the turn at the hips, his long thighs, became abstractions, pure equations, so that he engaged that part of my mind that also loves geometry or angels. (117)

Echoing the language of "Keeping Secrets," the slip that substitutes "angels" for the more appropriately geometric term "angles" at once reminds the reader of the narrator's own unreliability and bespeaks the idealizing fantasy that mediates his relation to the boy. This fantasy is also perceptible in the ways in which the scene's arrangement of its characters replicates the arrangement of the figures in the Picasso painting: as the boy leads the horse, so Stéphane leads the narrator through the streets of Paris. Their destination, the Paris school in which the young Allan Stein received his education, redoubles the linked meanings of movement and development that the narrator aims to freeze in moments of eroticized contemplation and narrative delays.

At certain points in the novel, these narrative asides become the basis for intimacies shared with other adult characters, who bond over the boy's idealized eroticism. The narrator's conversations with Miriam serve as one such example, but another, more explicit example occurs during a booze-soaked dinner with Deni and George, two gay men whom the narrator has met in Paris in the course of his research. Barely into their meal, the impostor Herbert lets slip about the details of his affair with Dogon. The narrator finds a "generous and keen" listener in Deni, who probes the narrator about his desire for another boy, Allan Stein (162). Space opens up within the novel's investigative plot in the form of a temporal delay: "the less we spoke the more powerfully the night ruptured, so that the billowing places where, for example, Allan or Stéphane came rushing in—that is, the idea of Allan or Stéphane (for they dwelt equally in these uncharted interstices between the pleasantries of conversation, those silences and sighs where crushed thoughts could breathe and become huge)—these opened up, and we had only to be still and courteous to allow them to inhabit us or be inhabited" (162). Laced with em dashes and a parenthetical aside, the syntax of the sentence replicates the narrator's description of a silent space that opens up within Deni and the narrator's sex talk, yielding an intimacy expressed in Deni's tender squeeze of the narrator's hand. The silent gesture also resonates with the narrator's previous description of his desire for Allan Stein as an erotically charged proximity, "—like in a photo, actually. The proximity is all that 'happens,' so I could touch him, though I never do. He's always poised there, but then nothing . . . proceeds'" (161). Given space to breath, the evening ends in the "swift and clear and pleasing" pleasures of the dinner, where "Allan Stein wavered and grew, emerging from the folds of someone else's history" (163).

The sense of comfort that the narrator enjoys with Deni in that moment contrasts with his acerbic take on US gay bars, according to which the commodification of gay sociability passes for progress. Ruminating within a Parisian gay bar where he has met Deni for a drink, the impostor Herbert muses to himself:

I don't know why conservative, drunk ex-husbands in tract houses watching TV news exposés are so easily convinced the gay demimonde is sex-saturated and glamorous. In fact it is just as tacky and crass as the worst G.I. Shenanigans bar in the most sexless highway strip mall of the most forlorn suburban development where *they* go. [. . .] As the Enlightenment proceeds, however, to its final totalizing end, the bright light of sexual liberation will shine out of the cities to reach the towns and sprawl, and everything will shift so that perversity will be allowed to thrive in that purgatory too. (153)

Taking similar aim at gay bars in "enviable high-rent districts of the city," what is proffered as evidence of progress is refigured as capture within the sprawl of late capitalism. "When I want to meet a new man I go to the dance," observes Deni of gay bars. "Boy is very exciting, and Le Palace. It's very easy in Paris to find the kind [of man] you want, if you know which place has him." Yet the narrator does not share this sense of variety and abundance, reflecting his own inability to place himself in them (152). In fact, the narrator won't find his type in any bar, as the exclusion of the boy from the bar is a condition of the gay bar's possibility. However, the boy returns in the bar's idealization of male youthfulness, an idealization that is sometimes rendered explicit within the venue's very name.

As the conventional place to mark a young gay man's coming of age, and thus of entering into gay society, the gay bar promises unsatisfying forms of closure for the novel's narrator, as he, Deni, and a motley crew of middle-aged art-world queers make a late-night voyage to Boy. There they plan to meet the elderly widow Roubina to discuss the Picasso sketches supposedly in her possession, but the narrator quickly finds himself bored and tired, distracting himself from the lively nightlife scene with soft-core fantasies of "the actual boy" Stéphane, lying in bed at home, his "boxers pushed down in front of a hand that holds his cock while he dreams" (233). As the hour grows late, Roubina arrives with Hank, a friend of Herbert who is unaware of the impostor's deceptions yet who has come to Paris to assist in securing the sketches. However, Hank reveals that the elderly widow no longer has them in her possession. With the location of the sketches unknown, the investigation comes to a dead end. The scene threatens a second form of closure in Hank's ability to expose the narrator's lies to his friends and to the Dupaignes, thus spoiling the connections to Deni and the others and, more significantly, eradicating the proximity he has enjoyed with Stéphane. This threat initiates the novel's final betrayal, as the narrator flees Boy in order to awaken Stéphane and prematurely begin the short journey they had planned to take together to visit Agay.

The novel's final chapter recounts the narrator and Stéphane's trip to the

South of France, where time dilates into an extended man-boy fantasy that the impostor Herbert aims to extend indefinitely. However, the past soon catches up to the pair: Miriam's letters arrive at the cabin where the narrator and Stéphane have been staying. While the boy's letter requests he return home immediately, the narrator's letter chastises him, not for having an affair with her son, but for both lying about it and using a false name: "It is with a kind of vertigo that I address you, since there is no one I know by that name, no man in this world to anchor the name to, and so I feel myself floating just to write it: Matthew. [. . .] I would not be upset by this trip with Stéphane if I could let myself believe that he was with *you*, with Herbert. But that has become impossible" (248). The exposure of the deception likewise spoils Matthew's relationship with Stéphane, who parts ways with him once the pair arrives in Agay. The moment highlights Matthew's own inability to connect his name to his desires: "Herbert," the narrator explains at an earlier point in the novel, "was a mask that trapped me at the same time as it made me visible" (169). Like the stalled political progress encapsulated in the gay bar, the false name cannot provide an adequate means to narrate Matthew's development, whose best option is either a repetitive sideways movement into pornographic fantasy or the erotically charged contemplation of the idealized boy's potential.

By the novel's end, Matthew is out of time and out of place. Wandering somewhere in the woods outside of Agay, where the unseasonal night air suggests that "it was summer when actually winter was still transpiring just over the next ridge," a drunken Matthew collapses into an old chair left near the river and delivers the novel's final lines: "I wondered where the boy had gone, dispersed into the air or locked in the ground in a crowded box? I have imagined that whole worlds dwell in the body of a boy and have pried with words to relax these meanings from their hiding place, to coax the boy into the open. He stood still for a moment, caught in the warmth of my regard, and when I reached for him he was gone" (252–53). By this point, the narrative has surpassed the time of the introductory section that contains the narrator's plea to the reader, and so this final scene exceeds both the spatial and temporal boundaries of that initial framing device. The statement also teases the question of what boy he has in mind, as the noun may refer as much to Stéphane as to Allan Stein, Dogon, the boy in Picasso's painting, or the narrator's own youthful self. That final possibility emphasizes the novel's narrative of stalled subject formation, yet it identifies neither a pathological cause for that arrested development nor a reparative frame for his reintegration into the world. Instead, there is simply the exhaustion of both the narrator and the fantasy of the boy he has unfolded, leaving Matthew largely indifferent to his predicament, collapsed in an abandoned chair like someone who has stuffed himself on a decadent meal.

In fact, the spatial-temporal ambiguity of the novel's ending provides a thematic and structural match for the novel's amoral take on man-boy intimacies. In contrast to both popular culture's clear-cut condemnation of the pedophile and the liberationist fantasies advanced in *Straight to Hell* or by NAMBLA's membership, Matthew concludes the narrative as neither a repentant pedophile, suitably condemned for his predatory ways, nor a posturing sex-radical, heroically upending society's values. Instead, he comprises something like a proto-version of Lee Edelman's future-negating queer, whose rejection of "the Child, as a disciplinary image of the Imaginary past or as a site of projective identification with an always impossible future," also amounts to a rejection of the modern social order and its foundational promise that, with the right politics, meaningful closure will eventually arrive.[70] However, Stadler's novel lacks the vehemence of Edelman's polemical critique of reproductive futurity: while Matthew holds little attachment to the names that might secure an identity for him, he is also eminently agreeable, gamely trying on the impressions of others as he encounters them, enjoying them intensely until they cease to function. Moreover, the two strongest connections that Matthew maintains are with Dogon and then Stéphane, whose sexual and gustatory appetites he indulges. However, the end of each attachment seems less like Matthew has coldly discarded his youthful lovers than his youthful lovers have outgrown him: while Dogon wisely turns down the offer to run away with Matthew to Paris, Stéphane, ailing from his indulgent diet and angered by Matthew's confessed deception, refuses to follow him off the train to Agay. While neither boy comes close to expressing the preternatural maturity of Nabokov's Lolita, they nonetheless intuit the moment when it's time to stop and return home.

If there's anything about the boys in *Allan Stein* that might render its depiction of intergenerational intimacy a bit more palatable for readers, then it's the fact that neither Stéphane nor Dogon is reliant on Matthew for his own survival. Their benign experiences as proto-gay boys in part reflect what Fischel terms the "conditions of gendered adolescence," which shape youths' intimate relations with adults yet whose variables become harder to apprehend before the far more compelling figures of the predatory pedophile and the erotic innocent. The inability to apprehend those conditions informs the use of blunt-force concepts when adjudicating sexual injury that produce their own collateral damage, from denying the sexual autonomy of youth to the further elaboration of the security state. Hence, Fischel argues, the goal is to make "relations, rather than bad persons, the object of intervention."[71] While neither of Matthew's boys is trapped in a relation of material dependence, they do lack the access he enjoys to the institutions of gay culture, which perhaps more than any other has developed the symbolic resources for making sense of man-boy intimacies as intimacies, rather than forms of predation. For Matthew, this is the gay bar and its sex public that yields up Deni as a sympathetic listener. For McDonald, it is the pornographic counterpublic of *Straight to Hell*, through which readers might share, respond to, and argue over the meaning of the man-boy experiences presented on its pages. As I have mentioned, the legal and normative exclusion of boys from participating in such counterpublics not only served as their enabling condition, but also contributed to the idealization of children. Hence, just as accounting for the conditions of gendered adolescence reveals the political inadequacy of abolishing of age-of-consent laws, so too does it reveal the problems with merely providing youth with access to the means of producing and consuming pornography.

Finally, and perhaps in keeping with its own indifference, Stadler's novel about man-boy love itself feels anachronistic in that its depictions of queer youth remain devoid of the digital technologies that have become a seemingly ever-present feature of contemporary youth cultures. While *Allan Stein* was published roughly a decade before what is sometimes referred to as the transition to an internet defined in terms of social media platforms, applications, and interactivity, personal computers and commercial internet access were an increasingly central feature of US homes by the late 1990s. In turn, the growing availability of the internet offered writers and readers a variety of new ways to write about their fantasies and organize their erotic practices, from dedicated websites to Usenet groups, electronic bulletin boards, and chat windows. However, beyond offering new means and venues to connect with one another, the internet also coincided with a structural change in the conditions of access that previously enabled the efflorescence of the print-based pornographic counterpublics that I have examined in the preceding chapters: namely, the internet has rendered the always-imperfect barriers to minors' access to consuming, producing, and distributing porn obsolete. As a result, the internet has touched off a new wave of moral panics focused on the perils that pornography poses to the development of White adolescent boys. To bring the history this book has told to its conclusion, the next and final chapter explores how these interrelated problems of digitally mediated pornographic writing, gay sexual sociability at the new millennium, and the development of White boys come together in Dennis Cooper's *The Sluts* (2004). While frequently read as a writer of transgressive fiction, the next chapter seeks a new way into Cooper's work, instead construing him, like Stadler, as eminently fascinated with the question of what it means for boys to grow up gay and what role pornography might play in that process.

Going Online

Dennis Cooper and the Piglets

The preceding chapters have described how a genre of pornographic writing took shape in the US during the late 1960s and subsequently influenced the production and consumption of literary fiction about gay sexuality for the rest of the century. Neither a merely private pleasure nor an overlooked trove of revolutionary political thought, gay pornographic writing was important precisely because its crudeness, marginality, political incoherence, and ephemerality convened counterpublics for which fantasies of sexual risk were the means to imagine modes of masculine gay subjectivity, intimacy, and sexual sociability. While pornographic writing was not itself new, it took specific shape during this period as a kind of lucrative popular writing oriented toward the body that gay writers with literary ambitions had to navigate, either by distancing their work from pornography or by incorporating its tropes and conventions within their own narratives. Beyond its ambivalent status as both obstacle to legitimation and source of aesthetic inspiration, gay pornographic writing helped to shape the formation of contemporary gay literary fiction in at least two additional ways. First, its counterpublics provided alternative contexts for the critical reception of novels either dismissed within mainstream venues of review or treated as sociological texts whose value lay in its capacity to explain homosexual subcultures to the national reading public. Second, it supplied a renewable resource both for publishing houses seeking to ballast the costs of publishing gay literary fiction and for the institutions of gay commercial culture, from bars to adult bookstores, who used porn to market their products and venues to gay men. As a result, gay pornographic writing had a central role to play in the subsequent legitimization of gay literary fiction as a distinct category of writing.

While the preceding chapters have highlighted the relations between gay pornographic writing and gay literary fiction, they have also shown the need for an expansion of the porn studies media archive. Emerging within feminist film and media studies during the 1980s, both porn studies and the verdant subfield of gay porn studies have exhibited a persistent bias toward still and moving images. This bias has been compounded in recent years as scholars have turned their attention to online pornography, whose vast and heterogeneous bulk has required the development of new frameworks that, as Susanna Paasonen has argued, can account for pornography as "a multifaceted assemblage—a historically evolving media genre. It is a field of labor, technological innovations, monetary exchange, carnal acts and sensations, regulatory practices, verbal definitions, and interpretations."[1] However, the image has continued to dominant even those such approaches, minimizing both the role that writing plays in the production and consumption of pornographic images online and drawing attention away from the substantial quantities of digital pornographic writing. To be sure, scholars such as Paasonen, Mica Hilson, and Steven Kruger have offered analysis of digital story archives, such as Nifty and Literotica, yet the story archive is only one way that pornographic writing appears on the internet.[2] In calling attention to how pornographic writing, including not just fiction but classified ads, personal correspondence, and other seemingly purely communicative genres, has both mediated forms of gay sexual sociability and influenced contemporary gay literary production, this book suggests the continuing need for scholars of pornography to attune themselves to the writing in that multifaceted assemblage, from story archives and self-published pornographic novels to promotional materials created by performers, the erotically elaborate profile text of apps and cruising websites, and the narrative captions appended to pornographic images on micro-blogging platforms. As much as the sound and images it may surround, such writing mediates men's relations to themselves and to others and thus provides an important resource for understanding how that mediation has changed over time.

To provide just one example, this book concludes with an analysis of Dennis Cooper's *The Sluts* (2004). Composed of various genres of digital writing associated with a website for advertising and reviewing gay escorts, the novel's narrative concerns the life and fate of an enigmatic hustler named Brad, whose boyish good looks, indeterminate age, and apparent willingness to conform to his clients most excessive desires quickly render him the stuff of internet legend. Visitors to the website's review pages and message boards share information about Brad and report on his arrangement with Brian, Brad's sadistic lover-turned-pimp, and each new encounter generates more writing that becomes its own source of pleasure: as William

Carney's nefarious uncle might have put it, a counterpublic of ghostly witnesses is always on hand, ready and waiting to read and comment upon the
latest news of Brad's sexual exploits. However, as reviews begin to surface
detailing Brad's brutal torture and death at the hands of Brian, his fan base
struggles to separate out the facts from the violent fantasies that brought
together the website's participants. Through the juxtaposition of a simple
mystery plot and a complex narrative structure, Cooper's novel offers a useful staging ground for considering how the qualities of risk, deferral, anonymity, and indefinite address that characterized the print-based publics
of gay pornography and which mediated specific forms of masculine gay
subjectivity were extended and transformed by the digital network.

Specifically, this chapter argues that *The Sluts* captures a transitional
moment between the pornographically mediated gay masculinities of the
late twentieth century and what João Florêncio terms the "gay pig masculinities" of the twenty-first century. In *Bareback Porn, Porous Masculinities,
Queer Futures: The Ethics of Becoming Pig* (2020), Florêncio offers a bracing
account of how the availability of pharmacological technologies capable of
managing HIV infection and thereby effectively preventing the spread of the
virus in Europe and North America has catalyzed a radical transformation
in masculine gay subjectivity and sexual sociability. In contrast to the Chel-
sea boy and other forms of internationalized gay masculinity, whose obsessive embrace of health, neatness, and bodily fitness comprised a reaction
to the stigma heaped on both penetrative anal sex and HIV-positive bodies during the 1980s and 1990s, pig masculinities are defined by an ethical
commitment to becoming pig through erotic practices that intensify one's
corporeal porousness: "'pig' has today become a form of self-identification
that is taken up by gay men who like to 'wallow in filth' as it were, who are
willing to test and push the boundaries of their bodies, and experiment with
horizons of bodily pleasures, opening themselves to exchanges of all kinds
of bodily fluids whilst no longer having to be haunted by the spectre of HIV
and AIDS, or by fears of emasculation through penetration."[3] While articulated from within and through contemporary biopolitical technologies
that generate self-surveilling and self-managing subjects of desire, gay pig
masculinities, according to Florêncio, may help in the generation of alternatives to the control society and its evermore diverse and inclusive array
of neoliberal subjectivities.

One of the many virtues of Florêncio's study is its willingness to engage
with the history of gay pornographic writing, revealing how the ethics of
becoming pig descend genealogically from the ethics of sexual risk elaborated through the pornography of the preceding decades. While gay pig
masculinities are very much embedded within a historical and geopolitical

context defined by the availability of new media and pharmaceutical technologies in the contemporary global North, references to pig sexuality date back to the 1970s, when magazines such as *Drummer* and European publications such as the German-language Swedish magazine *Kumpel* employed the respective terms "pig" and "Sau" or "Schwein" to describe forms of uninhibited erotic practice, including rough fucking, fisting, and piss and scat play.[4] Florêncio then tracks the history of similar terms into the 1990s with French publications such as *Projet X* before turning away from print and writing to the bareback subcultures mediated through the films of Paul Morris and Treasure Island Media. In contrast, *The Sluts* explores what it means to write like a pig, where the writing about sex is a part of the sex itself, yet it also poses a question to both Florêncio's account of gay pig masculinities and to the history that I have traced out in my previous chapters by focusing on a figure that has haunted the genre since the late 1960s. That is the figure of the adolescent boy, who comprises the obsessive fixation of the website's participants yet whose legal and social exclusion from the counterpublics of gay pornography serves as a significant condition for both contemporary pornography and the adolescent. In that sense, Cooper's *The Sluts* raises the question: how does a boy become a pig?

While the ethics of becoming pig entail a radical openness to the other, its subcultural articulations have gained clarity through their opposition to boys. On the one hand, the boy designates not a chronologically defined subject but an idealized norm of youth, fitness, and health, which contrasts with the pig's radical indifference to hygiene, contamination, and aging bodies.[5] On the other hand, it has been easy to maintain that clarifying distinction in light of the relative success that the US has had in hampering minors' access to both pornography and adult erotic subcultures, but the two figures may have more in common than it may at first seem. As Philippe Airés has shown, since the early modern period the adolescent has been defined as a stage in the life of the subject defined by transitivity and nonconformity. With the publication of G. Stanley Hall's magnum opus *Adolescence* (1904), the emergent discourses of psychology, psychoanalysis, and child development cast the adolescent as a specific kind of developmental problem, leading Airés to declare adolescence as "the privileged age of the twentieth century."[6] However, in addition to suddenly being redefined in terms of biological and psychological transformation, the adolescent was also incorporated into capitalist relations as a consumer of youth culture. In consuming media and products that promoted a sense of generational rebellion, youth culture also helped to integrate adolescent subjects into the circuits of socioeconomic reproduction, in many ways positioning them as the prototypical subject in the culture of consumption.[7] These interrelated ways of conceptualizing the adolescent, as a subject defiantly growing to adulthood and as a semi-independent consumer, have rendered it a porous and vulnerable subject, whom adults must protect from outside influences least they cause deviations in its normal development.

As Patricia Meyers Spacks has shown, adolescence has also been a primary preoccupation of the Anglophone novel since at least the eighteenth century, thus providing the narrative form for subsequent psychosexual models of adolescent development.[8] In turn, argues Jed Esty, arrested youth became prominent in the antidevelopmental plots of many modernist novels, which used the trope of deviated adolescence to explore how the linked terms of nation and adulthood failed to provide meaningful closure when faced with capitalism's perpetual disruption of national, geographic, and demographic boundaries. In this chapter, I read Cooper's *The Sluts* as continuing that tradition by proffering a vision of the queer boy as, in Esty's terms, a "figure who holds a position outside dominant discourses of progress at the level of individual self-formation and of social reproduction."[9] Deeply inspired by the French "poet of adolescence" Rimbaud, Cooper's fiction has similarly imagined youth not as a developmental stage but as an intensely vivid yet fleeting event largely disconnected from any sense of progressive sequence.[10] However, where Rimbaud preferred the antidevelopmental form of the *récit*, Cooper's *The Sluts* turns to digitally mediated pornographic writing, in particular the interactive, lust-driven chatter that pervades the online discussion boards of the novel's setting. With each chapter, the novel expands sideways into a complex series of interrelated repetitions that stall out just as they seem to develop into something substantial. To that extent, the novel's progress toward its conclusion and the resolution of its central mystery comes into stark and repeated contrast with its antidevelopmental movements into pornographic fantasies featuring the endlessly modifiable body of an adolescent boy.

Noting those qualities of the novel, readers have more often than not praised its online community as a kind of "queer commons," as Diarmund Hester terms it, demonstrating "the capacity of desire and celebrity to join various individuals together in a supple, noncoercive social structure."[11] However, these readings overlook two crucial facts about *The Sluts*: first, its setting on a website for gay escorts situates its online community in relation to a mode of contemporary capitalist relation whose "raw materials," argues Paul Preciado, "are excitation, erection, ejaculation, and pleasure and feelings of self-satisfaction, omnipotent control, and total destruction."[12] Second, while the community's discourse formalizes the antidevelopmental force of Cooperian adolescence, in which one is endlessly caught up within the pornographic spiral of its thrillingly transgressive pleasures, such readings overlook the novel's adolescent characters, who drive the website's traffic yet whose participation within its discourse is largely shaped and controlled by its adults. Through the presence of those exclusively included voices, the novel probes the stakes of adopting the adolescent as inspiration for an online pornographic community. In fact, while adolescent characters routinely fall prey to Brian and the other website's contributors, others repeatedly exploit and then deflate the fantasies that the website's participants work up for themselves, thereby marking out the place of barely perceptible adolescent subjects, hustlers and piglets, who desire to grow up into neither the website's pornographic collectivity nor a form of normative adulthood—gay or straight. If anything, *The Sluts* turns the antidevelopmental energies of adolescence against its deployment for *both* developmental *and* antidevelopmental ends.

Perhaps the contemporary obverse of Cooper's piglet is the adolescent porn addict, which a popular, pseudo-neuroscientific discourse imagines in terms of the White teenaged boy who finds himself locked into interminable and solitary acts of masturbation as he scours the internet for the next great perversely transgressive image that will finally bring him to climax. Corrupted by porn in his youth, the adult porn addict faces the terror of "porn-induced erectile dysfunction" that threatens his capacity to arrive as one of the nation's happily reproductive sexual citizens. Perhaps it's no surprise, then, that growing concern for the porn-addicted White boy more or less coincides with the public resurgence in the US of White supremacist movements that lionize the virile heterosexual male capable of keeping his desires masterfully in check. In stark contrast, Cooper's piglets highlight the continued limitations that gay youth face even as the internet established the possibility of their participation within the counterpublics that have been crucial for the mediation of masculine gay subjectivities and sexualities for much of the late twentieth century. As something that has been included within the history of gay pornographic writing precisely through its exclusion, the piglet is only minimally registered in Cooper's novel. Still, the traces he leaves point to new areas of investigation regarding representations of sexually active gay youth and queer growth in a world where online pornography is available as a form for the project of narrating the development of a sexual self. Yet before I get there, this chapter begins by briefly surveying the ways in which normative categories of childhood, adolescence, and adulthood have taken shape in relation to the historical processes that led up to the semi-apocryphal moment when, as Samuel Steward put it: "The gates were opened. The flood began. Suddenly all the old four-letter words (and some new ones) appeared in print, almost overnight."[13]

TRAPS FOR THE YOUNG

For at least the past one hundred and fifty years, the belief that pornography can inflict lasting harm on the minds of youth has served as the justification for imposing legal limits on minors' access to pornographic materials, providing one of the central logics driving the early formation of federal obscenity law in the United States. For much of the early nineteenth century, the regulation of sexually explicit materials remained relatively lax in US cities, and the rough patchwork of obscene libel laws that did exist went largely unused. However, the emergence of new printing technologies and the subsequent efflorescence of the flash press, whose bawdy tales of urban prostitution and satirical attacks on the city's power brokers were popular among increasingly literate working-class and immigrant communities, generated interest among Protestant elites in strengthening obscenity laws.[14] By the late nineteenth century, the popularity of the flash press, the growing trade in erotic "fancy" books and sexological tracts, and the availability of inexpensive erotic photosets and postcards energized reformers such as Anthony Comstock to lobby for a regulatory framework that could effectively combat the production and spread of obscene texts throughout the nation.[15] For Comstock, obscene publications posed both a spiritual and physical danger to youth, as their eroticism would tempt young readers into committing the dissipative act of masturbation and, as a result, put the future of the nation at stake. "The morals of our youth first, conventionalities afterward," Comstock concisely declared in his treatise *Traps for the Young* (1883): "These foul publications, as has been seen, breed lust. Lust brings disease, weakness, and suffering."[16] Highly successful in his efforts, the federal framework that Comstock helped to install would remain more or less intact for the next seventy years.

With the decision on *Roth v. United Sates* (1957), the US Supreme Court installed a new test for obscenity that reflected a significant softening of the court's certification of Comstock's policy work from half a century before. However, concerns about children, adults, and the differences between them remained central to the court's midcentury renegotiations of obscenity law. As Marjorie Heins has shown, in the same year that the court adopted a flexible test for obscenity, it also issued its ruling on *Butler v. Michigan* (1957), which overturned a Michigan state law that "criminalized any publication with a tendency 'to incite minors to violent or depraved or immoral acts, manifestly tending to the corruption of the morals of youth.'"[17] The court found that the law was overly broad because it prevented adults from accessing materials that might be appropriate for them, even if they were not appropriate for a child, a logic that Justice Felix Frankfurter derided as patently absurd in his majority opinion: "The State insists that, by thus quarantining the general reading public against books not too rugged for grown men and women in order to shield juvenile innocence, it is exercising its power to promote the general welfare. Surely, this is to burn the house to roast the pig."[18] Over the next ten years, the court continued to relativize its obscenity test in terms of the consumer's age. For example, its ruling on *Ginsberg v. New York* (1968), which upheld the state's conviction of a luncheonette owner for selling "girlie" magazines to a sixteen-year-old boy, found that pornographic materials otherwise freely available to adults could become obscene if they were distributed to youth. In doing so, the court continued to develop an understanding defined, not only by the content of a publication, but also by matters of context, access, and the psychological capacities of the reader involved.

The court's shifting position on obscenity reflected the ways in which notions of childhood and adolescence were inflected by the expert discourses of psychology, psychoanalysis, and child development during the twentieth century. For example, the court was not unanimous in its support of the New York state law at stake in *Ginsberg v. New York*. However, as Heins has argued, William Brennan nonetheless justified upholding Ginsberg's conviction by cobbling together a rationale that pulled from a wide array of psychological research that provided "a patina of scientific respectability to arguments that censorship was necessary to the proper socialization of youth even if, at bottom, these arguments were no different from the more frankly ideological ones that had turned on Victorian attitudes."[19] While Heins sees no difference between Brennan and Comstock, it's important to note that the body of scientific knowledge available to the former was not available to the latter, whose desire to regulate obscenity derived explicitly from his Congregationalist faith.[20] In other words, Comstock wanted to burn the house to roast the pig, and the federal regulatory framework he helped to install set a singular standard for all readers, even if obscenity laws themselves were not uniformly enforced. In contrast, Brennan's turn to psychological research reflects the ways in which the twentieth-century disciplines of childhood studies and child development had reimagined the child, in Kathryn Bond Stockton's terms, as "a creature of *gradual growth* and *managed delay*": while adolescents were previously associated with periods of tumultuous change, shifts in obscenity law reflected a uniquely twentieth-century understanding that youth growing into adulthood required formalized education, legal protections, and other forms of management that could successfully ensure the continuity of the social order.[21]

The point wasn't necessarily to produce a rigidly conformist subject, but to produce a subject capable of responsibly enacting its freedoms in the space of a market whose wares included pornographic materials.

As a subject undergoing a process of psychosexual development that adults needed to carefully orchestrate, the child retained the potential to handle the sexually explicit materials the law currently forbade it. Until that moment, which was the same moment in which the child became an adult, the child needed to undergo the proper forms of education that would allow them to manage any unsettling effects that sexually explicit representations might solicit from their bodies at a later point in their life.[22] As Ian Hunter, David Saunders, and Dugald Williamson have argued, the child had yet to be schooled in the practice of "*biblio-erotics* or book sex," a term they have coined to describe "the ethical and literary techniques of conscience-formation" that in the eighteenth century were rerouted from the Christian pastoral through the technology of the book and the act of contemplative reading.[23] Thus, the deregulation of obscenity marked the ongoing subordination of sovereign power to a deployment of sexuality conducted through various institutions tasked with shaping readers' engagements with print. For those scholars, the way in which biblio-erotics was conceived in the US during the twentieth century particularly as a problem of subject formation is especially clear in the recommendations of *The Report of the Commission on Obscenity and Pornography* (1970), informally known as the Lockhart Report, which called for an end to blanket censorship and advocated for "a massive sex education effort" involving "government, schools, families, churches, health practices, citizens' groups and the media, working with people of all age groups and in all sectors of society."[24] Under this regime, the state needed to intervene only in those cases when someone consumed pornography inappropriately, such as in the public where its visibility offended others, or when a person who had not yet acquired the appropriate techniques of self-management nevertheless had access to it. Pornography was something that one had to grow into, where growth was understood as a process that concerned the interrelated biological, psychological, and ethical capacities of the subject.

While the US never adopted the recommendations of the Lockhart Report, the biblio-erotics at its core provides greater clarity as to why the legalization of pornography required the law to operate like a semipermeable membrane, allowing porn to pass freely to certain populations of adults while restricting its flow to youth and deviant adults. In the hands of someone deemed incapable of handling the excitations it produced, for example, porn might once more inflame the criminally pathological behavior of the convicted sex offender released on parole. The spread of a biblio-erotics was also of a piece with the emergence of ratings systems for films and in the labeling of pornographic materials as for "adults only," thereby providing booksellers some level of protection from prosecution should the materials accidentally fall into the wrong hands. It is also evident in concerns regarding the detrimental effects of accidental exposure in the form of controversial speech overheard on the radio or seen on TV, or encountered in advertisements on the way to or from school. In fact, fears regarding the presence of adult bookstores in urban neighborhoods played an important role in the redevelopment of urban spaces during the 1980s and 1990s. During that period, not only did politicians such as Jesse Helms lean on the rhetorical figure of imperiled youth in order to strengthen the regulatory powers of the Federal Communications Commission, but also a number of municipal governments passed zoning ordinances that relocated sex-related businesses from urban neighborhoods to the city's fringes, far away from schools, churches, and other spaces in which children were thought to congregate.[25] Enacted in the name of protecting both youth and the expressive freedoms of adults, such measures decimated many of the queer urban sex publics that not only had relied on pornography as a significant mediator but also facilitated significant forms of cross-class contact.

Politicians presented such regulations as an ostensible solution to the proliferation of pornography during the late twentieth century, yet the introduction of the commercial internet once more exacerbated fears about minors' premature exposure to porn. The internet, it seemed, provided access to obscene representations in ways that put radio and television to shame. Such fears found expression in a number of ways, but perhaps their clearest expression came in the controversial 1995 *Time* magazine cover story "Cyberporn," the subhead of which read "A new study shows how pervasive and wild it really is. Can we protect our kids—and free speech?" As Wendy Hui Kyong Chun has shown in her extensive discussion of the story and its sensationalist illustrations, the internet intensified concerns that children not only would stumble across pornographic images during their otherwise innocent browsing but also would become accessible to sexual predators who could now groom them from within the presumed safety of the home.[26] This fear was succinctly expressed in one illustration that depicted a male child peering into a room where a male figure stands, holding a computer monitor at crotch level, its screen lit up with an image of a lollipop. Both the article itself and its accompanying imagery conveyed the feeling that the regulatory mechanisms that had been installed during the 1970s and 1980s were quickly becoming obsolete as new information technologies found their away around and through the barriers enacted in order to protect the normal development of youth.

In the same year that "Cyberporn" appeared, legislators attempted to engineer a form of relativized access appropriate to the digital age with the short-lived Communications Decency Act (CDA) and the Child Online Protection Act (COPA), which replaced the CDA in 1998. At stake in each piece of legislation was a set of dueling visions of computers and the internet that figured each, on the one hand, as a vital means to facilitate collaboration, improve the efficiency of work, and enable forms of personal and democratic enterprise, and, on the other hand, as an oppressive surveillance tool infiltrating homes and workplaces and allowing perverts, hackers, and other malicious figures to organize themselves and flood the internet with obscene and destructive content. As Chun explains, both the CDA and subsequently COPA sought to reconcile these visions by commercializing pornography: they prohibited sites that allowed unrestricted access to porn while providing safe harbor for those that sequestered pornographic content behind credit card–based age-verification systems.[27] The implicit logic of early internet legislation thus connected youth as a subject imperiled by its rapid psychosexual development to a notion of youth as proto-economic agent, such that by the time the adolescent came into possession of a credit card he would also possess the appropriate ethical and cultural techniques of consciousness formation. In other words, the youth was no longer a youth but an adult. Of course, legislators overlooked the fact that many teenagers often have credit cards well before they became eligible voters and thus would easily bypass the new form of regulation. Nonetheless, the effectiveness of the CDA and COPA was moot. Neither piece of legislation survived challenge in the courts, yet they had enabled a demonstration of adults' willingness to enter their credit card information into online forms, thereby generating interest in the possibilities of e-commerce.

While the CDA and COPA encouraged the expansion of a market and infrastructure for online pornography, the subsequent invention of wirelessly networked digital devices further exacerbated the anxieties regarding the dangers that porn posed to youth. These anxieties key into the ways that laptops, tablets, and mobile phones have become, not only ubiquitous, but also integral to many contemporary youth cultures and subcultures. A key source of that anxiety lies in the fact that new media technologies enable youth to access, produce, and distribute sexually explicit representations of themselves and by themselves. In fact, youth's sexual media practices have intensified the sex panics of the previous decade while continuing to outpace the conceptual and disciplinary frameworks that adults have devised to contain the spread of pornography. As Amy Hasinoff has pointed out, state and regional authorities overwhelmingly respond to minors' production and sharing of sexually explicit media with the child pornography laws that

had been developed to prevent the abuse of minors at the hands of predatory pedophiles. The enforcement of such laws is also often highly classed
and racialized, with middle-class White minors more likely to face rehabilitative disciplinary measures while working-class minors, queer minors, and
minors of color are more likely to face legal prosecution and sex offender
registration.[28] Responses to teens' sexting practices are also gendered in
significant ways, such that adults explain girls' consensual sexting practices
in terms of low self-esteem, the hypnotic influence of popular culture, or the
unruly influence of hormones on girls' decision-making abilities.[29] Where
the problem for girls lies in their production and sharing of sexual representations, explains Hasinoff, "the sexual risks of digital media for adolescent
boys are more often imagined in terms of their access to pornography, not
their creation of it."[30] In other words, the problem for boys is not that they
will appear in pornography, but that they will become consumers of pornography before they possess the capacities to handle such images appropriately.

In ways that I have already suggested, the role that gender has played
in shaping adults' concerns over youths' access to pornography and other
forms of popular culture is not necessarily unique to the digital age. Fears
about the harms of the flash press and the erotic postcards of the mid-
nineteenth century as well as anxieties over the sexually suggestive comic
books and popular films of the early twentieth century took shape in terms
of the deviations they may cause within a boy's developing masculinity,
whether it be inducing dissipative acts of masturbation or seeding sexual
perversion. During the late twentieth century, antiporn critics employed
media effects research to argue that porn and other forms of sexually explicit
and violent media would socialize boys into those behaviors, yet as critics
have since shown, media effects researchers repeatedly failed to establish
a causal link between the consumption of particular representations and
changes in behavior.[31] Nonetheless, the fears motivating adults' desires to
pin down pornography's morally and psychologically corrosive effects have
not gone away. The latest iteration has taken shape in terms of the antiporn
activists' efforts to rescue adolescent boys from the scourge of porn addiction. Steeped in computer metaphors and neuroscientific terminology, porn
addiction discourse holds that the mix of pornography and digital technologies pose a serious threat to the adolescent boy's developing sexuality
because they can overload his brain with an endless flow of sexual stimuli,
which are so powerful that a boy becomes incapable of having sex with
another person. As *Time* magazine's April 11, 2016, cover story "Porn and the
Threat to Virility" reported, many young men were now finding that "their

sexual responses have been sabotaged because their brains were virtually marinated in porn when they were adolescents."[32]

As with media effects research before it, research on pornography addiction is scant, and what research does exist suffers from the conceptual vagueness and covert moralism that plagues the diagnoses of sex addiction and compulsory sexual behavior from which it derives.[33] While one can find reference to pornography addiction as early as the mid-1970s, it has grown in popularity over the past twenty years among antiporn feminists for whom online pornography provides evidence for the "pornification" of everyday life.[34] Such criticism echoes many of the arguments advanced by antiporn activists during the early 1980s, yet it also differs in that it construes porn as primarily a problem not for women but for male adolescents.[35] Making very, very liberal use of brain-imaging and animal studies of drug addiction, porn addiction discourse uses the cover of scientific "fact" to disguise profoundly cultural anxieties about normative masculinity and the male body. In contrast to an idealized body defined by strength, self-mastery, and impenetrability, porn addiction discourse imagines the body of the adolescent boy as highly porous and thus vulnerable to contamination by external agents. Like a toxic drug, the stream of digitally mediated pornographic images locks the boy into a seemingly endless hunt for images of "extreme sex," a term used to denote an array of representations that range from conventional gay porn or porn featuring trans performers to porn depicting scat play or bestiality.[36] Yet the content of the image also matters little beyond its capacity to signify as deviant, as the repeated act of searching, clicking, and masturbating is what "rewires" the boy's neuronal networks and alters the flow of neurotransmitters in his brain. Bypassing consciousness altogether, online porn penetrates the boy's flesh and corrodes his masculine potential by undermining its naturalized foundation in the very material stuff of his body.

THE SLUTS AND THE LIMITS OF COLLABORATIVE PRODUCTION

Another way to understand those fears of male youth transformed via access to porn may come in the form of Dennis Cooper's *The Sluts* (2004). While the novel barely predates the second wave of panics about minors' sexual media practices that occurred during the first two decades of the twenty-first century, it is nonetheless both thematically and formally concerned with the relation between youth and the risky pleasures of online pornography. The novel initially conveys this focus through its chapter structure and titles, each of which invokes some form of electronic or digitally mediated communication technology. Respectively titled "Site 1" and "Site 2," chapters 1 and 5 consist of reviews posted to a website dedicated to advertising and evaluating gay escorts, while the action of chapter 3, "Board," occurs on a discussion forum set away from the site's main review pages. Chapter 2 is titled "Ad," and chapter 4 is titled "Email, Fax." While the former details a series of classified advertisements and the conversations they generate, the latter consists of one side of a series of emailed and faxed messages exchanged between two of the novel's central characters. Taken together as a sequence, the chapters comprise a rhythmic structure that alternates between scenes of public, multiparticipant communication and instances of seemingly private, two-way communication; moreover, subsequent even- and odd-numbered chapters recall and modify the structure of the previous corresponding chapter, such that chapter 4 echoes chapter 2 and chapter 5 builds off chapter 3, which in turn elaborates on chapter 1. In formal terms, the result is something like a pair of intersecting narrative spirals, within which the novel's action develops through an iterative process of revision and accretion.

At the core of the novel is the elusive character Brad, an adolescent hustler who quickly becomes the focus of the reviews that users post to the site. In "Site 1," the reviews comprise a narrative about Brad's involvement with Brian, a wealthy sadist who has created an arrangement with Brad that exchanges material support for the ability to murder him at some future point. As Brian explains in his first post to the site: "Before you decide that I'm a saint, I should explain that my all time fantasy is to murder a boy during the sex act" (15). Owing to the fact that Brad "has an advanced inoperable brain tumor" from which he will die in "six months," Brian provides Brad with "the ideal situation" (15–16): in Brian's terms, a stable living situation, a chance to earn some money, and a means to avoid a protracted and painful death. Brian concludes his review by offering the site's users an opportunity to arrange their own special encounters with Brad. Thus, the rest of the first section unfolds as something akin to a detective plot, whereby the site's other users struggle to determine how much of Brian's story and the subsequent posts about Brad's sexual encounters and eventual death are true. Further complicating matters is a significant subplot regarding the possibility that Brad is Stevie Sexed, an HIV-positive gay porn star who turns up murdered in his San Diego apartment after attempting to meet Brad in person. Posts to the site eventually reveal that the murder of Stevie Sexed is unrelated to the Brad-Brian story, and the chapter concludes with the rapid deflation of the tension that the reviews have slowly built up to that point: Brian confesses that while his relationship with Brad was in many respects real, other elements, including Brad's brain tumor and his murder were fictional. Instead, following a violent fight between them, Brad left Brian, ending their relationship and breaking all contact with him.

In short, like the anxieties informing contemporary antiporn discourse, the novel's plot concerns all the terrible things that can happen to youth when they get caught up in pornography. To that end, the intrigue of the Brad-Brian relationship of chapter 1 provides the renewable structure for subsequent odd-numbered chapters, as each takes up the Brad-Brian saga and elaborates it with new characters and scenarios only to end in a similar experience of deflation, disappointment, and frustration. In chapter 3, "Board," the webmaster has migrated the discussion about Brad onto the site's message boards where it quickly becomes wrapped up in the possibility that Brad is in Portland, Oregon. The chapter's narrative develops around a series of rumors pertaining to Brad's arrest and imprisonment for arson after destroying the business of builtlikeatruck44, a user who claims to have offered shelter and employment to Brad only to have Brad violently turn on him. Brad is also rumored to be romantically involved with a woman named Elaine, yet Brian seemingly resurfaces on the message board in an effort to reestablish contact with Brad, in the process boasting that he has also murdered another hustler named Jimmy Taylor as well as a young boy. However, "Board," like "Site 1," concludes by calling the most sensational bits of its narrative into doubt. In this case, the reveal comes through the exposure of Zack Young, described by one user as a "brilliant" and "gorgeous" HIV-positive top recently fired from his job as a "high level software designer at IBM" (160–61), who has been posting to the message board under several pseudonyms—including as the infamous Brian—in order to develop and continue the story from "Site 1." As Zack explains, the murders were in fact carefully plotted fictions: "I'm just obsessed with the whole Brad/Brian/Stevie Sexed mythology like you guys. The difference is that I won't sit on the sidelines with my tongue hanging out" (163). What began as a series of reviews has become in "Board" a kind of collaborative and interactive pornographic narrative, which adapts and responds to other users' reviews and posts.

However, Zack's exposure at the end of chapter 3 does not bring an end to the Brad-Brian saga. "Site 2" replicates the Brad-Brian saga of "Site 1," yet it is revealed by the end of the novel that the individuals posing as Brad and Brian on "Site 2" are in fact Zack and another adolescent hustler named Thad. However, as the clients that Zack-as-Brian arranges for Thad-as-Brad become increasingly violent, Thad develops second thoughts about their arrangement and escapes from Zack. Nonetheless, Zack-as-Brad continues to post a number of fictional reviews to the site detailing an escalating series of violent encounters between clients and Brad, which culminate once more in the boy's alleged murder. Shortly thereafter, Zack commits suicide, but not before sending an email to the webmaster containing his suicide note and a confession that all but the first few reviews about Brad posted in "Site 2" were fakes, crafted by Zack utilizing a range of pseudonyms similar to his work on the site's message board. The final post, which concludes the novel, contains the content of Zack's email to the webmaster, which Zack had asked the webmaster to keep secret: "I ask if you would keep this email between you and me, if you don't mind. At least that way people reading these reviews will feel like they got what they wanted even if they aren't happy about how it played out" (262). By violating Zack's final wish for privacy, the webmaster exposes everything that has happened to Brad as a part of a collectively articulated fantasy, masterminded by Zack and enhanced by the opacity and speed of online discourse.

The particular form of collaborative writing the novel imagines closely resembles the interactive exchanges that characterize websites dedicated to the production of user-generated pornographic fiction. As both Mica Hilson and Susan Paasonen have shown, such sites cultivate modes of interactivity through an array of design features, including rating systems, contact information, and comment sections, all of which encourage readers and writers to engage one another in ways that have significant implications for the narratives published on the site. On Literotica, explains Paasonen, the review and comment features serve as a means to derive value judgments about stories, and many writers view their success online as an important transitional stage in a professionalization process that culminates with the move from digital publication into print.[37] However, as Hilson has demonstrated, the interactive qualities of websites dedicated to pornographic writing have also enacted significant changes in the genre itself by pushing writers away from long-form fiction and toward shorter, serialized narratives that they can rapidly alter in response to readers' suggestions, requests, and complaints; in addition, "some authors deliberately leave their stories unresolved, offering to continue only if reader feedback demands it, and even authors who write single-part stories with clear conclusions are sometimes persuaded to write a second installment."[38] While it's possible to find narratives online that employ conventional plots that find closure in the protagonist's adoption of a self-actualized gay identity, the interactivity of the online story archive has also promoted narratives uniquely shaped by internet media. "Thus, although it would be wrong to assume that the medium of online gay erotic fiction always determines the genre's content," concludes Hilson, "it is valuable to view these stories in the context of desiring exchanges and interactions between authors, readers, and website designers."[39]

While critics of Cooper's novel have not necessarily connected it to the interactive narrative forms of online pornographic writing, they have nonetheless understood the interactions between its characters in similar terms to those that Hilson finds in the story archives. In his reading of *The Sluts*, for example, Patrick Hayes has argued that the "virtual spaces" of Cooper's novel "create a mode of pornographic writing in which, protected by anonymity, men can collaboratively, or competitively, fantasize through the idiom of the erotic confessional," and that their the transgressive qualities "[violate] the normal ways in which the self is immersed in cultural values," thereby posing a challenge to normative masculinity.[40] Likewise, Diarmuid Hester has argued that the novel's take on the collaborative production of transgressive sexual fantasies reflects a fascination with creative communities that has defined much of Cooper's career, beginning with his transformative curation of the Beyond Baroque reading series in Los Angeles during the 1980s. "Returning to the idea of community in the wake of widespread digitalization," writers Hester, "*The Sluts* finds Cooper at work sketching a fictional blueprint for an online community, drawn together by intrigue and held together by the promise of sex or fame or an elusive brush with celebrity. [. . .] In *The Sluts*, Cooper explores the ways that one might effect the development of a network—a social formation where relations between members are nonhierarchical."[41] Moreover, Hester suggests, the novel's effort to imagine a nonhierarchical community served as a model for the blog that Cooper launched in 2006 and which for more than a decade served as a "home to a dynamic and rapidly expanding network of queer subcultural producers and consumers."[42]

Such readings highlight important dimensions of the collectivity imagined at is core, and in Hester's case, the ways in which new media technologies shaped Cooper's writing of *The Sluts*. At the same time, their celebratory takes derive from a partial analysis focused on the odd-numbered chapters, with little discussion of the even-numbered chapters or their relation to the broader narrative the novel unfolds. As a consequence, Brad, who serves as the users' obsessive focus, becomes little more than a specter that, as Timothy Baker describes, "is completely unknowable: he is a blank identity that can be filled both by himself and others."[43] Similarly, Hester describes Brad as a "void" that allows Cooper to reorient the reader's attention to the novel's collectivity.[44] These kinds of claims aptly capture how Brad's enigmatic quality stirs up a tempest of fantasies for the site's users, yet they overlook the extent to which such fantasies—even as they challenge the idea that one can obtain an unmediated relation to the world—nonetheless find purchase in the material bodies of adolescent boys. Thus, the online community portrayed in *The Sluts* differs from the fiction websites that Hilson and others have analyzed to the extent that its narrative functions beyond the boundaries of a virtual space sanctioned for fantasy.

Far from being "cutting-edge escapism," the reviews and messages posted to the novel's central website both drive and are driven by an informal economy of youthful gay hustlers and escorts. In fact, this is one major source of the novel's transgressive force: not only do the site users offer up fantasies of proto-pig sex, in which bodily boundaries are violated and fluids are liberally exchanged, but they also place at the center of those practices a passive subject, the adolescent boy, widely believed to be deeply imperiled by his exposure to queer adults, gay pornography, and the sex economy.

As Hester's critical biography of Cooper suggests, the novel's iterative structure reflects the writer's own interests in horizonal forms of sociability, for which a kind of queer adolescence itself serves as a crucial source of inspiration. That is not adolescence understood as a stage in a linearly organized developmental process but the condition of solipsistic insularity that defines the subject's inability to have an unmediated relation to the world.[45] However, while Cooperian adolescence seems to establish "solitude, non-relationality, and ego-centrism [as] fundamental features of subjective experience," the pornographically mediated collectivity at the core of *The Sluts* imagines how those features might define instead a form or mode of intersubjective relation, within which the users' transgressive chatter holds them together in a collectively articulated fantasy.[46] To that extent, the long-standing belief that pornography is simply a form of aesthetic immaturity would be a perversely apt description of users' collaborative fantasizing. Yet, perhaps in keeping with the ways that, as Hester claims, Cooper continually puts pressure on his own vision of adolescence, the novel pits its adolescent boys against that insular collectivity, as the minimally perceptible voices of the boys introduced through the even-numbered chapters regularly pierce the pornographic solitude of the website's users. In doing so, the novel's youth highlight how the inclusive exclusion of the adolescent has been a necessary condition for the gay pornographic counterpublic, and thereby obliquely suggesting at least one reason why such transgressive gay sociability will not live up to the political hopes invested in it without coming to terms with its enabling exclusions. While it's been easier to ignore such conditions in the era of print publishing, the internet and the myriad of problems it has created for regulators seeking to safeguard children has rendered them harder to ignore. Yet, it's that weakness that the youth of Cooper's novel relentlessly probe.

PIGLETS AND HUSTLERS

As I've mentioned, the novel's critique of pornographic sociability unfolds through the economy of youthful hustlers and escorts it introduces through the even-numbered chapters, "Ad" (chapter 2) and "Email, Fax" (chapter 4), which consists of electronic communications conducted elsewhere than on the central website. "Ad" consists of messages exchanged between Brian and a series of boys whom Brian plans to have sex with and then murder. In chapter 1, Brian confesses to having had "sex with a number of boys who were perfectly willing to be killed, but something always stopped me from going all the way" (16). Chapter 2 then comprises the record of those aborted attempts, yet the foreknowledge of their failure does little to alleviate the chapter's transgressive effects, which culminate in a recorded conversation between Brian and a man who arranges to "loan" him his cognitively impaired teenaged son for a hefty sum. "Email, Fax" replicates the theme of "Ad" in recounting how Thad initially came into contact with Zack. "Email, Fax" consists of only one side of a communicative exchange, providing readers with the increasingly desperate messages that Thad, then living on the street and using drugs, sends to the man whom he thinks is Brian. Unlike the chapters that position the reader as a lurker on the website, chapters 2 and 4 situate the reader as someone overhearing a series of otherwise private communications. In doing so, they contrast with the odd-numbered chapters not only in form but also by emphasizing how the adolescents have a fundamentally different relation than the adult men to the pornographic discourse that circulates on the website. Thus, *The Sluts* both foregrounds the deceptions of the signifier yet also suggests that they are always and inextricably in relation to some material world: Brad may be a void, yet he's not a purely surface effect disconnected from the real.

Established in part by the novel's alternating chapter structure, the sense of a world beyond the fantasies spun out of the website helps to set up a familiar critique of the men who regularly use the site. At best, such men are so wrapped up in their fantasies that they fail to see the ways in which the boys and young men they hire comprise a precarious class of vulnerable and therefore easily exploitable youth. At worst, the men get off on the deliberate power they exercise over such hustlers and escorts. This critique targets characters such as Brian and reviewers such as llbean, whose username evokes the recreational clothing and sporting goods brand marketed to middle-class outdoorsmen yet which contrasts jarringly with the content of his posts: "I personally like my boys a little lived in. I met him at the door with a bottle of Jack Daniels, and he just took off the cap, and chugged about half of it down while I stripped him. He has a very tight, adolescent looking body with long, skinny arms and legs, and the smallest ass and about twelve pubic hairs. The earlier review stated Brad was spooky, and he has some mental problems for sure, but I'm not into being some kid's father, so I could care less" (6). llbean's botched rejection of a fatherly role bespeaks the ways in which Brad's vulnerabilities do not detract from the sex but instead enhance his appeal. Thus, instead of involving Brad in hunting, fishing, or other conventionally masculine outdoor pursuits, llbean handcuffs Brad to the bed and buries "bigger and bigger dildos in his ass" (6).

Of course, not all reviewers who post to the message board emulate llbean's cold instrumentalization of Brad, and some seem to express genuine concern for Brad's well-being. For example, immediately following llbean's review is one by JoseR72 in which he admonishes the website's users for taking advantage of someone in need: "Brad is one of the cutest twinks I've ever seen in fact. I don't know how a boy as cute and young as Brad ended up in the low end of his profession, but it's wrong to exploit him. He deserves better" (8). In doing so, JoseR72 gives voice to the critique a reader might direct at users like Brian and llbean. To that end, he concludes by explaining that he has set Brad up "in an outpatient program": "He is no longer at the phone number posted here and with any luck, you have heard the last of him. Shame on you" (8–9). Yet JoseR72's fatherly scold is immediately undercut by a follow-up post from Brad: "This guy's a fucking prick. I don't need help. He's a liar. I'm writing this on his computer. What does that tell you?" (9). Those interruptions provide one significant source of the novel's underappreciated humor, and Brad's cuttingly funny remark exposes JoseR72's concern for what it is: another form of control conducted under the guise of care. While precarious and vulnerable to exploitation, Brad also resists users' efforts to manage or control his actions, leading even Brian, who otherwise appears as a kind of wealthy master figure, to denounce his former lover as "a pathological liar and control freak who has no morality whatsoever. His only goal in life is to be desired and worshipped, and he'll do whatever it takes to addict men to him. He took me to psychological places I should never have gone, and pushed me to do things to him that no one should ever do to another human being" (64–65). Brad isn't simply the vulnerable teen addicted to drugs and sex, but also the dangerously addictive substance that repeatedly undermines Brian's pretense of mastery.

At once vulnerable and threatening, the resistance that Brad manifests to efforts at recovery or correction caution against reading his situation simply in terms of exploitation. Even within llbean's review, Brad seemingly expresses a responsiveness to his john's erotic torments: "It was clear that he could have gone on all night if I wanted" (6). Such reports about Brad are unsettling in part because they represent a queer youth who is in deliberate pursuit of what the professional porn performer Ty Mitchell has termed an "adult gay sex *life*."[47] In a review essay for the *New Inquiry*, Mitchell attempts to do justice to the ambivalence of "gay boyhood" through a series of brief autobiographical reflections on his own experiences of "gay male intimacy across stark differences of age, power, and money."[48] In doing so, Mitchell speaks to the desire of some queer youth to turn to older gay men in order to participate in an erotic world from which they have been formally excluded and over which they have little control. Mitchell's account overlooks how that exclusion in part constructs the categories of youth and adult, yet he nonetheless captures a significant set of conflicting conditions. The production of the gay boy renders him vulnerable to forms of cultivated dependency and physical abuse, yet such situations also become powerful figures for the kinds of eroticism the boy desires. In that context, an "adult gay sex life" does not mean mutualistic sex practices or romantic coupling, but sex that seeks to capture the kinds of unseemly fantasies illuminated within gay pornographic writing and BDSM practices, and so often associated with the ego-annihilating pleasure of self-shattering or, in the twenty-first century, the sticky porosities of pig sex. To be sure, the gay boy "doesn't want to die; he just wants to be undone." The dirty secret of "gay boyhood," Mitchell concludes, is that "we eagerly seek out pleasure alongside danger, that when a man gives it to us we feel shame and remorse unevenly, and that we are still blameless for all of it."[49]

In ways that echo Stockton's own analysis of queer children, Mitchell claims that the dirty secret of gay boyhood is "only available to us from the voice of the boy himself, a voice only intelligible in fiction and memoir."[50] Mitchell's essay provides a set of terms to understand Brad and the other boys who appear in Cooper's novel, including the troubling collection of anonymous boy voices that appear in chapter 2 in classified advertisements and in the transcripts of recorded exchanges with Brian. For example, in the first exchange of the chapter, between Brian and juicyLAboy, whose ad reads "Cute, slim, euro trash bottom, 19, 5' 10", 155 lbs, brown hair, blue eyes. Hot, deep, butt and mouth. Out only. $250 hr./$700 overnight. Will do anything for a price. No limits" (69), Brian attempts to gain juicy-LAboy's "permission" to kill him for $5,000 without being explicit about his desires, yet the prospect seems to appeal to the boy.

[Brian] **Do you want to explain the "no limits" thing?**
[juicyLAboy] Yeah, um . . . There's just nothing I won't do, I guess.
Nothing?
Not for $5000.
Okay.
I'm strange.
How so?
How so? Because I'm a slut.
It'll be heavy.
Really? I mean I don't care. (73)

Arranged as a series of alternating lines of dialogue with Brian's lines set off in bold, the exchange is troubling because it is immediately clear that Brian and the boy are speaking at cross-purposes, even as they go on to articulate together a fantasy of sadistic domination. While the events in chapter 2 take place chronologically prior to those in chapter 1, the placement of "Ad" after "Site 1" enhances that sense of miscommunication as the reader is already aware of Brian's history with Brad. The substantial sum of money that Brian offers maintains the boy's interest, even as Brian later ominously explains that he will "have to give it to charity" (74). However, the boy also feels out his own desires through the fantasy, attracted by the sense of danger and power that accrues to Brian. "I have a sick sense of humor too," the boy explains at one point during the exchange, yet perhaps the most significant moment is his self-identification as "a slut" (73). To treat these expressions as *merely* an effort for the boy to meet his needs too hastily overlooks the possibility that they are also at the same time genuine expressions of erotic curiosity or, in other words, a desire to become a pig.

In fact, more sophisticated ethical and political critiques of sex across significant power differentials become possible when one recognizes the possibility that the boy is driven by both need and desire rather than need alone. When Mitchell describes the gay boy as blameless, he crucially refrains from disavowing the boy's erotic autonomy. Instead, he recognizes that what is at stake between the boy and the adult is a relation, yet the boy is nonetheless composed through that relation as a kind of precarious life situated at the center of a contemporary mode of gay male sociality. To put that point differently, Mitchell and Cooper highlight the extent to which the adolescent boy, while marginalized in the sense of lacking resources and access to the institutions of law, provides a key element within a commercially mediated network of social relations. Calling the boy's actions "sex work," Mitchell explains, "misses the point—this not about going to work" and all the agency such activity might entail. Rather, "it's about running from home," a partially calculated escape from the oppressive strictures of normative childhood that establishes the gay boy as a form of what Preciado calls naked technolife. In contrast to the concept of bare or naked life developed by Giorgio Agamben, which imagines the biopolitical subject as "reduced to existing only physically and stripped of all legal status and citizenship," naked technolife lies at the center of "postindustrial democracies, forming part of a global, integrated multimedia laboratory-brothel, where the control of affect begins under the pop form of excitation-frustration."[51] Situated at the limit of the sphere of rights, protections, and privileges unevenly distributed among adult citizens, the boy becomes a biopolitical subjectivity through his insertion within the relations of power and pleasure that compose the digitally mediated economy of the novel's website.

Understood in terms of Preciado's naked technolife, juicyLAboy's self-description as a slut serves at once as an enticing boast and as a name for the various kinds of biopolitical subjectivity produced in the contemporary moment. The slutty teenaged boy, the piglet, comprises an inverse figure of the porn addict, for whom the transgressive erotic experiences generated through online pornography require, not only the renormalization of his desire, but also a multitude of networked technological supports aimed at the correct cultivation of his pleasures: after all, as one prominent spokesman for recovered porn addicts assures us, "quitting porn is one of the most sex-positive things people can do."[52] Yet while porn addiction discourse construes the boy as powerless before the image that corrupts him, Cooper's novel recognizes a mode of resistance available to the boy-slut whose desires were never "normal" to begin with. Brad, Brian complains, is like a drug who gets men hooked on him, yet perhaps the best example is Jimmy Taylor, the hustler whom Zack-as-Brian claims to have murdered in chapter 3. As with Brad's response to JoseR72, Jimmy posts to the message board, viciously deflating the users' fantasies: "I was gonna let you faggots stew in your sick juices, but it's too fucking hilarious" (152–53). In "Site 2," Jimmy returns to the board threatening to expose Zack's scam, then does so anyway even after Zack pays Jimmy $3,000 in hush money. "Never trust a whore," Jimmy admonishes the site's users: "Didn't your mothers ever tell you that?!" (249). My point here is not that Jimmy and Brad are revolutionary subjects; rather each of these characters embody a young slut or piglet working against the biopolitical controls shaping normative adolescence.

To put that point another way, Brad and Jimmy only ever appear at the edges of the narrative, yet they are nonetheless central to its action. To that extent, the novel formalizes the mutually constitutive relation between adolescence, and in particular male adolescence, and pornography. Adults' ability to consume the latter depends on the exclusive inclusion of the former, who not only should not appear in porn because of the potentially traumatic effects, but who has also not yet acquired the biblio-erotics necessary to cope with the desires and fantasies such texts may generate. If the predatory pornographer looms as an external threat, then porn addiction persists as an internal one. While the adolescent boy's liminal status enables the adult's free consumption of porn, it also invests the boy with an enigmatic intensity: it is precisely the vaguely apprehended truth of Brad's background or Jimmy's cold elusiveness that renders them sources of erotic fascination for the site's adult participants, stoking their fantasies about what could be and thus energizing rounds of pornographic chatter. In the process, Jimmy and Brad become fantastic boys with no limits. In Brad's case, the site's partic- ipants can repeatedly subject him to an escalating series of torments that open up the boundaries separating his insides from the outside world. Yet, after each death he returns, seemingly indifferent to the prospect of either stopping or continuing for another round. In Jimmy's case, he taunts his prospective clients by boasting about his big dick, even bigger libido, and a willingness to do anything—for the right price. To that end, Jimmy is per- haps not so much a piglet but a hustler, who turns to his advantage, as much as he is able, a set of communicative and economic relations that excludes his participation but nonetheless uses his image and the images of others to keep users hooked.

While not a central concern of this book, the material relations informing the creation of pornography has come up repeatedly in the preceding chap- ters, and the history of gay pornographic writing, as well as of pornographic writing in general, may have something crucial to tell us about the histori- cal processes shaping contemporary modes of artistic production. As both Jimmy portends and Mitchell's book review suggests, online pornography provides both direct and indirect means to market a variety of cultural prod- ucts to consumers, many of whom are now more likely to recognize Mitch- ell's name than Cooper's. However, that practice has its own long history, stretching back through Scott O'Hara's publication of excerpts from Samuel Delany's *The Mad Man*, Steward's promotion of *City of Night* in *Der Kreis*, or even Ed Franklin's praise of William Carney's *The Real Thing* on the pages of *Drummer* magazine. To that extent, the relations between the literary and the pornographic may serve as another useful site to consider what Lee Konstantinou has recently termed "Mass High Culture, in which ever more cultural practices reconfigure themselves as, or imagine themselves to be, arts," and whose cultural ascendance over the past fifty years may reflect a broader reconfiguration in the relations between the work of art and the operations of capital in the neoliberal era.[53] Neither Konstantinou nor the contributors included in his special dossier on the "seven neo-liberal arts" make much mention of pornography or its high-minded cousin "erotic lit- erature," yet the effort to bring pornography up and out of the muck has been a recurrent theme within the pornographic counterpublics of the late twentieth century and, arguably, within the broader history of contempo- rary US fiction. It's been my hope that this book will help provide one part of the story of how we arrived here and thus provide some sense, however crude, of what the future might hold.

Acknowledgments

So much of the work of writing a book entails the learning of how to write a book. Thankfully, I have benefited from the wisdom, assistance, and support of a number of talented people. First and foremost, I owe a deep debt to the amazing librarians and archivists who have assisted me in my research. I'd like to thank the staff at the Bancroft Library at the University of California, Berkeley; the Beinecke Rare Book and Manuscript Library at Yale University; the Human Sexuality Collection at Cornell University; the Kinsey Institute for Research in Sex, Gender, and Reproduction at Indiana University, Bloomington; the Leather Archives and Museum of Chicago, which awarded me a travel grant to conduct some of my early research in its archives; and the San Francisco Public Library. Special mention goes to Mel Leverich at the Leather Archives and Museum for her tireless research support. In fact, Mel's assistance was crucial as I worked to complete the manuscript revisions just as the spread of the novel coronavirus forced the California State University system to close down the majority of its campus operations, which made conducting last-minute research and the collecting of illustrations an interesting challenge. In any case, when it's safe to do so, I hope to return to the museum soon in order to thank y'all personally.

For their dialogue and encouragement, I would like to thank Elizabeth Adan, Leah Benedict, Brad Campbell, Loren Glass, Tavi Gonzalez, Graham Hammill, Ryan Hatch, Jayanta Hegde, Lizzie Lamore, Jane Lehr, Marcus McCann, Mireille Miller-Young, Emily Ryalls, Melissa Schindler, William Solomon, Catherine Waitinas, Roberta Wolfson, and Cynthia Wu. Many thanks to John Stadler for organizing the panel "The Pornographic and the Literary" at the 2016 Modern Language Association's annual convention, and thanks as well as to my fellow panelists Kathleen Lubey and Penelope Meyers Usher for their stimulating conversation. Similarly, Bri Watson organized the "Indigenous Obscenities and National Pornographies in America, 1940–90" panel at the Society for the History of Reading and Publishing's annual conference in 2019. The conversations I had with Jordan S. Carroll during that long weekend in Amherst, Massachusetts, were some of the most generative I've had in recent memory. Bernard Welt provided both encouraging words and last-minute assistance in securing permissions for many of the images in the book. At the California Polytechnic State University, San Luis Obispo, a number of students have contributed to this project in ways big and small. As my research assistants, Ares Bartell and Autumn Ford supplied crucial support for my research and manuscript preparations. From afar, David Squires served as my primary interlocutor and, dare I say, cheerleader throughout the writing process. Tim Dean remains both the most perceptive critic of my work and its most tireless supporter. His guidance played a central role in the development of this project, and his friendship helped me to complete it.

Speaking of completing things: At the University of Chicago Press, Alan Thomas and Randy Petilos deftly stewarded the manuscript through the approval process and then through publication. They also managed to locate two anonymous readers who not only read the manuscript but also crafted thoughtful reports just as the pandemic was ramping up in the spring of 2020. Thank you, whoever you are, for helping this book to become the best version of itself that it could possibly be. While Alan and Randy helped to get this book into print, it was Doug Mitchell who gave me the opportunity to try. I had the pleasure of meeting him in person only once, when he treated me and two other young scholars to dinner at a small Italian restaurant in Los Angeles, but his encouraging emails kept me writing when I needed them the most. I didn't know Doug nearly as well as many of the other scholars who had worked with him, but I am deeply thankful for the contact that I did have with him. Finally, I would like to thank Mark Reschke for the attention and care he devoted to the manuscript during the copyediting process.

· · ·

An earlier version of chapter 2 appeared under the title "The Law of Pornography: John Rechy and Samuel Steward" in the volume *Samuel Steward and the Pursuit of the Erotic*, edited by Debra A. Moddelmog and Martin Joseph Ponce, and published in 2017. Parts of chapter 4 appeared in an earlier version in *Porn Archives*, edited by Tim Dean, Steven Ruszczycky, and David

Squires (Durham, NC: Duke University Press, 2014), as "Stadler's Boys; or, The Fictions of Child Pornography." Finally, thank you Billy Miller for permission to reproduce images from Boyd McDonald's zine *Straight to Hell* and to the John Hay Library at Brown University for allowing me to reproduce the two maps from Scott O'Hara's journal *Steam*.

Notes

INTRODUCTION

1. Samuel Steward, *The Lost Autobiography of Samuel Steward: Recollections of an Extraordinary Twentieth-Century Gay Life*, ed. Jeremy Mulderig (Chicago: University of Chicago Press, 2018), 247.

2. Loren Glass, *Counterculture Colophon: Grove Press, "The Evergreen Review," and the Incorporation of the Avant-Garde* (Stanford, CA: Stanford University Press, 2013).

3. Charles Rembar, *The End of Obscenity: The Trials of "Lady Chatterley," "Tropic of Cancer," and "Fanny Hill" by the Lawyer Who Defended Them* (New York: Harper and Row Publishers, 1968).

4. Allison Pease, *Modernism, Mass Culture, and the Aesthetics of Obscenity* (Cambridge: Cambridge University Press, 2000).

5. Pease, 50–64.

6. In addition to Pease, see Florence Dore, *The Novel and the Obscene: Sexual Subjects in American Modernism* (Stanford, CA: Stanford University Press, 2005).

7. For an account of this history, see Rachel Potter, *Obscene Modernism: Literary Censorship and Experiment, 1900–1940* (Oxford: Oxford University Press, 2014), 153–73.

8. Elizabeth Ladenson, *Dirt for Art's Sake: Books on Trial from "Madame Bovary" to "Lolita"* (New York: Cornell University, 2007). Glass, *Counterculture Colophon*, 104–9.

9. Steven Marcus, *The Other Victorians: A Study of Sexuality and Pornography in Mid-Nineteenth-Century England* (New Brunswick, NJ: Transaction, 2009), 286.

10. Pease, *Modernism*, xi.

11. Phil Andros, *San Francisco Hustler* (San Francisco: Gay Parisian Press, 1970), 52–53.

12. Lynn Hunt, "Introduction: Obscenity and the Origins of Modernity, 1500–1800," in *The Invention of Pornography: Obscenity and the Origins of Modernity, 1500–1800*, ed. Lynn Hunt (New York: Zone Books, 1993), 23.

13. Quoted in Justin Spring, *Secret Historian: The Life and Times of Samuel Steward, Professor, Tattoo Artist, and Sexual Renegade* (New York: Farrar, Straus, Giroux, 2010), 181.

14. John D'Emilio, *Sexual Politics, Sexual Communities: The Making of a Homosexual Minority in the United States, 1950–1970*, 2nd ed. (Chicago: University of Chicago Press, 1998), 136.

15. Michael Bronski, *Pulp Friction: Uncovering the Golden Age of Gay Male Pulps* (New York: St. Martin's Griffin, 2003), 9.

16. Roger Austen, *Playing the Game: The Homosexual Novel in America* (New York: Bobbs-Merrill, 1977), 219.

17. Larry Townsend, "Plight of Gay Novelists: Who Gauges Market Correctly, Publishers or Writers?," *Advocate*, August 19, 1970, reprinted in Richard Amory, *Song of the Loon*, ed. Michael Bronski (Vancouver: Arsenal Pulp Press, 2005), 236.

18. Samuel M. Steward. "Erotica—the Purest Form of Entertainment," *Gay News* 5, no. 21 (August, 7–20, 1981): 26.

19. John Rechy, *My Life and the Kept Woman: A Memoir* (New York: Grove Press, 2008), 341.

20. Michael Lowenthal, "Introduction: Beyond Porn: Sex, Confession, and Honesty," in *Flesh and the Word 4*, ed. Michael Lowenthal (New York: Plume Books, 1997), xii.

21. Lowenthal, xii.

22. Lowenthal, xv.

23. Allen appears to have envisioned the production of an edited collection on the subject of Eros featuring the writers he had contacted, but archival documents suggest that the project never went further than his brief correspondence. Letter from Donald Allen to Samuel Delany, March 22, 1983, Donald Allen Correspondence Regarding Eros, 1983, James C. Hormel Gay and Lesbian Center, San Francisco Public Library. All citations of correspondence in this paragraph are from this collection.

24. Michael Rumaker, March 31, 1983.

25. Samuel Steward, "A Personal Letter on Erotica from the Bishop of Andros," n.d. Steward's letter to Allen comprised a revised version of his thoughts about gay pornographic writing printed in *Gay News* two year prior and contains a far less pessimistic take on the future of gay pornographic writing than he had expressed in that earlier version.

26. Pat Califia, n.d. I do my best to respect Califia's chosen name throughout this book, and in instances when I refer to "Pat" and not "Patrick," I do so in reference to the name as it appears on the archival documents from which I have constructed my history.

27. Samuel Delany, "Notes for the D.A.," March 26, 1983.

28. David Bergman, "The Cultural Work of Sixties Gay Pulp Fiction," in *The Queer Sixties*, ed. Patricia Juliana Smith (New York: Routledge, 1999). Bronski, *Pulp Frictions*. Christopher Nealon, *Foundlings: Lesbian and Gay Historical Emotion before Stonewall* (Durham, NC: Duke University Press, 2001). Susan Stryker, *Queer Pulp: Perverted Passions from the Golden Age of the Paperback* (San Francisco: Chronicle Books, 2001).

29. Whitney Strub, "Historicizing Pulp: Gay Male Pulp and the Narrativization of

Queer Cultural History," in *1960s Gay Pulp Fiction: The Misplaced Heritage*, ed.
Drewey Wayne Gunn and Jaime Harker (Amherst: University of Massachusetts
Press, 2013), 43–77. David K. Johnson, *Buying Gay: How Physique Entrepreneurs
Sparked a Movement* (New York: Columbia University Press, 2019). Martin
Meeker, *Contacts Desired: Gay and Lesbian Communications and Community,
1940s–1970s* (Chicago: University of Chicago Press, 2006).

30. Strub, "Historicizing Pulp," 71–72.

31. Drewey Wayne Gunn and Jamie Harker, "Introduction," in Gunn and Harker,
1960s Gay Pulp Fiction, 16.

32. "One advantage of this understanding of genre," Poovey explains, "is that it
enables us to view each text both as a member of a larger set (its genre) and in
relation to other texts produced at the same time that belong to other genres.
Another advantage is that it enables us to see that genres change: as the social
function of a particular genre changes, the hierarchy of its features and its relation
to other genres change too. Then, too, this model of genre allows us to understand the various genres produced at any given time as themselves hierarchically
arranged in relation to each other." Mary Poovey, *Genres of the Credit Economy:
Mediating Value in Eighteenth- and Nineteenth-Century Britain* (Chicago: University of Chicago Press, 2008), 421–22.

33. Samuel R. Delany, *The Mad Man* (New York: Richard Kasak Books, 1997), xiii.

34. Ross Chambers, *Untimely Interventions: AIDS Writing, Testimonial, and the Rhetoric of Haunting* (Ann Arbor: University of Michigan Press, 2004), 24–25.

35. Chambers, 33.

36. In the introduction to her study of race and Black pleasure in pornographic film
and video, Jennifer Nash provides a thorough and concise summary of this history, which helpfully highlights the contributions that different feminist critics
have made to contemporary understandings of porn, even as the stark limitations
in their respective approaches, and in Nash's case as those limitations pertain specifically to the often merely rhetorical deployment of race, have motivated porn
scholars to revisit the question of pornographic representation. See Jennifer Nash,
The Black Body in Ecstasy: Reading Race, Reading Representation (Durham, NC:
Duke University Press, 2014), 9–21.

37. Laura Kipnis, *Bound and Gagged: Pornography and the Politics of Fantasy in America* (Durham, NC: Duke University Press, 1999), 196.

38. Elizabeth Cowie, "Pornography and Fantasy: Psychoanalytic Perspectives," in
Sex Exposed: Sexuality and the Pornography Debate, ed. Lynne Segal and Mary
McIntosh (London: Virgo Press, 1992), 136.

39. Kipnis, *Bound and Gagged*, 167.

40. Tim Dean, *Unlimited Intimacy: Reflections on the Subculture of Barebacking* (Chicago: University of Chicago Press, 2009).

41. Ricky Varghese, ed., *Raw: PrEP, Pedagogy, and the Politics of Barebacking*
(Regina: University of Regina Press, 2019).

42. Dean, *Unlimited Intimacy*, 94–95. While the phrase "the traffic in women" comes
from Gayle Rubin's landmark essay on the subject, Eve Kosofsky Sedgwick
provided the first detailed analysis of the ways in which kinship between men frequently depends on sublimating homosocial desire through the bodies of women.
See Eve Kosofsky Sedgwick, *Between Men: English Literature and Male Homo-*

social Desire (New York: Columbia University Press, 1985). Gayle Rubin, "The Traffic in Women: Notes on the 'Political Economy' of Sex," in *Feminist Anthropology: A Reader*, ed. Ellen Lewin (Malden, MA: Blackwell Publishing, 2006), 87–106.

43. This is particularly true for the branch of gay porn studies that originates out of Thomas Waugh and Richard Dyer's early writing on gay porn for the journal *Jump Cut*. See Thomas Waugh, "Men's Pornography: Gay vs. Straight," *Jump Cut: A Review of Contemporary Cinema* 30 (1985): 30–36, and in the same issue Dyer, "Male Gay Porn," 27–29. Thomas Waugh, *Hard to Imagine: Gay Male Eroticism in Photography and Film from Their Beginnings to Stonewall* (New York: Columbia University Press, 1996). John Mercer, *Gay Pornography: Representations of Sexuality and Masculinity* (London: I. B. Taurus, 2017). John Mercer, ed., "Gay Porn Now!," *Porn Studies* 4, no. 2 (2017). Mercer's special issues samples the cutting edge of gay porn studies and features essays pertaining to a wide variety of media—except writing and print. In that, it reflects the general orientation of the journal *Porn Studies*, whose essays consist primarily of social scientific studies of photographic media, primarily film and video.

44. Lucas Hilderbrand, "Historical Fantasies: 1970s Gay Male Pornography in the Archives," in *Porno Chic and the Sex Wars: American Sexual Representation in the 1970s*, ed. Carolyn Bronstein and Whitney Strub (Amherst: University of Massachusetts Press, 2016), 327–46. Earl Jackson Jr. *Strategies of Deviance: Studies in Gay Representation* (Bloomington: Indiana University Press, 1995). Darieck Scott, "Porn and the N-Word: Lust, Samuel Delany's *The Mad Man*, and a Derangement of Body and Sense(s)," in *Extravagant Abjection: Blackness, Power, and Sexuality in the African American Literary Imagination* (New York: New York University Press, 2010): 204–56. While not a study of gay pornographic writing per se, Constance Penley's inspiring work on slash fiction has much to offer that project, as well as the broader project of expanding the field of porn studies beyond its near-exclusive focus on the image. See Constance Penley, *NASA/TREK: Popular Science and Sex in America* (New York: Verso, 1997).

45. Michael Davidson, *Guys Like Us: Citing Masculinity in Cold War Politics* (Chicago: University of Chicago Press, 2004), 16.

46. Glass, *Counterculture Colophon*, 123–28.

47. Jordan S. Carroll, "White-Collar Masochism: Grove Press and the Death of the Managerial Subject," *Twentieth Century Literature* 64, no. 1 (March 1, 2018): DOI: 10.1215/0041462X-4387677.

48. Glass, *Counterculture Colophon*, 127.

49. Peter Buitenhuis, "Nightmares in the Mirror," *New York Times*, June 30, 1963, 68. Throughout this book, I employ bracketed ellipses to indicate where I have omitted material from quotations for the sake of clarity and concision. I have done so only when I believe that such omissions do not alter the meaning of the original passage in any significant way.

50. Alfred Chester, "Fruit Salad," *New York Review of Books*, June 1, 1963. 6.

51. Chester, 6.

52. Merve Emre, *Paraliterary: The Making of Bad Readers in Postwar America* (Chicago: University of Chicago Press, 2017), 10.

53. Michael Trask provides a detailed examination of the ways different classes of

public intellectuals drew associations between effeminate male homosexuality and a willingness to engage in flights of fantasy in *Camp Sites: Sex, Politics, and Academic Style in Postwar America* (Stanford, CA: Stanford University Press, 2013).

54. Martin Levine, *Gay Macho: The Life and Death of the Homosexual Clone* (New York: New York University Press, 1998), 57.

55. Johnson, *Buying Gay*, 226.

56. Benedict Anderson, *Imagined Communities: Reflections on the Origins and Spread of Nationalism* (New York: Verso Books, 1983), 24.

57. Michael Warner, *The Letters of the Republic: Publication and the Public Sphere in Eighteenth-Century America* (Cambridge, MA: Harvard University Press, 1990), 63.

58. The term "imagined community" was also important for Kath Weston's study of how print and televisual representations of urban homosexuality fueled the "Great Gay migration" of the 1970s. As popular representations of urban homosexuality began to proliferate, Weston argues, they fostered a gay imaginary in which readers recognized their desires as something that tied them to an imaginary community of sexual minorities thriving in the nearest metropolis. While cities rarely turned out to be the queer utopias that readers often initially imagined them to be, their depiction as such helped to drive large numbers of sexual and gender minorities from rural areas to cities in search of others just like them. Kath Weston, "Get Thee to a Big City: Sexual Imaginary and the Great Gay Migration," *GLQ: A Journal of Gay and Lesbian Studies* 2, no. 3 (1995): 253–77. For a concise discussion of the ongoing relevance of Weston's work, see Karen Tongson and Scott Herring, "The Sexual Imaginarium: A Reappraisal," *GLQ: A Journal of Gay and Lesbian Studies* 25, no. 1 (2019): 51–56.

59. These critiques are collected in Craig Calhoun, ed., *Habermas and the Public Sphere* (Cambridge, MA: MIT Press, 1992).

60. Eric O. Clarke, *Virtuous Vice: Homoeroticism and the Public Sphere* (Durham, NC: Duke University Press, 2000). Michael Warner and Lauren Berlant, "Sex in Public," in *Publics and Counterpublics* (Zone Books: New York 2002), 187–208.

61. Michael Warner, "Publics and Counterpublics," in *Publics and Counterpublics*, 114.

62. It is important to stress the idea of "participation" here because, as Warner suggests, publics are not describable in terms of demography. Instead, they refer to imaginary projections constituted through expression, address, and language use. Thus, it is possible to participate in a counterpublic at one moment and in the dominant public the next. Warner, "Public and Private," 57.

63. Warner, "Publics and Counterpublics," 122.

64. In framing my own approach to these terms, I am inspired by the following statement from Darieck Scott, which appears in the introduction to his anthology of Black gay pornographic writing: "I cannot claim—I will disclaim—that there is anything about this collection that should be construed as 'revolutionary.'" And yet, "these jack-off stories begin to hint at the ways that pleasure is or can be political—even if the politics aren't 'correct' and maybe aren't recognizable in standard understandings of the political—and how pleasure can be found in circumstances politically defined as limited, disempowering, even degrading." Darieck Scott, "Introduction: Black Gay Pornotopias; or, When We Were Sluts," in *Best Black Gay Erotica* (San Francisco: Cleis Press, 2005), xi.

65. João Florêncio, *Bareback Porn, Porous Masculinities, Queer Futures: The Ethics of Becoming Pig* (New York, Routledge: 2020).

CHAPTER ONE

1. Gayle Rubin, "The Leather Menace: Comments on Politics and S/M," in *Sexual Revolution*, ed. Jeffery Escoffier (New York: Thunder's Mouth Press, 2003): 266–99.
2. Michael Warner, "Public and Private," 58.
3. For a concise history of the gay leather subculture in the Folsom area of San Francisco, see Rubin, "Sites, Settlements, and Urban Sex," in *Archaeologies of Sexuality*, edited by Robert Schmidt and Barbara Voss (London: Routledge, 2000), 62–88. Levine describes the influence of leather-centric BDSM on the rise of the gay macho social identity during the late 1970s. Levine, *Gay Macho*, 95–96. Peter Hennen offers a concise history in *Faeries, Bears, and Leathermen: Men in Community Queering the Masculine* (Chicago: University of Chicago Press, 2008), 136–44.
4. Hennen, *Faeries, Bears, and Leathermen*, 8.
5. Preston, "Introduction," in *The Leatherman's Handbook*, by Larry Townsend (Beverly Hills, CA: L. T. Publications, 1993). On the proliferation of leather styles, see Gayle Rubin, "Old Guard, New Guard," accessed July 2, 2016, http://www.evilmonk.org/a/grubin.cfm.
6. Davidson, *Guys Like Us*.
7. As this chapter will explore, I take this phrase as a recasting of Susan Sontag's observation that pornography is uninterested in the person in terms of "a certain state of her will" using a specifically gay idiom. Susan Sontag, "The Pornographic Imagination," in *Styles of Radical Will* (New York: Faber, Straus and Giroux, 1969), 53.
8. Townsend, *The Leatherman's Handbook*, 256.
9. "Homosexuality in America," *Life*, June 26, 1964. 66.
10. Lee Edelman, *Homographesis: Essays in Gay Literary and Cultural Theory* (New York: Routledge, 1994), 154.
11. Paul Welch, "The 'Gay' World Takes to the City Streets," *Life*, June 26, 1964, 68.
12. Welch, 70. Ernest Havemann, "Scientists Search for the Answers to a Touchy and Puzzling Question. Why?," *Life*, June 26, 1964, 76.
13. Johnson, *Buying Gay*, 11.
14. Johnson, 226.
15. Johnson, 94–103.
16. Craig M. Loftin, "Unacceptable Mannerisms: Gender Anxieties, Homosexual Activism, and Swish in the United States, 1945–1965," *Journal of Social History* 40, no. 3 (2007): 578.
17. Johnson, *Buying Gay*, 97.
18. Johnson, 34.
19. Larry Townsend, "Who Lit Up the 'Lit' of the Golden Age of *Drummer*?," in *Gay San Francisco: Eyewitness "Drummer" Magazine*, by Jack Fritscher (1995), 95–100, accessed July 1, 2016, www.JackFritscher.com.
20. Henry D. Thoreau, *Walden and Resistance to Civil Government*, ed. William Rossi, 2nd ed. (New York: W. W. Norton and Company, 1992), 217.

21. Jack Fritscher, "Artist Chuck Arnett: His Life/Our Times," in *Leatherfolk*, ed. Mark Thompson (Los Angeles: Alyson Books, 2001), 108.
22. Johnson, *Buying Gay*, 231.
23. Bob Opel, "Cycle Sluts," *Drummer* 9 (October 1976): 9.
24. Jack Fritscher, *Gay Pioneers: How "Drummer" Magazine Shaped Gay Popular Culture: 1965–1999* (San Francisco: Palm Drive Publishing, 2017), 68.
25. T. R. Witomski, "The Pink Triangle: Never Forgotten, Never Repeated," *Drummer* 104 (1986): 70.
26. Pat Califia, "Nazi Iconography Dispute," *Drummer* 106 (1986): 5.
27. Eric E. Rofes, "Fantasies vs. Politics," *Drummer* 109 (1986): 5.
28. Editorial note to "Witomski Replies," *Drummer* 106 (1986): 65.
29. John Preston, "Introduction," in *The Leatherman's Handbook*, n.p.
30. Larry Townsend, *Leather Ad: M* (New York: Bad Boy Press, 1996), 40. Subsequent references appear in text.
31. Linda Williams, *Hard Core: Power, Pleasure, and the "Frenzy of the Visible"* (Berkeley: University of California Press, 1999), 50.
32. Staci Newmahr, *Playing on the Edge: Sadomasochism, Risk, and Intimacy* (Bloomington: Indiana University Press, 2011), 163.
33. For example, "Blue Light" appears in Simon Sheppard, ed., *Homosex: Sixty Years of Gay Erotica* (New York: Carroll and Graff, 2007), 115–54; Aaron Travis's *The Flesh Fables* (New York: Bad Boy, 1994), 15–56; and John Preston, ed., *Flesh and the Word: An Anthology of Erotic Writing* (New York: Plume, 1992), 125–57.
34. Aaron Travis, "Blue Light," in *The Flesh Fables*, 15–56. Subsequent references appear in text.
35. On vulgar modernism, see Glass, *Counterculture Colophon*, 126–27. On the demographics of Grove's readership, see Glass, 130–31, and Carroll, "White-Collar Masochism."
36. William Carney, *The Real Thing* (New York: Richard Kasak Books, 1995), 10. Subsequent references appear in text.
37. Scott Herring, *Queering the Underworld: Slumming, Literature, and the Undoing of Gay and Lesbian History* (Chicago: University of Chicago Press, 2007).
38. William Carney, draft letter to Max Gartenberg, August 12, 1967, Carton 8, Folder 22, William Carney Papers, 1942–87, University of California, Berkeley.
39. Carney to Gartenberg, August 12, 1967, William Carney Papers. Despite his frustrations, it seems that Carney never sent this letter. Carney had a habit of handwriting and then typing his correspondence, yet no typed copy appears in his papers and the draft has the word "unsent" scrawled across it, suggesting that Carney may have second-guessed himself, perhaps not wanting to put the novel's prospects in jeopardy.
40. Alan Hull Walton, "Introduction," in *The Real Thing* (New York: G. P. Putnam's Sons, 1968), 7.
41. Walton, 7, 18.
42. Putnam's and Sons Advertisement, William Carney Papers, Carton 8, Folder 23, Bancroft Library, University of California, Berkeley.
43. Glass, *Counterculture Colophon*, 123.
44. Glass, 127.
45. Peter Buitenhuis, "Nightmares in the Mirror," *New York Times*, June 30, 1963, 68.
46. Buitenhuis, 68.

47. Phoebe Adams, *Atlantic,* June, 1968, William Carney Papers, Carton 8, Folder 23, Bancroft Library, University of California, Berkeley.

48. *Publisher's Weekly* 193, no. 10 (March 4, 1968), William Carney Papers, Carton 8, Folder 23, Bancroft Library, University of California, Berkeley.

49. Thom Gunn, Letter to William Carney, March 1968, Personal Correspondence, William Carney Papers, Carton 8, Bancroft Library, University of California, Berkeley.

50. *New York Mattachine Newsletter,* September 1968, William Carney Papers, Carton 8, Folder 23, Bancroft Library, University of California, Berkeley.

51. Townsend, *The Leatherman's Handbook,* 256.

52. Larry Townsend, *Run, Little Leather Boy* (Los Angeles: L. T. Publications, 2003), 41.

53. Ed Franklin, "Book Report," *Drummer,* July 7 1976, 57–58.

54. Fritscher, *Gay Pioneers,* 160.

55. William Carney, Letter to David Lewis, Personal Correspondence, March 12, 1981, William Carney Papers, Carton 10, Bancroft Library, University of California, Berkeley.

56. Nina Attwood and Barry Reay, "ANONYMOUS and Badboy Books: A 1990s Moment in the History of Pornography," *Porn Studies* 3, no. 3 (2016): 255–75.

57. Patrick Califia, *Hard Men* (Los Angeles: Alyson Books, 2004), ix.

58. Levine, *Gay Macho,* 79.

59. Fritscher, *Gay Pioneers,* 32.

60. In *Sex and Social Justice,* Martha Nussbaum offers an important corrective to Andrea Dworkin and Catherine MacKinnon's undertheorized notion of objectification, which treated a number of qualities including "instrumentality," "denial of autonomy," "inertness," "fungibility," "violability," "ownership," and "denial of subjectivity" as both inherently undesirable and logically entailing one another (218). Nussbaum finds that the moral quality of any specific instance of objectification is highly context dependent, such that the specific mode of objectification that transpires in one instance may be undesirable while its meaning might change under different conditions and with different people involved. "What this should tell us," she concludes, "is that the dehumanization and objectification of persons has many forms" (238). Time and space prevent a fuller elaboration of this point, but Nussbaum's account of objectification bears some significant resemblances to Frances Ferguson's account of pornography as social structure devoted to the temporary and localized objectification of actions for the purposes of generated instantaneous consensus about those actions relative value. Martha Nussbaum, *Sex and Social Justice* (Oxford and New York: Oxford University Press, 2000). On pornography, objectification, and its relation to utilitarian social theory, see Frances Ferguson, *Pornography the Theory: What Utilitarianism Did to Action* (Chicago: University of Chicago Press, 2004).

61. In addition to Scott's work cited elsewhere in this book, see Ariane Cruz, *The Color of Kink: Black Women, BDSM, and Pornography* (New York: New York University Press, 2016).

62. "It didn't matter that *Drummer* was a gay men's magazine," explains Johnson. "We read *Drummer,* learned from it and enjoyed it." Viola Johnson, "Drummer," *Carter/Johnson Leather Library Newsletter* 1, no. 3 (March 2011), http://carterjohnson library.com/the-stacks/library-docs/newsletters/2011-2/mar-2011/, accessed July 12, 2019.

63. Cain Berlinger, *Black Men in Leather* (Tempe, AZ: Third Millennium Publishing, 2006), 113.
64. Berlinger, 114.
65. Fritscher, *Gay Pioneers*, 128.
66. Fritscher, 31.
67. Fritscher, 17.

CHAPTER TWO

1. Phil Andros, "The Peachiest Fuzz," in *Below the Belt and Other Stories* (San Francisco: Perineum Press, 1982), 31.
2. Christopher Wilson, *Cop Knowledge: Police Power and Cultural Knowledge in Twentieth-Century Fiction* (Chicago: University of Chicago Press, 2000), 6.
3. James Baldwin, "A Report from Occupied Territory," in *The Price of the Ticket: Collected Nonfiction, 1948–1985* (New York: St Martin's Press, 1985), 424.
4. For a version of these arguments, see Jack Halberstam, *The Queer Art of Failure* (Durham, NC: Duke University Press, 2011). Against such criticisms, scholars of gay pulp culture such as Michael Bronski have noted how the pornographic novels of the 1970s expressed explicit sympathies with the militant politics of gay liberation, yet Bronski's important recovery of texts such as *Gay Rights* (1978) and *Gay Revolution* (1970) downplays the ways in which gay porn remained erotically fascinated by figures of White hetero-patriarchal authority. My argument in this chapter is not that Bronski lacks the nerve to address those representations, but that the terms of his recovery project make it conceptually harder to understand the meaning they acquired for writers and readers, and so they are left out of his consideration. See Michael Bronski, *Pulp Friction: Uncovering the Golden Age of Gay Male Pulps* (New York: St. Martin's Griffin, 2003).
5. On this point, Rechy's thinking about the police bears significant similarities to Guy Hocquenghem's claim that "[between] the police and the legal system on the one hand and the homosexual on the other, there is an inverted relation of desire." See *Homosexual Desire* (Durham, NC: Duke University Press, 1993), 61.
6. For examples of Rechy's views toward censorship, see "A Case for Cruising," in *Beneath the Skin: The Collected Essays of John Rechy* (New York: Carroll and Graff, 2004), 77–84.
7. Steward, *The Lost Autobiography of Samuel Steward*, 226.
8. Andros, "The Peachiest Fuzz," 33.
9. While the story lacks the explicit representations of sex conventional to gay porn, it utilizes a hustler to educate his readers on erotic matters in a manner that recalls the exchanges between novice and seasoned prostitutes that were a central convention within eighteenth-century French pornography. See Lynn Hunt, "Obscenity and the Origin of Modernity," in *The Invention of Pornography: Obscenity and the Origins of Modernity, 1500–1800*, ed. Lynn Hunt (New York: Zone Books, 1996), 24–25.
10. Andros, "The Peachiest Fuzz," 35.
11. Foucault, *The History of Sexuality, Volume 1*, translated by Robert Hurley (1978; New York: Vintage Books, 1990), 85.
12. Steward, *The Lost Autobiography of Samuel Steward*, 226.
13. Ann Marie Schott, "'Moonlight and Bosh and Bullshit': Phil Andros's *$tud* and the

Creation of a 'New Gay Ethic,'" in *1960s Gay Pulp Fiction: The Misplaced Heritage*, ed. Dewey Wayne Gunn and Jamie Harker (Amherst: University of Massachusetts Press, 2013), 153.

14. John Rechy, *This Day's Death* (New York: Grove Press, 1969), 36. Subsequent references appear in text.

15. See Eve Kosofsky Sedgwick, *Between Men*, 2–3, as well as her discussion of universalizing and minoritizing epistemologies in *Epistemology of the Closet* (Berkeley: University of California Press, 1990), 67–90.

16. Kevin Arnold, "'Male and Male and Male': John Rechy and the Scene of Representation," *Arizona Quarterly* 67, no. 1 (2011): 131.

17. While throughout this book I prefer the term "BDSM" to refer to the range of practices that deliberately eroticize power differentials, when discussing Rechy's critique of those practices I follow his usage of the somewhat narrower term "S&M" in reference primarily, although not exclusively, to sadism and masochism.

18. John Rechy, *City of Night* (New York: Grove Press, 1963), 263.

19. John Rechy, *The Sexual Outlaw: A Documentary* (New York: Grove Press, 1977), 261. Subsequent references appear in text. There is some contention over the best way to write about kinky sex practices. Rechy prefers "S&M" in his writing, although he subsumes a diverse array erotic practices, such as fisting or "fist-fucking" (260), under S&M, even though fisting need not (and often does not) involve elements recognizable in terms of either master/slave or sadism/masochism dynamics.

20. Manuel Betancourt, "Cruising and Screening John: John Rechy's *The Sexual Outlaw*, Documentary Form, and Gay Politics," *GLQ: A Journal of Gay and Lesbian Studies* 23, no. 1 (2017): 35.

21. Jonathan Kahana, *Intelligence Work: The Politics of American Documentary* (New York: Columbia University Press, 2008), 241–42.

22. Kahana, 205.

23. Kahana, 205.

24. In addition to Arnold, "'Male and Male and Male,'" see Ben Gove, *Cruising Culture: Promiscuity, Desire, and American Gay Literature* (Edinburgh: Edinburgh University Press, 2000). Ben Nichols, "Reductive: John Rechy, Queer Theory, and the Idea of Limitation," *GLQ: A Journal of Gay and Lesbian Studies* 22, no. 3 (2016). Ricardo L. Ortiz, "Sexuality Degree Zero: Pleasure and Power in the Novels of John Rechy, Arturo Islas, and Michael Nava," in *Critical Essays: Gay and Lesbian Writers of Color,* ed. Emmanuel S. Nelson (Philadelphia: Haworth, 1993).

25. Two examples that come at this from the two very different directions of intersectional feminism and deconstruction are, respectively, Marcelle Maese-Cohen, "'But It Should Begin in El Paso': Civil Identities, Immigrant 'World'-Traveling, and Pilgrimage Form in John Rechy's *City of Night*," *Arizona Quarterly: A Journal of American Literature, Culture, and Theory* 70, no. 2 (Summer 2014): 85–114, and David Johnson, "Intolerance, the Body, Community," *American Literary History* 10, no. 3 (1998): 446–70.

26. Kahana, *Intelligence Work*, 266.

27. John Preston, "Introduction," in *$tud*, by Phil Andros (Boston: Alyson Publications, 1982), 9.

28. Spring, *Secret Historian*, 306–7.

29. Spring, 306–7.

30. "About John Rechy, City of Night," *Der Kreis* 31 (1963): 35–36, Samuel Steward Papers, Box 3, 1960, Archives at Yale, "John Rechy." For Rechy's response, see his letter to Phil Sparrow dated July 11, 1963.

31. Phil Andros, *Shuttlecock* (San Francisco: Perineum Press, 1984), 103. Following the initial citation, subsequent references to Steward's Andros novels appear in text with abbreviations of the title of the relevant Grey Fox edition.

32. Phil Andros, *The Boys in Blue* (San Francisco: Perineum Press, 1983), 14.

33. Phil Andros, *Roman Conquests* (San Francisco: Perineum Press, 1983), 53.

34. Michel Foucault, "Sex, Power, and the Politics of Identity," in *Ethics: Subjectivity and Truth*, ed. Paul Rabinow, trans. Robert Hurley, Essential Works of Foucault: 1954–1984, vol. 1 (New York: New York University Press, 1997), 169. Foucault famously treated BDSM practices as his privileged example of practices that de-genitalized pleasure, yet he had little to say about how pornography also contribute to that process. For a more thorough exploration of this idea in relation to video pornography, see Tim Dean, "Stumped," in *Porn Archives*, ed. Tim Dean, Steven Ruszczycky, and David Squares (Durham, NC: Duke University Press, 2014).

35. Following Derrida, one might phrase this movement in terms of conventions that *belong* to no single genre, yet for that reason *participate* in a variety of genres. See Jacques Derrida and Avital Ronell, "The Law of Genre," *Critical Inquiry* 7 (1980): 65.

36. This conventional narrative and its associated figures pervade the long history of police procedurals, yet one particularly notorious example appears in Sid Davis's educational film *Boys Beware* (1961), in which a detective assigned to the Inglewood Police Department instructs its school-aged audience on the predatory dangers that mentally deranged homosexuals pose to teenaged boys.

37. Samuel M. Steward. "Erotica—the Purest Form of Entertainment," *Gay News* 5, no. 21 (August, 7–20, 1981), 26.

38. Steward, 26.

39. Dean, "Stumped," 431–32.

40. Martin Joseph Ponce, "Revisiting Racial Fetishism: Interracial Desire, Revenge, and Atonement in Samuel Steward's *\$tud*," in *Samuel Steward and the Pursuit of the Erotic*, ed. Debra A. Moddelmog and Martin Joseph Ponce (Columbus: Ohio State University Press, 2017), 176. In his biography, Steward describes how these scenes not only deliberately traded in fantasies of Black revenge and White guilt but were quite popular with the readers of the homophile magazines in which they first appeared. Steward, *The Lost Autobiography of Samuel Steward*, 246.

41. Michael Davidson, *Guys Like Us*, 16–17. However, unlike the communities that Davidson describes, the exclusion of women does not have the same political implications, insofar as the erotic innovation that the men engage in does little to advance their social status. In fact, it puts them at greater risk of losing what status they do have, as the conclusion of the book reveals. When Phil's hustler identity is exposed to his fellow police officers, he departs for Chicago in order to save Pete and Greg. However, Phil later receives word that the two men have been arrested when their new roommate, a fellow cop, unwittingly brings home a vice cop to replace Phil.

42. Samuel M. Steward, "Detachment: A Way of Life," *Der Kreis* (August 1958): 34.

43. Steward, 34.
44. Spring, *Secret Historian*, 412.
45. Michael Rowe, "Steven Saylor, Writing as 'Aaron Travis,'" in *Writing Below the Belt: Conversations with Erotic Authors* (New York: Hard Candy Books, 1997), 376.

CHAPTER THREE

1. Peter Alilunas, "Bridging the Gap: Adult Video News and the 'Long 1970s,'" in *Porno Chic and the Sex Wars: American Sexual Representation in the 1970s*, ed. Carolyn Bronstein and Whitney Strub (Amherst: University of Massachusetts Press, 2016), 305. See also Blaise Cronin, "Eros Unbound: Pornography and the Internet," in *The Internet and the American Business*, ed. William Aspray and Paul E. Ceruzzi (Cambridge, MA: MIT Press, 2008), 500–1.
2. Whitney Strub, *Perversion for Profit: The Politics of Pornography and the Rise of the New Right* (New York: Columbia University Press, 2011), 179–81.
3. For examples, see Ricky Varghese, ed., *Raw: PrEP, Pedagogy, and the Politics of Barebacking* (Regina: University of Regina Press, 2019).
4. Samuel R. Delany, *The Mad Man* (New York: Richard Kasak Books, 1994), xiii. Subsequent page references appear in text.
5. Jeffery Allen Tucker, "A Revolution from Within: Paraliterature as AIDS Activism," in *A Sense of Wonder: Samuel R. Delany, Race, Identity, and Difference* (Hanover, NH: Wesleyan University Press, 2004).
6. Scott, *Extravagant Abjection*, 257.
7. Tyler Bradway, "Bad Reading: The Affective Relations of Queer Experimental Literature after AIDS," *GLQ: A Journal of Gay and Lesbian Studies* 24, nos. 2–3 (2018): 191.
8. Bradway, 193.
9. Following Deborah Gould's study of emotion and AIDS-era politics, I understand these emotions as culturally and historically specific mediations of affect, or "the body's ongoing and relatively amorphous inventory-taking of coming into contact and interacting with the world" (20). Affect is a vague potential sensed in the body, for which the subject must draw on its "storehouse of knowledge, habit, and experience, as well as from culturally available labels and meanings" in order to render its felt intensities legible as emotion to oneself and others, without ever fully divesting affect of its felt, enigmatic quality (21). This chapter thinks of genre as one way to describe the array of preexisting symbolic frameworks available to subjects as they struggle to resolve affect into specific emotions and of gay pornographic writing as way in which such mediation occurs. Deborah Gould, *Moving Politics: Emotion and ACT UP's Fight against AIDS* (Chicago: University of Chicago Press, 2009), 20–22.
10. Since its initial publication, Delany has twice revised and republished *The Mad Man*, first in 2002 with Voyant Publishing and then again in 2015 as a digital edition with Open Road Media. To date, Delany considers the 2015 edition, which carries the full title of *The Mad Man: or, The Mysteries of Manhattan*, as the definitive version. However, given this chapter's interest in situating the novel historically, it focuses on the original edition.
11. John Paul Ricco, *The Logic of the Lure* (Chicago: University of Chicago Press, 2002), 148. In addition, this decade also witnessed the emergence of many Black-

owned publications, including Alan Bell's *BLK*, Ric Irick's *Malebox*, Gregory Victorianne's *Buti Voxx*, and Ajamu X's *Wickers & Bullers*, which mixed politics with
pornography in order to cultivate transatlantic Black gay sex publics. See Adri-
enne Adams, Alan Bell, Ric Irick, Gregory D. Victorianne, and Ajamu X, "Black
Gay Mail" (Roundtable, ONE Archives at USC Libraries, Los Angeles, California,
February 4, 2021), http://www.youtu.be/8FNPAvZ-feg.

12. Judith Lawrence Pastore, "Introduction," in *Confronting AIDS through Literature:
The Responsibilities of Representation* (Urbana and Chicago: University of Illinois
Press, 1993), 3.

13. Steven F. Kruger, *AIDS Narratives: Gender and Sexuality, Fiction and Science*
(New York: Garland Publishing, 1996), 4.

14. Kruger, *AIDS Narratives*, 173.

15. See Sander L. Gilman, "AIDS and Syphilis: The Iconography of Disease," in *AIDS:
Cultural Analysis/Cultural Activism*, ed. Douglas Crimp (Cambridge, MA: MIT
Press, 1988): 87–108, and Leo Bersani. "Is the Rectum a Grave?," in *Is the Rectum
a Grave? And Other Essays* (Chicago: University of Chicago Press, 2010): 3–30.

16. Paula Treichler, *How to Have Theory in an Epidemic: Cultural Chronicles of AIDS*
(Durham, NC: Duke University Press, 1999), 11.

17. Crimp, "How to Have Promiscuity in an Epidemic," in *Melancholia and Moralism:
Essays on AIDS and Queer Politics* (Cambridge, MA: MIT Press, 2002), 245.

18. Richard Canning, "The Literature of AIDS," in *The Cambridge Companion to Gay
and Lesbian Writing*, ed. Hugh Stevens (Cambridge: Cambridge University Press,
2011), 133–34.

19. See Cindy Patton, *Fatal Advice: How Safe Sex Education Went Wrong* (Durham,
NC: Duke University Press, 1996), 133, 124.

20. Patton, 124.

21. John Preston, "Introduction," in *Hot Living: Erotic Stories about Safer Sex*, ed.
John Preston (Boston: Alyson Publications, 1985), 11.

22. Phil Andros, "The Broken Vessel," in Preston, *Hot Living*, 18.

23. Andros, 18.

24. Foucault, "Sex, Power, and the Politics of Identity," 165.

25. Andros, "The Broken Vessel," 21. Kinsey's *Sexual Behavior in the Human Male*
(1948) contains no mention of phantom feelings, yet his *Sexual Behavior in the
Human Female* (1953) does. In the chapter titled "Neural Mechanisms of Sexual
Response," Kinsey describes the case of a paraplegic woman for whom "psychological stimulation did not bring any pelvic reactions [. . .] [yet] tactile stimulation of the upper end of her body (apparently centered about the breasts)
did bring sexual response which led to complete orgasm." The two cases, one
pornographic and one clinical, are not identical, but are similar enough to suggest
that Steward had Kinsey's work on female sexual behavior in mind. Alfred C.
Kinsey et al., *Sexual Behavior in the Human Female* (Bloomington: Indiana University Press, 1998), 700.

26. Edward I. Koch, "Senator Helms's Callousness toward AIDS Victims," *New York
Times*, November 7, 1987, NYTimes.com, accessed November 27, 2015. Crimp,
"How to Have Promiscuity in an Epidemic," 65.

27. Dan Royles, *To Make the Wounded Whole: The African American Struggle against
HIV/AIDS* (Chapel Hill: University of North Carolina Press, 2020), 63–64.

28. Royles, 66.

29. In addition to Alilunas, "Bridging the Gap," see Jeffrey Escoffier, *Bigger than Life: The History of Gay Porn Cinema from Beefcake to Hardcore* (Philadelphia: Running Press, 2009), 189, and Cronin, "Eros Unbound," 499–500.

30. "Codebreaker—Is It Evil? Ep: 2 Internet Porn," *Codebreaker*, by Marketplace and Tech Insider, hosted by Ben Johnson and Clare Toenisskoetter, released November 18, 2015, accessed November 25, 2015, http://www.marketplace.org/2015/11 /18/tech/codebreaker-marketplace-and-tech-insider%E2%84%A2/codebreaker -it-evil-ep-2-internet-porn.

31. Escoffier, *Bigger than Life*, 197–98.

32. T. R. Witomski, "'Unsafe' Porno," in *Kvetch* (Berkeley, CA: Celestial Arts, 1989), 90.

33. "CAUTION," *Drummer* 100 (October 1986): 2.

34. Michael Rowe, "Steven Saylor, Writing as 'Aaron Travis,'" 369.

35. Patrick Califia, "Introduction to the Original Edition," in *Macho Sluts* (Vancouver: Arsenal Pulp Press, 2009), 61.

36. Califia, 61.

37. Bersani, "Is the Rectum a Grave?," 18.

38. Tucker, "A Revolution from Within," 275.

39. Gabriel Rotello, *Sexual Ecology: AIDS and the Destiny of Gay Men* (New York: Dutton Books, 1997), 156.

40. David L. Chambers, "Gay Men, AIDS, and the Code of the Condom," *Harvard Civil-Rights Liberties Law Review* 29 (1994): 359.

41. Chambers, 357.

42. Chambers, 362.

43. Scott, *Extravagant Abjection*, 247.

44. Scott, 247.

45. Scott, 245.

46. Tim Dean, *Unlimited Intimacy*, 56–57.

47. Scott O'Hara, *Autopornography: A Memoir of Life in the Lust Lane* (New York: Harrington Park Press, 1997), 129.

48. Ray Davis, "Delany's Dirt," in *Ash of Stars: On the Writing of Samuel R. Delany*, ed. James Sallis (Jackson: University of Mississippi Press, 1996), 181.

49. Reed Woodhouse, *Unlimited Embrace: A Canon of Gay Fiction, 1945–1995* (Amherst: University of Massachusetts Press, 1998), 220.

50. Woodhouse, 220.

51. Samuel R. Delany, "The Thomas L. Long Interview," in *Shorter Views: Queer Thoughts and the Politics of the Paraliterary* (Hanover, NH: Wesleyan University Press, 1999), 133–34.

52. Dwight Garner, "Pulp Friction: A Conversation with the '90s Prince of Porn Paperbacks," Salon.com, July 29, 1996, accessed August 8, 2020, https://www .salon.com/1996/07/29/kasak/.

53. Attwood and Reay, "ANONYMOUS and Badboy Books," 255–75.

54. Gould, *Moving Politics*, 136.

55. Scott O'Hara, "Ed," *Steam: A Quarterly Journal for Men* 1, no. 2 (Summer 1993): 71.

56. Scott O'Hara, "Editorial: Change Is Growth," *Steam: A Quarterly Journal for Men* 3, no. 4 (Winter 1995/1996): 362–63.

57. "Excerpt from Samuel R. Delany, *The Mad Man*," in *Steam: A Quarterly Journal for Men* 2, no. 2 (Summer 1994): 172.

58. Scott O'Hara, "Editorial: Just Sex," *Steam: A Quarterly Journal for Men* 2, no. 1 (Spring 1994): 2–3, 2.

59. Delany, *Times Square Red, Times Square Blue* (New York: New York University Press, 1999), 78–79.

60. Delany, 63.

61. Bill Andriette, "Queerest Queers: Man/Boy Love Faces Violence Out of Control," *Steam: A Quarterly Journal for Men* 2, no. 2 (Summer 1994): 167, 165–67.

CHAPTER FOUR

1. Matthew Stadler, *Allan Stein* (New York: Grove Press, 1999), 5. Subsequent page references appear in text.

2. Jed Esty, *Unseasonable Youth: Modernism, Colonialism, and the Fiction of Development* (Oxford: Oxford University Press, 2012).

3. Esty, 205.

4. Kadji Amin, *Disturbing Attachments: Genet, Modern Pederasty, and Queer History* (Durham, NC: Duke University Press, 2017), 39. I take Amin's point of regarding the inescapability of the social inequalities that characterize modern pederasty, yet this chapter more frequently employs the term "intergenerational intimacy" in order to emphasize the wide array of fantasies and desires that inform such relations, such that the adult's exertion of his physical or material power over the youth is not always the principal source of the relation's eroticism, even as it remains an important mediator of that force.

5. Amin, 39.

6. John Heywood, "'The Object of Desire Is the Object of Contempt': Representations of Masculinity in *Straight to Hell* Magazine," in *Language and Masculinity*, ed. Sally Johnson and Ulrike Hanna Meinhof (Oxford: Oxford University Press, 1997), 193.

7. Bernard Welt, *Mythomania: Fantasies, Fables, and Sheer Lies in Contemporary American Popular Art* (Los Angeles: Art Issues Press, 1996), 59.

8. Philip Jenkins, *Moral Panic: Changing Concepts of the Child Molester in America* (New Haven, CT: Yale University Press, 1998).

9. As Fischel has shown, the efforts of children's advocates to claim innocence for Black children has been an important political strategy in a climate where the racist presumption of an inherent sexual precocity justifies the preemptive criminalization of their actions or the underreporting of their experiences of abuse. See Joseph Fischel, "Pornographic Protections? Itineraries of Childhood Innocence," *Law, Culture, and the Humanities* 12, no. 2 (June 2016): 206–20. Similarly, Harkins warns against revaluing the pedophile sex offender as a figure of radical politics because the pedophile's implicit Whiteness and masculinity renders him an exception to the empirical reality that "those vulnerable to other modes of racial profiling are disproportionately targeted for sexually and gender non-conforming practices in public spaces." Gillian Harkins, "Lost Sociality of Skin: Security and the Pedophilic Function," *American Literary History* 28, no. 4 (2016): 744.

10. William E. Jones, *True Homosexual Experiences: Boyd McDonald and "Straight to Hell"* (Los Angeles: We Heard You Like Books, 2016), 84.

11. Scott Weiner, "What I Learned When QAnon Came for Me," NYTimes.com,

October 19, 2020, https://www.nytimes.com/2020/10/19/opinion/scott-wiener -qanon.htm.

12. Jenkins, *Moral Panic*. In particular, see chapters 6 and 7.
13. Ian Hacking, "The Making and Molding of Child Abuse," *Critical Inquiry* 17, no. 2 (Winter 1991): 266–69.
14. Roger Lancaster, *Sex Panic and the Punitive State* (Berkeley: University of California Press, 2011), 56–59.
15. Carolyn E. Cocca, *Jailbait: The Politics of Statutory Rape Laws in the United States* (Albany: State University of New York Press, 2004), 18–19. Joseph Fischel, "Per Se or Power? Age and Sexual Consent," *Yale Journal of Law and Feminism* 22, no. 2 (2010): 287–90.
16. James Kincaid, *Erotic Innocence: The Culture of Child Molesting* (Durham, NC: Duke University Press, 1998), 15.
17. Lancaster, *Sex Panic*, 42–43.
18. Lancaster, 44–45.
19. Lancaster, 92–93.
20. Greg Youmans, "Supporting the Revolt of the Perverts: Gay Activist Filmmaking and the Child Pornography Panic of the Late 1970s," in *Porno Chic and the Sex Wars: American Sexual Representation in the 1970s*, ed. Carolyn Bronstein and Whitney Strub (Amherst: University of Massachusetts Press, 2016), 276.
21. As Chuck Kleinhans notes, the laws concerning the indexical quality of the pornographic image helped to set the terms for defining child pornography in terms of photographic rather than written representations. Chuck Kleinhans, "Virtual Child Porn: The Law and the Semiotics of the Image," in *More Dirty Looks: Gender, Pornography, and Power*, ed. Pamela Church Gibson (London: British Film Institute, 2004), 73.
22. Henry Cohen, *Obscenity, Child Pornography, and Indecency* (New York: Novinka Books, 2002), 3.
23. Youmans, "Suppressing the Revolt of the Perverts," 282.
24. Cohen, *Obscenity, Child Pornography, and Indecency*, 239–40.
25. For examples, see Ian O'Donnell and Claire Milner, *Child Pornography: Crime, Computers, and Society* (Portland: Wilian Publishing, 2007), 70, and Max Taylor and Ethel Quayle, *Child Pornography: An Internet Crime* (New York: Brunner-Routledge, 2003), 4.
26. Quoted in Adler, "The Perverse Law of Child Pornography," 262.
27. Adler, 262.
28. Philip Jenkins, *Moral Panic*, 155.
29. Jon Davis, "Imagining Intergenerationality: Representation and Rhetoric in the Pedophile Movie," *GLQ: A Journal of Lesbian and Gay Studies* 13, nos. 2–3 (2007): 377.
30. Kathryn Bond Stockton, *The Queer Child; or, Growing Sideways in the Twentieth Century* (Durham, NC: Duke University Press, 2009), 40.
31. Kleinhans, "Virtual Child Porn," 75.
32. Stockton, *The Queer Child*, 10.
33. Adam Baran, "Billy Miller, Editor of Iconic True Sex Story Zine 'Straight-to-Hell,' Talks about the Early Days of Gay Erotica," *The Sword*, February 9, 2015, accessed October 11, 2020, https://www.thesword.com/billy-miller-interview.html.
34. Jones, *True Homosexual Experiences*, 67.

35. Jones, 106–7.
36. Boyd McDonald, *Straight to Hell* 1, no. 27 (1975): 1.
37. Boyd McDonald, "Memories and Desires," *Straight to Hell* 1, no. 29 (1976): 9.
38. Jones, *True Homosexual Experiences*, 86.
39. McDonald succinctly expressed this attitude in a nasty comment made after attending a dinner party with Quentin Crisp: "'We don't have to wear dresses to be gay.'" Jones, *True Homosexual Experiences*, 136.
40. Baran, "Billy Miller"
41. "4 Boys Raped Me—Thank God," in *Meat: How Men Look, Act, Walk, Talk, Dress, Undress, Taste, and Smell; True Homosexual Experiences from S.T.H.*, ed. Boyd McDonald (San Francisco: Gay Sunshine Press, 1981), 95.
42. "4 Boys," 96.
43. "In the Park," *Straight to Hell* 1, no. 26 (1975): 2.
44. Bruce Rogers, *Gay Talk: A (Sometimes Outrageous) Dictionary of Gay Slang* (New York: Paragon Books, 1972), 46. For a detailed discussion of the foreskin and its various significations in porn, see Harri Kalha, "Fantasy Uncut: Foreskin Fetishism and the Morphology of Desire," in *Porn Archives*, ed. Tim Dean, Steven Ruszczycky, and David Squires (Durham, NC: Duke University Press, 2014), 375–98. Kalha does not consider explicitly matters of coloniality, yet his discussion of the foreskin in Bel Ami videos as a signifier for "Eastern European ethnic alterity, of Slavic sexiness," and by extension an archaic realm untouched by Western civilization, seems apt in this context (391).
45. Eng-Beng Lim, *Brown Boys and Rice Queens: Spellbinding Performance in the Asias* (New York: New York University Press, 2014), 9.
46. "Raped," *Straight to Hell* 1, no. 27 (1975): 3.
47. "Raped," 3.
48. "Raped," 3.
49. Scott, *Extravagant Abjection*, 206.
50. Scott, 217.
51. "Raped," 2.
52. Charley Shively, "Introduction," in McDonald, *Meat*, n.p.
53. Shively, n.p.
54. Hocquenghem, *Homosexual Desire*, 99.
55. Hocquenghem, 110.
56. Hocquenghem, 111.
57. To that extent, the collages of McDonald's zine seem to predict the modes of becoming imagined through the images of *Butt* magazine. See Peter Rehberg, "Male Becomings: Queer Bodies as Aesthetic Forms in the Post-Pornographic Fanzine *Butt*," in *Art as Revolt: Thinking Politics through Immanent Aesthetics*, ed. David Fancy and Hans Skott-Myhre (Montreal: McGill-Queen's University Press, 2019), 167–82.
58. Youmans, "Suppressing the Revolt of the Perverts," 288.
59. Kate Millett and Mark Blasius, untitled interview, *Semiotext(e)*, Summer 1980, 38.
60. Amin, *Disturbing Attachments*, 39.
61. Matthew Stadler, "Keeping Secrets: NAMBLA, the Idealization of Children, and the Contradictions of Gay Politics," *The Stranger*, March 20, 1997, 10.
62. Stadler, 9.
63. Stadler, 8–9.

64. Shively's own commitments to the legitimization of man-boy love were voiced explicitly in his study of Walt Whitman's correspondence with male soldiers during the Civil War. Charley Shively, *Drum Beats: Walt Whitman's Civil War Boy Lovers* (San Francisco: Gay Sunshine Press, 1989).
65. While Stadler provides an overview history in his feature story, Jenkins provides a fuller account in *Moral Panic*, 157–58. See also Youmans, "Suppressing the Revolt of the Perverts," 287–88.
66. Stadler, "Keeping Secrets," 15.
67. Stadler, 12.
68. Stadler, 15.
69. Stadler, 15.
70. Lee Edelman, *No Future: Queer Theory and the Death Drive* (Durham, NC: Duke University Press, 2004), 31.
71. Joseph Fischel, *Sex and Harm in the Age of Consent* (Minneapolis: University of Minnesota Press, 2016), 14.

CONCLUSION

1. Susanna Paasonen, *Carnal Resonance: Affect and Online Pornography* (Cambridge, MA: MIT Press, 2011), 8.
2. Mica Ars Hilson, "Sharing Economies and Value Systems on the Nifty Archive," in *The Feminist and Queer Information Studies Reader*, ed. Patrick Keilty (Sacramento, CA: Litwin Books, 2012), 431–39. Steven Kruger, "Gay Internet Medievalism: Erotic Story Archives, the Middle Ages, and Contemporary Gay Identity," *American Literary History* 22, no. 4 (Winter 2010): 913–44. Susanna Paasonen also discusses interactivity in her study of the website Literotica. See Paasonen, "Good Amateurs: Erotica Writing and Notions of Quality," in *Porn.com: Making Sense of Online Pornography*, ed. Feona Attwood (New York: Peter Lang, 2010), 138–54.
3. Florêncio, *Bareback Porn*, 85.
4. Florêncio, 62–67.
5. Perry N. Halkitis, "Masculinity in the Age of AIDS: HIV-Seropositive Gay Men and the 'Buff Agenda,'" in *Gay Masculinities*, ed. Peter Nardi (New York: Sage Publications, 1999), 132.
6. Philippe Airés, *Centuries of Childhood: A Social History of Family Life*, trans. Robert Baldick (New York: Random House, 1962), 32.
7. Rob Latham, *Consuming Youth: Vampires, Cyborgs, and the Culture of Consumption* (Chicago: University of Chicago Press, 2002), 10–19.
8. Patricia Meyers Spacks, *The Adolescent Idea: Myths of Youth and the Adult Imagination* (New York: Basic Books, 1981), 15.
9. Esty, *Unseasonable Youth*, 23.
10. Diarmuid Hester, *Wrong: A Critical Biography of Dennis Cooper* (Iowa City: University of Iowa Press, 2020), 29–31.
11. Hester, 206.
12. Paul Preciado, *Testo Junkie: Sex, Drugs, and Biopolitics in the Pharmacopornographic Era*, trans. Bruce Benderson (New York: Feminist Press, 2013), 39.
13. Steward, *The Lost Autobiography of Samuel Steward*, 247.
14. Donna Dennis, *Licentious Gotham: Erotic Publishing and Its Prosecution in*

Nineteenth-Century New York (Cambridge, MA: Harvard University Press, 2009), 57–70. See also Whitney Strub, *Obscenity Rules: Roth v. United States and the Long Struggle over Sexual Expression* (Lawrence: University Press of Kansas, 2013), 18–19.

15. Amy Werbel, *Lust on Trial: Censorship and the Rise of American Obscenity in the Age of Anthony Comstock* (New York: Columbia University Press, 2018), 68–69.

16. Anthony Comstock, *Traps for the Young* (Cambridge, MA: Belknap Press of Harvard University Press, 1967), 147.

17. Marjorie Heins, *Not in Front of the Children: "Indecency," Censorship, and the Innocence of Youth* (New Brunswick, NJ: Rutgers University Press, 2001), 60.

18. *Butler v. Michigan*, 352 U.S. 380 (1957).

19. Heins, *Not in Front of the Children*, 73–74.

20. Werbel, *Lust on Trial*, 29–30.

21. Stockton, *The Queer Child*, 40.

22. Ian Hunter, David Saunders, and Dugald Williamson, *On Pornography: Literature, Sexuality, and Obscenity Law* (London: MacMillan Press, 1993), 40.

23. Hunter, Saunders, and Williamson, 40.

24. Hunter, Saunders, and Williamson, 203.

25. Michael Warner, *The Trouble with Normal: Sex, Politics, and the Ethics of Queer Life* (New York: Zone Books, 1999), 175–88.

26. Wendy Hui Kyong Chun, *Control and Freedom: Power and Paranoia in the Age of Fiber Optics* (Cambridge, MA: MIT Press, 2006), 91–96.

27. Chun, 78–79.

28. Amy Hasinoff, *Sexting Panic: Rethinking Criminalization, Privacy, and Consent* (Urbana: University of Illinois Press, 2016), 39.

29. Hasinoff, 4.

30. Hasinoff, 57.

31. For a concise account of the problems pertaining to media effects research, see Heins, *Not in Front of the Children*, 228–53.

32. Belinda Luscombe, "Porn and the Threat to Virility," *Time*, April 11, 2016, https://time.com/4277510/porn-and-the-threat-to-virility/?iid=toc_033116.

33. David Ley, Nicole Prause, and Peter Finn, "The Emperor Has No Clothes," *Current Sexual Health Reports* 6, no. 2 (June 2014): 100–101.

34. Clarissa Smith and Feona Attwood, "Emotional Truths and Thrilling Slide Shows: The Resurgence of Antiporn Feminism," in *The Feminist Porn Book: The Politics of Producing Pleasure*, ed. Tristan Taormino, Celine Parreñas Shimizu, Constance Penley, and Mireille Miller-Young (New York: Feminist Press, 2013), 41–42.

35. Jamie Stoops, "Just Like Heroin: Science, Pornography, and Heteronormativity in the Virtual Public Sphere," *Porn Studies* 4, no. 4 (2017): 369.

36. For a sampling of these confessionals, see Gary Wilson, *Your Brain on Porn: Internet Pornography and the Emerging Science of Addiction* (Kent: Commonwealth Publishing, 2015). A retired biologist, Gary Wilson is one prominent face of the porn addiction movement, which he warns against on his website yourbrainonporn.com and his popular TEDx lecture "The Great Porn Experiment."

37. Paasonen, "Good Amateurs," 142, 147–52.

38. Hilson, "Sharing Economies," 438.

39. Hilson, 438.
40. Patrick Hayes, "Human 2.0? Life-Writing in the Digital Age," in *On Life Writing*, ed. Zachary Leader (Oxford: Oxford University Press, 2015), 252.
41. Hester, *Wrong*, 205.
42. Diarmuid Hester, "The Anarcho-Queer Commons of Dennis Cooper's Blog, *The Weaklings*: A Brief History," *GLQ: A Journal of Lesbian and Gay Studies* 24, no. 4 (2018): 522–27, 523.
43. Timothy Baker, "The Whole Is Untrue: Experience and Community in *The Sluts*," in *Dennis Cooper*, ed. Paul Hegarty and Danny Kennedy (Brighton, UK: Sussex Academic Press, 2008), 57.
44. Hester, *Wrong*, 203.
45. Hester, 32.
46. Hester, 32.
47. Mitchell, "Boy Problems," *New Inquiry*, May 29, 2019, http://thenewinquiry.com/boy-problems/.
48. Mitchell.
49. Mitchell.
50. Mitchell.
51. Preciado, *Testo Junkie*, 49–50.
52. Luscombe, "Porn and the Threat to Virility."
53. Lee Konstantinou, "The 7 Neoliberal Arts; or, Art in the Age of High Mass Culture," Post45.org. August 31, 2020, http://post45.org/2020/08/the-7-neoliberal-arts-or-art-in-the-age-of-mass-high-culture/.

Bibliography

Adler, Amy. "The Perverse Law of Child Pornography." *Columbia Law Review* 101, no. 2 (March 2001): 239–40.

Airés, Philippe. *Centuries of Childhood: A Social History of Family Life*, translated by Robert Baldick. New York: Random House, 1962.

Alilunas, Peter. "Bridging the Gap: Adult Video News and the 'Long 1970s.'" In *Porno Chic and the Sex Wars: American Sexual Representation in the 1970s*, edited by Carolyn Bronstein and Whitney Strub, 303–26. Amherst: University of Massachusetts Press, 2016.

Amin, Kadji. *Disturbing Attachments: Genet, Modern Pederasty, and Queer History*. Durham, NC: Duke University Press, 2017.

Anderson, Benedict. *Imagined Communities: Reflections on the Origins and Spread of Nationalism*. New York: Verso Books, 1983.

Andriette, Bill. "Queerest Queers: Man/Boy Love Faces Violence Out of Control." *Steam: A Quarterly Journal for Men* 2, no. 2 (Summer 1994): 165–67.

Andros, Phil. "A Better Samaritan." In *Below the Belt and Other Stories*, 81–92. San Francisco: Perineum Press, 1982.

Andros, Phil. *The Boys in Blue*. San Francisco: Perineum Press, 1983.

Andros, Phil. "The Broken Vessel." In *Hot Living: Erotic Stories about Safer Sex*, edited by John Preston, 14–23. Boston: Alyson Publications, 1985.

Andros, Phil. *Greek Ways*. San Francisco: Perineum Press, 1984.

Andros, Phil. "The Peachiest Fuzz." In *Below the Belt and Other Stories*, 24–35. San Francisco: Perineum Press, 1982.

Andros, Phil. *Roman Conquests*. San Francisco: Perineum Press, 1983.

Andros, Phil. *San Francisco Hustler*. San Francisco: Gay Parisian Press, 1970.

Andros, Phil. *Shuttlecock*. San Francisco: Perineum Press, 1984.

Arnold, Kevin. "'Male and Male and Male': John Rechy and the Scene of Representation." *Arizona Quarterly* 67, no. 1 (2011): 115–34.

Attwood, Nina, and Barry Reay. "ANONYMOUS and Badboy Books: A 1990s Moment in the History of Pornography." *Porn Studies* 3, no. 3 (2016): 255–75.

Austen, Roger. *Playing the Game: The Homosexual Novel in America*. New York: Bobbs-Merrill, 1977.

Baker, Timothy. "The Whole Is Untrue: Experience and Community in *The Sluts*." In *Dennis Cooper*, edited by Paul Hegarty and Danny Kennedy, 52–57. Brighton, UK: Sussex Academic Press, 2008.

Baldwin, James. "A Report from Occupied Territory." In *The Price of the Ticket: Collected Nonfiction, 1948–1985*, 415–24. New York: St. Martin's Press, 1985.

Bergman, David. "The Cultural Work of Sixties Gay Pulp Fiction." In *The Queer Sixties*, edited by Patricia Juliana Smith, 22–42. New York: Routledge, 1999.

Berlant, Lauren, and Michael Warner. "Sex in Public." In *Publics and Counterpublics*, 187–208. Zone Books: New York, 2002.

Berlinger, Cain. *Black Men in Leather*. Tempe, AZ: Third Millennium Publishing, 2006.

Bersani, Leo. "Is The Rectum a Grave?" In *Is The Rectum a Grave? And Other Essays*, 3–30. Chicago: University of Chicago Press, 2010.

Betancourt, Manuel. "Cruising and Screening John: John Rechy's *The Sexual Outlaw*, Documentary Form, and Gay Politics." *GLQ: A Journal of Lesbian and Gay Studies* 23, no. 1 (2017): 31–49.

Bittner, Egon. *The Functions of Police in Modern Society*. Chevy Chase, MD: National Institute of Mental Health, Center for Studies of Crime and Delinquency, 1970.

Boyd, Nan Alamilla. "Policing Queers in the 1940s and 1950s: Harassment, Prosecution, and the Legal Defense of Gay Bars." In *Wide-Open Town: A History of Queer San Francisco*, 108–47. Berkeley: University of California Press, 2003.

Bradway, Tyler. "Bad Reading: The Affective Relations of Queer Experimental Literature after AIDS." *GLQ: A Journal of Lesbian and Gay Studies* 24, nos. 2–3 (2018): 189–212.

Bronski, Michael. *Pulp Friction: Uncovering the Golden Age of Gay Male Pulps*. New York: St. Martin's Press, 2003.

Calhoun, Craig, ed. *Habermas and the Public Sphere*. Cambridge, MA: MIT Press, 1992.

Califia, Pat. "The Limits of the S/M Relationship, or, Mr. Benson Doesn't Live Here Anymore." In Thompson, *Leatherfolk*, 221–32.

Califia, Pat. "No Minor Issues: Age of Consent, Child Pornography, and Cross-Generational Relationships." In *Public Sex: The Culture of Radical Sex*, 2nd ed., 54–96. San Francisco: Cleis Press, 2000.

Califia, Patrick. *Hard Men*. Los Angeles: Alyson Books, 2004.

Califia, Patrick. "Introduction to the Original Edition." In *Macho Sluts*. Vancouver: Arsenal Pulp Press, 2009.

Canning, Richard. "The Literature of AIDS." In *The Cambridge Companion to Gay and Lesbian Writing*, edited by Hugh Stevens, 132–47. Cambridge: Cambridge University Press, 2011.

Carney, William. *The Real Thing*. New York: Richard Kasak Books, 1995.

Carroll, Jordan S. "White-Collar Masochism: Grove Press and the Death of the Managerial Subject." *Twentieth Century Literature* 64, no. 1 (March 1, 2018). DOI: 10.1215/0041462X-4387677.

Castillo, Debra, and John Rechy. "Interview: John Rechy." *Diacritics* 25, no. 1 (Spring 1995): 113–25.

Chambers, David L. "Gay Men, AIDS, and the Code of the Condom." *Harvard Civil-Rights Liberties Law Review* 29 (1994): 353–85.

Chambers, Ross. *Untimely Interventions: AIDS Writing, Testimonial, and the Rhetoric of Haunting*. Ann Arbor: University of Michigan Press, 2004.

Chauncy, George. *Gay New York: Gender, Urban Culture, and the Making of the Gay Male World: 1890–1940*. New York: Basic Books, 1995.

Chun, Wendy Hui Kyong. *Control and Freedom: Power and Paranoia in the Age of Fiber Optics*. Cambridge, MA: MIT Press, 2006.

Clancy, Susan A. *The Trauma Myth: The Truth about the Sexual Abuse of Children—and Its Aftermath*. New York: Basic Books, 2009.

Clarke, Eric O. *Virtuous Vice: Homoeroticism and the Public Sphere*. Durham, NC: Duke University Press, 2000.

Cocca, Carolyn E. *Jailbait: The Politics of Statutory Rape Laws in the United States*. Albany: State University of New York Press, 2004.

Cohen, Henry. *Obscenity, Child Pornography, and Indecency*. New York: Novinka Books, 2002.

Comstock, Anthony. *Traps for the Young*. Cambridge, MA: Belknap Press, 1967.

Cooper, Dennis. *The Sluts*. New York: Carroll and Graff, 2004.

Cowie, Elizabeth. "Pornography and Fantasy: Psychoanalytic Perspectives." In *Sex Exposed: Sexuality and the Pornography Debate*, edited by Lynne Segal and Mary McIntosh, 132–54. London: Virgo Press, 1992.

Crimp, Douglas. "How to Have Promiscuity in an Epidemic." In *Melancholia and Moralism: Essays on AIDS and Queer Politics*, 43–82. Cambridge, MA: MIT Press, 2002.

Cronin, Blaise. "Eros Unbound: Pornography and the Internet." In *The Internet and the American Business*, edited by William Aspray and Paul E. Ceruzzi, 491–537. Cambridge, MA: MIT Press, 2008.

Cruz, Ariane. *The Color of Kink: Black Women, BDSM, and Pornography*. New York: New York University Press, 2016.

Davidson, Michael. *Guys Like Us: Citing Masculinity in Cold War Poetics*. Chicago: University of Chicago Press, 2003.

Davis, Jon. "Imagining Intergenerationality: Representation and Rhetoric in the Pedophile Movie." *GLQ: A Journal of Lesbian and Gay Studies* 13, nos. 2–3 (2007): 369–86.

Davis, Ray. "Delany's Dirt." In *Ash of Stars: On the Writing of Samuel R. Delany*, edited by James Sallis, 162–88. Jackson: University of Mississippi Press, 1996.

Dean, Tim. "Bareback Time." In *Queer Times, Queer Becomings*, edited by E. L. McCallum and Mikko Tuhkanen, 75–99. Albany: State University of New York Press, 2011.

Dean, Tim. *Beyond Sexuality*. Chicago: University of Chicago Press, 2000.

Dean, Tim. "The Erotics of Transgression." In *The Cambridge Companion to Gay and Lesbian Writing*, edited by Hugh Stevens, 65–80. Cambridge: Cambridge University Press, 2011.

Dean, Tim. "Foucault and Sex." In *After Foucault: Culture, Theory, and Criticism in the 21st Century*, edited by Lisa Downing, 141–55. Cambridge: Cambridge University Press, 2018.

Dean, Tim. "Stumped." In Dean, Ruszczycky, and Squires, *Porn Archives*, 420–40.

Dean, Tim. *Unlimited Intimacy: Reflections on the Subculture of Barebacking*. Chicago: University of Chicago Press, 2009.

Dean, Tim, Steven Ruszczycky, and David Squires, eds. *Porn Archives*. Durham, NC: Duke University Press, 2014.

Delany, Samuel R. *The Mad Man*. New York: Richard Kasak Books, 1997.

Delany, Samuel R. "The Thomas L. Long Interview." In *Shorter Views: Queer Thoughts and the Politics of the Paraliterary*, 123–40. Hanover, NH: Wesleyan University Press, 1999.

Delany, Samuel R. *Times Square Red, Times Square Blue*. New York: New York University Press, 1999.

Delany, Samuel R. "Excerpt from Samuel R. Delany, *The Mad Man*." *Steam: A Quarterly Journal for Men* 2, no. 2 (Summer 1994): 168–75.

D'Emilio, John. *Sexual Politics, Sexual Communities: The Making of a Homosexual Minority in the United States, 1950–1970*. 2nd ed. Chicago: University of Chicago Press, 1998.

Dennis, Donna. *Licentious Gotham: Erotic Publishing and Its Prosecution in Nineteenth-Century New York*. Cambridge, MA: Harvard University Press, 2009.

Derrida, Jacques, and Avital Ronell. "The Law of Genre." *Critical Inquiry* 7, no. 1 (1980): 55–81.

Dewhurst, Robert. "Gay Sunshine, Pornopoetic Collage, and Queer Archive." In Dean, Ruszczycky, and Squires, *Porn Archives*, 213–33.

Doidge, Norman. *The Brain That Changes Itself: Stories of Personal Triumph from the Frontiers of Brain Science*. New York: Penguin Books, 2007.

Dore, Florence. *The Novel and the Obscene: Sexual Subjects in American Modernism*. Stanford, CA: Stanford University Press, 2005.

Dyer, Richard. "Male Gay Porn: Coming to Terms." *Jump Cut* 30 (1985): 27–29.

Echols, Alice. "The Homo Superiors: Disco and the Rise of the Gay Macho." In *Hot Stuff: Disco and the Remaking of American Culture*, 121–58. New York: Norton, 2010.

Edelman, Lee. *Homographesis: Essays in Gay Literary and Cultural Theory*. New York: Routledge, 1994.

Edelman, Lee. *No Future: Queer Theory and the Death Drive*. Durham, NC: Duke University Press, 2004.

Eighner, Lars. *Travels with Lizbeth*. New York: St. Martin's Press, 2013.

Emre, Merve. *Paraliterary: The Making of Bad Readers in Postwar America*. Chicago: University of Chicago Press, 2017.

Escoffier, Jeffrey. *Bigger than Life: The History of Gay Porn Cinema from Beefcake to Hardcore*. Philadelphia: Running Press, 2009.

Esty, Jed. *Unseasonable Youth: Modernism, Colonialism, and the Fiction of Development*. Oxford: Oxford University Press, 2012.

Ferguson, Frances. *Pornography, the Theory: What Utilitarianism Did to Action*. Chicago: University of Chicago Press, 2004.

Fiedler, Leslie. "Come Back to the Raft Ag'in, Huck, Honey." In *A New Fiedler Reader*, 3–13. Amherst, MA: Prometheus Books, 1999.

Fischel, Joseph. "Pornographic Protections? Itineraries of Childhood Innocence." *Law, Culture, and the Humanities* 12, no. 2 (June 2016): 206–20.

Fischel, Joseph. *Sex and Harm in the Age of Consent*. Minneapolis: University of Minnesota Press, 2016.

Florêncio, João. *Bareback Porn, Porous Masculinities, Queer Futures: The Ethics of Becoming Pig*. New York: Routledge, 2020.

Foucault, Michel. "About the Concept of the 'Dangerous Individual' in Nineteenth-Century Legal Psychiatry." In *The Essential Works of Foucault: 1954–1984: Power*, edited by James D. Faubion, 176–200. New York: New Press, 2000.

Foucault, Michel. *The History of Sexuality, Volume 1: An Introduction*, translated by Robert Hurley. 1978; New York: Vintage Books, 1990.

Foucault, Michel. "Sex, Power, and the Politics of Identity." In *Ethics: Subjectivity and Truth*, edited by Paul Rabinow and translated by Robert Hurley and others, 163–64. The Essential Works of Foucault: 1954–1984, vol. 1. New York: New Press, 1997.

Fritscher, Jack. "Artist Chuck Arnett: His Life/Our Times." In Thompson, *Leatherfolk*, 106–18.

Fritscher, Jack. *Gay Pioneers: How "Drummer" Magazine Shaped Gay Popular Culture: 1965–1999*. San Francisco: Palm Drive Publishing, 2017.

Gilman, Sander L. "AIDS and Syphilis: The Iconography of Disease." In *AIDS: Cultural Analysis/Cultural Activism*, edited by Douglas Crimp, 87–108. Cambridge, MA: MIT Press, 1988.

Glass, Loren. *Counterculture Colophon: Grove Press, "The Evergreen Review," and the Incorporation of the Avant-Garde*. Stanford, CA: Stanford University Press, 2013.

Glass, Loren. "Redeeming Value: Obscenity and Anglo-American Modernism." *Critical Inquiry* 32, no. 2 (Winter 2006): 341–61.

Gould, Deborah. *Moving Politics: Emotion and ACT UP's Fight against AIDS*. Chicago: University of Chicago Press, 2009.

Gove, Ben. *Cruising Culture: Promiscuity, Desire, and American Gay Literature*. Edinburgh: Edinburgh University Press, 2000.

Gunn, Drewey Wayne, and Jamie Harker. "Introduction." In Gunn and Harker, *1960s Gay Pulp Fiction*, 1–28.

Gunn, Drewey Wayne, and Jamie Harker, eds. *1960s Gay Pulp Fiction: The Misplaced Heritage*. Amherst: University of Massachusetts Press, 2013.

Hacking, Ian. "The Making and Molding of Child Abuse." *Critical Inquiry* 17, no. 2 (Winter 1991): 253–88.

Halkitis, Perry N. "Masculinity in the Age of AIDS: HIV-Seropositive Gay Men and the 'Buff Agenda.'" In *Gay Masculinities*, edited by Peter Nard, 130–51. New York: Sage Publications, 1999.

Harkins, Gillian. "Lost Sociality of Skin: Security and the Pedophilic Function." *American Literary History* 28, no. 4 (2016): 740–58.

Hasinoff, Amy. *Sexting Panic: Rethinking Criminalization, Privacy, and Consent*. Urbana: University of Illinois Press, 2016.

Hayes, Patrick. "Human 2.0? Life-Writing in the Digital Age." In *On Life Writing*, edited by Zachary Leader, 233–56. Oxford: Oxford University Press, 2015.

Heins, Marjorie. *Not in Front of the Children: "Indecency," Censorship, and the Innocence of Youth*. New Brunswick, NJ: Rutgers University Press, 2001.

Hennen, Peter. *Faeries, Bears, and Leathermen: Men in Community Queering the Masculine*. Chicago: University of Chicago Press, 2008.

Herring, Scott. "On Late-Life Samuel Steward." In *Samuel Steward and the Pursuit of the Erotic*, edited by Debra A. Moddelmog and Martin Joseph Ponce, 68–84. Columbus: Ohio State University Press, 2017.

Herring, Scott. *Queering the Underworld: Slumming, Literature, and the Undoing of Gay and Lesbian History*. Chicago: University of Chicago Press, 2007.

Hester, Diarmuid. "The Anarcho-Queer Commons of Dennis Cooper's Blog, *The Weaklings*: A Brief History." *GLQ: A Journal of Gay and Lesbian Studies* 24, no. 4 (2018): 522–27.

Hester, Diarmuid. *Wrong: A Critical Biography of Dennis Cooper*. Iowa City: University of Iowa Press, 2020.

Heywood, John. "'The Object of Desire Is the Object of Contempt': Representations of Masculinity in *Straight to Hell* Magazine." In *Language and Masculinity*, edited by Sally Johnson and Ulrike Hanna Meinhof, 188–207. Oxford: Oxford University Press, 1997.

Hilderbrand, Lucas. "Historical Fantasies: 1970s Gay Male Pornography in the Archives." In *Porno Chic and the Sex Wars: American Sexual Representation in the 1970s*, edited by Carolyn Bronstein and Whitney Strub, 327–46. Amherst: University of Massachusetts Press, 2016.

Hilson, Mica Ars. "Sharing Economies and Value Systems on the Nifty Archive." In *The Feminist and Queer Information Studies Reader*, edited by Patrick Keilty, 431–39. Sacramento, CA: Litwin Books, 2012.

Hocquenghem, Guy. *Homosexual Desire*, translated by Daniella Dangoor. Durham, NC: Duke University Press, 1993.

Hunt, Lynn. "Obscenity and the Origin of Modernity." In *The Invention of Pornography: Obscenity and the Origins of Modernity, 1500–1800*, edited by Lynn Hunt, 9–48. New York: Zone Books, 1996.

Hunter, Ian, David Saunders, and Dugald Williamson. *On Pornography: Literature, Sexuality, and Obscenity Law*. London: MacMillan Press, 1993.

Irvine, Janice. "Reinventing Perversion: Sex Addiction and Cultural Anxieties." *Journal of the History of Sexuality* 5, no. 3 (January 1995): 429–50.

Jackson, Earl, Jr. *Strategies of Deviance: Studies in Gay Male Representation*. Bloomington: Indiana University Press, 1995.

Jenkins, Philip. *Beyond Tolerance: Child Pornography and the Internet*. New York: New York University Press, 2001.

Jenkins, Philip. *Moral Panic: Changing Concepts of the Child Molester in America*. New Haven, CT: Yale University Press, 1998.

Johnson, David. "Intolerance, the Body, Community." *American Literary History* 10, no. 3 (1998): 446–70.

Johnson, David K. *Buying Gay: How Physique Entrepreneurs Sparked a Movement*. New York: Columbia University Press, 2019.

Johnson, Viola M. *To Love, to Obey, to Serve: Diary of an Old Guard Slave*. Fairfield, CT: Mystic Rose Press, 1999.

Jones, William E. *True Homosexual Experiences: Boyd McDonald and "Straight to Hell."* Los Angeles: We Heard You Like Books, 2016.

Kahana, Johnathan. *Intelligence Work: The Politics of American Documentary*. New York: Columbia University Press, 2008.

Kalha, Harri. "Fantasy Uncut: Foreskin Fetishism and the Morphology of Desire." In Dean, Ruszczycky, and Squires, *Porn Archives*, 375–98.

Kincaid, James. *Erotic Innocence: The Culture of Child Molesting*. Durham, NC: Duke University Press, 1998.

Kinsey, Alfred C., Wardell B. Pomeroy, Clyde E. Martin, and Paul H. Gebhard.

Sexual Behavior in the Human Female. Bloomington: Indiana University Press, 1998.

Kipnis, Laura. *Bound and Gagged: Pornography and the Politics of Fantasy in America*. Durham, NC: Duke University Press, 1996.

Kleinhans, Chuck. "Virtual Child Porn: The Law and the Semiotics of the Image." In *More Dirty Looks: Gender, Pornography, and Power*, edited by Pamela Church Gibson, 71–84. London: British Film Institute, 2004.

Kruger, Stephen F. "Gay Internet Medievalism: Erotic Story Archives, the Middle Ages, and Contemporary Gay Identity." *American Literary History* 22, no. 4 (Winter 2010): 913–44.

Kruger, Stephen F. *AIDS Narratives: Gender and Sexuality, Fiction and Science*. New York: Garland Publishing, 1996.

Ladenson, Elizabeth. *Dirt for Art's Sake: Books on Trial from "Madame Bovary" to "Lolita."* New York: Cornell University Press, 2007.

Lancaster, Roger. *Sex Panic and the Punitive State*. Berkeley: University of California Press, 2011.

Laplanche, Jean, and Jean-Bertrand Pontalis. "Fantasy and the Origins of Sexuality." In *Formations of Fantasy*, edited by Victor Burgin, James Donald, and Cora Kaplan, 5–26. New York: Routledge, 1989.

Latham, Rob. *Consuming Youth: Vampires, Cyborgs, and the Culture of Consumption*. Chicago: University of Chicago Press, 2002.

Levine, Martin. *Gay Macho: The Life and Death of the Homosexual Clone*. New York: New York University Press, 1998.

Ley, David, Nicole Prause, and Peter Finn. "The Emperor Has No Clothes: A Review of the 'Pornography Addiction' Model." *Current Sexual Health Reports* 6, no. 2 (2014): 94–105.

Lim, Eng-Beng. *Brown Boys and Rice Queens: Spellbinding Performance in the Asias*. New York: New York University Press, 2014.

Loftin, Craig M. "Unacceptable Mannerisms: Gender Anxieties, Homosexual Activism, and Swish in the United States, 1945–1965." *Journal of Social History* 40, no. 3 (2007): 577–96.

Lowenthal, Michael. "Introduction: Beyond Porn; Sex, Confession, and Honesty." In *Flesh and the Word 4*, edited by Michael Lowenthal, ix–xvi. New York: Plume Books, 1997.

Maese-Cohen, Marcelle. "'But It Should Begin in El Paso': Civil Identities, Immigrant 'World'-Traveling, and Pilgrimage Form in John Rechy's *City of Night*." *Arizona Quarterly* 70, no. 2 (Summer 2014): 85–114.

Marcus, Steven. *The Other Victorians: A Study of Sexuality and Pornography in Mid-Nineteenth-Century England*. New Brunswick, NJ: Transaction, 2009.

McDonald, Boyd. "Memories and Desires." *Straight to Hell* 1, no. 29 (1976): 9.

McKay, Richard A. *Patient Zero and the Making of the AIDS Epidemic*. Chicago: University of Chicago Press, 2017.

Meeker, Martin. *Contacts Desired: Gay and Lesbian Communications and Community, 1940s–1970s*. Chicago: University of Chicago Press, 2006.

Mercer, John. "Gay Porn Now!" *Porn Studies* 4, no. 2 (2017).

Mercer, John. *Gay Pornography: Representations of Sexuality and Masculinity*. London: I. B. Taurus, 2017.

Meyers Spacks, Patricia. *The Adolescent Idea: Myths of Youth and the Adult Imagination*. New York: Basic Books, 1981.

Nash, Jennifer. *The Black Body in Ecstasy: Reading Race, Reading Representation*. Durham, NC: Duke University Press, 2014.

Nealon, Christopher. *Foundlings: Lesbian and Gay Historical Emotion before Stonewall*. Durham, NC: Duke University Press, 2001.

Newmahr, Staci. *Playing on the Edge: Sadomasochism, Risk, and Intimacy*. Bloomington: Indiana University Press, 2011.

Nichols, Ben. "Reductive: John Rechy, Queer Theory, and the Idea of Limitation." *GLQ: A Journal of Lesbian and Gay Studies* 22, no. 3 (2016): 409–35.

Nussbaum, Martha. *Sex and Social Justice*. Oxford and New York: Oxford University Press, 2000.

O'Donnell, Ian, and Claire Milner. *Child Pornography: Crime, Computers, and Society*. Portland: Wilian Publishing, 2007.

O'Hara, Scott. *Autopornography: A Memoir of Life in the Lust Lane*. New York: Harrington Park Press, 1997.

O'Hara, Scott. "Ed." *Steam: A Quarterly Journal for Men* 1, no. 2 (Summer 1993): 71.

O'Hara, Scott. "Editorial: Change Is Growth." *Steam: A Quarterly Journal for Men* 3, no. 4 (Winter 1995/1996): 362–63.

O'Hara, Scott. "Editorial: Just Sex." *Steam: A Quarterly Journal for Men* 2, no. 1 (Spring 1994): 2–3.

Ortiz, Ricardo L. "Sexuality Degree Zero: Pleasure and Power in the Novels of John Rechy, Arturo Islas, and Michael Nava." In *Critical Essays: Gay and Lesbian Writers of Color*, edited by Emmanuel S. Nelson, 111–26. Philadelphia: Haworth, 1993.

Paasonen, Susanna. *Carnal Resonance: Affect and Online Pornography*. Cambridge, MA: MIT Press, 2011.

Paasonen, Susanna. "Good Amateurs: Erotica Writing and Notions of Quality." In *Porn.com: Making Sense of Online Pornography*, edited by Feona Attwood, 138–54. New York: Peter Lang, 2010.

Pastore, Judith Lawrence. "Introduction." In *Confronting AIDS through Literature: The Responsibilities of Representation*, 1–14. Urbana and Chicago: University of Illinois Press, 1993.

Patton, Cindy. *Fatal Advice: How Safe Sex Education Went Wrong*. Durham, NC: Duke University Press, 1996.

Patton, Cindy. *L.A. Plays Itself/Boys in the Sand*. Vancouver: Arsenal Pulp Press, 2014.

Pease, Allison. *Modernism, Mass Culture, and the Aesthetics of Obscenity* Cambridge: Cambridge University Press, 2000.

Penley, Constance. *NASA/TREK: Popular Science and Sex in America*. New York: Verso, 1997.

Pérez-Torres, Rafael. *Fictions of Masculinity: Crossing Cultures, Crossing Sexualities*. New York: New York University Press, 1994.

Ponce, Martin Joseph. "Revisiting Racial Fetishism: Interracial Desire, Revenge, and Atonement in Samuel Steward's *$tud*." In *Samuel Steward and the Pursuit of the Erotic*, edited by Debra A. Moddelmog and Martin Joseph Ponce, 162–78. Columbus: Ohio State University Press, 2017.

Poovey, Mary. *Genres of the Credit Economy: Mediating Value in Eighteenth- and Nineteenth-Century Britain*. Chicago: University of Chicago Press, 2008.

Potter, Rachel. *Obscene Modernism: Literary Censorship and Experiment, 1900–1940*. Oxford: Oxford University Press, 2014.

Preciado, Paul. *Testo Junkie: Sex, Drugs, and Biopolitics in the Pharmacopornographic Era*, translated by Bruce Benderson. New York: Feminist Press, 2013.

Preston, John. "Introduction." In *Hot Living: Erotic Stories about Safer Sex*, edited by John Preston, 7–13. Boston: Alyson Publications, 1985.

Preston, John. "Introduction." In *The Leatherman's Handbook*, by Larry Townsend, n.p. Beverly Hills, CA: L. T. Publications, 1993.

Preston, John. "Introduction." In *$tud*, by Phil Andros. Boston: Alyson Publications, 1982.

Preston, John. "What Happened?" In Thompson, *Leatherfolk*, 210–20.

Rechy, John. "A Case for Cruising." In *Beneath the Skin: The Collected Essays of John Rechy*, 77–84. New York: Carroll and Graff, 2004.

Rechy, John. *City of Night*. New York: Grove Press, 1963.

Rechy, John. *My Life and the Kept Woman: A Memoir*. New York: Grove Press, 2008.

Rechy, John. *The Sexual Outlaw: A Documentary*. New York: Grove Press, 1977.

Rechy, John. *This Day's Death*. New York: Grove Press, 1969.

Rehberg, Peter. "Male Becomings: Queer Bodies as Aesthetic Forms in the Post-Pornographic Fanzine *Butt*." In *Art as Revolt: Thinking Politics through Immanent Aesthetics*, edited by David Fancy and Hans Skott-Myhre, 167–82. Montreal: McGill-Queen's University Press, 2019.

Rembar, Charles. *The End of Obscenity: The Trials of "Lady Chatterley," "Tropic of Cancer," and "Fanny Hill" by the Lawyer Who Defended Them*. New York: Harper and Row Publishers, 1968.

Rico, John Paul. *The Logic of the Lure*. Chicago: University of Chicago Press, 2002.

Rogers, Bruce. *Gay Talk: A (Sometimes Outrageous) Dictionary of Gay Slang*. New York: Paragon Books, 1972.

Rotello, Gabriel. *Sexual Ecology: AIDS and the Destiny of Gay Men*. New York: Dutton Books, 1997.

Rowe, Michael. "Steven Saylor, Writing as 'Aaron Travis.'" In *Writing Below the Belt: Conversations with Erotic Authors*, 347–78. New York: Hard Candy Books, 1997.

Royles, Dan. *To Make the Wounded Whole: The African American Struggle against HIV/AIDS*. Chapel Hill: University of North Carolina Press, 2020.

Rubin, Gayle. "The Leather Menace: Comments on Politics and S/M." In *Sexual Revolution*, edited by Jeffrey Escoffier, 266–99. New York: Thunder's Mouth Press, 2003.

Rubin, Gayle. "Sites, Settlements, and Urban Sex: Archaeology and the Study of Gay Leathermen in San Francisco, 1955–1995." In *Archaeologies of Sexuality*, edited by Robert Schmidt and Barbara Voss, 62–88. London: Routledge, 2000.

Rubin, Gayle. "Thinking Sex: Notes for a Radical Theory of the Politics of Sexuality." In *The Lesbian and Gay Studies Reader*, edited by Henry Ablove, Michèle Aina Barale, and David Halperin, 3–44. New York: Routledge, 1993.

Rubin, Gayle. "The Traffic in Women: Notes on the 'Political Economy' of Sex." In *Feminist Anthropology: A Reader*, edited by Ellen Lewin, 87–106. Malden, MA: Blackwell Publishing, 2006.

Rubin, Marian, et al. "'Not a Pretty Picture.'" In *Porn 101: Eroticism, Pornography, and the First Amendment*, edited by James Elias and others, 213–27. New York: Prometheus Books, 1999.

Schott, Ann Marie. "'Moonlight and Bosh and Bullshit': Phil Andros's $tud and the Creation of a 'New Gay Ethic.'" In *1960s Gay Pulp Fiction: The Misplaced Heritage*, edited by Dewey Wayne Gunn and Jamie Harker, 143–66. Amherst: University of Massachusetts Press, 2013.

Scott, Darieck. *Extravagant Abjection: Blackness, Power, and Sexuality in the African American Imagination*. New York: New York University Press, 2010.

Scott, Darieck. "Introduction: Black Gay Pornotopias; or, When We Were Sluts." In *Best Black Gay Erotica*, edited by Darieck Scott, ix–xiv. San Francisco: Cleis Press, 2005.

Sedgwick, Eve Kosofsky. *Between Men: English Literature and Male Homosocial Desire*. New York: Columbia University Press, 1985.

Sedgwick, Eve Kosofsky. *Epistemology of the Closet*. Berkeley: University of California Press, 1990.

Shilts, Randy. *And the Band Played On: Politics, People, and the AIDS Epidemic*. New York: St. Martin's Griffin, 2007.

Shively, Charley. *Drum Beats: Walt Whitman's Civil War Boy Lovers*. San Francisco: Gay Sunshine Press, 1989.

Shively, Charley. "Introduction." In *Meat: How Men Look, Act, Walk, Talk, Dress, Undress, Taste, and Smell; True Homosexual Experiences from S.T.H*, volume 1, edited by Boyd McDonald. San Francisco: Gay Sunshine Press, 1981, 1994.

Smith, Clarissa, and Feona Attwood. "Emotional Truths and Thrilling Slide Shows: The Resurgence of Antiporn Feminism." In *The Feminist Porn Book: The Politics of Producing Pleasure*, edited by Tristan Taormino, Celine Parreñas Shimizu, Constance Penley, and Mireille Miller-Young, 41–57. New York: Feminist Press, 2013.

Sonenschein, David. "Sources of Reaction to 'Child Pornography.'" In *Porn 101: Eroticism, Pornography, and the First Amendment*, edited by James Elias, 527–33. New York: Prometheus Books, 199.

Sontag, Susan. "The Pornographic Imagination." In *Styles of Radical Will*, 35–73. New York: Faber, Straus and Giroux, 1969.

Spring, Justin. *Secret Historian: The Life and Times of Samuel Steward, Professor, Tattoo Artist, and Sexual Renegade*. New York: Farrar, Straus, and Giroux, 2010.

Stadler, Matthew. *Allan Stein*. New York: Grove Press, 1999.

Stadler, Matthew. "Keeping Secrets: NAMBLA, the Idealization of Children, and the Contradictions of Gay Politics." *The Stranger*, March 20, 1997.

Steward, Samuel. *The Lost Autobiography of Samuel Steward: Reflections of an Extraordinary Twentieth-Century Gay Life*. Edited by Jeremy Mulderig. Chicago: University of Chicago Press, 2018.

Samuel M. Steward. "Detachment: A Way of Life." *Der Kreis*, August 1958, 34–36.

Stockton, Kathryn Bond. *The Queer Child; or, Growing Sideways in the Twentieth Century*. Durham, NC: Duke University Press, 2009.

Stoops, Jamie. "Just Like Heroin: Science, Pornography, and Heteronormativity in the Virtual Public Sphere." *Porn Studies* 4, no. 4 (2017): 364–80.

Strub, Whitney. "Historicizing Pulp: Gay Male Pulp and the Narrativization of Queer Cultural History." In Gunn and Harker, *1960s Gay Pulp Fiction*, 43–77.

Strub, Whitney. *Obscenity Rules: Roth v. United States and the Long Struggle over Sexual Expression*. Lawrence: University Press of Kansas, 2013.

Strub, Whitney. *Perversion for Profit: The Politics of Pornography and the Rise of the New Right*. New York: Columbia University Press, 2011.

Stryker, Susan. *Queer Pulp: Perverted Passions from the Golden Age of the Paperback*. San Francisco: Chronicle Books, 2001.

Taylor, Max, and Ethel Quayle. *Child Pornography: An Internet Crime*. New York: Brunner-Routledge, 2003.

Thoreau, Henry D. *Walden and Resistance to Civil Government*. Edited by William Rossi. 2nd ed. New York: W. W. Norton and Company, 1992.

Thompson, Mark, ed. *Leatherfolk*. Los Angeles: Alyson Books, 2001.

Tongson, Karen, and Scott Herring. "The Sexual Imaginarium: A Reappraisal." *GLQ: A Journal of Gay and Lesbian Studies* 25, no. 1 (2019): 51–56.

Townsend, Larry. *Leather Ad: M*. New York: Bad Boy Press, 1996.

Townsend, Larry. *The Leatherman's Handbook*. Beverly Hills, CA: L. T. Publications, 1993.

Townsend, Larry. *Run, Little Leather Boy*. Los Angeles: L. T. Publications, 2003.

Townsend, Larry. "Who Lit Up the 'Lit' of the Golden Age of *Drummer*?" In *Gay San Francisco: Eyewitness "Drummer" Magazine*, by Jack Fritscher, 95–100. www.JackFritscher.com. 1995; accessed July 1, 2016.

Trask, Michael. *Camp Sites: Sex, Politics, and Academic Style in Postwar America*. Stanford, CA: Stanford University Press, 2013.

Travis, Aaron. "Blue Light." In *The Flesh Fables*, 15–56. New York: Bad Boy, 1994.

Treichler, Paula. *How to Have Theory in an Epidemic: Cultural Chronicles of AIDS*. Durham, NC: Duke University Press, 1999.

Tucker, Jeffery Allen. *A Sense of Wonder: Samuel R. Delany, Race, Identity, and Difference*. Hanover, NH: Wesleyan University Press, 2004.

Turner, Fred. *From Counterculture to Cyberculture: Stewart Brand, the Whole Earth Network, and the Rise of Digital Utopianism*. Chicago: University of Chicago Press, 2006.

van Dijck, José. *The Culture of Connectivity: A Critical History of Social Media*. Oxford: Oxford University Press, 2013.

Varghese, Ricky, ed. *Raw: PrEP, Pedagogy, and the Politics of Barebacking*. Regina: University of Regina Press, 2019.

Walton, Allan Hull. "Introduction." In *The Real Thing*. New York: G. P. Putnam's Sons, 1968.

Warner, Michael. *The Letters of the Republic: Publication and the Public Sphere in Eighteenth-Century America*. Cambridge, MA: Harvard University Press, 1990.

Warner, Michael. "Public and Private." In *Publics and Counterpublics*, 21–64. New York: Zone Books, 2002.

Warner, Michael. "Publics and Counterpublics." In *Publics and Counterpublics*, 65–124. New York: Zone Books, 2002.

Warner, Michael. *The Trouble with Normal: Sex, Politics, and the Ethics of Queer Life*. Cambridge, MA: Harvard University Press, 1999.

Waugh, Thomas. *Hard to Imagine: Gay Male Eroticism in Photography and Film from Their Beginnings to Stonewall.* New York: Columbia University Press, 1996.

Waugh, Thomas. "Men's Pornography: Gay vs. Straight." *Jump Cut* 30 (1985): 30–36

Welt, Bernard. *Mythomania: Fantasies, Fables, and Sheer Lies in Contemporary American Popular Art.* Los Angeles: Art Issues Press, 1996.

Werbel, Amy. *Lust on Trial: Censorship and the Rise of American Obscenity in the Age of Anthony Comstock.* New York: Columbia University Press, 2018.

Weston, Kath. "'Get Thee to a Big City': Sexual Imaginary and the Great Gay Migration." *GLQ: A Journal of Gay and Lesbian Studies* 2, no. 3 (1995): 253–77.

Williams, Linda. *Hard Core: Power, Pleasure, and the "Frenzy of the Visible."* Berkeley: University of California Press, 1999.

Wilson, Christopher. *Cop Knowledge: Police Power and Cultural Knowledge in Twentieth-Century Fiction.* Chicago: University of Chicago Press, 2000.

Wilson, Gary. *Your Brain on Porn: Internet Pornography and the Emerging Science of Addiction.* Kent: Commonwealth Publishing, 2015.

Witomski, T. R. *Kvetch.* Berkeley, CA: Celestial Arts, 1989.

Woodhouse, Reed. *Unlimited Embrace: A Canon of Gay Fiction, 1945–1995.* Amherst: University of Massachusetts Press, 1998.

Youmans, Greg. "Supporting the Revolt of the Perverts: Gay Activist Filmmaking and the Child Pornography Panic of the Late 1970s." In *Porno Chic and the Sex Wars: American Sexual Representation in the 1970s*, edited by Carolyn Bronstein and Whitney Strub, 274–302. Amherst: University of Massachusetts Press, 2016.

Index

Made in the USA
Columbia, SC
19 March 2024